Brian Freemantle

has worked in more than thirty countries, including Russia, Vietnam and America. In 1975 he organised the only British airlift of Vietnamese orphans immediately prior to the collapse of South Vietnam, rescuing 96 children only hours before Saigon fell to the communists.

In 1975 Freemantle quit journalism to write novels. He is published in thirteen countries, with a worldwide sale in excess of seven million. The first of his eleven Charlie Muffin novels was filmed, with David Hemmings playing the title role.

In 1979, in their archive of twentieth century literary and entertainment figures, Boston University opened a section in his name. In 1986 he was nominated for the Edgar Allan Poe Award by the Mystery Writers of America.

Charlie's Choice

The First Charlie Muffin Omnibus

Brian Freemantle

BLOODLINES

This omnibus edition first published in Great Britain in 1997 by
The Do-Not Press
PO Box 4215
London SE23 2QD

Charlie Muffin by Brian Freemantle © 1977
by Innslodge Publications Ltd
Clap Hands, Here Comes Charlie by Brian Freemantle © 1978
by Innslodge Publications Ltd
The Inscrutable Charlie Muffin by Brian Freemantle © 1979
by Innslodge Publications Ltd
Introduction © 1997 by Brian Freemantle.
All rights reserved

ISBN 1 899344 26 8

British Library Cataloguing in Publication Data. A catalogue record for this book is available from the British Library.

All rights reserved. No part of this publication may be reproduced, transmitted or stored in a retrieval system, in any form or by any means without the express permission in writing of The Do-Not Press having first been obtained.

This book is sold on the condition that it shall not, by way of trade or otherwise, be lent, resold or hired out or otherwise circulated without the publisher's prior consent in any form of binding or cover other than that in which it is published and without a similar condition being imposed on the subsequent purchaser.

Printed and bound in Great Britain by The Guernsey Press Co. Ltd.

Contents

Introduction 7
Charlie Muffin 9
Clap Hands, Here Comes Charlie 143
The Inscrutable Charlie Muffin 287

Introduction

On painful feet, Charlie Muffin shuffled into print at the height of the Cold War, that period of international history when Russian espionage agents, the bad guys in the black hats, gazed over the Wall that divided Europe at the good guys of Western intelligence, allocated the white hats to prove their squeaky cleanness. That, at least, was the conventional Western wisdom. In reality it was certainly a time of one simple espionage code for both sides: screw the opposition before they screw you.

Charlie Muffin didn't wear a hat of any colour and the Hush Puppies had to be broken in by long wear to comfort those permanently aching feet. He moulded the creed to his personal comfort, too. Charlie Muffin's axiom was to screw anyone from anywhere to avoid it happening to him. He did it so well that the first of what became an eleven book series was filmed in 1979 for international movie distribution.

Charlie, dishevelled, cantankerous and disrespectful, is a survivor at any cost in the wilderness of mirrors in which the life of a professional intelligence agent is reflected.

That cost is too great, in *Clap Hands, Here Comes Charlie*, the sequel to the introductory book: too great for him and greater still for those to whom he illustrates yet again his own very personal interpretation of the secret agent's code.

It is an interpretation that puts Charlie, always the outsider, beyond any redemption in *The Inscrutable Charlie Muffin*. And forces him into a new career and into hiding, in faraway Hong Kong. Charlie still plays by his own rules, of course. And as always there's a cost but this time Charlie doesn't pay. Not much, anyway.

It was American financier-philosophist Bernard Baruch who, in 1946, first used the expression 'Cold War' to describe the frigid, non-shooting state of frigidity between the monolithic Soviet Union – then ruled by Stalin who'd viewed the Second World War as a stepping stone for the communist domination of Europe – and the West. A year earlier, in Fulton, Missouri, Britain's wartime leader Winston Churchill had talked of Europe being divided by an Iron Curtain.

By 1977, when *Charlie Muffin* was published, the Cold War was at its iciest. During the three year period in which the Charlie Muffin series grew with *Clap Hands, Here Comes Charlie* and *The Inscrutable Charlie Muffin*, Rhodesia – now Zimbabwe – declared independence. Britain had its last Labour government for eighteen years and had to be rescued from financial catastrophe by an IMF loan of £2,300 million. The Queen celebrated her Silver Jubilee. The IRA terrorist campaign in Britain escalated. *Rocky*, staring Sylvester Stallone, won the Oscar for best film. The average house price in London and the South East was £16,731 and a colour TV licence cost £21. Elvis Presley died and Princess Anne gave birth to a son, Peter. 'Don't Cry for Me Argentina' got into the hit parade and disco fever was stoked by John Travolta in *Saturday Night Fever*. And in the hostile Soviet Union, one of its most corrupt leaders ever, Leonid Brezhnev, came to power.

Brian Freemantle, Winchester, 1997

Charlie Muffin

1.

Like tombstones of forgotten graves, the decayed apartment buildings in the Friedrichstrasse pooled haphazard shadows in the approaching dusk and both men expertly used the cover, walking close to the walls. Although together, they carefully avoided physical contact and there was no conversation.

They stopped just before the open-spaced, free-fire area leading to Checkpoint Charlie, the taller, younger man using the pretence of taking a light for his cigarette from his companion to gaze over the outstretched arm towards the crossing point into West Berlin. On either side of the road, the criss-cross of tank traps indicated the limits of the minefield.

'Looks all right,' he said, shielding the cigarette in a cupped hand. He was shaking, saw Charlie Muffin.

'It would, wouldn't it?' Charlie said dismissively.

Brian Snare managed to intrude his irritation into the noisy inhalation. The damned man never stopped, he thought.

'There's not the slightest sign of activity,' insisted Snare. The wind drove the wispy fair hair over his face. Quickly he brushed it back, carefully smoothing it down.

'Don't be stupid,' said Charlie. 'Every border from the Baltic to the Mediterranean will be on full alert.'

'Our documents are in order.'

'So were Berenkov's. And I got him.'

Snare looked from the border to the other man, arrested by the 'I'. Muffin had coordinated Berenkov's capture, probably the most important single spy arrest in Europe since the Second World War, and was frightened the credit for it was being taken away. Silly old sod. Another indication that he was past it, this constant need to prove himself.

'Well, we can't stay here all fucking night. Our visas expire in eight hours.'

The carefully modulated obscenity sounded out of place from the Cambridge graduate. Had there still been National Service, thought Charlie, Snare would have rolled his own cigarettes in the barracks to prove he was an ordinary bloke and made up stories about NAAFI girls he'd screwed. No he wouldn't, he corrected immediately. The man would have used his family connections to obtain a commission, just as he was invoking them to push himself in the service. He'd have still lied about the NAAFI girls, though.

'Harrison crossed easily enough,' argued Snare.

Three hours earlier, from the concealment of one of the former insurance office buildings further back in Leipzigerstrasse, they had watched the third member of the team, Douglas Harrison, go through the checkpoint unchallenged.

'That doesn't mean anything,' dismissed Charlie. The habit of the other two men to address each other by their surnames irritated the older man, in whose world partners upon whom your life depended were called by their Christian names. He knew they used the public school practice to annoy him.

'You mean mates,' Harrison had sneered when Charlie's anger had erupted months ago, at the start of the operation that was concluding that afternoon.

Like so many others, he'd lost the encounter, he remembered. The ill-considered retort – 'I'd rather have a mate than a rich father and a public school accent' – had been laughed down in derision.

'I wouldn't, Charles,' Snare had replied. 'But that's not the point, is it? Why ever can't you drop this inverted snobbery? We'll try hard to be your chums, even though you don't like us.'

'We've stood here too long,' warned Snare. It was his turn to cross next.

Charlie nodded, moving back into the deeper shadows. The other man's shaking had worsened, he saw.

'The car-crossing documents are in the door pocket,' said Snare, who had driven the hired Volkswagen with Harrison from West to East Berlin a week earlier. Cuthbertson had decreed they separate to avoid suspicion, so Charlie had arrived by train. But Cuthbertson had ordered him to bring the car back.

'We'll be waiting for you on the other side,' added Snare, attempting a smile. 'We'll have a celebration dinner in the Kempinski tonight.'

But first they'd ring London, Charlie knew, to get in early with their account of the completed phase of the operation. His part in the affair was going to be undermined: he was sure of it. Bastards.

'What about the rest?' demanded Charlie.

Again Snare allowed the sigh of irritation.

'The original documents are in the car, too,' said Snare. 'But that's almost academic. Harrison had photocopies and by now they're in the West Berlin embassy waiting for the next diplomatic pouch. That'll satisfy the court.'

'You've got photostats, too?' insisted Charlie.

Snare looked curiously at the older man.

'You know I have.'

For several moments they stood like foreign language students seeking the proper words to express themselves.

'All right then,' said Charlie, inadequately. He nodded, like a schoolmaster agreeing to a pupil's exit from the classroom.

Snare's face stiffened at the attitude. Supercilious fool.

'I'll see you at the Kempinski,' said Snare, feeling words were expected from him.

'Book a table,' said Charlie. 'For three,' he added, pointedly.

Abruptly Snare moved off, head hunched down into the collar of the British warm, hands thrust into the pockets, well-polished brogues sounding against the pavement. A man assured of his future, thought Charlie, briefly, turning in the other direction to walk back up Friedrichstrasse into East Berlin. Of what, he wondered, was he assured? Bugger all, he decided.

Just before the checkpoint, Snare turned, a typical tourist, raising his camera for the last picture of the divided city. Through the viewfinder, he strained to locate the retreating figure of Charlie Muffin.

It took over a minute, which Snare covered by jiggling with the light-meter and range adjustment. Muffin was very good, conceded Snare, reluctantly. The man was moving deep against the protection of the buildings again: no one from the observation points near the Wall would have detected him.

A professional. But still an out-of-date anachronism, concluded Snare contemptuously. Muffin was an oddity, like his name, a middle-aged field operative who had entered in the vacuum after the war, when manpower desperation had forced the service to reduce its standards to recruit from grammar schools and a class structure inherently suspect, and had risen to become one of the best-regarded officers in Whitehall.

Until the recent changes, that was. Now Sir Henry Cuthbertson was the Controller, with only George Wilberforce, a permanent civil servant and an excellent fellow, retained as his second-in-command. So from now on it was going to be different. It was going to be restored to its former, proper level and so Charlie Muffin was a disposable embarrassment, with his scuffed suede Hush Puppies, the Marks & Spencer shirts he didn't change daily and the flat, Mancunian accent.

But he was too stupid to realise it. Odd, how someone so insensitive had lasted so long. Snare supposed it was what his tutor at Cambridge had called the native intelligence of the working class. In the field for twenty-five years, reflected Snare, turning back towards the Wall. An amazing achievement, he conceded, still reluctantly. An exception should be made to the Official Secrets Act, mused Snare, enjoying his private joke, to enable Muffin to be listed in the *Guinness Book of Records*, along with all the other freaks.

Five hundred yards away inside East Berlin, Charlie turned from the Friedrichstrasse on to Leipzigerstrasse, feeling safe. It was important to see Snare cross, he had decided. From the shelter of the doorway from which they'd both watched Harrison go over, he observed the man approach the booth and present his passport, hardly pausing in his stride in the briefest of formalities.

Slowly Charlie released the breath he had been holding, purposely creating a sad sound.

'Just like that,' he said, quietly. In moments of puzzlement, when facts refused to correlate, Charlie unashamedly talked to himself, enumerating the factors worrying him, counting them off one by one on his fingers.

He was aware that the habit, as with everything else, amused Snare and Harrison. They'd even used it as an indicator of character imbalance in discussions with Cuthbertson, he knew. And Wilberforce, who had never liked him, would have joined in the criticism, Charlie guessed.

'Because of Berenkov's arrest, every border station should be tighter than a duck's bum,' Charlie lectured himself. 'Yet they go through, just like that.'

He shook his head, sadly. So a decision had been made in that teak-lined office with its Grade One fitted carpet, bone china tea-cups and oil paintings of bewigged Chancellors of the Exchequer staring out unseeing into Parliament Square.

Tit for tat.

'But I'm not a tit,' Charlie told the empty doorway.

Charlie sighed again, the depression deepening. Poor Günther.

But he had no choice, Charlie reasoned. It was a question of survival. Always the same justification, he thought, bitterly. Charlie Muffin had to survive, no matter how unacceptable the method. Or the way. Everyone before Cuthbertson had realised that: capitalised upon it even. But Cuthbertson had arrived with his punctilious, Army-trained attitudes and preconceived ideas, contemptuous of what might have happened before him.

But he had been clever enough to realise the importance of Berenkov, thought Charlie, tempering the disparagement. That would have been Wilberforce, he guessed, asshole crawling to ingratiate himself, showing Cuthbertson the way. Neither had had anything to do with it. But three months from now, Charlie knew, the affair would be established as a coup for the new regime. Fucking civil service.

He was purposely letting his mind drift to avoid what he had to do, Charlie accepted, realistically. Charlie's first visit on the Berenkov affair had been more than a year ago, during the days when he'd been properly acknowledged as the leading operative.

It wasn't until much later, when the potential of the investigation had been fully recognised and there had been the changes in Whitehall, that Snare and Harrison had been thrust upon him. And by then it didn't matter because Charlie had established, unknown to any of them, one of the many lifelines along which he could claw to safety, fertilising the protective association with Günther Bayer, gradually convincing the dissident student who believed him a traveller in engineering components, that one day he would help his defection.

What had happened thirty minutes before at Checkpoint Charlie meant that day had arrived.

Charlie had two brandies, in quick succession, in the gaudy cocktail bar of the Hotel Unter den Linden before calling the memorised number. Bayer responded immediately. The conversation was brief and guarded, conceding nothing, but Charlie could discern the tension in the other man. Poor sod, he thought. Yes, agreed the East German quickly, he could be at the hotel within an hour.

Charlie returned to the bar, deciding against the brandy he wanted. Drunkenness didn't help: it never did. He ordered beer instead, needing the excuse to sit there, gazing into the diminishing froth.

Did personal survival justify this? he recriminated. Perhaps his fears were unfounded, he countered hopefully. Perhaps he'd end up making a fool of himself and provide more ammunition for the two men already in West Berlin's Kempinski Hotel. And if that happened, Bayer would be the only beneficiary, a free man.

He shrugged away the reassurance. That was weak reasoning: people died because of weak reasoning.

There had been other instances like this, but it had never worried him so much before. Perhaps he was getting as old and ineffectual as Snare and Harrison were attempting to portray him. Cuthbertson and Wilberforce would be eager listeners, Charlie knew.

Bayer arrived in a rush, perspiration flecking his upper lip. He kept smiling, like a child anticipating a promised Christmas gift.

The two men moved immediately to a table away from the bar, Charlie ordering more beer as they went. They stayed silent until they were served, the East German fidgeting with impatience. I bet he always hunted for his presents early in December, thought Charlie.

'You've found a way?' demanded Bayer, as soon as the waiter moved off.

'I think so.'

Bayer made a noise drinking his beer. Snare would have been distressed, thought Charlie, at the man's table manners.

'You've got the passport?' asked the Englishman.

Bayer reached towards his jacket pocket, but Charlie leaned across, stopping the movement.

'Not here,' he said, annoyed.

Bayer winced, worried by his mistake.

'Sorry,' he apologised. 'I'm just excited, that's all.' It was a good forgery, Charlie knew. He'd had it prepared months before just off West Berlin's Kurfürstendamm, using one of the best forgers among those who made a business trading people across the Wall. It had cost £150 and Charlie had only managed to retrieve £75 back on expenses; even then there'd been queries. He'd make up on this trip, though.

'How can it be done?' asked Bayer.

'When I came in, a week ago, I used the railway,' said Charlie, gesturing out towards the overhead S Bahn linking East and West. That *had* been the first indication, decided Charlie, positively: Cuthbertson's explanation about the chances of detection had been banal. Bayer nodded, urging him on.

'But the samples were brought in by another traveller, by car.'

Bayer frowned, doubtfully.

'...but...'

'...And he's gone back, on foot,' enlarged Charlie. 'The car is here and the crossing papers are in order.'

Bayer patted his pocket, where the passport lay.

'There's no entry date,' he protested.

Charlie slid a small packet across the table.

'A date stamp,' he said. 'From the same man that made the passport. It'll match the documents in the car perfectly.'

Bayer reached forward, seizing the other man's hand and holding it.

'I don't have the words to thank you,' he said. His eyes were clouded, Charlie saw.

The Briton shrugged, uncomfortably.

'You must have dinner with Gretel and me, tomorrow, when it's all over.'

'Gretel?'

'The girl I'm going to marry. I've already telephoned, telling her something could be happening.'

Charlie concentrated on the beer before him.

'Was that wise?' he queried. 'The call has to go through a manned exchange to the West.'

'No one would have learned anything from the conversation,' assured Bayer. 'But Gretel knows.'

Charlie looked at his watch, wanting to end the encounter. Perhaps he *was* getting too old, he thought.

'You've got three hours,' he warned. 'And you'll need time to enter the visa stamp.'

The other man was having difficulty in speaking, Charlie saw.

'You're a marvellous man,' Bayer struggled, at last, reaching over the table again.

Charlie shrugged his hand off, irritably.

'Just don't panic. Remember, everything is properly documented.'

From the lounge, Charlie watched the student collect the hired car and move off unsteadily into the traffic stream. He stayed, staring into the beer, thoughts fluttering through his mind like the clues in a paper-chase, scattered pieces creating nothing but a jagged line. Reluctantly he rose, paying the bill.

He had waited for an hour in that familiar Leipzigerstrasse doorway when he recognised the number of the approaching Volkswagen. Bayer was driving with confidence, more used to the vehicle. He passed the Briton, unseen in the shadows, slowing at the border approach to edge dutifully into the yellow smear of light.

The sudden glare of the spotlight, instantly joined by others that had obviously been specially positioned, was the first indication, and later Charlie reflected that it had been a mistake, throwing the switch so soon. A professional would have managed to reverse, to make a run for it. The manoeuvre wouldn't have achieved anything, of course, because immediately State Police vehicles and even armoured cars swarmed from the roads and alleys behind, blocking any retreat. For a few seconds, the Volkswagen actually continued forward, then jerked to a stop, like an insect suddenly impaled under a microscope.

'Stay there,' said Charlie, opening his private conversation. 'They'll shoot if you move.'

The driver's door thrust open, bouncing on its hinges, and Bayer darted out, crouching, trying to shield his face from the light.

'Halt!'

The command echoed over the checkpoint from several amplifiers. On the fringe of the illumination, Charlie could detect a frieze of white faces as the Americans formed to watch from their side of the border. Would Snare and Harrison be there? he wondered.

Bayer began to run, without direction, plunging towards the mines before realising the error and twisting back to the roadway.

'Blinded,' Charlie told himself.

'Halt!'

Louder this time, with more amplifiers turned on.

'Stop, you bloody fool,' intoned Charlie.

Bayer was running back towards East Berlin now, towards the road-blocks he couldn't see, head thrown back, eyes bulging.

In the report to Cuthbertson two weeks later, Charlie wrote that those first shots were premature, like the lights, but by then the hysteria would have been gripping everyone. Given the lead, there was firing from all sides, even from the armoured vehicles towards which the student was fleeing. Bayer was thrown up by the crossfire, his feet snatched from the ground and then he collapsed, flopping and shapeless, like a rag-doll from which the stuffing had escaped.

The Volkswagen was sprayed in the shooting, too, and a bullet must have entered the petrol tank, which exploded in a red and yellow eruption. Debris fell on to the body, setting some of the clothing alight.

It took Charlie ten minutes to reach Bahnhof Friedrichstrasse and the tram arrived almost immediately.

I'd have liked to see the Reichstag in Hitler's day, thought Charlie, as the train carried him to safety past the silhouette. By the time he'd reached Berlin it had been 1956 and most of the landmarks were skeletons of brick and girders. Günther's father had been a tank commander in a Panzer division, he remembered the student telling him: he carried a yellowed, fading picture in his wallet and was fond of producing it. Poor Günther.

The crossing formalities were brief and within thirty minutes he was disembarking at Bahnhof Zoo, selecting the main station because the crush of people would have confused any East German sent in immediate pursuit when they discovered their mistake.

He bathed leisurely at the Kempinski, even waiting while his second suit was pressed, enjoying the thought of the confrontation that was to come.

Snare and Harrison were already in the bar, both slightly drunk as he had anticipated they would be. Snare saw him first, stopping with his hand outstretched towards his glass.

'Oh my God,' he managed, badly.

Harrison tried, but couldn't locate the words, standing with his head shaking refusal.

'You're dead,' insisted Snare, finally. 'We saw it happen.'

And stayed quite unmoved, guessed Charlie. They really *had* tried to set him up.

'Brandy,' he ordered, ignoring the two men. He made a measure between finger and thumb, indicating the large size to the barman.

Snare and Harrison really weren't good operatives, decided Charlie. No matter what the circumstances, they shouldn't have permitted such reaction.

'So you're having a wake for me,' he suggested, sarcastically, nodding towards the drinks. He raised his own glass. 'To my continued good health.'

Both grabbed for their glasses, joining in the toast. Like hopefuls in a school play, thought Charlie, watching the performance.

They were losing their surprise now, recognising the stupidity of their response and embarrassed by it.

'Charles,' said Snare. 'This is fantastic! Absolutely fantastic!'

'I thought you'd be pleased,' goaded Charlie. 'Booked a table for the celebration?'

'But we thought you'd been killed,' said Harrison, speaking at last. He was a heavy, ponderous man, with a face that flushed easily beneath a disordered scrub of red hair and with thick, butcher's fingers. A genetic throw-back, Charlie guessed, to a dalliance with a tradeswoman by one of his beknighted ancestors.

'Better fix it then, hadn't you?' replied Charlie.

'Of course,' agreed Harrison, flustered more than Snare by the reappearance. He gestured to the barman to inform the restaurant.

'How did you do it, Charles?' asked Snare. He was fully recovered now, Charlie saw. They'd have already informed London of his death, Charlie knew. That had been the main reason for delaying his entry into the bar, to enable them to make every mistake. Cuthbertson would have told the Minister: the two would get a terrible bollocking.

Charlie waited until they had been ushered into the rebooked table and had ordered before replying.

'A bit of luck,' he said, purposely deepening his accent. He paused, then made the decision.

'...There was this mate...'

'...who...?' broke off Harrison, stupidly.

Charlie considered the interruption for several minutes, robbed of the annoyance he had hoped to cause the other two men.

'His name was Bayer,' he said, seriously. 'Günther Bayer.'

The waiter began serving the oysters, breaking the conversation again. Charlie gazed out of the restaurant window at the necklace of lights around the city. Somewhere out there, he thought, was a girl called Gretel. She wouldn't know yet, he realised. She'd still be preparing her own celebration meal.

'Tabasco?' enquired the waiter.

'No,' answered Charlie, smiling. 'Just lemon.'

2.

The grilled, narrow windows of the special interview room at Wormwood Scrubs were set high into the wall, making it impossible to see anything but a rectangle of grey sky. Charlie gazed up, trying to determine whether it had started raining. He could feel the edge of the matting through the sole of his left shoe; if the weather broke, he'd get wet going back to Whitehall.

He turned back into the room, studying it expertly. The camera was set into the ventilation grid behind him, he knew. Then there'd be a microphone in the light socket. And another concealed in the over-large locking mechanism on the door. And it would be easy to have inserted another monitor in the edging around the table at which they would sit. Cuthbertson would have had it done, he guessed. The man liked electronic gadgetry.

Welcome the invention of the tape recorder, mused Charlie, his interest waning. He could still remember the days of silent note-takers and the irritable disagreements after a six-hour debriefing between operatives trying to remember precisely what had been said.

He heard footsteps and turned to the door expectantly, looking forward to the meeting with the Russian.

He liked Alexei Berenkov, he decided.

The Russian entered smiling, a shambling man with a bulging stomach, a tumble of coal-black hair and ready-to-laugh eyes set in a florid, over-indulged face. The cover of a wine importer, which had allowed frequent trips abroad, was well chosen, thought Charlie. Berenkov had had his own private wine bin at the Ritz and Claridge's and a permanent box at Ascot.

'Charlie!' greeted the Russian, expansively. He spread his arms and moved forward. Muffin made to shake hands, but Berenkov swept on, enveloping him in a hug. It wasn't a sham, remembered Charlie. They'd kept the man under observation for six months, before even beginning the concentrated investigation. Berenkov was a naturally exuberant extrovert, using the very attention he constantly attracted as a shield behind which to hide. Charlie stood with the man's arms around him, feeling foolish.

Thank God Snare and Harrison weren't there.

'It's good to see you, Alexei,' he said, disentangling himself. He looked beyond, to the warder who stood uncertainly inside the door, frowning at the greeting.

'You can go,' dismissed Charlie. Cuthbertson had arranged the meeting with his child-like interpretation of psychology and insisted just the two of them be in the room.

'I'm quite safe,' Berenkov told the official. He thought the assurance amusing and shouted with laughter, slapping Charlie's shoulder. The warder still hesitated. After several minutes, he shuffled away, flat-footedly. He'd stay very close, guessed Charlie. Cuthbertson would insist on a report from the man, despite all the recording apparatus.

Berenkov turned back, still smiling.

'The only thing missing is some wine,' apologised the Russian, playing the host. 'It's a pity. This year I'd selected some really sensational Aloxe Corton.'

Charlie smiled back, enjoying the performance.

'So they've sent you to find out what you can, thinking I'll be off-guard after the trial. And probably shocked by the sentence,' attacked the Russian, suddenly. The smile had gone, like a light being extinguished.

Charlie shrugged, sitting in one of the padded chairs by the table. Berenkov was very clever, he decided.

'I'm sorry,' said Charlie, in genuine embarrassment. 'I know it's bloody ridiculous. But they wouldn't listen.'

Berenkov moved to the table, glancing up at the heavy light fitting.

'Probably,' agreed Charlie, following Berenkov's look and recalling his earlier thoughts. 'It's the most obvious place.'

'Who are they, these fools who employ you?' demanded Berenkov.

Charlie settled comfortably. This was going to be enjoyable, he decided.

'It's no good, Alexei,' he said, wanting to prolong it. 'I made the point, saying you were obviously a professional who wouldn't break, even now. But they insisted. I've said I'm sorry.'

Berenkov puffed his cheeks, indignantly. Aware every remark was being relayed, he rose to the meeting, like the actor he was.

'They're cunts,' he said, offended. 'I'm a loyal Russian.'

'I know,' agreed Charlie, sincerely. 'But it was easier to come than to argue that you wouldn't give anything away about your system...'

He smiled, genuinely. 'Anyway,' he added, 'I wanted to see you again.'

It was an odd relationship between them, reflected Charlie. It was basically deep admiration from one professional to another, he supposed. Berenkov had realised, months before his arrest, that he was under observation. Charlie had made it obvious, in the end, hoping to frighten the man into an ill-considered move. Berenkov hadn't made one, of course. Instead, the knowledge had piqued his conceit and it had become a battle between them, an exercise in wits, like a game of postal chess. And Charlie had won, proving he was slightly the better of the two. So, added to Berenkov's admiration was an attitude of respect.

'Why weren't you at the trial?' Berenkov asked, settling at the table and taking, uninvited, one of Charlie's cigarettes.

'It was decided it was too dangerous,' said Charlie, unconvincingly repeating Cuthbertson's explanation. 'We didn't want to risk identification. Your people would have photographed everyone going into the Old Bailey, wouldn't they?'

Berenkov frowned for a moment, then smiled at Charlie's lead, looking up at the light.

'Oh yes,' he agreed. 'Every picture will be in Moscow by now.'

That would put the fear of Christ up the Special Branch and Cuthbertson, Charlie knew. They'd had four men of their own photographing everyone within a quarter of a mile vicinity during the week-long trial. It would take them months to identify every face; but Cuthbertson would insist upon it – 'mountains are just pieces of dust, all gathered together' was a new catch phrase from the department controller. Now he'd be shit scared there was the risk of his own men being identified.

'So Snare and Harrison got all the credit,' jabbed Berenkov.

The Russian *was* bloody good, thought Charlie. It was not surprising he'd held the rank of General in the KGB for the twenty years he'd operated in the West. His capture would be an enormous blow to Russia: perhaps even greater than they had realised.

'Something like that,' agreed Charlie.

'They're no good,' dismissed the prisoner. 'Too smart... too keen to shine and impress people. Their performance in court was more like *Sunday Night at the London Palladium*. Send them on a field operation and we'd use it as a training exercise.

Oh God, how I'd like to be with Cuthbertson when the tapes are played back, thought Charlie. Please God let Snare and Harrison be there.

The Briton thought again of the life style that Berenkov had followed until his arrest six months earlier: despite the apparent *bonhomie*, the man must be suffering, he decided.

'What's it like here?' asked Charlie, curiously, gesturing to the prison around them.

'Known worse,' replied Berenkov, lightly.

And he would have done, Charlie knew. The Russian admitted to being fifty, but Charlie assessed him ten years older. He'd have served in the Russian army during the war, probably as a field officer on the German Front. Certainly it was from Germany that he had appeared, posing as a refugee displaced by the division of his country, to enter Britain.

'But forty years!' reminded Charlie.

Berenkov stared at him, frowning, imagining for a moment that the Briton was serious. He shrugged, agreeing to whatever Charlie wanted to achieve.

'Don't be stupid,' he answered. 'I won't serve forty years and we all know it. I guess two, but it might be shorter. I'm very highly regarded in the Soviet Union. They'll arrange an exchange. All they need is a body.'

And they almost had one four months ago at Checkpoint Charlie, remembered the Briton.

The KGB general leaned back, reflectively.

'I tried to outwit you, Charlie. You know I did,' he began, unexpectedly. 'But more to cover up my network than for myself.'

He was being truthful now, realised Charlie, the recording apparatus disregarded.

'You know what my feelings were, realising you were after me?' Berenkov stared across the table, intently.

'What?' prompted Charlie.

'Relief,' answered Berenkov, simply. He leaned forward, arms on the table, gazing straight at the other man.

'You know what I mean, Charlie,' he said, urgently. 'Look at us. Apart from being born in different countries and being absolutely committed to opposite sides, we're practically identical. And we're freaks, Charlie. Whoever heard of two spies, both out in the field, alive and nudging fifty?'

Charlie shrugged, uncomfortably. 'I know,' he agreed.

'I was losing my grip, Charlie,' admitted Berenkov. 'And I think Moscow was beginning to realise it. I've been scared for the last two years. But now everything is all right.'

'Sure?' questioned Charlie.

'Positive,' insisted Berenkov, with his usual confidence. 'Look at the facts. I'll spend a couple of years here, warm, safe and comfortable as a guest of Her Majesty's Government, then be exchanged...'

He leaned back, eyes distant, reflecting his future.

'I've retired, Charlie,' he said. 'Waiting for me in Moscow is a wife I've only ever seen for two or three weeks a year, on phoney wine-buying trips to Europe. And a son of eighteen I've met just once...'

He came back to the Briton.

'...he's studying engineering at Moscow University,' continued Berenkov. 'He'll pass with a First. I'm very proud.'

Charlie nodded, knowing it would be wrong to interrupt the reminiscence.

'I shall go back to full honours, feted as a hero. I've a government apartment I've never seen and a dacha in the hills outside Moscow. I'll teach at the spy college and spend the summers in the sun at Sochi. Think of it, Charlie – won't it be wonderful!'

'Wonderful,' said Charlie.

The Russian hesitated, appearing uncertain. The need to hit back at someone who had proved himself superior surfaced.

'What about you, Charlie?' worried the Russian. 'What's your future... where's your sunshine...?'

Outside, the rain finally broke, driven against the windows with sharp, hissing sounds by the growing wind. Charlie moved his foot inside the worn-out shoe. Bugger it, he thought.

'If I hadn't been caught, Charlie, I'd have been withdrawn. Operatives our age are expendable.'

The memory of the exploding Volkswagen and the way it had ignited the body of Günther Bayer pushed itself into Charlie's mind.

'I know,' he said, softly.

'But there is a difference,' said Berenkov, scoring still. 'Russia never forgets a spy... my release is guaranteed...'

He paused, allowing the point to register.

'...but Britain couldn't give a bugger,' he sneered. 'I'd hate to work in your service, Charlie.'

The man was right, accepted the Briton. The eagerness of the British Government to dissociate itself from a captured operative had always been obscene. How much enjoyment Cuthbertson and Wilberforce would get, cutting him off, thought Charlie, bitterly.

'It's a great incentive not to get caught,' said Charlie, hollowly.

'Bullshit,' replied Berenkov quickly. 'How your people can ever expect anyone to work for them I'll never understand. Russia might have its faults... and it's got them, millions of them. But at least it's got loyalty.'

'Moscow will be very strange to you, after so long,' Charlie tried to recover.

Berenkov shrugged, uncaring. 'But I'll be able to wake up in the morning without those sixty seconds of gut-churning fear while you wait to see if you're alone... without having to turn immediately, to ensure that the pistol is still under the pillow and hasn't been taken by the man you always expect to be waiting at the end of the bed.'

It was as if the other man were dictating the fears that he was daily experiencing, thought Charlie.

'How many more jobs will there be, Charlie?' pressed the Russian. 'Will we get you next time? Or will you be lucky and survive a little longer?'

Charlie sighed, unable to answer.

'Perhaps I'll get a Whitehall desk and a travel organiser's job.'

Berenkov shook his head.

'That's not the way your people work, Charlie,' he replied, correctly. 'You'll be for the dump.'

Cuthbertson *had* been prepared to sacrifice him, Charlie knew. Ordering the three of them to return from East Berlin separately, then leaking the number of the Volkswagen that would be crossing last, had been a brilliant manoeuvre, guaranteeing that two operatives crossed ahead of it with the complete list of all Berenkov's East European contacts to make the Old Bailey prosecution foolproof.

It had just meant the demise of Charlie Muffin, that's all. Expendable, like Berenkov said.

'Worried about your network?' tried Charlie.

Berenkov smiled. 'Of course not.'

'So it hasn't been closed down,' snatched Charlie.

Berenkov's smile faltered.

'How would I know?' he said. 'I've been in custody for seven months already.'

'We managed to get five,' revealed Charlie.

The expression barely reached Berenkov's face. So there were more, discerned Charlie.

'Well, they had a good run and made some money,' dismissed the Russian, lightly. 'And I always let them have their wine wholesale.'

Charlie wondered the price of Aloxe Corton. It would be nice to take a bottle to Janet's flat. He had £5 and might be able to get some expenses from Cuthbertson. Then again, he contradicted, he might not. Accounts claimed he was £60 overdrawn and Cuthbertson had sent him two memoranda about getting the debt cleared before the end of the financial year. Bloody clerk.

'Will you come to see me?' asked the Russian. Quickly he added: 'Socially, I mean.'

'I'll try,' promised Charlie.

'I'd appreciate it,' replied Berenkov, honestly. 'They have given me a job in the library, so I'll have books. But I'll need conversation.'

The Russian *would* suffer, thought Charlie, looking around the prison room: the whole place had the institutionalised smell of dust, urine and paraffin heaters. It was a frightening contrast to the life he had known for so long. Charlie heard the scuff of the hovering warder outside the door. It had been a useful meeting, he decided. He wondered if Cuthbertson would realise it.

He rose, stretching.

'I really will try,' he undertook.

Again there was the bear-hug of departure: the man still retained the odour of expensive cologne.

'Remember what I said, Charlie,' warned Berenkov. 'Be careful.'
'Sure,' agreed Charlie, easily.
Berenkov held him, refusing to let him turn away.
'I mean it, Charlie...'
He dropped his restraining hands, almost embarrassed.
'...You've got a feel about you, Charlie... the feel of a loser...'

General Valery Kalenin was a short, square-bodied Georgian who regarded Alexei Berenkov as the best friend he had ever known, and recognised with complete honesty that the reason for this was that the other man had spent so much time away from Russia that it had been impossible for him to tire of the association, like everyone else did.

General Kalenin was a man with a brilliant, calculating mind and absolutely no social ability, which he accepted, like a person aware of bad breath or offensive perspiration. Because of a psychological quirk, which had long ceased bothering him, he had no sexual inclination, either male or female. The lack of interest was immediately detected by women, who resented it, and by men, who usually misinterpreted it, and were offended by what they regarded as hostile coldness, verging on contempt for their shortcomings compared to his intellect.

With virtually nothing to distract him apart from his absorption in the history of tank warfare, in which he was an acknowledged expert, Kalenin's entire existence was devoted to the *Komitet Gosudarstvennoy Bezopasnosti* and he had become a revered figure in the KGB of which he was now chief tactician and planner.

Utterly dedicated, he worked sixteen hours a day in Dzerzhinsky Square or in any of the capitals of the Warsaw Pact, of which he was over-all intelligence commander. Any surplus time was spent organising solitary war games with his toy tanks on the kitchen floor of his apartment in Kutuzovsky Prospekt. Only during the war games did General Kalenin feel his loneliness and regret his inability to make friends: it was always difficult to perform as the leader of both sides, even though he was scrupulously fair, never cheating with the dice.

The arrest of Berenkov had affected him deeply, although it would have been impossible for anyone to have realised it from his composure in the small conference chamber in the Kremlin complex.

'Berenkov *must* be exchanged,' said the committee chairman, Boris Kastanazy, breaking into the General's reflections.

Kalenin looked warily at the man who formed the link between the Praesidium and the KGB. It was the fourth occasion he'd uttered the same sentence. Kalenin wondered if he were completely secure or whether he should be worried by this man.

'I know,' responded Kalenin. There was no trace of irritation in his voice.

'And will be,' he added. He wasn't frightened, he decided. And Kastanazy knew it. The man would be annoyed. He enjoyed scaring people.

'Not if the attempt to ensnare a British operative is handled with the stupidity surrounding the East Berlin border crossing.'

'The officers who reacted prematurely have been reprimanded,' reminded Kalenin.

Kastanazy moved, irritably.

'That's a stupid gesture; it wasn't the right man, so what does it matter? The important thing is that one of the best operatives the service ever had is rotting in a filthy jail and we're doing nothing about it.'

Kastanazy was a pinch-faced, expressionless man who wore spectacles with which he fidgeted constantly, like some men use worry beads.

'At the last full session of the Praesidium,' said the chairman, slowly, gazing down at the revolving spectacles, 'a lengthy discussion was held on the matter.'

'I am aware how this committee was formed,' said Kalenin. He would not be intimidated by the man, he decided.

'But I don't get the impression, Comrade General, that you fully appreciate the determination to retrieve General Berenkov.'

'I assure you, Comrade Chairman,' retorted the tiny KGB chief, 'that I do.'

'Have plans been made?'

'I am in the course of formulating proposals,' Kalenin tried to avoid.

'You mean you've done nothing?' demanded Kastanazy, sharply.

'I mean I do not intend embarking on anything that will worsen, rather than improve, the position of General Berenkov.'

Kastanazy sighed, noisily, staring directly at the other man. When he spoke, he did so with care, wanting the words to register. He talked directly to the secretary sitting alongside, ensuring everything was correctly recorded for later submission to the Presidium.

'I want you to leave the meeting understanding one thing…'

He paused, but Kalenin refused to prompt him, knowing it would show nervousness.

'I want you to fully appreciate,' said Kastanazy, 'that if General Berenkov isn't being received with full honours at Sheremetyevo airport reasonably soon, the most stringent enquiry will be held…'

He hesitated again and Kalenin knew he had not finished.

'…an enquiry, Comrade General, in which you will be the central character…'

3.

Charlie Muffin wedged the saturated suede boots beneath the radiator, then spread his socks over the metal ribs to dry. There was a faint hissing sound.

The bottoms of his trousers, where the raincoat had ended, were concertinaed and sodden and he felt cold, knowing his shirt was wet where the coat had leaked. It was the newer of the two suits he possessed and now it would have to be dry-cleaned. It wouldn't be long before it started getting shiny at the seat, he thought, miserably.

Charlie wondered if he would catch influenza or a cold from his soaking; it would provide an excuse to stay away from the office for a few days. He stopped at the hope. The last time he'd had such a thought he had been a fifth former, trying to avoid an English examination at Manchester Grammar School.

'Steady, Charlie,' he advised himself. 'Things aren't that bad.'

He would have kept drier, he reflected, had he caught a taxi back from Wormwood Scrubs, instead of travelling by bus and underground from Shepherd's Bush. The sacrifice had been worth it, he decided. It meant an expenses profit of £2 and a bottle of wine for tonight.

'Aloxe Corton,' he reminded himself. 'Mustn't forget the name.'

The dye had come out of his boots, staining his heels and between his toes a khaki colour. Barefoot, he padded into the lavatory opposite his office, from which he could always hear the flush and usually the reason for it, filled a water glass with hot water and returned towards his office, pausing at the door. He'd only occupied it for three months, since Cuthbertson had decreed that the room adjoining his own suite and in which Charlie had worked during home periods for the past twenty years was big enough for two men. So Snare and Harrison had got the airy, oak-panelled room with its views of the Cenotaph. And Charlie – 'as a senior operative, you'll have to be alone, old boy' – had been relegated to what had once been the secretaries' rest room, overlooking an inner courtyard where the canteen dustbins were kept. On the wall by the window there was still a white outline where the sanitary-towel dispenser had been: Janet had identified the mark and Charlie refused to have it painted over, knowing it offended Cuthbertson.

He entered the cramped room, sitting carefully at the desk, which was wedged tight against one wall. The wet trousers clung to his ankles and he grimaced, unhappily. Even with two men in it, he remembered, his old office was still bigger than that he was now forced to occupy. And it had had an electric fire, too, where he could have dried his trousers.

He stripped some blotting paper, soaked it in the glass and began sponging his feet, reflecting on his meeting with Berenkov Had the Russian meant to tell him so much? he wondered. It could hardly have been a mistake; he wasn't the sort of man to allow errors. He'd been caught, contradicted Charlie. *That* had been a mistake. Or had it? Had Berenkov been incredibly clever, accepting his self-confessed fear and manoeuvred the whole thing, confident of repatriation as a hero after sentence?

He paused, left ankle across his right knee. Were his feelings for Berenkov admiration or envy? he wondered, suddenly.

'Good God!'

Snare stood at the doorway, gazing down at him.

'What the hell do you think you are doing?' demanded the younger man.

'Washing my feet,' retorted Charlie, obviously. Snare's expressions of horror were encompassing the entire religious gamut, Charlie thought. He was embarrassed at being caught by the other man.

Snare leaned on the doorpost knowing the discomfort and enjoying it.

'Very biblical,' mocked Snare. 'Can you do miracles too?'

'Yes,' said Charlie, irritably. 'I can come back from the dead out of burning Volkswagens.'

The smile left Snare's face and he moved away from the doorway. The bastard *had* known, Charlie decided, even before they'd gone into East Berlin.

'The Director wants to see you,' said Snare. Wanting to score, he quickly added, 'With your shoes on.'

'Then he'll have to wait,' said Charlie. A faint mist was rising from his drying socks and shoes. And there was a smell, realised Charlie, uncomfortably.

'Shall I tell him ten minutes?'

'Tell him what you like,' said Charlie. 'I'm waiting for my socks to dry.'

He was ready in fifteen minutes, but was delayed another ten by comparing two sheets in the Berenkov file.

'Charlie boy, you're a genius,' he assured himself. They were waiting for him. Charlie saw Snare was standing at the window, appearing preoccupied with the view below. Harrison was sitting by the small table containing the newspapers and magazines, his back to the wall, determined to miss nothing. Wilberforce was in the leather-backed lounging chair to the side of Cuthbertson's desk disembowelling a pipe he never seemed to light with a set of attachments that retracted into a single gold case. The second-in-command was a slightly built but very tall fine featured man with fingers so long they appeared to have an extra joint and of which he was over conscious, frequently making washing movements, covering one with the other, which drew attention to their oddness. He invariably wore gloves even in the summer, and had a predilection for pastel-shaded shirts that he always wore with matching socks. Probably dryer than mine, thought Charlie, who still felt damp. He decided Wilberforce carried the pipe as a symbol of masculinity.

'More comfortable now?' greeted Cuthbertson, heavily.

The new Director was a very large but precise man, with a face permanently reddened by a sub-lieutenant's liking for curry at the beginning of his career in Calcutta, and a later tendency to blood pressure on the British General Staff. He had a distressingly phlegmy voice, which meant he bubbled rather than spoke words. Charlie found this offensive. But then he found most things about Cuthbertson offensive. The man's family was probably traceable back to Elizabethan times and there had been generals in it for three hundred years. It was with that rank, plus a DSO and the inherited baronetcy originally conferred by George III, that Cuthbertson had left the Chief of Staff to head the department. His outlook and demeanour were as regimented as his brigade or Eton tie, the family-crested signet ring and the daily lunch at Boodle's. Which was precisely why he had been appointed, a government experiment to improve by strict discipline and army-type order a department that had suffered two humiliating – and worse, public – mistakes in attempting to establish systems in Poland and Czechoslovakia.

Charlie wondered how long it would take before they suffered their biggest mistake to date. Not long, he decided, confidently.

'Much more comfortable, thank you, sir,' replied Charlie. The term of respect sounded offensive. No one offered him a chair, so he stood casually at ease. On a parade ground, he thought, Cuthbertson would have put him on a charge.

'Which is more than I can say for myself,' said Cuthbertson, softly. It was an affectation never to be seen to lose his temper, so it was impossible to gauge any mood from the gurgling tone in which the man spoke.

'Sir?'

'It has been my misfortune…'

He paused, gesturing to the others in the room.

'...and the misfortune and embarrassment of my colleagues, to have listened to a tape recording that many people might construe as being almost treasonable...'

He stopped again, as if expecting Charlie to speak, but the man remained silent, eyes fixed on the Director's forehead. If he wriggled his toes, Charlie discovered, he could make a tiny squelching sound with his left boot.

'Psychologically,' continued Cuthbertson, 'today was the ideal time to interrogate Berenkov... bewildered and frightened by the severity of his sentence, cut off from life and eager to exchange every confidence with someone conducting an examination in a proper, sympathetic way...'

Charlie wondered at the text-book from which Cuthbertson would have read that thesis. It was probably a do-it-yourself paperback from WH Smith's, he decided.

Snare turned away from the window, wanting to see Charlie suffer.

'Instead,' continued the former army officer, 'we got the meanderings of two men play-acting for the benefit of the recorders... recorders that Berenkov could only have learned about from you...'

It would have been a severe exercise of will to maintain the monotone, thought Charlie. He wondered why the man never cleared his throat. A nerve in Cuthbertson's left eye-lid began twitching, indicating his anger. The man felt on his desk for a transcript.

'...The Russian made a remark about age,' said Cuthbertson, apparently reading. He'd rehearsed this part, Charlie realised.

The Director stood up, trying to hold Charlie's eyes.

'For you, it was a prophecy,' declared Cuthbertson. 'I've already sent to the Minister a copy of the transcript and my appreciation of it, together with my recommendation of your immediate, premature departure from any position of authority in this department... I don't want traitors working with me, Muffin.'

Snare and Harrison were smirking, Charlie saw.

Silence settled like frost in the room. Charlie stayed unmoving, wanting Cuthbertson to finish completely, with no opportunity for retreat. What idiots they all were, he thought.

'Have you anything to say?' demanded Wilberforce, still rummaging into the bowl of his pipe. He would find it impossible to confront directly anyone being disciplined, Charlie realised. The permanent civil servant had waited a long time for this scene, Charlie knew. Why, he wondered, did Wilberforce hate him so?

'Does that mean I'm fired?' he asked, hopefully. He purposely omitted the 'sir'.

'It does not,' said Cuthbertson. 'I want you under constant supervision, where I can ensure you don't forget the terms of the Official Secrets Act by which you're bound for a lifetime but which, judging from this morning's performance, you have forgotten.'

'Demotion?' asked Charlie.

'As far down as I can possibly achieve,' confirmed Cuthbertson.

'So my allowance and salary will be cut?'

Cuthbertson nodded.

'And you've suggested all this in the letter to the Minister?' demanded Charlie. He was enjoying himself, he realised.

'That's an impudent question,' said Cuthbertson huffily. 'But yes, I have.'

'Oh dear,' said Charlie. 'That was a silly thing to have done.'

The silence this time was far more oppressive than that of a few moments before when Cuthbertson had announced his decision on Charlie's future. Wilberforce had stopped working on his pipe, but remained staring fixedly at it, as if he expected to find a clue in the blackened bowl. Harrison shifted uncomfortably in the chair, as if he wanted to use a lavatory, and Snare looked hurriedly from person to person, seeking a clue from the others on what reaction to make. The lobes of Cuthbertson's ears flushed and the nerve in his eye increased its tic.

'Impudence will not gain the dismissal to get whatever redundancy pay you imagine is owed you,' rejected Cuthbertson, haughtily.

For the first time, Charlie lowered his eyes from the man's forehead, staring directly at him. Cuthbertson appeared to realise Charlie was not scared and blinked, irritably. It was very rare for Cuthbertson to encounter somebody not in awe of him, Charlie guessed.

He'd make them suffer, he decided; he had very little to lose. Nothing, in fact. Their decision about Charlie Muffin had been made months ago. He supposed he should consider himself lucky he was still alive.

'There is a procedure,' he began, slowly. 'Innovated by your predecessors... a procedure that the Minister likes followed because it has shown such success in the past...'

'But one which was overlooked in the Czechoslovakian and Polish disasters,' tried Snare, eager to impress his mentor.

Charlie turned to him, frowning.

'I'm sorry?' he said, knowing the effect would be destroyed if the man were forced to repeat it.

'Nothing,' said Snare. 'Just a comment.'

'Oh,' said Charlie. He still waited, as if expecting Snare to repeat himself. Wince, you bastard, he thought. At last he looked back to Cuthbertson.

'I'm sure it will be followed in the case of my interview with

Berenkov,' he continued. 'Once established, procedures are rigidly followed. And *you've* decreed that, of course.'

Cuthbertson nodded, cautiously. The man's left eye twitched and Charlie thought he detected Wilberforce looking surreptitiously at him.

'What are you talking about?' demanded the Director.

He was beginning to become unsettled, Charlie decided, happily, detecting the apprehension in that unpleasant voice.

'The detailed analysis,' said Charlie. 'By psychological experts, not only of the tapes but of the film that was shot in the interview room.'

'What about it?'

'Your reaction to the meeting and your recommendation was made without waiting for the results of that analysis.'

'There was no need to wait,' defended Cuthbertson.

'As I said,' reminded Charlie. 'A silly thing to have done.' They were all frightened, he knew, without being able to appreciate their mistake. It was time to change his approach, he determined.

'My meeting with Berenkov was one of the most productive I can remember having had with a captured spy,' asserted Charlie, brutally. 'And the analyst's department will confirm it…'

He paused, deciding to allow himself the conceit.

'…They always have in the past,' he added.

Wilberforce was back at his pipe but the other three were staring at him, unmoving.

'Close examination of the transcript,' continued Charlie, hesitating for another aside, '…much closer than you've allowed yourselves… will confirm several things. Berenkov admitted his nerve had gone. If he knew it, then Moscow certainly did. And the Kremlin would have acted upon that knowledge. A replacement would have been installed in London, long before we got on to Berenkov. He's important, certainly. But because of what he'd done in the past, not for what he might have done in the future. We haven't broken the Russians' European spy system. I estimate his successor will have been here for a year, at least… so you've got to begin all over again…'

The vibration in Cuthbertson's eye was now so severe he put his hand up to cover it.

'There are a number of his existing network whom we haven't caught, either,' enlarged Charlie. 'Consider the film and watch the facial reaction when I announced, quite purposely, that we have caught five. Slow the film: it will show a second's look of triumph, indicating there are some still free…

Charlie stopped again, swallowing. They were so innocent, he thought, looking at the four men. Wilberforce was like them, he decided, institutionalised by training according to a rule book and completely unaware of what they should be doing.

'...And he told us how to find them,' Charlie threw out.

He waited. They would have to crawl, he determined.

'How?' asked Cuthbertson, at last.

'By boasting,' explained Charlie. 'Letting them have their wine wholesale wasn't a smart, throwaway remark. It was exactly the grandiose sort of thing that an extrovert like Berenkov would have done. And he would have kept scrupulous records; a spy always complies with every civil law of any country in which he's operating. Check every wholesale outlet against income tax returns and you'll find the rest of the network. The five we've got are all on it – I checked while my socks were drying.'

He looked carefully at each man, allowing his head to shake almost imperceptibly.

'I'm *really* sorry that the meeting was regarded by you all as such a failure,' he insisted, straining for the final insult. 'And I'm sure the Minister will be surprised when he considers your views against those of the detailed analysis. Now, if you'll excuse me, I'll clear my desk...'

He drew almost to attention, coming back to Cuthbertson.

'Have I your permission to leave, sir?'

The Director seemed intent on the papers lying before him and it was several minutes before he spoke.

'We could have been a little premature in our assessment,' he conceded. The words were very difficult for him, Charlie knew. He noted the pronoun; within the day, the mistake would be shown not to be Cuthbertson's but someone else wrongly guiding him.

Charlie said nothing, knowing that silence was his best weapon now.

'Perhaps,' continued the Director, 'we should re-examine the tape and discuss it tomorrow.'

'Re-examine the tape by all means,' agreed Charlie, deciding to abandon the 'sir'; Cuthbertson didn't deserve any respect. 'I'm sure the Minister will expect a more detailed knowledge of it at the meeting you will inevitably have,' he added. 'But tomorrow I'm going on leave... you've already approved it, you'll remember?'

'Of course,' said Cuthbertson, groping on the desk again, as if seeking the memorandum of agreement.

'So perhaps we'll discuss my future in a fortnight?'

Cuthbertson nodded, half concurring, half dismissing. His presence embarrassed them, Charlie knew. They would welcome the two-week gap more than he.

'I can go?' pressed Charlie.

'Yes,' said Cuthbertson, shortly.

Outside the office, Charlie turned right, away from his own room, feeling very happy.

Janet was sitting expectantly at her desk, solemn-faced.

'I've been dumped,' announced Charlie.

'I know,' said Cuthbertson's secretary. 'I typed the report to the Minister. Oh Charlie, I'm so sorry.'

'So are they,' said Charlie, brightly. 'They've made a balls of it. Tonight still OK?'

The girl stared at him, uncertainly.

'Does it mean you won't be demoted to some sort of clerk?'

'Don't know,' said Charlie. 'Seven o'clock?'

She nodded, bewildered.

Whistling tunelessly, Charlie wandered back to his cramped room. The affair with Janet had only begun four weeks ago and still had the excitement of newness about it. Pity the holiday would intrude; but that was important. Edith needed a vacation, he decided, thinking fondly of his wife.

And so did he, though for different reasons.

General Kalenin pushed aside the file containing the questionable plans for Berenkov's release, lounging back in his chair to look over the Kremlin complex. Most of the office lights were out, he saw. How different it had been in Stalin's time, he remembered, when people remained both day and night at their desks, afraid of a summons from the megalomaniac insomniac.

He looked back to the unsatisfactory dossier. He was more apprehensive now than he had ever been then, he decided. The Berenkov affair could topple him, Kalenin realised. It wasn't the purge and disgrace that frightened him. It was being physically removed from the office in the Lubyanka buildings in Dzerzhinsky Square. Without a job, he would have nothing, he thought. He'd commit suicide, he decided, quite rationally. It wasn't the first time he'd thought of such a thing and there was no fear in the consideration. A revolver, he determined. Very quick. And befitting an officer.

He sighed, hearing midnight strike. Slowly he packed the papers into his personal safe, trying to arouse some anticipation for the war game he had prepared when he got to his apartment.

Tonight he was going to start the Battle of Kursk, the greatest tank engagement in history. But his mind wouldn't be on it, he knew.

4.

Charlie had seen advertised in the *New Yorker* the orange Gucci lounging pyjamas, with the matching rhinestone-encrusted sandals in which Janet greeted him.

She smelt fresh and expensive and when he kissed her, just inside the doorway of the Cadogan Square flat, he could feel she was still warm from her bath. It was nice of her to go to all the trouble, thought Charlie.

'I've bought some wine,' he announced.

She accepted the bag from him and extracted the bottle.

'Lovely,' she said. 'Spanish burgundy.'

'They didn't have Aloxe Corton,' he said. They had, but it had been priced at £4.

'What?' she said, moving further into the flat.

It wasn't important, decided Charlie. 'Nothing,' he said. Janet was using him, he decided, as he entered the antique-adorned living-room behind her, watching her body beneath the silk. She had a lovely ass.

Had she been born in a council house instead of on a country estate and attended a state school instead of Roedean, Janet would have been a slag, Charlie decided. She had an amorality sometimes found in the rich that made her sexually promiscuous, experimental and constantly avaricious. Rich enough – first from an aunt's, then a cousin's inheritance – to do nothing, Janet worked for £4,000 a year as Cuthbertson's private secretary and never had any money. To get it, she had even whored, in a dilettante, friends-only way – 'making a hobby pay for itself' – and enjoyed boasting about it, imagining Charlie would be impressed or excited by it. Charlie felt she was exactly his sort of woman. And in addition, very useful. And she really was very good at her hobby between those silk sheets that always slipped off the bed, so that his bum got cold.

Quite unoffended, Charlie knew he was another experiment, like working for Sir Henry Cuthbertson, who was her godfather, and drinking warm bitter, which she had done for the first time on their initial date in the dive bar of the Red Lion, near Old Scotland Yard, and declared it, politely, to be lovely. Charlie was 'other people', a person to be studied like she had examined dissected frogs at her Zürich finishing school after leaving Sussex.

'Like the duchess screwing the dustman,' he reflected, aloud, stretching his feet towards the electric fire. They were still damp, he saw, watching the steam rise.

She reappeared from the kitchen, corkscrew in hand. She was a tall girl, hair looped long to her shoulders, bordering a face that needed only a little accent around the deep brown, languorous eyes and an outline for the lips that were inclined to pout.

'What about a duchess?' she queried.

'You look like one,' said Charlie, easily.

Who was using whom? he wondered, smiling up at her. Poor Janet.

He pulled the wine, filling the glasses she offered.

'Love or what you will,' he toasted.

She drank, swallowing heavily.

'Very nice,' she said bravely.

They had bred good manners in Switzerland, thought Charlie. He smiled, imagining Berenkov's reaction to the wine. It was bloody awful.

'For a man who has been demoted, you're remarkably unconcerned,' said Janet, sitting opposite. She wasn't wearing a bra, he realised.

'I told you, they've made a balls,' he said. Rough talk would fit the image she wanted, he decided. He refilled his glass, ignoring her; it was unfair to expect her to drink it.

'How?'

'Completely misread the interview,' he reported. 'They have determined to get rid of me, certainly. But it won't work this time.'

'Cuthbertson won't apologise,' predicted Janet.

The fact that she was his god-daughter was incredibly useful, reflected Charlie; no one in the department knew the man like she did.

'He'll have to.'

She shook her head.

'I know Sir Henry. He's a bastard.'

'So am I,' responded Charlie. 'Funny thing is, nobody has realised it. It'll be the ruin of them.'

She smiled at the boast. It was a normal reaction, she supposed. His pride must be badly bruised; he'd once been the most important operative in the department.

'I've cooked a meal, so we can eat here,' she announced, wanting to move him away from the afternoon.

And not run the risk of being seen by any of your friends, thought Charlie. She would be very embarrassed by him, he knew. He was very happy with the proposal; there was no outing they would mutually enjoy and whatever they tried would have cost money and he didn't have any. And she would never think of paying.

'What happened after I left?' asked Charlie, spreading the salmon mousse on the toast.

The girl sighed. The preoccupation was to be expected, she thought, but it made him boring.

'They went potty,' said Janet. 'Wilberforce was sent to retrieve the report to the Minister, but it had already gone. So Sir Henry dictated a contradicting amendment, then scrapped it because it seemed ridiculous. When I left, he was making arrangements to dine the Minister at Lockets to explain everything.'

'And who got the blame?' queried Charlie.

'Wilberforce,' answered Janet. 'Poor man. Uncle treats him almost like a court jester.'

'Masochist,' identified Charlie. 'Gets a sexual thrill out of being tongue-lashed.'

She believed him, realised Charlie, seeing the interested look on her face. To correct the misunderstanding seemed too much bother.

He cut into the *steak au poivre*, sipping the wine she had provided.

'This is good,' he complimented.

'Margaux,' explained Janet, patiently. 'Daddy takes the production of the vineyard. This is '62.'

Charlie nodded, as if he'd recognised the vintage.

'Where did you learn to cook like this?'

'They thought it important at school.'

'What have Snare and Harrison been told to do?' he probed, insistently. She obviously hadn't understood the wording of the Official Secrets Act she had promised to obey seven months earlier.

'Interrogate Berenkov again.'

'Oh Christ,' said Charlie, putting aside his knife and fork. 'That's a tape I'd love to hear.'

She pushed away her plate, fingering the stem of her wine glass.

'I'm very fond of you, Charlie,' she announced, suddenly.

At least she didn't make any pretence of love, he thought. He hoped she wasn't moving to end the affair; he wasn't ready for it to end yet. He gazed across the table, admiring her. Certainly not yet.

He waited, apprehensively.

'What are you going to do? They're determined to get you out,' she said.

Charlie stopped eating, appetite gone.

'I know,' he said, completely serious. 'And it frightens me to death. They won't let me go, because they want me under observation. Or stay, because they detest me. So I'm faced with working for the next fifteen years as a poxy clerk.'

'You couldn't stand that, Charlie.'

'I've got no bloody choice, have I? I've devoted my life to the service. I love it. There's not another sodding thing I could do, even if they'd let me.'

He *did* love the life, he decided, adding to both their glasses. Because he was so good at it.

It had been wonderful before Cuthbertson and the army mafia had arrived, when his ability had been properly recognised.

The Director had been Sir Archibald Willoughby, who'd led paratroopers into Arnhem with his batman carrying a £20 hamper from Fortnum & Mason, and Venetian goblets for the claret in special leather cases. He was cultivating Queen Elizabeth and Montana Star roses in Rye now, hating every moment of it. There'd been two written invitations to visit him since his summary retirement, but so far Charlie had avoided it. They'd drink too much whisky and become maudlin about previous operations, he knew. And there was no way they could have kept the conversation off Bill Elliot.

On the day of the purge, Elliot had been sent home early because Cuthbertson, who read spy novels, imagined he would find evidence of a traitor if he turned out every desk and safe in the department.

So the second in-command had arrived in Pulborough three hours earlier than usual for a Tuesday to find his wife in bed with her brother.

Elliot had walked from the room without a word, gone directly to the hide at the bottom of the garden from which he had earned the reputation of one of Britain's leading amateur ornithologists and blown the top of his head away with an army-issue Webley fired through the mouth. He had been crying and he'd made a muck of it, so it had taken two days for him to die.

The suicide had slotted neatly into Cuthbertson's 'who's to blame' mentality, despite the wife's unashamed account to the police, and Elliot had been labelled responsible for the Warsaw and Prague débâcles. It would be nice, reflected Charlie, to prove Cuthbertson wrong about that. Like everything else.

'Sure they wouldn't let you retire, prematurely?' asked Janet, breaking Charlie's silent reminiscence.

'Positive,' asserted Charlie. 'And I don't think I'd want to. At least rotting as a clerk would mean a salary of some sort. I wouldn't live off a reduced pension.'

'I thought Edith had money.'

'She's loaded,' confirmed Charlie. 'But my wife is tighter than a seal's asshole.'

She smiled, nodding. It really was the sort of language she expected, Charlie realised.

'Do you know there are receipted bills at home dating back ten years. And if you asked her the amount, she could remember,' he added.

'Why not leave her?'

'What for?' challenged Charlie. 'Would you have me move in here, a worn-out old bugger of forty-one without a bank account of his own who can only afford Spanish plonk.'

She reached across, squeezing his hand.

'From the performance so far, you're hardly worn out,' contradicted Janet. 'But no, Charlie. I wouldn't.'

'So I've got to stay, haven't I? – tethered to a job that doesn't want me. And at home, to a wife who's not very interested.'

'Poor Charlie,' she said. She didn't sound sad, he thought. He gestured round the apartment, then nodded towards her.

'All this will end, when I'm transferred, won't it?'

'I expect so,' she said, always honest, looking straight at him.

'Pity.'

'It's been fun,' she said. She made it sound like a skiing lesson or a day out at Ascot when she'd picked a winner.

'Shall we go to bed?' he suggested.

'That's what you came here for.'

They took a long time with each other, exploring; like children in bicycle sheds at school, thought Charlie, biting at her thigh. Just more comfortable, that's all.

'Don't. That hurts.'

'So does what you're doing. I can feel your teeth.'

'Want me to stop?'

'No.'

'Charlie.'

'What?'

'Your feet are a funny brown colour.'

'My shoes leaked. The dye won't come off.'

'Poor Charlie.'

Then:

'I like what you're doing, Charlie.'

'Where did you learn to do *that*?' he said, with difficulty.

'At school.'

All that and cooking too, reflected Charlie. He winced, conscious of her teeth again. He should have washed his feet a second time, he told himself. She'd bathed, after all.

Charlie and his wife crossed on the following night's ferry from Southampton, so they were in Cherbourg by 6.30 in the morning.

Charlie liked driving Edith's Porsche, enjoying the power of machinery performing fully in the manner for which it was designed. I perform best fully extended, he thought, looking sideways at the woman as they climbed the curling road out of the French port and thinking of the previous night. Had Janet been acting her whore's role when she'd cried, he wondered.

Edith was a handsome woman, decided Charlie, as she smiled back at him. She had wound the window down, so that her naturally blonde hair tangled in the wind. She was definitely very lovely, he thought, her face almost unlined and no sag to the skin around her throat. He was very lucky to have her as a wife.

They stopped at Caen to look around the war museum and still easily reached Paris by noon. While Edith sipped kir on the pavement outside Fouquet's, Charlie telephoned their lunch reservation.

They ate at the Tour d'Argent, fond of the view across the Quai de la Tournelle to the Notre Dame. With the *filet de sole cardinale*, Charlie ordered Corton Charlemagne and then – 'we're on holiday, after all' – a half bottle of Louis Roederer with the *soufflé vallesse*, which he later agreed was an ostentatious mistake.

'You enjoy spending money, don't you, Charlie?' she said, as they unpacked at the Métropole-Opéra.

'Do you begrudge it?' he asked, immediately.

'You know I don't,' she said, quickly, frightened of offending him. 'But I saw the bill. It was over £50.'

'But worth it,' he defended.

He sat watching her change, enjoying her body. She was very well preserved, he thought, admiringly. Her waist was bubbled only slightly over the panty girdle, which he didn't think she needed anyway, and her legs were firm and unveined. Her full breasts fell forward as she unclipped her bra and she became conscious of his attention, covering herself like a surprised schoolgirl.

'What are you looking at?'

'What do you think?'

'Don't,' she protested, emptily, pleased at the attention. She loved him very much and it frightened her sometimes.

Janet liked him admiring her body, Charlie compared, even insisting they made love with the light on. Edith always wanted it dark. Women were funny, he thought. His wife had much the better body. She should learn to be proud of it, not shy.

Edith was a comfortable woman to be with, he decided, the sort you didn't have to talk to all the time. With Janet three minutes of silence was construed either as boredom or boring so there was always a frenzy of meaningless chatter, like annoying insects on a summer's picnic. He definitely preferred Edith, he decided. They were friends, more than lovers, he thought. But very much lovers; Edith had a remarkable appetite for a woman of forty.

She backed towards him, the zip of her dress undone.

'Do me up.'

'Why don't we undo it?'
'There isn't time.'
'For what?'
'Don't muck about, Charlie. Tonight.'

He fastened the dress; she didn't bulge it anywhere, he saw.

He gave every indication of loving her, she thought, patting her hair into place before the dressing table.

'Promise me something, Charlie,' she said, crossing the room to him and placing her hands upon his shoulders. She was very serious, he realised. Her eyes were quite wet.

'What?'

'You won't leave me because of this office business, will you?'

'You know I won't,' chided Charlie. 'I've told you not to worry.'

'I can't help it,' said Edith, who ten years earlier had occupied the position that Janet now held as secretary to Sir Archibald Willoughby. Charlie had told her in detail of his treatment since Cuthbertson's arrival.

He stood up, coming level with her.

'I *love* you, Edith,' he insisted, putting his hands round her waist. 'I promise you that everything will work out. They're bloody fools.'

'They can't be as stupid as you think.'

'You wouldn't believe it!'

He kissed her, very softly, and she clung to him, head deep into his shoulder.

'I'm so worried about you, Charlie.'

He stroked her neck, lips against her hair.

'I'm a survivor, Edith. Don't forget that. I always have been.'

She shook her head, dismissing the assurance.

'Not this time, Charlie.'

'We'll see, darling. We'll see.'

Edith had allotted £100 a day for their holiday and Charlie drove eastwards from Paris the following morning £10 under budget, which pleased her.

Financial security meant everything to Edith, he knew, as it always had to her family. She couldn't temper her attitude, despite what had happened to her father. He had been a bank manager in Reigate, a respected Freemason, church deacon and treasurer to the local Rotary Club. And he'd embezzled £600 to cover stupidly incurred gambling debts he was too proud to ask his rich wife to settle, shocking her and Edith by the knowledge that he feared their contempt and attitude to money more than the ignominy of a jail sentence.

Edith had never forgotten the barrier that money had created between her parents and tried desperately to avoid it arising between her and Charlie. She was terrified that she was failing.

Charlie had planned the holiday with care, determined they should enjoy themselves. In Reims, they stayed at La Paix but ate at Le Florence, on the Boulevard Foch, dining off *pâté de canard truffé* and *langoustine au ratafia*, drinking the house-recommended Maureuil. The next day, Charlie drove hard, wanting to reach the German border by the evening. They stayed in Sarreguemines, where Charlie remembered the *Rôtisserie Ducs de Lorraine* on Rue Chamborand from an operation eight years earlier.

'The duck is as good as it ever was,' he declared at the table that night.

'I wish we could stay in France,' said Edith, almost to herself.

'I thought you were looking forward to seeing Austria and Germany in the autumn.'

'I was,' she agreed. 'But not any more. Not now.'

'What's wrong?' he asked.

'You do love me, don't you, Charlie?'

'Yes, Edith,' he answered, holding her eyes.

'I know I'm inclined to keep a pretty close check on money,' she said, looking down into her wine glass and embarking upon a familiar path. 'But I can't help it; it's bred into me. But I regard it as our money, Charlie. Not just mine. Spend all of it, if you want to.'

He waited.

'I mean, it wouldn't matter if you were downgraded... we wouldn't starve or anything. And it would be safer, after all.'

'I'll have Cuthbertson begging me for help,' predicted Charlie. 'And it'll be my money that supports us.'

Why, thought the woman sadly, did he have to have that bloody grammar-school pride. Just like her damned father.

5.

The priority coded warning had come from the CIA Resident at the Moscow embassy in advance of the diplomatic bag containing the full report, so the Director was already alerted and waiting when the messenger arrived at Langley.

He spent an hour examining the messages, then analysing the station head's assessment, reading it alongside the report that had come in two days earlier from the agency monitoring station in Vienna, which had fed his excitement the moment the initial Moscow report had been received.

Finally he stood up, gazing out over the Virginia countryside, where the leaves were already rusting into autumn.

Garson Ruttgers was a diminutive, frail man who deliberately cultivated a clerk-like appearance with half-lens spectacles that always appeared about to fall off his nose and slightly shabby, Brooks Brothers suits, invariably worn with waistcoats, and blue, button-down-collared shirts. He smoked forty cigarettes a day against doctor's advice, convincing himself he compensated by an almost total abstinence from liquor, and was consumed by the ambition to become to the CIA what Hoover had been to the FBI.

In a period that included the last year of the Second World War – when he had been a major in the OSS – and then in the Korean conflict, he had killed (by hand because weapons would have made a noise and attracted attention) ten men who had threatened his exposure as an agent. Never, even in moments of recollection, had he reproached himself about it, even though two of his victims had been Americans whose loyalty he only suspected but could not disprove, and so had disposed of just in case.

That more people had not been killed with the same detachment was only because he had spent nearly eighteen years in Washington and the need had not arisen. He was, Garson Ruttgers convinced himself, a complete professional. A psychiatrist, knowing of his tendency to kill without compunction, would have diagnosed him a psychopath.

Ruttgers shivered, suddenly frightened by the information that lay before him. There could only be one conclusion, he judged. And the British, whom he regarded as amateurs, were bound to screw it up.

He dispatched a 'most urgent' classified instruction to the embassy, ordering the Resident back to Washington on the next civilian aircraft, guaranteeing the man's presence in the capital at dawn the following day by arranging for a military plane to be specially available at the first airfield in the west.

Building a margin for any flight problems, he arranged the meeting with the Secretary of State, Willard Keys, at noon, cautioning in their telephone conversation that Keys might want to request an immediate meeting with the President.

From the computer in the Langley headquarters Ruttgers had within two hours a complete print-out on the man named in the report lying on his desk. It was very brief, as Ruttgers had anticipated; a man like General Valery Kalenin used anonymity like a cloak, he knew. Annexed to the print-out was the brief confirmation: 'no photograph known to exist'.

It had to be right, assessed Ruttgers, summarily cancelling all appointments and meetings during the next week.

There had never been an opportunity like this, he reflected. If they could get involved, the Agency would wipe away all the post-Watergate criticism. Internal telephone tapping, the Bay of Pigs and the Rockefeller Commission would be laughed at. And Garson Ruttgers would achieve the awe that had surrounded Hoover.

That night Ruttgers broke his habit and had two brandies after dinner; without them, he decided, he wouldn't he able to sleep. He looked upon the second drink as a celebration in advance.

William Braley's cover as CIA Resident in Moscow was as cultural attaché to the US embassy. He was a puffy-faced, anaemic-looking man with a glandular condition that put him two stone overweight, pebble glasses that made him squint and the tendency to asthma when under pressure. He arrived in Washington at 10 a.m., delayed by fog at Frankfurt, gravel-eyed through lack of sleep and wheezing from apprehension.

Ruttgers would be furious if it transpired he had overreacted, he knew, thrusting the inhaler into his mouth in the back of the Pontiac taking him and the Director into Washington.

The prospect of meeting the Secretary of State terrified him; he wouldn't be able to use the breathing aid at the meeting, he thought, worriedly. Keys might he offended. He was rumoured to have a phobia about health.

'It could be nothing,' Braley cautioned Ruttgers, hopefully. If he expressed doubt in advance, perhaps the recriminations wouldn't be so bad.

Ruttgers shook his head, determined.

'No way, Bill,' dismissed the Director, who took pride in his hunches and knew this had the feel of a defection. 'You got it right the first time. I'm proud of you.'

Keys was waiting for them in his office in the Executive Building, a taciturn, aloof man, whose careful enunciation, like a bored educationalist in a school for retarded children, concealed a word-stumbling shyness. He knew the shell of arrogance beneath which he concealed himself caused dislike, which exacerbated the speech defect when meeting strangers for the first time.

Ruttgers had submitted a full report overnight and it lay now, dishevelled, on the Secretary of State's desk.

'Don't you think we're assuming a lot?' asked Keys, seating them considerately in armchairs before the fire. Braley remained silent, taking his lead from his superior sitting opposite. The fat man seemed unwell, thought the Secretary, distastefully. He hoped it wasn't anything contagious.

'I don't think so, Mr Secretary,' argued Ruttgers. 'Consider the facts and equate them against the computer information.'

Keys waited, nodding encouragement. Ruttgers would think him obtuse, the Secretary knew, unhappily.

'Until last week,' explained Ruttgers, 'there wasn't a Western embassy in Moscow who had a clue what Kalenin looked like... no one even knew for sure that he existed. Then, without any apparent reason, he turns up at one of our own receptions, a party considered so unimportant that apart from our own ambassador, it was only attended by First Secretaries and freeloaders with nowhere else to go on a dull night.'

He nodded sideways to Braley, aware of the man's apprehension and trying to relax him.

'Thank God Bill was there, able to realise the significance.'

'And what was that?' asked Keys, seeking facts rather than impressions.

'A man known only by an incredible reputation attends an unimportant function,' he repeated. 'He stays for two hours and makes a point of speaking almost exclusively to the British military attaché...'

Ruttgers grew discomforted at Keys's complete lack of reaction.

'...And if that isn't odd enough,' the Director hurried on, desperately, 'a man of whom no photographs are known to exist, willingly poses for his picture to be taken...'

'How do we know it is Kalenin,' butted in Keys, 'if there haven't been any pictures.'

'*Known* pictures,' qualified Ruttgers. 'We've had photographs compared with every Praesidium group taken over the last twenty years. The one established fact about Kalenin is his incredible survival... he appears in official pictures dating back two decades...'

Ruttgers waved his own file, like a flag. '...examine it,' he exhorted the Secretary. 'Six photographs of the most secretive man in the Soviet Union...'

Keys sighed. On amorphous interpretations such as this, he thought, the policies of a nation could be changed. It was little wonder there were so many crises.

'All this,' stressed Ruttgers, 'just three days after one of the most vicious diatribes ever published in *Pravda* and by *Izvestia* about lack of State security... an attack that can only be construed as a direct criticism of Kalenin...'

Keys waved a hand, still unconvinced.

'What do you think, Mr Braley?' he asked. He was not interested, but it would give him time to consider what he'd read in the file and consider it against Ruttgers's conviction.

'It's strange, sir,' managed the fat man, breathily. 'I know it appears vague. But I seriously interpret it as indicating that Kalenin is considering the idea of coming across. Which is what worries me...

'Worries you...?'

'Our reception was the only Western diplomatic function that week... Kalenin used us, just to reach the British. As soon as we realised who he was, I and the ambassador tried to get involved. The man was positively rude in rejecting us.'

Keys pursed his lips, with growing acceptance. On the other side of the desk, Ruttgers frowned, annoyed the Secretary wasn't showing the enthusiasm he had expected. He gestured towards the dossier.

'And don't forget the Viennese reports,' he continued encouragingly. 'In Prague, according to our Austrian monitor, *Rude Pravo* have actually named Kalenin. No newspaper in the East does that without specific Praesidium instructions...the man's being purged. There can't be any doubt about it. He knows it and wants to run.'

'To the British?'

'That's how it looks.'

'I'd like more information upon which to make a judgment,' complained Keys, cautiously. He'd use the antiseptic spray in the office when the two had gone; Braley looked as if he could be consumptive.

'As far as Russia is concerned, sir,' offered Braley, 'the indications we've got so far and those which are in the last report, are amazingly informative.'

'Have you tried the British?'

'Of course,' said Braley. 'Their attitude encourages our conviction.'

Keys waited.

'They've gone completely silent,' reported Braley. He paused, like Ruttgers expecting some reaction. When none came, he added: 'For a closed community like Moscow, that's unheard of. We live so cut off from everything that embassy-to-embassy contact, particularly between ourselves and the British, is far greater than anywhere else. For the past five days, I've tried to encourage a meeting, on any level...'

'And?'

'The British Embassy is tighter than the Kremlin itself.'

'It certainly looks unusual,' conceded Keys, finally. 'If Kalenin is thinking of coming over, for whatever reason, how close are we to the British for access?'

Ruttgers controlled the sigh of impatience. He wasn't waiting until the British had finished, he had decided. That could take years.

'That's what made me request this meeting,' said the Director. 'The British have just had a major overhaul, throwing out nearly everyone.'

'So?'

'I don't think they could properly handle something this big. It'll go wrong.'

'How important is Kalenin?' asked Keys.

Ruttgers hesitated. At last, he thought, the doubtful son of a bitch is coming round.

'I don't think,' he replied, slowly, 'that I can think of a Russian whose defection would be more important in the entire history of communism... except perhaps Stalin.'

Keys sat back, bemused at the analysis. Ruttgers was absolutely convinced, he decided.

'But surely...' he started to protest.

'...he's lived through it all,' insisted Ruttgers. 'Stalin... Beria... Krushchev and Bulganin... Brezhnev... there is not one single Russian better able to tell us not only what happened in the past, but what might occur in the future. His value is incalculable.'

Ruttgers *had* been right in seeking the meeting, decided Keys. He'd tell the President at the afternoon briefing.

'I agree,' said the Secretary. 'We've got to get involved.'

Ruttgers smiled and Braley found his breathing easier.

'But be careful,' added Keys. 'If the shit hits the fan, I want us wearing clean white suits. Handshakes in space and *détente* is important at the moment.'

'I know,' assured Ruttgers. He paused, uncertain about the commitment at the final moment of making it. The risks were enormous. But then so was the chance of glory.

'I thought I'd do it personally,' he announced.

Keys stared at the CIA chief, the words jamming in the back of his throat.

'Do you think that's wise?' he queried, finally.

'It's got to be someone of authority... someone who can make decisions on the spot,' argued Ruttgers.

Keys looked down at the photographs of Kalenin smiling up at him from the desk. Such an ordinary little man, he thought. Was he really worth it?

'I think it's very dangerous,' judged Keys.

'So do I,' agreed Ruttgers. 'But I think the potential rewards justify it.'

Keys nodded slowly, indicating Braley.

'I think you should be seconded to it, as well,' he said. 'You've encountered Kalenin, after all. And if the need to go into Moscow arrives, your visa is valid.'

Braley smiled and felt his lungs tighten again.

The Secretary of State turned back to the Director.

'Keep me completely informed... at all times,' he instructed. 'I don't like it... I don't like it at all.'

Kalenin crouched on the kitchen floor of his apartment, frowning at the tank displacement before him. He'd been fighting the Battle of Kursk for over a week now and it wasn't going at all well. Unless there was a sudden change of luck, the Germans were going to reverse historical fact and win. He stood up, bored with the game.

What, he wondered, would be his worth to the West? It was important to calculate the amount to reflect his value, without being ridiculous. He smiled, happy at the thought. Five hundred thousand dollars, he decided. Yes – that was just about right.

The Customs inspector at Southampton located the second litre of brandy in Charlie's overnight case and sighed, irritably. Why was there always a bloody fool? He held up the bottle, not bothering with the question.

'Forgot,' offered Charlie, shortly. 'Bought it on the way out and forgot.'

'Even though it's wrapped in underwear you packed last night?' accused the official. He made them unpack all their luggage, searching it slowly, so their departure would be delayed. If his dinner was going to be ruined, so would their homecoming.

'It'll cost you £4 in duty,' he said, finally, surveying their wrecked suitcases.

It was another hour before they reached the M3 on the way to London.

'Sometimes,' said Edith, breaking the silence, 'I really don't understand you, Charlie.'

'Bollocks,' he said.

6.

Cuthbertson had telephoned ahead, so Snare and Harrison were already waiting in the office when the Director and Wilberforce flurried in from their meeting with the Cabinet. It was the first occasion it had happened and he'd impressed them, Cuthbertson knew. There'd be other meetings at Downing Street, after today.

Cuthbertson was purple-faced with excitement, smiling for no reason, moving around the room without direction, nerves too tight to permit him to sit down.

'Everyone agrees,' he announced, generally. He giggled, stupidly. The other three men pretended not to notice.

Since the disaster of the Berenkov debriefing, Cuthbertson had always waited for an independent judgment. With Kalenin, he had insisted on two assessments and then met with the Foreign Secretary before bringing it before the full cabinet. The Prime Minister had been incredibly flattering, remembered Cuthbertson. He felt warm and knew his blood pressure would be dangerously high.

'This is going to be the sensation of the year... any year,' insisted Cuthbertson, as if challenging a denial. He looked at the others in the office. Wilberforce probed his pipe. Snare and Harrison nodded agreement.

'Kalenin didn't actually say anything about defection, did he?' queried Snare, selecting a bad moment.

Cuthbertson stared at the man as if he had emitted an offensive smell.

'Good Lord, man, of course not. But you've read the Moscow reports from Colonel Wilcox. He used to be in my regiment... know the man's integrity as well as I know my own. There can be only one possible interpretation.'

'So what happens now?' asked Harrison, pleased at the rebuff to Snare.

'He's given us our lead. Now we've got to follow it.'

'How?' said Snare, anxious to recover.

'The Queen's Birthday,' declared Cuthbertson, quickly, leaning back in his chair and smiling up at the ceiling.

Christ, it was better than soldiering, he thought.

'There's going to be a party at the Moscow embassy to celebrate it. And then there's the Leipzig Fair.'

Snare frowned, but stayed silent. He could easily understand how the Director annoyed Charles Muffin, he thought.

'If Kalenin turns up at either we'll get our proof.'

'I don't quite see...' Wilberforce stumbled.

'Because we'll be at both places, to speak to him,' enlarged the Director.

'Are you sure he'll go to Leipzig? It'll be unusual attending a trade fair, surely?' questioned Harrison.

Irritably, Cuthbertson rummaged in the file, extracting the report from the trade counsellor at the Moscow embassy that had accompanied that of the military attaché.

'..."Trade is important between our two countries,"' quoted the Director. '"...I personally hope to see it first hand at this year's convention... Through trade, there will be peace, not war..."'

He looked up, fixing Harrison, who shifted uncomfortably.

'...Where's the Easter trade delegation?' he demanded, needlessly. 'Leipzig, of course.'

'Will we be able to get visas in time?' smirked Snare.

'There's a vacancy on the embassy establishment in Moscow,' said Cuthbertson, airily. 'It'll be easy to get you accredited.'

Colour began to suffuse Snare's face.

'So I'm going to Moscow?' he clarified.

'Of course,' said Cuthbertson. 'And Harrison to East Germany.'

He gazed at Snare. 'Wilcox is a good man... he'll cooperate fully,' predicted the Director.

Neither operative looked enthusiastic.

'This is going to stamp our control indelibly upon the service,' continued Cuthbertson. 'We'll be the envy of every country in the West... they'll come to us cap in hand for any crumbs we can spare...'

'It won't be easy,' said Harrison. It would be disastrous if he made a mistake, he thought. Fleetingly, the vision of the burning Volkswagen and the body he had thought to be that of Charles Muffin flickered into his mind.

'Of course it won't be easy. The Russians will do anything to prevent Kalenin from leaving...' agreed Cuthbertson. He paused, looking carefully from one to the other. '...You'll have to be bloody careful. Let Kalenin make the running all the time.'

'And if he doesn't?'

The hope in Snare's voice was evident to everyone in the room.

'Then you'll stay in Moscow for a few months until we can withdraw you without it being too obvious. And Harrison can come out when the Fair is over.'

'If nothing happens,' enthused Harrison, later, as the two operatives sat in the office formerly occupied by Charlie Muffin, 'think of all the wonderful ballet you'll be able to see. I hear the Bolshoi are marvellous.'

Snare stayed gazing out of the window into Whitehall. At least those killed in the war had a public monument, he thought, looking at the Cenotaph.

'I don't like ballet,' he said, bitterly.

Back in Cuthbertson's office, Janet carried in the carefully brewed Earl Grey tea, placing the transparent bone china cups gently alongside the Director and Wilberforce, then returned within minutes with two plates, each containing four chocolate digestive biscuits.

She stood, waiting.

'What is it?' demanded Cuthbertson, impatiently.

'I thought you might have forgotten,' offered Janet. 'Mr Muffin returned this morning. He's been in the office, all day.'

'Oh Christ!' said Cuthbertson. He stared at Wilberforce, deciding to delegate. Muffin wasn't important any more.

'You see him,' he ordered the second man.

'What shall I tell him to do?'

Cuthbertson shrugged, dismissively, taking care to break his biscuits so that no crumbs fell away from the plate.

'Oh, I don't know,' he said, consumed by the Kalenin development. 'Let him see Berenkov again.'

'So Muffin isn't to be demoted?' probed Wilberforce, anxious to avoid being blamed for another mistake.

The Director paused, teacup to his lips. 'Of course he is,' he snapped, definitely. Even though the man had been right, showing them the way to uncover three other members of Berenkov's system, Cuthbertson didn't intend admitting the error.

'But for God's sake, man, consider the priority,' he insisted. 'The last thing that matters is somebody as unimportant as Muffin. Kalenin is the only consideration now.'

Charlie lay exhausted in the darkness, feeling the sweat dry coldly upon him. He hooked his feet under the slippery sheet, trying to drag it over him, finally unclasping his hands from behind his head to complete the task. He didn't like silk bed-linen, he decided.

'So he won't even see me?' he said.

'He's very busy,' defended Janet, loyally, intrigued by the self-pity in Charlie's voice. She hoped he wasn't going to become a bore; she'd almost decided to take him to a party the coming Saturday, to show him to her friends.

'What's happening?' asked Charlie turning to her. In the darkness, she wouldn't detect his attention.

'There's a hell of a flap,' reported the girl. 'We're trying to get Snare a visa for Moscow. And Harrison into East Germany under Department of Trade cover for the Leipzig Fair.'

'Why?'

'Cuthbertson thinks some General or Colonel or something wants to defect from Russia.'

'Who?'

'He won't identify him. Even the memorandum to the Prime Minister refers to the man by code.'

Charlie smiled in the darkness. The bloody fools.

'You'll be annoyed tomorrow, Charlie,' predicted the girl, suddenly.

He waited.

'Remember the last time you saw Berenkov... the day your shoes leaked...?'

'Yes.'

'Cuthbertson has cut the taxi fare off your expenses. He dictated a memo today, saying you'd obviously walked.'

The girl went silent, expecting an angry reaction. Instead she detected him laughing and smiled, too. Charlie was such an unpredictable man, she thought, fondly. She would take him to Jennifer's twenty-first.

'I did miss you, Charlie.'

'Yes,' he said, distantly, his mind on other things.

'Charlie.'

'What?'

'Make love to me again… the way I like it…' The trouble with her preference, thought Charlie, pushing the sheet away, was that he always got cramp in his legs.

He sighed. And it was going to be a cold walk home, he thought. He'd been relying on those expenses; now he couldn't afford a taxi.

7.

Hesitant and uncomfortable, like a couple selected by a computer dating service, the two Directors finally met at Cuthbertson's club in St James's Street, agreeing its security. Each had had detailed biographies prepared by their services on the other, and had memorised them. Purposely, phrases were introduced into the small talk, showing the preparation, each wanting the other to know that he was aware it wasn't really a social occasion.

He'd been right, decided Ruttgers, smiling across the lunch table at the man. Sir Henry Cuthbertson was lost outside the barrack square and the benefit of Queen's Regulations.

The Kalenin approach had been made at an American embassy function, recalled Cuthbertson, answering the smile. Their awareness and the consequent approach was hardly surprising. That the Director had come from Washington was unexpected, though. He'd impress Ruttgers, like he'd impressed the Prime Minister, three weeks earlier, determined the Briton.

'These Arbroath smokies are very good,' complimented the American, boning the smoked fish. 'It's something we don't have in America.'

'I'm very fond of your cherrystone clams,' Cuthbertson countered. Advantage Cuthbertson, he decided.

'I was very glad when the Secretary of State suggested I come to make your acquaintance.'

The American lifted the Chablis at the end of the sentence.

'Cheers.'

'Cheers,' accepted Cuthbertson. 'Yes, liaison is very important.'

'Vitally important,' said Ruttgers.

Deuce, decided Cuthbertson, irritably.

The waiter came to clear the plates, saving him.

'In every field,' he generalised.

'But I'm interested in one particular aspect,' pressed Ruttgers. 'The immediate future plans of a certain General.'

Cuthbertson stared around him, alarmed. He was going to lose the encounter, he thought, worriedly.

The artificial reaction amused the American, who waited until the other man had come back to him. This was going to be comparatively easy, thought Ruttgers.

'We know all about it,' exaggerated the CIA chief. 'We know you're expecting further contact within a week or two.'

It had been easy in the closed environment of Moscow to discover the impending arrival of the man named Snare. Already, the operative who had been Braley's deputy in the Soviet capital had been ordered to keep the Briton under permanent observation once he arrived. They'd know immediately there was a move, Ruttgers hoped.

'I find it difficult to understand what you're talking about,' said Cuthbertson, stiffly. This wasn't going at all like the Downing Street meeting. No one had pushed him then, just listened with polite attention.

'Come now, Sir Henry,' protested Ruttgers, lightly, carefully lifting the mollusc from the top of his steak and kidney pudding and frowning at it.

'It's an oyster,' said the Briton helpfully. 'You're supposed to eat it with the pudding.'

Ruttgers pushed it to the side of his plate.

'There is no other man in the world to whom I would dream of talking as directly as this,' continued Ruttgers, flatteringly, holding Cuthbertson's eyes in a gaze of honesty. 'We don't have to be coy with each other, surely?'

Cuthbertson speared several marinated kidneys, filling his mouth so he could avoid an immediate reaction. The other man's directness flustered him, as it was intended to do.

'There *is* a development in the East which is quite interesting,' conceded the Briton, at last. He sipped his Château Latour reflectively. 'And I'm sure you won't be offended,' he hurried on, disclosing his apprehension, 'when I say I don't see that at the moment it affects you in the slightest...'

He paused, growing bolder.

'...There is an excellent liaison between us, as we have agreed. If anything transpires, you'll hear about it through the normal channels.'

Bloody prig, thought Ruttgers, smiling broadly in open friendship. He hadn't believed people talked of 'normal channels' any more.

'Sir Henry,' he placated, 'let's not misunderstand each other.'

'I don't think there's any misunderstanding,' insisted Cuthbertson. The game was swinging back his way, he decided.

Ruttgers spread his hands, recognising the cul-de-sac.

'The Kalenin affair is spectacular,' he announced, selecting a different path and trying to shock the man into concessions.

Cuthbertson curbed any concern this time.

'It really is too much for one service,' said the American.

'I can recommend the Stilton,' said Cuthbertson, twisting away. 'With a glass of Taylors, perhaps?'

Ruttgers nodded his acceptance, feeling the anger surface. Arrogant, stupid old bugger. How, he wondered, desperately, would the professional soldier react to the suggestion of higher authority?

'I have it on the direct instructions of the President himself,' disclosed Ruttgers, grandly, 'that I can offer the full and complete services of the CIA on this operation.'

'That's very nice,' replied Cuthbertson.

The American was unsure whether he was referring to the offer or the cheese.

'It would be an absolute disaster for the West if anything went wrong,' bullied Ruttgers.

'I'm quite confident nothing will,' said Cuthbertson, dabbing his lips with the linen napkin. The two men sat looking at each other.

'I shall be staying in London for some time,' said Ruttgers, maintaining the smile. 'Now that we've opened up this personal contact between our two services, I think it should continue.'

'Oh,' prompted Cuthbertson, uncertainly.

'By regular meetings,' expanded Ruttgers.

'Of course,' agreed the British Director, surprised that the other man had capitulated so easily. 'I'd like that.'

And he would, decided Cuthbertson, leaving the club for his waiting car. People appeared remarkably easy to handle. This job wasn't going to be as difficult as he had feared, after all.

He smiled, settling back against the leather upholstery. It had been game, set and match, he decided.

The greetings weren't the same any more, recognised Charlie, as Berenkov entered the interview room. The Russian's exuberance was strained, as if he were constantly having to force his attitude and recall the exaggerated gestures. His skin had that grey, shining look of a man deprived of fresh air for a long period, and the familiar mane of hair was flecked with grey, too. The prison denims were freshly laundered and pressed, but the hands that lay flaccid on the table between them were rough, the once immaculate nails chipped and rimmed with dirt.

'It's good of you to come so often, Charlie,' thanked Berenkov.

Since his return from holiday, Charlie had visited the spy every week; the decline in that time could be almost measured on a graph, thought the Briton.

'How is it?' Charlie asked, concerned.

Berenkov shrugged. He sat hunched over the table, as if he were guarding something between his fingers. Charlie saw the palm of his right hand was nicotine-stained where he smoked in the prison fashion, cigarette cupped inwards against detection. A year ago, thought Charlie, Berenkov had had a gold holder for the Havana Havanas. The Russian appeared to notice the dirtiness of his nails for the first time and began trying to pick away the dirt.

'It's not easy to adjust to a place like this, Charlie.'

'You'll get used to it,' said Charlie, immediately offended by his own platitude.

Berenkov looked directly at him for the first time, a sad expression.

'I'm sorry,' apologised Charlie. He should be careful to avoid banal remarks, he decided.

'What's happening outside?' asked Berenkov.

'It's a rotten spring,' replied Charlie. 'More like winter – bloody cold and wet.'

'I used to like the English winters,' said Berenkov, nostalgically. 'Some Sundays I used to go to Bournemouth and walk along the seafront, watching the sand driven over the promenade by the sea.'

Bournemouth, noted Charlie. Too far for a casual, afternoon stroll. So Berenkov had had a source at the Navy's Underwater Weapons Establishment at Portland. He'd have to submit a report to Cuthbertson; they thought they had plugged the leak by the arrest of Houghton and Gee after the detection of Lonsdale, back in the 1960s.

'You've been taken off the active rota,' challenged Berenkov, unexpectedly.

Charlie smiled. The Russian wasn't completely numbed by his imprisonment, he thought. But it was a fairly obvious deduction from the frequency of the visits.

'I suppose so,' admitted Charlie.

'What happened?'

'Face didn't fit,' reported the Briton. 'There was a new regime; I upset them.'

The Russian carefully examined the man sitting before him, easily able to understand how he could have offended the British caste system.

Charlie Muffin was the sort of man whose shirt tail always escaped from his trousers, like a rude tongue.

Apart from the flat-vowelled accent, Charlie wore his fair hair too long and without any style, flopped back from his forehead. He perspired easily and thus rarely looked washed and the fading collars of his shirts sat uncomfortably over a haphazardly knotted tie, so it was possible to see that the top button was missing. It was a department store suit, bagged and shapeless from daily wearing, the pockets bulging like a schoolboy's with unseen things stored in readiness for a use that never arose.

Yet about this man, decided the Russian, there was the indefinable ambience of ruthless toughness he had detected among the long-term prisoners with whom he was having daily contact. In Charlie it was cloaked by an overall impression of down-at-heel shabbiness. But it was definitely there.

It was almost impossible to believe the man possessed such an incredible mind, thought Berenkov.

'Is it a change for the good?' asked the Russian.

The recorders were probably still operating, thought Charlie, despite the lack of interest now in Berenkov.

'They've a different approach,' sidestepped Charlie. 'Very regimental.'

'Soldiers can't run spy systems,' declared Berenkov, positively, picking up the clue that Charlie had offered.

'You're a General,' said Charlie. 'And so is Kalenin.'

'Honorary titles, really,' said the Russian, easily. He seemed to brighten. 'More for the salary scale and emoluments than for anything else.'

'Just like the capitalist societies,' picked up Charlie, noting the change of attitude. 'Every job has got its perks.' The Russian became serious again.

'You haven't forgotten what I said, Charlie,' he urged, reaching across the table and seizing the other man's wrist. 'Be careful... even though they've pushed you aside, be careful.'

Charlie freed his wrist, embarrassed.

'I'll be all right,' he said. He sounded like a child protesting his bravery in the dark, he thought.

The Russian stared around the interview room. 'Don't ever let yourself get put in jail,' he said, very seriously.

'I won't,' agreed Charlie, too easily.

'I mean it,' insisted Berenkov. 'If you get jailed, Charlie, your lot wouldn't bother to get you out. Kill yourself rather than get caught.'

Charlie frowned at the statement. He would have thought Berenkov could have withstood the loss of freedom better than this. He felt suddenly frightened and wanted to leave the prison.

'Come again?' pleaded Berenkov.

'If I can,' said Charlie, as he always did. At the door he turned, on impulse. Berenkov was standing in the middle of the room, shoulders bowed, gazing after him. There was a look of enormous sadness on his face.

'Charlie,' he told himself, waiting in Du Cane Road for the bus. 'You're getting too arrogant. And arrogance breeds carelessness.'

A woman in the queue looked at him curiously. She'd seen his lips move, Charlie realised.

'So it didn't work?' queried Braley, perched on the windowsill of the room that had been made available to them in the American embassy in Grosvenor Square.

'No,' snapped Ruttgers. His face burned with anger. 'Pompous bugger spent most of the time trying to teach me how to eat oysters.'

Braley frowned, trying to understand, but said nothing. 'We can't do anything unless they let us in,' said the Moscow Resident.

'I know,' agreed Ruttgers, slowly.

'So what now?' asked Braley.

Ruttgers smiled, an expression entirely devoid of humour.

'Lean on them,' said the Director. 'In every way.'

Braley waited, expectantly.

'And if something started happening to their operatives,' continued Ruttgers, 'then they'd need assistance, wouldn't they?'

'Yes,' agreed Braley. 'They would.'

Ruttgers, he thought, looking at the mild little man, was a rare sort of bastard. It was right to be frightened of him.

8.

General Valery Kalenin entered the Leipzig Convention Hall at precisely 11.15 a.m. on March 11. Harrison noted the exact time, determined to prepare an impeccable report to Cuthbertson on his first absolutely solo operation. A bubble of excitement formed in his stomach and he bunched his hands in his pockets, trying to curtail the shaking.

The Russian was in plain clothes, a neat, fussy little figure who appeared to listen constantly, but say hardly anything. The deference towards him was very obvious, Harrison saw.

The General moved in the middle of a body of men, three of whom Harrison had seen during the previous two days at the Fair. The recognition annoyed him; he hadn't isolated them as secret policemen. One had got quite drunk at the opening ceremony and Harrison had marked the three as relaxing communist businessmen. The episode would have been a ploy, he realised now, a clever attempt to tempt people into unconsidered words or action. The mistake worried him. Charles Muffin would have probably recognised them.

Kalenin appeared in no hurry, hesitating at exhibition stands and closely examining products. Any questions, Harrison noted, were usually addressed through one of the other people in the party, so avoiding direct contact.

Harrison's entry documents described him as an export specialist in the Department of Trade and Industry, enabling him free movement to any British exhibition. Impatiently, he shifted between the stalls and platforms, accepting the nods and smiles of recognition; with the obedience instilled by his army training, he had dutifully followed instructions and befriended those businessmen providing his cover.

'Let Kalenin take the lead' – He recalled Cuthbertson's orders, watching the agonisingly slow progress of the Russian party, but holding back from direct approach. It would have been impossible to achieve anyway, he thought; there needed to be an excuse for the meeting to prevent surprise in the rest of the party.

At noon, by Harrison's close time-keeping, Kalenin was only two stalls away, lingering with the Australian exhibitors. The Briton imagined he detected growing attention from the diminutive, squat man at the approach to the British section. Harrison positioned himself away from the first display, an office equipment stand, remaining near an exhibit of farm machinery. It comprised tractors and harvesters, among which it was possible for a man to remain inconspicuous, Harrison reasoned.

At the office equipment stall, Kalenin abandoned for the first time the practice of talking through the men with him, instead posing direct questions to the stallholders.

'Wants to show off his English,' commented the salesman by Harrison's side. The operative turned sideways, smiling. The man's name was Dalton or Walton, he thought. Prided himself as a wit and had spent the previous evening telling blue jokes at the convention hotel.

'Any idea who he is?' floated Harrison.

'Looks important from the entourage,' guessed the salesman.

Harrison went back to the Russian party, detecting movement, but the farm machinery salesman was ahead of him, beaming.

'Reminds me of a T-54,' Kalenin said hopefully, pointing to a combine harvester and looking to his companions in anticipation. There was a scattering of smiles and Kalenin appeared disappointed at the response.

'But more useful than a tank, surely, sir,' intruded Harrison, seeing the blank look on the stallholder's face.

Kalenin stared directly at him, gratefully.

'Do you know tanks?' asked the General. 'They're a hobby of mine.'

'Only of them,' said Harrison.

'A man of peace, not war,' judged the Russian, smiling.

'A man whom my country much admires, once remarked that through trade there will be peace, not war…' tried Harrison, quickly, wondering if the man would remember quoted verbatim what he had said at the American embassy reception. If Kalenin missed the significance, he would have to be more direct and that would be dangerous in such an open situation.

Harrison was conscious of a very intense examination. Please God, don't let him misconstrue it, thought the Englishman.

'A wise comment,' accepted Kalenin.

He *had* remembered, decided Harrison. He felt very nervous, aware that the attention of the entire party was upon them and that the tractor salesman was desperately attempting to edge back into the conversation, believing Kalenin to be a trade official. The man thrust forward a square of pasteboard, eagerly.

'Bolton, sir,' he introduced. 'Joseph Bolton.'

'And a remark my country remembered,' overrode Harrison, desperate not to lose the opportunity. He was attempting to reduce the sound of his voice, so it would not be heard by the others.

'Perhaps there should be a wider exchange of views between the two?' suggested Kalenin.

'They're looking forward very eagerly to such a possibility,' responded Harrison. Elation swept through him. The last time he had experienced such a sensation, he remembered, was when he had collected his Double First at university and seen his parents, who had been separated for ten years, holding hands and crying.

He'd done it, he knew. In four minutes of apparently innocuous banter, he had brilliantly achieved what he had been sent to do.

Kalenin turned to the salesman, accepting the card at last. None of the others would have suspected anything, decided Harrison. It was perfect.

'Show me the engine,' said Kalenin, then immediately proceeded to ask three technical questions showing his knowledge of machinery. The visit was consummately timed, assessed Harrison, admiringly. The Russian allowed exactly the proper amount of attention before disengaging himself to move back into the group.

'It was a pleasant meeting, sir,' said Harrison, walking with him towards the edge of the stand. 'Perhaps on another occasion?'

'I don't know,' countered Kalenin. 'I'm leaving Leipzig tonight.'

The Russian spoke in the short, precise sentences of a dedicated man who had learned English in a language laboratory.

'It would be nice, possibly, to extend the conversation,' said Harrison, dangerously.

'Yes. I'd like that,' replied Kalenin, already moving on. Harrison stood, savouring the knowledge of success, watching the party involve themselves in other displays. From no one came a backward glance that would have hinted suspicion.

'If you'd spend less time getting in the bloody way, I might have made some progress there.'

Harrison turned to the annoyed salesman; Bolton, he remembered.

'He took your card, Mr Bolton,' pointed out Harrison.

'You damned DTI men are all the same,' went on Bolton, unmollified. 'Out for a bloody social occasion. Some of us live by selling, not as parasites off the taxpayer.

Harrison was conscious of the amused attention of the adjacent stalls and smiled. Nothing could upset him after the preceding fifteen minutes.

'He devoted more time to you than any other English exhibit,' offered Harrison, moving away.

'For sod all,' echoed behind him.

Harrison spent the afternoon preparing a verbatim transcript of the encounter, sipping frequently from the duty-free whisky he'd bought on the outward journey and which he felt he deserved, in celebration. Charlie Muffin, whom everybody had considered so damned good, couldn't have done as well, he convinced himself, belching and grimacing at the fumes that rose in his throat. The whole meeting had been magnificent; it didn't matter if the others with Kalenin had heard every word. To anyone but the two of them, it was just a meaningless exchange of pleasantries.

He felt quite light-headed when he located the rest of the government party and entrusted the security-sealed envelope to the courier for transmission to the East Berlin embassy and then the diplomatic bag to London next day.

He had a five-day holiday, he realised, suddenly, sitting in the hotel bar that evening. He looked around the drab room. Hardly the place he would have chosen to spend it.

In the far corner, Bolton was in his accustomed role, the centre of a raucous group and involved in a story which needed much hand-waving.

Harrison smiled and nodded, but the tractor-salesman pointedly ignored him.

The CIA cover for the Fair was through a legitimate firm of timber exporters based in Vancouver, British Columbia. From their observer, five stools further down the bar, had already gone the report of the unexpected presence that day of General Kalenin, following Ruttgers's alert to all Warsaw Pact stations to react immediately to the appearance of the man whose face they knew after twenty-five years' anonymity.

'Bolton's bloody angry,' reported the Australian with the stall adjoining the British office equipment exhibit, nodding along the bar.

'Why?' asked the CIA man, politely. The Australian's tendency to drink beer until he was sick offended the American.

'Reckons the bloody man screwed up an order from that important-looking Russian delegation that came through this morning.'

The CIA man looked towards Harrison with growing interest.

'Who is he?' asked the American.

The Australian, who had served in Vietnam and retained the vernacular like a medal, wanting people to recognise it, moved closer and affirmed, 'I reckon a spook... a bleedin' pommie spook. From the questions he's been asking the exhibitors, he knows fuck all about trade.'

'Excuse me,' said the CIA man. 'Reports to write for head office.'

Four days later, Harrison set off alone in a hired Skoda, driving slowly, unsure of the way, wishing within an hour of departure he had curbed his boredom and returned in convoy with the main British contingent.

He was moving along the wide, tree-lined highway about twenty miles outside of East Berlin when he first became conscious of the following car in his rear-view mirror. It was too far away to determine the number of occupants and Harrison kept glancing at the reflection, expecting it to overtake. It appeared to be keeping a regular distance and Harrison experienced the first jerk of fear. Immediately he subdued it; his trade cover was perfect and he carried no incriminating material whatsoever. There couldn't be the slightest danger.

So occupied was he with what was following that for those first few seconds Harrison thought the traffic ahead had slowed because of an accident. Then he realised it was a road block. He recognised soldiers as well as People's Police and saw that, in addition to the vans that completely closed the highway, strips of spiked metal had been laid zigzag in front of them to rip out the tyres of any vehicle that didn't slow to less than walking pace to negotiate the barrier.

Then he realised the following car had closed behind him. There were only five yards between them now and he could see five men jammed uncomfortably in the other vehicle.

'Oh my God,' said Harrison, aloud.

In the first few seconds of unthinking confusion, he braked, accelerated, then braked again, so that the car leapfrogged towards the obstruction. Two soldiers in front of the spikes motioned him to stop and men began fanning out along either side of the road. The recollection of the burning Volkswagen and the dull, thudding sound that the bullets had made, hitting the body, forced itself into his mind and again he braked, sharply and with design this time, trying to spin the car in its own length so that he could be facing back up the road. The vehicle stuck, halfway around, the bonnet pointing uselessly towards the bordering field. To his right, Harrison saw the following car had anticipated the manoeuvre and turned across the road, blocking any retreat.

Harrison was sobbing now, the breath shuddering from him. There was no reason why he should be detained, he assured himself, his lips moving. No reason. Or excuse. Don't panic. Act in the outraged manner of any important government official irritated by being stopped. The car episode was easily explained; just dismiss it as lack of control in an emergency situation in a hired car.

He thrust out of the vehicle and began walking purposefully towards the road block, protest disordered in his mind. But then he saw the uniforms and fear got control of him and he stopped. His mouth opened, but no sound emerged. And then he ran, stupidly, first towards the waiting soldiers, then sideways, trying to leap the ditch.

There was no sound of warning before the firing, which came almost casually from a machine gun mounted on a pivot near the driving position of the leading armoured car. Harrison was hit in mid-air and dropped, quite silently, into the ditch he was trying to leap.

The driver and one of the men from the following car walked slowly up the road, hands buried into the pockets of their leather topcoats, breath forming tiny clouds in front of them as they walked. For several minutes they stood staring down into the ditch, alert for any movement that would indicate he was still alive. Only Harrison's legs were visible, the rest of him submerged in the black, leaf-covered water. His foot jerked spasmodically, furrowing a tiny groove in the opposite bank. It only lasted a few seconds and then it was quite still.

'It's not possible to spin a Skoda like that,' said the driver, as they turned to go back to their own vehicle.

'No?'

'No. Something to do with the suspension and the angle that the wheels are splayed.'

'Must be safe on ice, then?'

'I suppose so.'

'We won't tell Snare,' decreed Cuthbertson. He stood at the window, watching a snake of tourists slowly enter the Houses of Parliament. They were Japanese, he saw, armoured in camera equipment and wearing coloured lapel pins identifying them with their guides, who carried corresponding standards in greens and reds and yellows.

'All right,' agreed Wilberforce.

'It would be quite wrong,' justified Cuthbertson, turning back into the room. 'He'd go to Moscow frightened. A frightened man can't be expected to operate properly. It's basic training.'

'Need he go at all?' asked Wilberforce. 'Surely Harrison's report is pretty conclusive.'

'Oh yes,' insisted Cuthbertson. 'He's got to go. I'm convinced now, but we need to know the conditions that Kalenin will impose. And if he's made his own escape plans. A man like Kalenin won't just walk into an embassy and give himself up.'

'Yes,' concurred Wilberforce. 'I suppose you're right.'

They remained silent while Janet served the tea. It was several minutes after she had left the office before the conversation was resumed.

'Was it a surprise?' asked Wilberforce, nodding to the door through which the girl had left the room.

'What?' demanded Cuthbertson, pretending not to know what the other man was talking about.

'To discover from the security reports that Janet was having an affair with that man Muffin.'

'Not really,' lied the Director. 'I gather he has a reputation for that sort of thing. Rutting always has been the pastime of the working class.'

He shook his head, like a man confronted with a distasteful sight.

'Imagine!' he invited. 'With someone like that!'

'What are you going to do?' asked the second-in-command. 'He's married and she's the daughter of a fellow officer, for God's sake.'

Cuthbertson opened the other file on his desk, containing the report of Harrison's death.

'Let's see how Snare gets on,' he said, guardedly.

'Over six months have passed since Comrade General Berenkov was sentenced,' recorded Kastanazy, gazing over his desk at Kalenin.

'Yes,' said the KGB officer.

'Most of yesterday's Praesidium meeting was devoted to discussing the affair.'

'Yes,' said the General.

'Please understand, Comrade Kalenin, that the patience of everyone is growing increasingly shorter.'

'Yes,' agreed the General.

Had Kastanazy purposely dropped his rank? he wondered.

9.

Snare hated Moscow, he decided. It was claustrophobic and petty-minded and inefficient and irritating. He had attended the Bolshoi and been unmoved, the State Circus and been bored and the Armoury and been unimpressed with the Romanov jewellery, even the Fabergé clocks. The body of Lenin, enclosed behind glass in that mausoleum, was not, he had concluded, the embalmed body at all, but a waxwork. And a bad waxwork at that. He'd seen better at Madame Tussaud's, when he'd taken his young nephew for an Easter outing. The child had wet himself, he remembered, distastefully, and made the car smell.

The flattery of being lionised as a new face in an embassy starved of outside contact had worn off now and he pitied the diplomats and secretaries whose constant opening gambit was to refer to his thoughtfulness in bringing as gifts from London, Heinz baked beans, Walls pork sausages and Fortnum & Mason Guinness cake. It had been Muffin's advice, recalled Snare. Just the sort of sycophantic rubbish in which the man would have indulged, a gesture to make people like him.

He'd spent several evenings with the Director's friend, Colonel Wilcox, and rehearsed their approach if Kalenin attended the official function. But even Wilcox had erected a barrier, afraid any mistake could create an embarrassing diplomatic incident. So no one liked him, decided Snare. He didn't give a damn. Thank Christ, he thought, gazing out of the embassy window, that the stupid party was tonight and he could start thinking of his return to London. It was raining heavily, smearing the houses and roads with a dull, grey colour. It was hardly surprising, he thought, that the Russians seemed so miserable.

The interest of the Americans slightly worried him. They knew who he was, he accepted. That absurdly tall man who kept talking about basketball, moving his hands in a flapping motion as if he were bouncing a ball against the ground, was definitely an Agency man. Snare groped for the man's name, but had forgotten it. Odd how sportsmen liked to boast their chosen recreation, he considered. Harrison was always driving imaginary golf balls with his reversed umbrella.

Someone in the British embassy must have disclosed his identity, he thought. When he got back to London, he'd complain to Sir Henry Cuthbertson and get an investigation ordered. Bloody diplomats were all the same; trying to show off their knowledge, gossiping their secrets.

The fact that he was known to be an operative didn't matter, he rationalised. They'd be expecting him to do something befitting his role and all he had to do was attend an embassy party and, if Kalenin were there, carry on where Harrison had left the conversation in East Germany.

And because no one, apart from the British, knew what that conversation was, then all he would appear to be doing was behaving in a normal, social manner.

The thought of achieving his mission while they all watched, unaware of what was happening, amused him. It would have been pleasant, letting them know afterwards how stupid they had been. But probably dangerous. He sighed, abandoning the idea.

Snare turned away from the window, taking from the desk immediately behind it the coded report that had come from Whitehall three weeks earlier giving a complete account of Harrison's meeting with the General.

Harrison had done bloody well, congratulated Snare. When he got back to London, he'd take the man out for a celebration meal, to l'Étoile or l'Épicure. Some decent food would be welcome after what he had endured for the past month, when he'd been lucky enough to get any service at all in a hotel or restaurant.

Carefully, he traced the responses that Kalenin had given in Leipzig. There could be no doubt, he agreed, turning to Cuthbertson's assessment, that the General was a potential defector. The East German encounter had shown him the pathway, thought Snare. But it was still going to be difficult if Kalenin turned up, discovering the undoubted conditions that the man would impose. Secretly he hoped Kalenin wouldn't appear; then he could just go home. Yes, he thought, it would be better if Kalenin didn't attend. Because whatever he achieved tonight, if anything at all, would be secondary to Harrison's initial success. It was bloody unfair, thought Snare, irritably, that the other man had just got six days in East Germany and all the glory and he'd been stuck in Moscow for four weeks and had to perform the most difficult part of the whole operation.

He descended early to the ballroom, arriving with the first of the British party. He spoke briefly to the ambassador and Colonel Wilcox, discussed the quality of the Cambridge eight with the cultural attaché who had been his senior at King's and had got a rowing blue, and then edged away, to be alone. Being disliked had its advantages, he thought; no one bothered to follow.

The American contingent arrived early and there were more of them than Snare had expected. What an appalling life, sympathised Snare, playing follow-my-leader from one embassy gathering to another, repeating the same conversations like a litany and attempting to keep sane. Almost immediately behind the Americans, the rest of the diplomatic corps arrived, crushing into the entrance and slowly funnelling past the hosts towards the drinks tray and tables of canapés. Whatever did these people, all of whom had seen each other in the last week and to which absolutely nothing had happened in the interim, find to talk about? wondered the Briton.

At the far end of the chandeliered room, an orchestra was attempting Gilbert and Sullivan and Snare was reminded of the amateur musical society at his prep school.

'Hi.'

Snare turned to the fat man who had appeared at his elbow. He seemed to be experiencing some difficulty in his breathing.

'Braley,' the man introduced. 'American embassy.'

Another CIA man? wondered the Briton.

'Hello,' he returned, minimally.

'Could be a good party.'

Snare looked at him, but didn't bother to reply.

'Not seen you before. Been in Washington on leave, myself.'

'I envy you,' said Snare, with feeling.

'Don't you like Moscow?'

'No.'

'How long will you be stationed here?'

'As briefly as possible,' said Snare.

Christ, thought Braley. And the man was supposed to have diplomatic cover; hadn't anyone briefed him?

'Believe you've met my colleague, Jim Cox?' said Braley, brightly.

Snare looked at the second American and nodded. He wasn't practising his basket approach tonight, Snare saw. What had really offended him about Cox, a thin-faced, urgent-demeanoured man who did callisthenics every morning and jogged, according to his own confession, for an hour in the US embassy compound in the afternoon, was the discovery that the price he was offering Snare for the duty-free, embassy-issued Scotch would have only allowed a profit of twenty pence a bottle. The offence was not monetary, but the knowledge that others in the embassy would have learned about it and laughed at him for being gullible, particularly after the apparent well-travelled act of bringing in the beans and sausages. Everyone would know now that it wasn't his idea, but somebody else's. They'd probably guess Charlie Muffin, he thought; in his first few days in the Soviet capital, there had been several friendly enquiries about the bloody man.

Snare looked back to Braley. So he was an Agency man, too. Best not to encourage them.

'Excuse me,' said Snare, edging away. 'I've just seen somebody I must talk to.'

'An idiot,' judged Braley, watching the Englishman disappear through the crowd.

'I told you he wasn't liked,' reminded Cox.

Apart from the invisible basketball practice, Cox had the habit of rising and falling on the balls of his feet, to strengthen his calf muscles. He did it now and Braley frowned with annoyance. Cox would probably die of a heart attack when he was forty, thought the unfit operative.

'I thought you were exaggerating,' confessed Braley. 'He's unbelievable.'

'It's been like this all the time.'

'The Director said there had been changes. I wasn't aware how bad their service had got. They certainly need our involvement.'

Cox dropped an imagined ball perfectly through the shade of a wall light, nodding seriously to his superior.

'The Russians must have spotted him,' he predicted.

Braley looked at him, sadly.

'They know us *all*,' he cautioned. 'Don't…'

'Here he is,' broke off Cox, urgently.

Braley stopped talking, looking towards the entrance. There were ten in the Russian party. Kalenin was the last to come through the door, separated from the others by a gap of about five yards. He wore uniform, which seemed to engulf him, and moved awkwardly, as if uncomfortable among so many people.

Politely he stood last in line as his colleagues eased forward, greeting the ambassador and the assembled diplomatic corps.

'And there goes Snare,' completed Cox, needlessly.

The Englishman had positioned himself near the side table laid out with cocktail snacks. He moved away as the Russians entered, remaining halfway between it and the greeting officials, permitting him a second chance of an encounter, as they came to eat, if Colonel Wilcox failed to hold Kalenin sufficiently for the rehearsed meeting.

But Wilcox didn't fail. Soldierly obedient to his instructions, the distinguished, moustached officer immediately moved to engage Kalenin, and Snare continued forward. He estimated he had ten minutes in which to confirm absolutely the conviction about the Russian General by discovering the conditions.

Wilcox saw his expected approach and smiled, half turning in feigned invitation. It was going almost too well, thought Snare, apprehensively, entering the group.

'General, I don't believe you've met the newest recruit to our embassy, Brian Snare.'

The Englishman waited, uncertain whether to extend his hand. Kalenin gave a stiff little bow, nodding his head.

Befitting the Gilbert and Sullivan string ensemble, decided Snare, answering the bow.

'A pleasure, General,' he began. It would, he guessed, be another fencing session, like that which Harrison had recorded so well from East Germany.

'And mine,' responded the Russian.

'Your command of English is remarkably good,' praised Snare, seeking an opening. He glanced almost imperceptibly at Wilcox, who twisted, seeking an excuse to ease himself from the conversation and avoid the involvement that so worried him.

'It's a language I enjoy,' replied Kalenin. 'Sometimes I listen to your BBC Overseas broadcasts.'

An unexpected confession, judged Snare. And one that could create problems for the man.

'They're very good,' offered Snare, inadequately.

'Sometimes a little misguided and biased,' returned Kalenin.

The reply a Russian should make, assessed Snare. Now there was no danger in the original remark.

Although a small man, the Russian looked remarkably fit, despite the rumoured dedication to work. Snare found him vaguely unsettling; Kalenin had the tendency to remain completely unmoving, using no physical or facial gestures in conversation. The man reminded Snare of a church-hall actor, reciting his responses word-perfect, mindless of their meaning.

'Excuse me,' muttered Wilcox, indicating the British ambassador who stood about ten feet away. 'I think I'm needed.'

Good man, judged Snare. He'd exonerate him from any criticism of the embassy when he returned to London. He saw the faintest frown ripple Kalenin's face at the departure.

'There are other opportunities for practising the language, of course,' said Snare, conscious of the time at his disposal.

'At receptions like this,' suggested Kalenin, mildly.

'Or at trade gatherings, like those of Leipzig,' said Snare. He had to hurry, risking rebuttal, he decided.

Kalenin was looking at him quite expressionlessly. It would never be possible to guess what the man was thinking, realised Snare. Debriefing him would take years; and a cleverer man than Charlie Muffin.

'In fact,' continued the Englishman. 'I think you met a colleague of mine recently at Leipzig.'

'Wonder what they're talking about,' said Braley, leaning against the far wall forty feet away.

'Our turn will come, if all goes well,' said Cox, descending two inches from his calf exercise.

'I wish you'd stop doing that,' protested Braley, breathily. 'I find it irritating.'

Cox looked at him, surprised.

'Sorry,' he apologised. Sensitivity of a sick man confronted with good health, he rationalised. Poor guy.

Cox was a joke who needed replacing, decided Braley, enjoying his new intimacy with the CIA Director. He'd get the man moved as soon as possible.

'A colleague?' Kalenin was questioning, accepting champagne from a passing tray. He didn't drink, Snare noted, holding his own glass untouched. Kalenin was a careful man, he decided, unlikely to make any mistakes.

'Yes. At the British tractor stand.'

'Ah,' said Kalenin, like someone remembering a chance encounter he had forgotten.

Taking the lead, he said: 'Have you seen your friend lately?'

'No,' said Snare, intently. 'But I know fully of your conversation.'

Kalenin had his head to one side, examining him curiously, Snare saw. His reply did not appear to be that which Kalenin had anticipated, he thought.

'My friend found the conversation most interesting,' he tried to recover, momentarily unsettled.

'Did he?' responded Kalenin, unhelpfully.

Snare felt the perspiration pricking out and wanted to wipe his forehead. It would be wrong to produce a handkerchief, he knew, resisting the move. There could only be a few minutes left before an inevitable interruption and the damned man was making it very difficult.

Harrison had been *bloody* lucky.

'In fact,' Snare went on, 'he would very much like to continue it.

The curious look persisted.

'But that would be difficult, wouldn't it?' said Kalenin. He smiled for the first time, an on-off expression like someone following an etiquette manual that recommended a relaxed expression exactly five minutes after the first meeting.

'Difficult,' agreed Snare. 'But not impossible.'

Kalenin frowned again, then shrugged. What did that mean? wondered Snare. Quickly he pulled his hand over his forehead; the sweat had begun to irritate his skin. Kalenin would have seen it, realising his nervousness, he thought, worriedly.

'Perhaps that's a matter of interpretation. And differing opinion,' said Kalenin, obscurely.

Cuthbertson was right, thought Snare. There were to be conditions.

'I'm sure the difficulties could be resolved to the satisfaction of both interpretations,' assured Snare.

Kalenin had probably survived for so long by being so cautious, decided the Briton. He felt happier at the new direction of their conversation.

'It would need the most detailed discussion.'

'Of course,' agreed Snare.

'And would probably involve expense.'

Snare swallowed, nervously. The meeting *would* be as successful as Harrison's, he determined. Despite the outward calm, he guessed Kalenin was a desperately scared man.

'I don't see expenditure being a problem,' said Snare. '

'Not half a million dollars?' questioned the General, eyebrows raised.

Snare paused, momentarily. 'Anything,' Cuthbertson had said. 'Anything at all.'

'Certainly not half a million dollars,' guaranteed Snare.

Kalenin smiled, a more genuine expression this time.

'Do you know the Neskuchny Sad, Mr Snare?'

For a moment Snare didn't understand the question, then remembered the gardens bordering the Moskva River. He nodded.

'I've taken to walking there most Sundays,' reported the Russian. 'I feel it's important for an inactive man to get proper exercise.'

'Indeed,' concurred Snare, wondering the route towards which the Russian was guiding the conversation.

'I've made it a very regular habit. Usually about 11 a.m.'

'I see,' said Snare, relaxing further. It was almost too simple, he thought.

'I really am most anxious about my health,' expanded Kalenin. 'I'm quite an old man and old men believe that misfortune will befall them any day.'

Wrong to relax, corrected Snare. There was a very real reason for this apparently aimless conversation.

'But that is often a groundless apprehension,' he responded. 'I've every reason to suppose that your health will remain good for a number of years.'

'It really is most important that I *know* that,' insisted Kalenin. 'In fact, if I thought these Sunday constitutional walks were doing me more harm than good, I'd immediately suspend them.'

'I think the walks are most beneficial. Certainly at this time of the year,' said Snare.

From his left, the Briton detected Colonel Wilcox returning, conforming to their rehearsal. Snare turned to greet Cuthbertson's friend.

'We've been discussing health,' threw out Kalenin, eyes upon Snare.

'Very important,' said the attaché, unsure of the response expected.

'I've been telling Mr Snare of exercises I've begun, to ensure I remain healthy for many years.'

Wilcox hesitated, waiting for Snare's lead.

'And I've been assuring the General,' helped the operative, 'that continuing good health, into a very old age, has become a subject of growing interest in England.'

Wilcox frowned, baffled by the ambiguity. What a stupid occupation espionage was, he decided. Silly buggers.

'Quite,' he said, hopefully.

Kalenin looked across the room, to the rest of the Russian contingent.

'I must rejoin my colleagues,' he apologised.

'I've enjoyed our meeting,' said Snare.

'And so have I,' said Kalenin. 'And remember the importance of good health.'

'I will,' accepted Snare. 'In fact, I might take up walking for the few remaining weeks I have in Moscow.'

'Do that,' encouraged Kalenin. 'I can recommend it.'

'Appeared to go well,' said Braley, watching the two men part. 'I'd just love to get my hands on Snare's report.'

'We will,' predicted Cox, stationary now. 'When the British are forced to admit us, officially, we can demand the files already created.'

'We've got to get in first,' cautioned Braley.

Snare coded his report that night, determined it would exceed in detail and clarity Harrison's account from East Germany. It hadn't been difficult to prepare a better report, decided Snare, reading the file that had taken him three hours to complete. The evidence was incontestable now. When this operation was successfully concluded, he decided, Britain would be regarded as having the best espionage service in the Western world. He sealed the envelope, personally delivering it to the ambassador's office for the diplomatic pouch. And I will be known to be part of that service, he thought, happily. A vitally important part. He would keep the Sunday appointment with Kalenin, he decided, then return to London the following week; perhaps Cuthbertson would insist that he accompany him to the personal briefing of the Prime Minister.

As the weekend approached, Snare felt the euphoria of a man ending a prison sentence, ticking off the last days of his incarceration. Just eight more days and he would be back in London, he consoled himself; it would be a triumphant homecoming.

On the Thursday, he decided to buy souvenirs, assembling the currency coupons that would give him concessions in the foreign exchange shops. Some of the intricately painted dolls, he decided, preferably in national costumes.

He was arrested walking along Gorky Street, towards the GUM department store. It was meticulously planned, taking little more than two minutes. The leading Zil pulled up five yards ahead, disgorging four men before it stopped and when he half turned, instinctively, he saw the second car, immediately behind. Four men were already spread over the pavement, blocking any retreat.

To his back was the wall. And the gap between the two cars was filled by both drivers, standing side-by-side and completing the box.

'Please don't run,' cautioned a man, from his right. He spoke English.

'I won't,' promised Snare. There was no fear in his voice, he realised, proudly.

'Good,' said the spokesman and everyone seemed to relax.

Charlie gazed around the lounge of his Dulwich home, revolving the after-dinner brandy between his hands.

'You've made a good home, darling,' he said. There was an odd sound in his voice, almost like nostalgia.

Edith smiled, a mixture of gratitude and apprehension. Her money had bought everything.

'I try very hard to please you, Charlie,' she reminded.

He concentrated completely upon her, reaching over and squeezing her hand.

'And you *do*, Edith. You know you do.'

'I don't mind about affairs, Charlie,' she blurted.

He remained silent.

'I'm just frightened it'll go wrong, I suppose.'

'Edith,' protested Charlie, easily. 'Don't be silly. How could that happen?'

'Love me, Charlie?'

'You know I do.'

'Promise?'

'I promise.'

'You're the only man I see colours with, Charlie,' she said, desperately. 'I wish to Christ I'd never inherited the bloody money to build a barrier between us.'

'Don't be silly, Edith,' he said. 'There's no barrier.'

The phone rang, a jagged sound.

'That girl from the office,' said Edith, accusingly, holding the receiver towards him.

'Sorry to trouble you at home so late,' said Janet, formally.

'What is it?' demanded Charlie, irritation obvious in his voice.

'You were to go directly to Wormwood Scrubs tomorrow?'

'Yes.'

'Sir Henry wants that cancelled. You're to be at the office at nine o'clock. Sharp.'

Very military, mused Charlie; just like her godfather's parade ground.

'But that...' began Charlie.

'Nine o'clock,' repeated the girl, peremptorily. 'I've already informed the prison authorities you won't be coming.'

'Thank you,' said Charlie, but the telephone had been replaced destroying the sarcasm.

'What is it?' asked Edith, as he put down the telephone.

'My meeting with Berenkov has been scrapped,' reported Charlie. 'I've got to see Sir Henry at 9.00 a.m.'

'What does that mean?' asked the woman, worriedly.

'What I've argued for the past ten months,' replied Charlie. 'That you can't run the service like an army cadet corps. I told you they'd need me.'

'Don't get too confident, will you, Charlie?'

'You know me better than that.'

'It's just so bloody dangerous.'

'It always has been,' said Charlie, tritely.

10.

It took Sir Henry Cuthbertson an hour to explain the operation upon which they had been engaged for the past four months, culminating in Harrison's death and Snare's capture.

Charlie sat relaxed in the enormous office, aware of Wilberforce's eyes upon him, his face masked against any emotion. Several times the Director stopped during the account, but Charlie's complete lack of response kept forcing him into further details.

'That's it,' completed Cuthbertson, at last. 'The whole story.'

Still Charlie said nothing.

'I was very wrong about you, Muffin,' offered the Director, finally.

'Really?' prompted Charlie. Now I know how Gulliver felt among the little people of Lilliput, he fantasised. Edith's warning of the previous night presented itself and he subdued the conceit. It *would* be stupid to get too confident, as she had warned.

'Your debriefing of Berenkov has been brilliant, absolutely brilliant. I've written a special memorandum to the Minister, telling him so.'

He must remember to question Janet about it, he thought. Cuthbertson was a lying sod.

'Thank you,' said Charlie.

'And you were quite right about Berenkov having a contact at the research station at Portland. Naval intelligence got him a week ago.'

'I'm glad,' said Charlie. Berenkov would be upset at the cancelled visit, Charlie knew.

Silence descended in the room like a dust sheet in an empty house. Charlie gazed over Cuthbertson's shoulder, watching the minute hand on Big Ben slowly descend towards the half-hour position. It would be the size of four men, he guessed; maybe even bigger. It would be a noisy job, cleaning it, he decided. How Wilberforce, with his irrational dislike, would be hating this interview, he thought.

Cuthbertson looked at Wilberforce and Wilberforce returned the stare.

'I would like you to accept my apology,' capitulated Cuthbertson.

'I was to be demoted,' reminded Charlie. He'd let Cuthbertson get away with nothing, he determined.

'Another mistake,' admitted the Director. 'Of course there's no question of that now.'

Because your balls are on a hook, completed Charlie, mentally.

'And some expenses...?' coaxed Charlie.

Cuthbertson stared directly at him. He really hates my guts, thought Charlie.

'Already reinstated,' promised Cuthbertson.

Another query to put to Janet, thought Charlie. Wilberforce shifted. Was it embarrassment for his superior or irritation? wondered Charlie.

'I will accept that although they initially did well, I sent inexperienced men into the field on this latest operation,' confessed Cuthbertson. He snapped his mouth shut after the sentence, like a man realising he was dribbling.

Never before in his life, Charlie knew, would Cuthbertson have been forced to make so many admissions of error. He would not be a man to forget such humiliation. His head pulled up, so that he was looking directly across his desk.

'So we need your help, Charles.'

'Charlie,' corrected the operative.

'What?'

'Charlie,' he repeated, unrelentingly. 'My friends call me Charlie.'

Cuthbertson swallowed. The man would have enjoyed standing on one of those elevated platforms, watching over the Wall the body of the man he believed to be me burning beside the Volkswagen, Charlie decided. What, he wondered, had happened to the girl called Gretel?

'We need your help, Charlie,' recited Cuthbertson, the words strained.

Charlie looked at him, allowing the surprise to show.

'How?' he asked.

Cuthbertson covered the exasperation by concentrating on the blank blotter before him. After several moments, he looked up again, under control.

'I want you to establish the link with Kalenin and bring him across,' announced the Director.

It was a mocking laugh from Charlie, an amazed refusal to accept the words he was hearing.

'There is nothing – nothing at all – that is funny about what I've said,' insisted Cuthbertson, taut-lipped.

Impulsively, Charlie stood up, pacing around his chair.

'No,' he agreed. 'Nothing funny whatsoever...'

He stood behind the chair, hands resting on its high back, like a man at a lecture.

'...It is just madness,' completed Charlie. 'Stark, raving madness...'

'I don't see...' tried Wilberforce, but Charlie refused the interruption.

'Please,' he said. 'Please, just listen to me. A year ago we broke a European spy ring, headed in this country by Alexei Berenkov...'

'For God's sake, forget the bloody man Berenkov,' erupted Cuthbertson, releasing his anger. 'He's got nothing to do with what we're discussing...'

'He's got *everything* to do with it,' rebuked Charlie, emphatically. 'Can't you see it, for Christ's sake?'

Cuthbertson winced, but said nothing; a court martial offence, judged Charlie.

'What do you mean?' asked Wilberforce, trying to buffer the feeling between the two men.

Ignoring Edith's warning of the previous night, Charlie burst on, 'I'm astonished you can't see what's happening...'

The outburst had gained him the attention of both men, he saw. Cuthbertson would be worried he'd made the wrong assessment, like all the others.

'We destroyed their system... a system that had cost them time and money and which we now know was enormously important to them,' elaborated Charlie. 'Suddenly, from the shadows, appears General Kalenin, the genius of the KGB, a man no one has seen for two decades, asserting he wants to defect. With the same remarkable timing, there are stories in all the major communist publications that he's under pressure, giving the defection credence.'

He stopped, looking to both men. Neither spoke.

'Like a rabbit coming out of a hat, he appears at Leipzig, exactly as he's indicated to Colonel Wilcox...'

Cuthbertson was doodling flowers on to his blotter and Wilberforce had begun mining his pipe; as a child, the second-in-command would have had a comfort blanket, Charlie decided.

'...and, like simple innocents, we grab at it,' took up Charlie. 'We expose an operative, get fed a load of defection bullshit and then our man, who has identified himself, gets shot. As if this weren't warning enough, we go through the same procedure a month later in Russia and lose a second man.'

They weren't accepting his arguments, Charlie realised.

'It's the oldest intelligence trick there is,' Charlie insisted. 'Make the bait big enough and so many fish will swarm you can catch them by hand.'

Cuthbertson shook his head. 'I can't agree... we've been unlucky, that's all. Others agree with me.'

'Others?' jumped Charlie, immediately.

'The analysis section, upon which you place such reliance,' said Cuthbertson, quickly.

There was more, Charlie knew, remaining silent.

'The initial approach was made at the American embassy,' reminded Cuthbertson, reluctantly. 'The CIA assessed the media attacks on Kalenin and made the same decision as we did.'

Charlie threw back his head, theatrically, braying his laughter.

'Oh Jesus!' he said. 'This is too much. Don't tell me the Americans are riding shotgun on the whole operation.'

'They've sought involvement,' conceded the Director. 'But I'm keeping the whole project British; they can have access to the debriefing in the course of time.'

Charlie made much of walking back around the chair and seating himself. Washington would be furious at being kept out, he knew.

'I am aware,' he began, speaking very quietly and with control, 'that I am badly regarded in this department, a reminder of a British intelligence system that made some very bad mistakes... mistakes that meant changes were almost inevitable...'

He hesitated. They were back with him now, he saw.

'But I have proved myself, if proof were needed, with the Berenkov debriefing,' he continued. 'I know espionage intimately... I'm an expert at it. You are a soldier, used to a different environment... a different set of rules...'

'What is the point you are trying to make,' broke in Cuthbertson, testily.

'That we're being set up,' said Charlie, urgently. 'A trap is being created and you are walking blindly into it...'

Again, Cuthbertson shook his head in refusal.

'...Cut off now, before it's too late,' pleaded Charlie. 'A committed man like Kalenin wouldn't defect in a million years.'

'You're scared,' accused the Director, suddenly.

'You're damned right I'm scared,' agreed Charlie, open in his irritation. 'Two agents plucked off within days of encountering Kalenin! We should all be terrified. If he has his way, he'll wreck the whole bloody department.'

'I want Kalenin,' declared Cuthbertson, pedantically.

'But he isn't *coming*,' insisted Charlie.

'He is,' said the Director.

'Then tell me why Harrison and Snare have been hit,' demanded Charlie.

'Because Kalenin is frightened.'

Charlie frowned, genuinely confused. 'What the hell does that mean?'

Cuthbertson paused at the impertinence, then dismissed it.

'On each occasion,' enlarged the Director, 'sufficient time elapsed for both men to dispatch full reports to London. Kalenin has allowed that, wanting the meetings to be relayed here. Both meetings were in public places... they would have been noted. And Kalenin would have known that. So he protected his back by going for them, once they'd served their purpose...'

He groped among the papers that leafed his desk.

'...Snare refers several times to Kalenin's ill-concealed fear...'

'Bloody right,' said Charlie. 'And I might concede your point if Snare had been killed too. But he's alive. By now, scientifically and without any pain, they will have taken apart the man's mind, right back to the age of two. Kalenin wouldn't have risked the inevitable exposure of his defection by letting Snare live, if the defection were genuine.'

'They've promised us consular access in three weeks,' rejected Cuthbertson, triumphantly. 'They wouldn't do that if Snare wasn't perfectly fit and had been subjected to any torture, physical or mental...'

Charlie sat, waiting, opening and closing his hands.

'Rubbish,' he said, at last. 'They will have stripped him to the bone.'

'The terms of your employment with the department do not allow you to refuse an assignment,' reminded the Director.

'I know,' said Charlie quietly.

'And I am ordering you to go.'

Charlie knuckled his eyes, then looked up at the men who despised him. He sighed openly. He'd given them the chance to avoid making fools of themselves, he decided. Now it was entirely their fault.

'Did American intelligence know how Harrison and Snare were making contact?'

'Not that we know of,' said Wilberforce.

Charlie sat, unconvinced. 'Both meetings were at public functions,' he said, talking almost to himself. 'Washington would have known.'

He looked up to Cuthbertson.

'They want involvement?' he queried.

'Desperately,' agreed the Director.

'Give it to them,' advised Charlie. 'The payment stipulates dollars. Let the money be their entry.'

'Why?' demanded Cuthbertson.

'To give me the opportunity for contact,' said Charlie. 'I don't want the Americans to have any idea that anyone is trying to pick up from Harrison or Snare. String them along by discussing money for a week, to give me time...'

'That won't work,' warned Wilberforce, happy to have found a flaw. 'Our embassy cover for you to go to Moscow doesn't come into operation for another three weeks.'

'I'm not going to Moscow under your cover,' lectured Charlie.

Again he was reminded of Edith's warning about conceit, but discarded it.

'...In the last three months you've arranged the crossing into Eastern Europe of two men whom you regarded highly,' he said. 'One is dead, the other is in Lubyanka. I'll get to Moscow myself.'

'Don't be ridiculous, Charles,' rebuffed Cuthbertson. 'No one can enter Russia like that.'

'Charlie,' reminded the operative.

'Charlie,' accepted the Director, tightly.

Charlie smiled, openly, so both men could see. He would have to be very careful not to go too far, he decided.

'Do you want the defection... if defection there is... to work?' asked Charlie.

'Yes,' said the other man, instantly.

'Then I want to operate as I always have done.'

'If it goes wrong,' cautioned the Director, 'then you'll be the sufferer.'

'Sir Henry,' accepted Charlie, smiling. 'We both know why I'm being brought back into active service. And what will happen if I fail.'

Cuthbertson did not answer the accusation.

'I'll need a large petty cash advance,' stipulated Charlie. He'd take some good wine to Janet's flat that evening, he decided.

The Director nodded, defeated.

'I'll want to know what's happening all the time,' said Cuthbertson, hopefully. 'And I'll need receipts.'

Charlie nodded. 'Of course,' he agreed.

Cuthbertson waited, guessing there was more.

'...And it would help to have my old office back,' said Charlie. 'If we're going to work on this, we'll need instant contact with each other...'

Cuthbertson nodded, his normally red face puce with emotion.

'I'm very worried about this,' said Wilberforce, after Charlie had left.

'I'm terrified,' confessed Cuthbertson. Why couldn't it have been Charlie Muffin shot in an East German ditch, he thought, regretfully. Even if he succeeded in this operation, decided the Director, he'd still ease him from the department, despite the promises he'd given. The man was quite insufferable.

The orange blossom trees were in full bloom, whitening the shrubbery outside Keys's office. Far away, people wandered ant-like into the Lincoln memorial, and in the park in front teenagers were clustered around an improvised guitar recital. It was very American and comforting, he thought.

'So how do you assess it?' demanded the Secretary of State, turning back into the room.

Ruttgers, who had arrived in Washington just one hour before and knew he would be affected by jet-lag very soon, shrugged, unwilling to commit himself.

'I don't honestly know,' he said. 'Kalenin has appeared, almost too easily. And from my last meeting with the British Director, it's obvious the man is discussing asylum.'

'Do you believe it's genuine?'

'I don't know enough about it to make a judgment,' avoided Ruttgers, easily.

'Do the British suspect why their operatives have been hit?'

'They haven't a clue,' assured Ruttgers, confidently. 'They think it's just KGB surveillance and Kalenin being over-cautious.'

'What about the request for money?'

'A stalling operation,' guessed the CIA chief. 'They are trying to send someone else in.'

'Will we be able to spot him?'

Ruttgers shifted, uncomfortable at the question. 'I don't know,' he replied, honestly. 'I've got the Moscow embassy on full alert; the man will have to have some official cover, so we should be able to pick him up.'

Knowing the Secretary of State's health fetish, Ruttgers never smoked in the man's presence. The need for a cigarette was growing by the minute.

It was time he came to the point of the meeting, decided the Director.

'The British are incredibly arrogant,' he embarked. 'It's about time they forgot they were ever a world power and realised how unimportant they've become these days.'

'What do you mean?' demanded the Secretary of State, aware now that Ruttgers had a proposition.

'The President is due to tour Europe in November?'

Keys nodded.

'It would be a terrible snub if he visited every capital except London,' predicted the CIA chief.

'You've got to be joking,' rebuked Keys. 'I could never make a threat like that.'

'You wouldn't have to,' insisted Ruttgers. 'Just to hint would be enough. Cuthbertson's a pompous old fool... he'd collapse the moment any ministerial pressure was put upon him. And there would be pressure, without the need for an outright threat.'

Keys shook his head, still doubtful.

'This could go badly wrong,' he said.

'Or be the most overwhelming success,' balanced Ruttgers.

'We'll provide the money?' guessed Keys.

'Oh yes,' agreed Ruttgers. 'I'm going to make it available. Once we're financially involved, we've got another lever to demand greater access.'

'Keep a check on the money,' said Keys. 'Congress are almost insisting on petty cash vouchers these days.'

Ruttgers looked pained.

'Of course we will,' he guaranteed. 'The numbers are being fed through the computer now. We'll have a trace on each note.'

'I don't like this,' repeated Keys, looking out over the gardens again. The police had begun to break up the guitar session, he saw. Why couldn't the kids have been allowed to continue? he wondered. They hadn't been causing any harm.

'It worries me,' he added.

'It'll worry us more if the British get away with Kalenin by themselves,' insisted Ruttgers.

'True,' agreed Keys, sighing.

'Will you make the threat about cancelling the London visit?' asked the Director.

'I suppose so,' said Keys, reluctantly.

Janet sat easily in the chair before her godfather, quite unembarrassed at his discovery of her affair with Charlie.

'But why, for God's sake?' pleaded the soldier. 'You can have absolutely nothing in common.'

Janet smiled, enjoying herself.

'At first,' she explained, 'he intrigued me... he was so different from any man I'd encountered before... more masculine, I suppose...'

She paused, preparing her shock.

'...and actually,' she went on, alert for the old man's reactions, 'he's really quite remarkable in bed.'

Cuthbertson's face went redder than normal and he gazed down at his desk to avoid her look.

'Do you love him?' he asked, still not looking at her.

'Of course not,' said Janet, astonished at the question.

'Good,' said the Director, coming back to her.

Janet frowned, waiting.

'I've involved him in the most vital operation in which he's ever been engaged...'

'...The Russian thing that killed Harrison?'

Cuthbertson nodded, apprehensively, but his goddaughter showed no feeling.

'It is imperative that he succeeds,' he said simply.

'Why are you telling me this?' demanded the girl.

'Because from this moment on I want to know everything that the man does during every minute of his existence. I've got him under constant surveillance... and I want to know your pillow talk as well.'

Janet grinned at the expression; he must have got it from a women's magazine, she supposed, the sort they read in Cheltenham.

'...ask him the odd question... he'll need to relax with someone... find out how he feels...'

Imperceptibly, he glanced at his watch. The electronic division would have completely bugged her flat by now, he estimated. Particularly the bedroom; some of what they heard would be unsettling, he thought, looking at the girl. Imagine, he recalled, he'd once held her in his arms in a baby's shawl!

'I know how he feels,' reported Janet. She hesitated, then went on. 'He resents your appointment... and the people you've brought in with you... the department is something to which he is deeply committed. Actually, I think it's the only thing for which he has any real feeling.'

The Director sat nodding, accepting her assessment.

'So he'll do his best?'

'For the department... not for you.'

Cuthbertson shrugged. 'I still want to know how he feels about this assignment.'

'You want me to spy on him?' asked the girl.

Cuthbertson nodded. 'Will you do it?'

'I suppose so,' she agreed, after a few seconds. 'It all seems a bit daft, really.'

'Good girl,' praised Cuthbertson. 'Oh,' he suddenly remembered, 'two more things.'

The girl sat, waiting.

'Get those expenses back that I cut,' he instructed. 'I'm restoring them. And take a note for the Minister...' He paused, assembling his words, then dictated the memorandum of praise for Charlie Muffin's handling of the Berenkov affair. He had the girl read it back, then said: 'One final paragraph.'

'In fact,' he dictated, 'Charles Muffin was one of my most able and eager workers in the very difficult capture of Alexei Berenkov, which I initiated and headed.'

He smiled across the desk. 'That'll do,' he dismissed, contentedly.

'What you're asking me to do is in the nature of an assignment, isn't it?' asked Janet, remaining seated.

'Yes,' he agreed, curiously.

'So there'll be some expenses, won't there? Good expenses?'

'Yes,' he accepted, sadly. 'there'll be liberal expenses.

Later, after she'd typed the memorandum, Janet sat back in her chair in the outer office and smiled down at her lover's name.

'Everyone in the world is trying to screw you, Charlie Muffin,' she said softly.

'Poor Charlie,' she added.

11.

In other circumstances, decided Charlie, as the coach left Sheremetyevo airport and picked up the Moscow road, he'd have enjoyed the experience. Perhaps he and Edith would be able to take one of the weekend holidays, some time. Then again, perhaps not.

His method of getting to Moscow had been simple and he was confident that neither Cuthbertson nor the CIA, who surrounded their activities with mystique and confusion, would realise how it had been done.

He'd simply gone to the Soviet-authorised travel agency in South London, knowing they issued the Intourist coupons for Russian vacations, and bought himself a £56 weekend package tour to the Russian capital.

The visa had taken a week and he'd had a pleasant flight out with a clerk from Maidenhead on his first trip abroad ('I read in a travel magazine that you need bath plugs; you can borrow mine if you like.') and fifteen members of a ladies' luncheon club from Chelmsford fervently anxious to experience romance without actual seduction ('There's such excitement about forbidden places, don't you think?').

By now Cuthbertson would have discovered he'd left England, decided Charlie, gazing out at the Soviet woodland.

The observation in London had been rather obvious and easy to evade. He glanced at his watch; the men outside the Dulwich house, which he'd left under a clearly visible pile of cleaning in the Porsche driven by Edith, would probably still be assuring Cuthbertson he hadn't left.

Would Cuthbertson approach Edith directly? he wondered. Unlikely, decided Charlie. But if the Director did summon his wife, Charlie was confident Edith would have no difficulty convincing the former soldier that when she had left on her cleaning expedition, Charlie had been inside the house. Edith had always found it easy to lie, he thought, reflectively.

Which was different from Janet, he thought. Her sudden interest in the operation ('I know what happened to Harrison; isn't it natural I should worry about you?') had amused him. Poor Janet, he thought. He wondered what incentive Cuthbertson had offered. Money, probably. She was a greedy girl.

The coach crossed the river and then pulled along the Moskva embankment towards the Rossiya hotel. Charlie disembarked as instructed by the officious Intourist guide and stood patiently for thirty-five minutes to be allocated a room, assuring the Maidenhead clerk when he finally collected his key, that he wouldn't forget the bath-plug offer.

There was still twenty-four hours before Kalenin was supposed to appear in Neskuchny Sad, so Charlie continued to be the tourist, prompt for the regimented meal times, always waiting for the coaches taking them in their pre-paid tours, diligent in his purchases of souvenirs. He'd surprise Janet, he decided, by taking her Beluga caviar.

I should feel nervous, he thought, during the interminable wait for dinner on Saturday night. Almost immediately, he corrected the thought. Not yet. So far there was nothing about which to be apprehensive. But there would be, soon, he knew. Then he would need the control of which he had always been so confident.

He was able to avoid the Sunday morning tour with less difficulty than he had expected, placating the Russian woman with the promise that he would be ready for the Basil Church and Lenin's tomb in the afternoon, then happily watching the Maidenhead clerk depart in close conversation with the secretary of the ladies' luncheon club who appeared likely to admit access to forbidden places.

'To work,' Charlie told himself, stepping out on to the embankment. He touched his jacket, in needless reassurance; the pocket recorder that he had checked and rewound lay snugly against his hip, quite comfortably.

It would be a long walk, he realised, striding out towards the Karmeni Bridge. But it would be safer to travel on foot, he knew. It was a fine, clear morning and he found the exercise stimulating; if it all goes wrong, he thought, wryly, then the only exercise he would know for the rest of his life would be the sort that Berenkov was getting in Wormwood Scrubs.

In the middle of the bridge spanning the Moskva, he rested, gazing over the parapet at the island in the middle, apparently an aimless tourist with time to waste. After fifteen minutes, he determined he was not being followed and continued his walk, turning down towards the Alexandre Palace.

It was 10.45 a.m. when he entered the park. A standing man is conspicuous, according to the instruction manual, he reminded himself. He meandered along the pathway leading towards the river, pacing the journey, turning back in perfect time to the entrance. The walk had reassured him. The park was not under obvious observation, he decided. His close survey didn't preclude watching and listening points immediately outside, of course.

Kalenin entered exactly on time, a short, chunky figure in an overcoat too long for him and a trilby hat that seemed to fit oddly upon his head. The General hesitated, then began strolling along the same path that Charlie had taken a few minutes earlier, gazing curiously from side to side, a man hopeful of an appointment.

The Englishman watched him go, making no effort to follow. It was ten minutes before Charlie accepted Kalenin was free from close surveillance and another ten minutes before he located the man again.

The General had stopped walking, sitting on a seat halfway down one of the longest paths, the uncomfortable hat alongside him on the bench. The man was so short his feet scarcely touched the ground, Charlie saw, as he approached. It was difficult to believe he was one of the most feared and powerful men in Russia.

General Kalenin turned to him, his eyes sweeping Charlie's westernised clothes and appearance as he smiled, very slightly.

Charlie gave no response, but sat at the far end of the bench, stretching in the pale sun. It would be too cold to sit there very long, he decided. He hoped Kalenin didn't engage in the ambiguity he'd shown Snare and Harrison. There was little reason why he should.

'A wise man always breaks his exercise by sensible rest periods,' opened Charlie.

'Yes,' agreed Kalenin.

Both spoke without looking at each other.

'This is my fourth Sunday here,' complained Kalenin. 'I was beginning to think Snare had missed the point during our conversation at the embassy.'

'How is he?' asked Charlie. Snare wouldn't have enquired after his well-being had the situation been reversed, Charlie reflected. He was glad Kalenin was going to avoid nuance and innuendo.

'Perfectly all right,' assured the Russian.

'There'll be a suspicion if he's not accused or released soon,' warned Charlie.

'I know,' agreed Kalenin, looking along the bench for the first time. 'I want to get it over with as soon as possible.'

'How soon?'

'Three weeks?'

Charlie looked back at the Russian, frowning.

'That's very short,' he protested.

'But very possible,' argued Kalenin. 'There has been arranged for months that I should make a visit to Czechoslovakia...'

'So the crossing would be into Austria?'

Kalenin nodded. 'Difficult?' he queried.

'I don't think so,' said Charlie. 'We've got a pretty strong system there.'

'So it would suit you?'

'Yes. I think it would be perfect.'

Kalenin shivered, conscious of the cold.

'The Americans are deeply involved,' announced the General, unexpectedly.

Charlie was suddenly attentive.

'What do you mean?'

'They identified both Snare and Harrison to our people... I had to act...'

Charlie laughed, surprised.

'The bastards,' he judged mildly.

'If Harrison hadn't run, our people wouldn't have shot him. They're trained to react that way.'

'I know,' accepted the Briton, remembering Checkpoint Charlie. 'Why do people always run?'

'Lack of experience,' recorded Kalenin, sadly. 'And neither he nor Snare were very good. It would have been difficult for them to have avoided suspicion.'

The same assessment that Berenkov had made, recalled Charlie. He was glad he had the tape recorder.

'Why would Washington do it?' probed Charlie, still conscious of the recording.

'Involvement,' said Kalenin, looking surprised at Charlie's question. 'They don't know of you, do they?'

'I hope not.'

'They suspect somebody is here, though,' said the General. 'They've alerted their embassy staff.'

The KGB would have an excellent monitoring system on the American embassy, Charlie knew. He supposed Washington would be aware of it; it would have been safer for them to have sent the instructions in the diplomatic bag. The mistake showed a lack of planning, decided Charlie. Or panic.

'Have they listed the name of Charles Muffin?' asked the Briton. He'd had to register in the hotel under his real identity and knew it would take little more than a day to check the hotels on the Intourist list.

'No,' reassured the General. 'They just know somebody is coming.'

So Cuthbertson was keeping him anonymous to the Americans. Thank God.

'Who's working on the request?' asked Charlie.

'The new CIA station chief is a man called Cox,' identified Kalenin. 'A sportsman... runs around the embassy.'

'We won't meet again,' stipulated Charlie, protectively. He was leaving the following night and knew that unless he monitored Kalenin's movements, which was virtually impossible, Cox could never discover his presence in the capital. If there *were* a confrontation, he'd kill the man. It would be necessary for his own protection; and Cox's organisation had been responsible for a British operative's death, which would give the killing some justification in Cuthbertson's view.

'There'll be no need,' said Kalenin. He was silent for several moments. Then he asked, 'Will Washington provide the money?'

'On the promise of participation, I would expect so,' responded Charlie. 'If they won't, Whitehall will...' he smiled. '...they're extraordinarily keen to get you across.'

Kalenin grinned back.

'It feels strange to be so important.'

'You never had any doubts, did you?' asked Charlie.

Kalenin shrugged. 'I was concerned the request wouldn't have been taken seriously.'

Charlie thought back to the last dispute with the Director and Cuthbertson's insistence that the defection was genuine. The little man was very convincing, thought Charlie. But then security men were often excellent actors.

The Briton became conscious that Kalenin was studying him minutely.

'You're recording this meeting?' the Russian demanded, expectantly.

'Whitehall will need some proof, other than my word.'

'Of course,' accepted Kalenin. 'But it would be awkward if the tape were found at the airport.'

'It won't be,' promised Charlie.

'Just in case, I'd better guarantee the flight,' cautioned Kalenin.

Momentarily Charlie hesitated, then gave the flight number of the aircraft in which he was leaving Moscow on the Monday night. It was getting very cold and there was still a lot to discuss, Charlie realised.

'Shall we walk?' invited Kalenin and Charlie stood, gratefully, falling into step beside the Russian. The man couldn't be more than five feet tall, thought Charlie. Maybe less.

'The Americans will mark the dollar notes,' warned the Russian.

'I expect so,' agreed Charlie.

'So the money will be worthless.'

'Yes,' agreed Charlie.

'That won't do,' protested Kalenin.

'I can ask for it in advance of the cross-over and "wash" it,' offered Charlie.

'It's important to do so.'

'I know that,' said Charlie.

'I'll need to know that it's been done.'

They turned on to a bisecting path. 'What date do you have in mind?'

'The nineteenth,' said Kalenin. 'That will give me a week in Prague.'

'We'll need to meet again,' said Charlie.

'You'll have to be careful of the Americans,' continued Kalenin. 'They might leak it to the *Statni Tajna Bezpecnost* and the involvement of the Czech secret police could be embarrassing.'

'I'll think of something,' promised Charlie. After today's meeting there could be protection in American presence, he decided.

They walked in silence for several minutes.

'Alexei Berenkov is probably my best friend,' Kalenin announced, suddenly.

'Yes,' prompted Charlie.

'How is he adapting to prison?'

'Badly,' said Charlie, honestly.

'He would,' agreed Kalenin. 'He's not a man to be caged.' Kalenin would have adjusted fairly easily, assessed Charlie. The General was a man who lived completely within himself.

'Poor Alexei,' said the Russian. Again there was silence.

'Do you think there'll be any serious problems?' demanded Kalenin, suddenly, stopping on the pathway to reinforce the question and looking intently up at the Briton.

Charlie answered the look.

'I don't know,' he replied. 'Are you frightened?'

Kalenin considered the question, hands deep inside the pockets of his overlarge coat. He was right to feel uncomfortable in that hat, decided Charlie; he looked ridiculous.

'Yes,' replied the General, finally, 'I'm a planner, not a field operative like you. So I'm very scared. I'm under intense pressure from a man in the Praesidium. That's why I want it all over so quickly.'

'Being a field operative doesn't help,' offered Charlie. 'I'm nervous too. I always am.'

The smaller man stood examining him for several moments.

'The other two men wouldn't have admitted that, Mr Muffin,' he complimented. 'I'd heard you're very sensible.'

It came as no surprise to learn the KGB had a file on him.

'I'm a survivor,' agreed Charlie.

'Aren't we all?'

'We'll know the answer to that on the nineteenth,' said Charlie.

They stopped inside the park gate, hidden by shrubbery. 'If the crossing is to be on the nineteenth, then I will be in Prague by the thirteenth,' undertook Charlie.

'It should be a casual encounter, like that of today,' advised Kalenin.

'Do you know the Charles Bridge?'

The Russian nodded.

'Let it be at midday on the fourteenth, on the side looking away from Hradcany Castle towards the sluices.'

Kalenin nodded, but stayed on the pathway, looking downwards. His shoes were brightly polished, Charlie saw.

'The Americans frighten me,' said Kalenin. Charlie waited, frowning.

'I could arrange quite easily for you to have a minder,' offered the Russian.

Charlie laughed, genuinely amused. 'A British operative guarded by the KGB?' he queried. 'Oh, come on!'

'It could be done without suspicion,' insisted Kalenin.

Such detailed surveillance would pad the file already existing upon him in Dzerzhinsky Square, he realised. The awareness alarmed him.

'I prefer to work completely alone,' reminded Charlie. 'I always have.'

'As you wish,' said Kalenin. 'But sometimes that's not possible.'

So I'm to be watched, realised Charlie. In Kalenin's position, able to invent any reason for such observation, he would have taken the same precautions, he knew. The irony amused him. It would soon need a small bus to accommodate the number of people assigned to him.

'Until the thirteenth,' said Kalenin, offering his hand.

'Yes,' agreed Charlie.

'Isn't that number considered unlucky in your country?' asked the Russian, suddenly.

'I'm not superstitious,' rejected Charlie.

'No,' said Kalenin. 'But I am.'

Charlie arrived back at the hotel in time for the afternoon tour, content with the morning's encounter. He was very alert, conscious of everyone around him, but was unable to identify anybody who could obviously have been an American paying special attention to his party.

When he attempted to run his bath that night, he discovered the plug missing. Smiling, he crossed the corridor and paused outside the clerk's doorway, listening before knocking. The noise they were making, thought Charlie as he turned away, was quite astonishing. But then, some girls were inclined to shout a lot. At the top of the corridor, he saw one of the women concierges who occupy a desk on every floor of Russian hotels. She had a pen in her hand and a book was open before her. She was staring fixedly towards the sounds.

'My friend suffers from catarrh,' said Charlie, smiling.

The woman looked expressionlessly at him, then began writing.

'Miserable sod,' judged Charlie, going back to his own room and jamming the bath with a wad of toilet paper.

'I have been asked,' said Cuthbertson, stiffly, 'to make this operation a joint one between our two services.'

'Yes,' said Ruttgers, happily. He looked appreciatively around the Whitehall office; the British knew how to live, he thought. All the furniture was genuine antique.

'It might not be easy,' protested the Briton. Ruttgers spread his hands, expansively.

'Not a matter for us, surely?' he said, soothingly. 'We merely have to obey the instructions from our superiors.'

Cuthbertson sat staring at him, saying nothing. The left eye flickered its irritation and Ruttgers looked down at the cigarette in his hand; just like Keys, he thought. There was a hostility in the man beyond that which the American had expected from being told to co-operate.

'I'm sure it will work fine,' said Ruttgers, briskly. 'Now what I want to do is send in one of my men to make contact with Kalenin. You haven't had much success so far, after all.'

From Moscow that morning he'd been assured that no new operatives had been posted to the British Embassy. Now was the time to make demands, when they were unsure of themselves.

'I'm afraid things have progressed beyond that point,' said Cuthbertson, smirking.

Ruttgers waited, apprehensively.

'We have made very successful contact with Kalenin and arranged a crossing,' continued Cuthbertson, condescendingly. 'There really is very little that we will need you for.'

Ruttgers flushed, furiously. Braley had been right, he thought. Cox was an incompetent idiot to have placed him in this position. He'd order the withdrawal immediately.

'It's a ministerial order that we co-operate,' reminded Ruttgers. He was confused, trying to recover his composure.

'I wonder,' mused Cuthbertson, completely sure of himself, 'if that order would have been issued had the Cabinet had the opportunity to listen to what Kalenin had to tell my man in Moscow.'

'What?' demanded the CIA Director, nervously. 'I know how Harrison and Snare were detected, Mr Ruttgers,' said the Briton.

'It's a lie,' snapped the American, instinctively.

'What?' pounced Cuthbertson.

Ruttgers fidgeted, annoyed with himself.

'Any allegation about my service,' he insisted, inadequately.

'I'm accepting your presence, under protest, because it's an order,' said Cuthbertson, in his familiar monotone. 'I'm making the transcript available to the Cabinet, together with my feelings about it. But make no mistake, Mr Ruttgers. The part you and your service play in this matter will be a very subservient one.'

The matryoshkas dolls, the rotund, Russian figures that fit one in the other, making a family of eight, were displayed on the dressing-table, reflected into the bedroom by the mirror. She'd liked the caviar, too, thought Charlie.

Janet lay, damp with perspiration, against his chest, nudging him with her tongue. He'd have to do it again in a minute, he knew. He really was getting too old.

'Sir Henry is very impressed,' she said.

'So he should be.'

'But I gather he and Wilberforce are annoyed you made the trip without their knowing.'

'Too bad.'

'What's Kalenin like?'

'Little bloke. Frightened, but he doesn't show it.'

'Half a million is a lot of money.'

'But worth it,' insisted Charlie. What would she do for half a million, wondered Charlie, stroking her hair.

She pulled away from him and wedged herself upon one arm.

'Do you think it will work, Charlie?'

'It's got to,' replied the man.

'For whom?' she demanded. 'You. Or the department?'

'Both,' said Charlie, immediately. 'It's equally important for both.'

'They're only using you, darling,' warned Janet, stretching back again. 'They'll fuck you in the end if it serves a purpose.'

'Yes,' agreed Charlie, softly. 'That's the worrying thought.'

12.

The distrust was tangible, a positive obstruction between them, thought Charlie, sitting comfortably in the Director's office. He'd created the situation and was contented with it, examining the reactions like a researcher studying slides beneath a microscope.

Wilberforce was in his accustomed chair, examining his peculiar hands as if seeing their oddness for the first time and Cuthbertson was attempting to improve the design on an already tattooed blotter. He regretted now his earlier agreement to the Moscow tape recording being played in full, guessed Charlie.

Ruttgers stood by the window, driven there by the anger that had pulled him from the chair as the Neskuchny Sad recording had echoed in the lofty room. The American Director was swirled in a cloud of tobacco smoke.

Braley perched in the stiff, uncomfortable chair, pumping at his inhaler.

'I repeat what I have already told Sir Henry,' protested Ruttgers, staring out into Parliament Square. 'Kalenin, if indeed the voice we have heard is that of Kalenin, is lying.'

'To what purpose?' enquired Charlie, in apparent innocence.

'What right have you got to question me?' demanded the American, imperiously.

'The right of a man whose two colleagues have already perished as a result of CIA involvement and whose neck is currently on the block,' retorted Charlie, judging the offence.

Ruttgers looked at Cuthbertson for rebuke, but when none came reiterated, 'The CIA did not inform upon your operatives.'

'Then what can it mean?' coaxed Charlie. This encounter couldn't have gone better, he thought.

'That he was lying,' said Ruttgers, without thought. 'Or that it isn't really Kalenin.'

'Do you really feel that?' seized Cuthbertson, ahead of Charlie, but prompting for different reasons.

'It's a reasonable assumption,' said the American.

'Then it's an equally reasonable assumption that the whole episode is phoney – as I have argued for many weeks now. And that we should stop this thing now without any more risk to either service or any more people,' said Charlie.

Ruttgers stayed at the window, recognising the alley into which he had been backed.

The cracking of Wilberforce's knuckles came over the sound of Braley's wheezing; it was like being a sick visitor in a terminal ward, thought Charlie.

'It *must* be pursued to the end,' asserted Ruttgers, finally.

Cuthbertson looked up from his defaced blotter.

'By my service,' he qualified.

Ruttgers said nothing.

'And on my terms,' stipulated the ex-soldier.

Ruttgers sighed, accepting he had no bargaining counters. He nodded, briefly.

'On our terms,' demanded the British Director, insistent on a commitment.

'Agreed,' confirmed the American, tightly.

'Which means I want somebody...' Charlie paused, looking at the asthmatic Braley, '... him, with me in Czechoslovakia. At all times, in fact...'

Cuthbertson and Wilberforce looked up, frowning curiously.

'Because having a CIA man with me guarantees I won't be exposed by them, doesn't it?' smiled Charlie, looking between the two Americans for reaction.

Ruttgers turned away from the window, his face clearing.

'...But that's...'

'...me setting *you* up,' interrupted Charlie. 'I want him with me, but taking as little part as I determine in the discussions I have. He's just always got to be within ten yards.'

'Ten yards?' queried Braley, the inhaler held loosely in his hand, like a blackboard pointer.

'From that range, I'm classified as an expert shot,' said Charlie, simply. 'I'd see an arrest coming, long before ten yards...'

He stared directly at Ruttgers.

'...I shall draw a gun from the British embassy,' he recorded. 'And before any arrest, I'll kill your man. And that would create an embarrassing international *cause célèbre*, wouldn't it?'

'This is preposterous!' complained the American, going to Cuthbertson.

'Yes,' agreed the British Director, 'it is, isn't it? But after the misfortunes that have occurred so far, I can see Muffin's point of view.'

'You want constant involvement,' contributed Wilberforce. 'This is surely what's being proposed?'

Another blocked alley, saw Ruttgers.

'I want to make it quite clear,' began Ruttgers, formally, 'that a full account of this meeting will be sent to the Secretary of State, Willard Keys, for whatever use he might see fit to make of it in his discussions with the President about the forthcoming European visit. I'm sure he'll find it sad that the special relationship between our two countries has reached such a point.'

'I'm sure he will,' picked up Cuthbertson, unafraid. 'I hope his distress will be matched by that of the British cabinet when they have had the opportunity fully to study the transcript of the Kalenin conversation.'

This was very bad, realised Ruttgers. If the British pressed the point, Keys would abandon him, assuring the President he had no knowledge of the entrapment of Snare and Harrison. He could be brought down by this débâcle, realised the American.

'I think we are allowing stupid, unwarranted animosity to cloud the point of this meeting,' he attempted.

'Which is to bring successfully to the West the most important Russian defector since 1945?' lured Charlie.

Ruttgers nodded, suspiciously.

'To a scenario which you don't accept?' said Braley, to help his superior.

'Doesn't it seem to you that, Harrison and Snare apart, the whole thing has gone just a little too easily?' asked Charlie.

'Yes,' agreed Ruttgers, immediately. 'But then again, how else could it have gone? Kalenin is in a unique position to manipulate circumstances to his own advantage and to behave in a manner that others would find impossible.'

'So now you accept it's genuine?' said Wilberforce, head sunk deeply on his chest so that the words were difficult to hear.

'I'm saying we...' Ruttgers paused, remembering the rebuke, '...you,' he corrected, 'should make the Prague meeting.'

'Have your analysts examined every report and transcript?' asked Charlie.

'Yes,' said Braley, shortly.

'To what conclusion?' demanded Charlie.

'Apprehension,' accepted Ruttgers. 'But not the outright doubt that you're expressing, Charles.'

'Charlie,' stopped the Englishman.

Ruttgers frowned. 'What the hell are you talking about?' demanded the American Director.

'If you must use it, the Christian name is Charlie,' he corrected.

Ruttgers looked in bewildered exasperation at Cuthbertson, who shrugged. Muffin was amazingly vindictive, decided Cuthbertson. Almost childishly so.

'It just doesn't feel right,' swept on Charlie, enjoying his control of the meeting. They were all uncomfortable and confused, he saw, happily.

'I know what you mean,' said the American, staring at the peculiar Englishman. 'But at this stage, we've got no choice but to go along with it.'

'What about access to Snare?' reminded Charlie, coming back to Cuthbertson.

'Deferred,' reported the permanently red-faced man. 'Without any explanation.'

Charlie shook his head, unhappily, as if the delay confirmed his concern.

'We can do nothing except follow Kalenin's lead,' stressed Braley, again taking his chief's lead.

'I believe Kalenin when he said he's putting me under surveillance,' said Charlie, opening a new course of discussion. 'Even here, in London.'

Both Ruttgers and Cuthbertson frowned.

'Have you been aware of it?' asked Wilberforce.

'No,' said Charlie. 'But if they were good, and they will be, then I wouldn't know of it, would I?'

'So?' queried Ruttgers. He examined the Englishman with interest. He was a complete professional, thought the CIA Director; the only one, apart from himself and Braley, in the room.

'So we *must* wash the money.'

Ruttgers moved, uncomfortably, like a subordinate aware of an indiscretion in front of the managing director at a firm's Christmas party.

'Now wait a minute...'

'...we can't wait a minute,' cut off Charlie. 'If that money isn't broken down, Kalenin will know about it. You heard the tape. He just won't cross.'

'What'll that involve?' asked Braley.

'To do it sufficiently publicly?' said Charlie, rhetorically. 'I'd say about two weeks to cover London, the South of France and Austria. And that's not allowing for any unforeseen difficulties.'

'We *did* record the numbers,' confessed Ruttgers. 'And it took us nearly a week, even feeding into a computer.'

'We'll still be able to keep a check,' said Charlie.

'How?' asked Ruttgers.

'Knowing every number is the optimum. And unnecessary,' Charlie lectured. 'To trace the money, if you need to, we'd need just a sample. Braley and I could use a pocket assessor and feed in a section of the cleaned money.'

Ruttgers frowned, doubtfully.

'And let's face it, you're being incredibly cautious,' stressed Charlie. 'At a conservative estimate, it'll take two years completely to debrief Kalenin. And even then he'll need and probably demand help with a new identity, place to live and permanent guards. We'll be aware of his location for ten to fifteen years from now. The money is very unimportant, except to him.'

And to the American Congress, thought Ruttgers. But the Briton was talking complete common sense. It really didn't matter and Keys would have to accept that ground conditions made the change necessary. Equated against the amount of money the CIA spent yearly, sometimes on madcap projects, this investment was infinitesimal, anyway. Ruttgers nodded acceptance, shifting from the window.

The man found it difficult to remain in any one position, thought Charlie, watching Ruttgers settle into the chair he had already quit four times during the course of the meeting.

Like Charlie, Ruttgers felt there was something indefinably wrong about the whole thing. But he did have what he wanted, a man involved from this moment in every aspect of the crossing, the American Director reassured himself.

'Right,' he accepted. 'We'll do what you suggest and hope it's right.'

'That's the trouble,' seized Charlie. 'None of us knows whether we're right or not. And we won't for three weeks.'

Berenkov looked a caricature of the man he had once been, thought Charlie. The Russian edged almost apprehensively into the room, all exuberance gone, standing just inside the door and staring at his visitor, awaiting permission to advance further.

The man's skin looked oily, but flaking, as if he were suffering from some kind of dermatitis and there was a curtain of disinterest over his eyes. He shuffled rather than walked, scarcely lifting his feet and when he spoke it was in the prison fashion, his lips unmoving.

'Good of you to come, Charlie,' he said. The voice was flat, completely devoid of expression.

'You don't look good, Alexei.'

The man stayed where he was, just inside the entrance.

'Come in, Alexei. Sit down,' invited Charlie. He felt patronising.

'It's been over a year,' mumbled Berenkov, through those unmoving lips, disordering his hair with a nervous hand as he settled at the table. 'One year, three months and two weeks.'

And two days, knew Charlie. How long, he wondered, before men with a sentence as long as Berenkov's stopped marking the calendar?

He had nothing to say, realised Charlie.

'I brought some magazines,' he tried, hopefully. 'They're being examined by the prison authorities, but it'll only take a few minutes. You should have them by tonight.'

'Thank you,' said Berenkov, unresponsively.

He wouldn't read them, Charlie realised. The degree of apathy into which the Russian had sunk would mean he spent all his cell-time staring at the wall, his mind empty. Berenkov had the smell of cheap soap and the proximity of too many bodies, thought Charlie, distastefully.

'Any tobacco?' cadged the Russian, hopefully. Charlie pushed some cigarettes across the table. Berenkov took one, hesitated, then slid the rest into his pocket. He stopped, frozen for a second to await the challenge from Charlie. The Briton said nothing and Berenkov relaxed.

'Doing anything interesting?' asked the Russian. Charlie looked at him curiously. It was a question without hidden point, he decided.

'No,' he generalised. 'Just clerking.'

Berenkov nodded. He'd barely assimilated the words, Charlie saw.

'But I'm going away on holiday for a few weeks,' covered Charlie. 'I won't be able to see you for a while.'

Momentarily the curtain lifted and Berenkov frowned, like a child being deprived without reason of a Sunday treat.

'You won't abandon me, Charlie?' he pleaded.

'Of course I won't,' assured Charlie, holding without any self-consciousness the hand that Berenkov thrust forward. 'I made you a promise, didn't I?'

'Don't let me down, Charlie. Please don't let me down.'

In Janet's flat, three hours later, he swilled brandy around the bowl, watching it cling to the side. He looked up suddenly at the girl.

'You know what?' he demanded.

'What?' responded Janet.

'Berenkov was right. All those months ago.'

'About what?'

'Me and imprisonment. He said I wouldn't be able to stand it and he was right. I'd collapse even before he's done.'

'So what would you do?' asked the girl, seriously.

'If I knew capture was inevitable,' asserted Charlie, 'then I'd kill myself.'

She was going to cry, realised Janet. Shit, she thought.

Kalenin began setting out the tanks for Rommel's assault upon Tobruk and then stopped the displacement, half completed. He wouldn't play tonight, he decided. He straightened, staring down at the models. The forthcoming Czech visit and what was to follow made it unlikely that he would recreate the battle for some weeks.

If ever. The thought came suddenly, worrying him. Why, he wondered, was Kastanazy being so implacable in his campaign? It was an over-commitment in the circumstances and therefore stupid, likely to cause him problems. And Kastanazy wasn't usually a stupid man.

Kalenin shrugged, replacing the tanks into their boxes. Perhaps it was time Kastanazy was taught a lesson, he thought, sighing. The man wasn't liked in the Praesidium, Kalenin knew.

The General went into the regimented living-room, carefully positioned the cover over the headrest of the easy chair and sat down, looking with satisfaction around the apartment, enjoying its clinical neatness. Not one thing out of place, he thought. He smiled at the thought. The words that could sum up his life, he decided; everything in the right place at the right time.

He rose abruptly, without direction, bored with the inactivity. The next month was going to be difficult to endure, he realised.

He poured a goblet of Georgian wine, then stood examining it. Berenkov had been disparaging about his country's products, recalled Kalenin. 'Bordeaux has much more body. And a better nose,' his friend had lectured, during their last meeting.

He envied Berenkov, Kalenin suddenly realised. The man was all he had ever wanted to be. But Berenkov had been caught, Kalenin rationalised. Which made him fallible.

Will I be detected? wondered Kalenin, finishing his wine.

13.

A large map table had been brought into Cuthbertson's office and several two-inch ordnance sheets pinned out in sequence showing the Czech border with Austria, with all the routings into the capital. Beside the maps were boxes of blue and green flags, awaiting insertion.

It was an exercise that Cuthbertson understood and he moved around the table assuredly, aided by Ruttgers, who had returned that morning from Washington and from a meeting with both Keys and the President. The CIA Director was pleased the President was involved; it elevated the operation to exactly the sort of status he considered necessary.

'By the thirteenth, we'll have moved over a hundred men into

Austria,' recorded Ruttgers. 'And we're airlifting in sufficient electronic equipment to guarantee a complete radio link-up between every operative.'

Cuthbertson nodded. The previous day there had been a full Cabinet meeting which he had attended and he knew that afterwards there had been direct telephone calls between the Prime Minister and the American leader.

'We're matching that commitment,' he confirmed. 'Man for man.'

The resentment at the American involvement still rankled with him; the Cabinet hadn't shown sufficient outrage, he thought, critically.

Cuthbertson stared fixedly at Ruttgers, then at the map table.

'Your cigarette is smouldering,' he complained. 'Can't you extinguish it?'

'Once Kalenin crosses that border,' said Ruttgers, casually stubbing the offensive butt and looking down at the map, 'the net will be so tight that a fly couldn't escape.'

'I'm still a little concerned about Austria,' said Wilberforce, 'we can't mount an operation of this size without them learning about it.'

'We can and we will,' bullied Ruttgers, immediately. 'By the time they discover anything, it'll be all over.'

'It still seems diplomatically discourteous,' protested the tall man.

'That's not the way they'll see it,' guaranteed the CIA chief. 'Austria is the bridge between East and West, don't forget. They'd be scared gutless knowing in advance someone of Kalenin's importance was going to move through their territory. Sure they'll bleat and complain at the United Nations and both our governments will dutifully apologise at the intrusion. But privately Austria will be bloody glad we kept them out so their relations with Moscow don't suffer.'

Cuthbertson smiled patronisingly at Wilberforce, indicating he shared the American's assessment.

'It'll be difficult to make all our displacements until we know when and how Kalenin intends crossing. But we can bottle up the city.'

He paused, looking at Ruttgers.

'You sure your house is safe?'

'For Christ's sake,' said Ruttgers, 'the CIA have owned it for twenty years...'

'...which means the KGB probably know about it,' intruded Wilberforce.

'Not this one,' promised Ruttgers, who regarded it as vitally important that Kalenin should be lodged instantly at an American-owned property. He was growing increasingly confident he could elbow the British aside once Kalenin had defected.

'Do you think I'd run the risk if I wasn't a hundred per cent certain?' he added.

Cuthbertson nodded, accepting the assurance. He took a gold flag indicating Kalenin from a third box and inserted it into the marked house on Wipplingerstrasse.

'Anyway,' pointed out the British Director, 'he won't be there longer than an hour. It will just be somewhere to stop, change his clothes and then leave for the airport.'

'You've fixed that?' queried the American.

Cuthbertson, who had already entered another gold marker in Schwechat, nodded.

'We've officially informed the Austrians we want to shift embassy furniture and equipment over a three-week period. There will be four dummy flights, moving things around for no reason except to get them used to it.'

As he talked, Cuthbertson was flagging the area around the house where Kalenin would be held. He worked on a grid pattern, marking down from the Danube Canal, bordered by the post office and Aspern Square across to the old city hall and Am Hof Square and embracing the Hofburg Palace, the Spanish Riding School and running up to Volksgarten. Blue flags indicated concealed observations; green designated open surveillance, on foot or in cars.

'That's a hell of an area,' remarked Ruttgers, echoing Wilberforce's thoughts.

'But necessary, insisted Cuthbertson. 'This outline covers the situation for a concealed, unpursued crossing...'

He opened a drawer and took out some red-headed pins.

'...I think there should be a contingency situation for an emergency flight, possibly under pursuit...'

He held up the crimson markers.

'...and we won't be able to insert these, showing it, until Muffin's meeting on the thirteenth from which I hope to know the crossing point.'

'Then what?' queried Ruttgers.

Cuthbertson sighed.

'I hope it doesn't happen,' he said. 'But in case it does, we'll want a back-up team at the crossing spot. If the Russians learn it's Kalenin, they'll come across without bothering whose country they're violating. I'll have a transfer car waiting, into which we can put Kalenin...'

He hesitated at the American's frown.

'I'll only need three minutes at the outside,' he said. 'If the Russians chase, I want them to be able to locate almost immediately the crossing car, which will take off to loop Vienna and apparently make for the Italian border...'

'While the real car completes the journey to the airport?' accurately guessed Ruttgers.

'There's a lot wrong with that,' argued Wilberforce. The two Directors stood, waiting.

'What do you imagine the Austrian authorities are going to do while all this is happening?' criticised the civil servant.

'As much as possible,' said Cuthbertson, confidently. 'All I want is the transfer. The Austrians will be chasing the car that crossed and which the Russians or Czechs followed. Not one of my operatives – or an American – will be involved, apart from the initial holding operation. From then on, Austrian police pursuit is exactly the sort of diversion I want.'

'What about the driver of Kalenin's original car?' probed Wilberforce, obstinately.

'He'll have to be sacrificed,' said Cuthbertson, easily. 'I want an explosive device fitted, during the transfer. To detonate within five minutes.'

'So who will be driving?' asked Wilberforce.

'I had thought of Muffin,' said Cuthbertson.

'He's too valuable; he'll have to travel on with Kalenin,' protested Ruttgers.

'You're right, of course,' accepted the British Director. 'It'll have to be somebody else.'

'There's Cox, currently attached to our Moscow embassy,' offered Ruttgers, remembering his annoyance at the man's inability to detect Charlie's entry into Russia. 'His involvement would be very natural. And he speaks Russian, which gives added validity for his secondment.'

'All right,' agreed Cuthbertson, carelessly. 'Let's use him.'

Wilberforce stood studying both men, wondering if either was really medically sane. He supposed the sacrifice of one life was justified, but he would have expected some distaste from those making the decisions. Ruttgers and Cuthbertson appeared almost to be enjoying it.

'Our debriefing team will be arriving in London next week,' reported Ruttgers, avoiding looking directly at Cuthbertson.

'Yes,' said the ex-soldier. He still hoped to persuade the Cabinet to retract permission for the interviews with Kalenin to be Anglo-American.

'We've houses available here?' asked Ruttgers.

'Four,' replied Cuthbertson. 'Each is as secure as the other. They're all in the Home Counties.'

'We'd like to examine them first,' said Ruttgers.

The clerk-like American had been born out of his time, decided Wilberforce. He would have enjoyed bear-baiting or cock-fighting, watching animals gradually tearing themselves to pieces.

'A pointless precaution,' defended Cuthbertson, holding his temper. 'I will not have that sort of interference.'

Ruttgers smiled. 'I'd still like to be satisfied,' he said.

'I'll raise it at the Cabinet meeting,' undertook Cuthbertson, trying to avoid the commitment. 'They might object, too.'

'They won't,' predicted Ruttgers. 'But if you need authority,' he continued, 'go ahead.'

Ruttgers was an easy man to dislike, thought Wilberforce.

'There's one other thing,' said the American.

Cuthbertson concentrated upon his map positions, appearing disinterested.

'I thought one of us should go to Vienna personally to meet him.'

Cuthbertson frowned, off-balanced by the suggestion.

'We'll *both* go,' insisted the Briton, anticipating what Ruttgers was going to say and determined not to be upstaged by the other man.

'It's an American house,' protested Ruttgers, who had wanted the opportunity to begin his persuasion upon the Russian.

'But a joint operation,' reminded the former soldier, definitely.

Ruttgers nodded in curt agreement. He'd blown it, he decided, annoyed at himself.

Charlie Muffin relaxed happily in his former office, with space in which to move and its pleasant view of Whitehall. Like a child who has had its ball returned from a neighbour's garden, he smiled at Braley. He liked the man, he decided. Braley was a professional, which always gained his esteem; little else did, reflected Charlie.

They had finished the public laundering of the money the previous night, one day before each departed for Prague under embassy cover. The debriefing with Ruttgers and Cuthbertson had been easy and almost perfunctory, both Directors preoccupied with their pinned and flagged series of maps.

There had not, anyway, been any reason for a lengthy meeting, remembered Charlie. The operation had gone perfectly and had been identical in the casinos of Vienna, Monte Carlo, Nice and the Clermont and National Sporting Clubs in London.

Each night for the previous two-and-a-half weeks they had entered the high game rooms and changed fifty thousand dollars into gambling chips. After three hours mingling with the gamblers but never playing, they returned to the *caisse*, changed the chips back into unmarked currency and left the casino. The mornings of each day had been spent taking sample records, Charlie selecting notes at random and dictating their numbers to Braley, who had operated the pocket recorder.

The American was bent over it now, making the final calculation.

'According to my figures, we've a trace on fifty-five thousand dollars. That's twenty thousand in sterling, fifteen in French francs and twenty thousand in Austrian Schillings.'

'Sufficient,' judged Charlie, dismissively.

'It was very necessary though, wasn't it?' he added.

Braley nodded, positively. In Vienna, Braley had identified two known KGB operatives and Charlie had located a third in Monte Carlo. For that number to have been seen meant the surveillance on Charlie had been absolute, they had decided at their meeting with the Directors.

'At least Kalenin knows we're following his stipulations to the letter,' said Braley.

'He knows exactly what we're doing,' agreed Charlie. 'What bothers me is that I haven't a clue about him.'

'Still apprehensive?' queried Braley.

Charlie nodded. 'Very,' he admitted.

The man's nervousness was unsettling, thought the American. He wondered how the Englishman would behave if things went wrong in Czechoslovakia.

14.

Charlie spent the day before his Prague flight in Rye. He had telephoned from London, so when he arrived at the station, Wilkins, who had been manservant and chauffeur to Sir Archibald throughout his directorship of the department and retired on reduced pension rather than work for another man, was there to meet him.

They had known each other for twenty years, but Wilkins greeted him formally, allowing just the briefest, almost embarrassed handshake, before opening the car door.

It was a magnificent Silver Shadow, maintained by a chauffeur who adored it in a condition of first-day newness.

'Car looks as good as ever,' complimented Charlie.

'Thank you, sir,' said Wilkins, steering it from the parking space.

'If ever Sir Archibald fires you, come and drive for me,' invited Charlie, attempting what had once been a familiar joke between them.

'Thank you, sir,' replied Wilkins. He'd forgotten, thought Charlie, sadly. The response should have disparaged a Ford Anglia, a troublesome vehicle that Charlie had once owned.

'Sir Archibald was sorry he couldn't come to the station,' recorded Wilkins.

'Isn't he well?'

'He's waiting at the house,' avoided the chauffeur.

'Isn't he well?' repeated Charlie, but Wilkins didn't reply and after several minutes Charlie relaxed against the shining leather, knowing the conversation was over.

No, thought Charlie, as he hesitantly entered the lounge of Sir Archibald's home, darkened by drawn curtains against the summer brightness. Sir Archibald wasn't well. It was incredible, Charlie thought, remembering his last meeting in Wormwood Scrubs with Berenkov, how quickly people collapsed. The former Cambridge cricket blue who had captained his county until his fiftieth birthday and who, three years before, had been an upright six-foot-three who could command attention by a look, was now a bowed, hollowed-out figure, with rheumy eyes and a palsied shake in his left hand. He'd developed the habit of twitching his head in a curious, sideways motion, like a bird pecking at garden crumbs apprehensive of attack, and he blinked, rapidly and constantly, as if there were a permanent need for clear vision.

'Charlie' he greeted. 'It's good to see you.'

The blinking increased. He was very wet-eyed, Charlie saw.

'And you, sir,' replied Charlie. Odd, he thought, how instinctive it was to accord Sir Archibald the respect he found so difficult with Cuthbertson.

'Sit down, lad, sit down. We'll drink a little whisky. I've some excellent Islay malt.'

Charlie had already detected it on the old man's breath. Sir Archibald filled two cut-glass goblets, raised his and said: 'To you, Charlie. And to the department.'

'Cheers,' said Charlie, embarrassed. It had been a forced toast and he wished the old man hadn't made it.

Sir Archibald sat in a facing chair and Charlie tried to avoid looking at the shading hand. The old man had always detested physical weakness, remembered Charlie. During his tenure as Director, medical examinations had been obligatory every three months.

'Been unwell,' complained Sir Archibald, confirming the expected irritation at his own infirmity. 'Caught flu, then pneumonia. Spent too much time in the garden on the damned roses. Lovely blooms, though. Have to see them before you go.'

'Yes,' agreed Charlie. 'I'd like that.'

Sir Archibald drank noisily, sucking the whisky through his teeth. Charlie became conscious of the stains on his jacket and trousers and sighed. Sir Archibald was a very shabby, neglected old man, he thought.

'Good of you to come at last,' said the former Director, floating the criticism.

'Been busy,' apologised Charlie, inadequately.

Sir Archibald nodded, accepting the excuse.

'Course you have, course you have. See from the newspapers that you finally got Berenkov.'

'Yes,' conceded Charlie, modestly. 'It was all very successful.'

Sir Archibald added whisky to both their glasses, looking cheerfully over the rim of the decanter.

'Got a commendation, too, I shouldn't wonder? Your job after all.'

'No,' said Charlie, staring down into the pale liquid. 'I didn't get a commendation. Two other operatives did though. Names of Harrison and Snare. You wouldn't know them; they arrived after you left.'

'Oh,' said Sir Archibald, glass untouched on his knee. The old man knew it would be improper to ask the question, Charlie realised, but the curiosity would be bunched inside him.

'It's very different, now, sir, said Charlie, briefly.

'Well, it had to be, didn't it?' offered Sir Archibald, generously.

'For two unpredictable, entirely coincidental bits of bad luck?' refuted Charlie, suddenly overcome by sadness at the figure sitting before him. 'I don't think so.'

'Come now, Charlie,' lectured his old boss. 'There had to be a shake-up and you know it.'

'It hasn't achieved much.'

'It got Berenkov,' pointed out Sir Archibald.

'I got Berenkov, operating a plan evolved by you and Elliot before the changes were made,' contradicted Charlie.

'It was sad about Elliot,' reflected Sir Archibald, reminded of his former assistant and trying to defuse Charlie's growing outrage. 'I visit the grave sometimes. Put a few roses on it and ensure the verger is keeping it tidy. Feel it's the least I can do.'

'I've never been,' confessed Charlie, suddenly embarrassed. 'I was in East Germany when the funeral took place.'

'Yes, I remember,' said Sir Archibald. 'Not important. It's the living that matter, not the dead.'

It had been one of Sir Archibald's favourite remarks, remembered Charlie.

'Yes,' he agreed, shielding his goblet from another addition from his persistent host.

'Is it going to be difficult, Charlie?' demanded Sir Archibald, suddenly.

'What?' frowned Charlie.

'Oh, I know you can't give me details... wouldn't expect it. But is the operation you're involved in going to be difficult?'

Charlie smiled, nodding his head at his former chief's insight.

'Very,' he confirmed. 'The most difficult yet.'

'Thought it was,' said the old man. 'Knew there had to be some reason for the visit.'

Quickly he raised his shaky hand, to withdraw any offence.

'Appreciate it,' Sir Archibald insisted. 'Consider it an honour to be thought of like this, by you.'

'It'll probably go off perfectly,' tried Charlie, cheerfully.

'If you believed that, you wouldn't have bothered to come here to say goodbye,' responded the former Director.

Charlie said nothing.

'Anything I can possibly do to help?' offered the old man, hopefully.

'No,' thanked Charlie. 'Nothing.'

'Ah,' accepted Sir Archibald. 'So you could die?'

'Easily,' agreed Charlie. 'Or be caught.'

Charlie paused, remembering Berenkov. 'I'm not sure of which I'm more frightened, death or a long imprisonment,' he added.

Sir Archibald gazed around the room. 'No, Charlie,' he agreed. 'I don't know, either. But the risk isn't new; it's been there on every job upon which you've ever been engaged.'

'This one is different,' insisted Charlie.

The decanter was empty and Sir Archibald took another bottle from beneath the cabinet. They were regimented in lines, Charlie saw, before the door was closed. The former Director fumbled with the bottle, finally giving it to Charlie to open for him.

'Have the department handled it right?' demanded Sir Archibald, defiantly.

He was getting very drunk, Charlie saw.

'Competently,' he said.

'But I'd have done better?' prompted the old man, eager for the compliment.

'I think you'd have had more answers by now,' said Charlie. It wasn't an exaggeration, he thought. Sir Archibald could always pick his way through deceit with the care of a tightrope-walker performing without a net.

Sir Archibald smiled, head dropped forward on to his chest.

'Thank you, Charlie,' he said, gratefully.

It was becoming difficult to understand him.

'For coming,' the old man added. 'And for the compliment.'

'I meant it,' insisted Charlie.

Sir Archibald nodded. The glass was lopsided in his hand, spilling occasionally on to his already smeared trousers.

'Be very careful, Charlie,' he said.

'I will, sir.'

'Remember the first rule – always secure an escape route,' cautioned Sir Archibald.

The training that got me back alive from East Germany, recollected Charlie.

'Of course.'

Sir Archibald hadn't heard him, Charlie realised. His head had gone fully forward against his chest and he had begun to snore in noisy, bubbling sounds. Carefully Charlie reached forward and extracted the goblet from the slack fingers and put it carefully on to a side table.

He stood for several minutes, gazing down at the collapsed figure. Every day would end like this, he realised; it was another form of imprisonment, like that of Berenkov.

'Goodbye, sir,' said Charlie, quietly, not wanting to rouse the man. He snored on, oblivious.

Wilkins was standing outside the room, waiting for him to leave.

'He's gone to sleep,' said Charlie.

Wilkins nodded.

'He's not been well, sir,' reminded the chauffeur.

'No,' accepted Charlie.

'He misses the department... misses it terribly,' said Wilkins in what Charlie accepted was the nearest the man had ever come to an indiscretion.

'And we miss him,' assured Charlie. 'Tell him that, will you?'

'Yes, sir,' promised Wilkins. 'It would please him to be told that.'

The man turned to the hall table.

'He wanted you to have these, sir,' said Wilkins, offering him a huge bunch of Queen Elizabeth roses. 'He's very proud of them.'

'Tell him I was very grateful.'

'Perhaps we'll see you again, sir,' said Wilkins, knowing it was unlikely.

'I hope so,' said Charlie, politely, knowing he would not make a return visit.

'What lovely flowers,' enthused Janet, as Charlie handed her the roses three hours later.

'I got them from Sir Archibald Willoughby,' reported Charlie.

The girl looked sharply at him.

'The Director wouldn't like it if he knew you'd seen him,' said Janet, formally.

'Fuck the Director, he'll know anyway because his watchers followed me, all the time. They were so bloody obvious they should have worn signs around their necks.'

'It's still improper,' insisted the girl.

'If he doesn't like it, he can go to Prague tomorrow and put his head in the noose, instead of staying behind in a comfortable office sticking pins in maps.'

The First Secretary, Vladimir Zemskov, was being cautious, judged Kalenin, unwilling to be openly critical before the full Praesidium.

'It is distasteful to us to have to demand an explanation from such an experienced officer as yourself, Comrade General,' he said.

Kalenin nodded, appreciatively.

'But Comrade Kastanazy has made the complaint about the progress so far,' hardened the Soviet leader. He waited, pointedly. 'And the consensus of opinion,' he continued, 'is that insufficient thought and planning has been put into proposals to repatriate General Berenkov...'

'I refute that,' said Kalenin, bravely.

Several members of the Praesidium frowned at the apparent impertinence.

'...I asked to be given a certain period of time,' reminded Kalenin. 'I understood from Comrade Kastanazy that I was being allowed that time. To my reckoning, it has yet to expire...'

'...There are only a few more days,' reminded Zemskov. The man was offended, Kalenin saw, and the ambivalent attitude was disappearing in favour of Kastanazy. They'd all follow Zemskov's lead, he knew.

'Allow me those days,' pleaded Kalenin.

'But no more,' said Zemskov, curtly.

I won't need any more, thought Kalenin.

15.

Charlie invariably grew nostalgic about the East European capitals he visited, trying to envisage the life of centuries before and those years free of concerted oppression when the people delighted in grandiose architecture and extravagant monuments to their own conceit.

'Prague would have been a women's city,' he told himself, in the taxi negotiating its way over the Manesuv Bridge. He stared along the Vlatva river towards the Charles Bridge upon which he was scheduled to meet Kalenin the following day.

'Please God, make it be all right,' he mumbled. He became aware of the driver's attention in the rear-view mirror and stopped the personal conversation. A psychiatrist would find a worrying reason for the habit, Charlie knew.

The car began to go along Letenska and Charlie gazed up at Hradcany Castle on the hill. The remains of King Wenceslaus were reported to be there, he remembered. He should try to visit the cathedral before he left.

The reception at the embassy was stiffly formal, which Charlie had expected. It was an embassy unlike most others, in which he had no friends, and he guessed no one there would make it easy. The high-priority message from Downing Street to the ambassador would have indicated the importance of Charlie's mission, but equally it would have alerted the diplomat to the risk of having his embassy and himself exposed in an international incident that could retard for years the man's progress through the Foreign Office. It was right they should resent his intrusion, he accepted.

'I hope to leave within days,' Charlie assured the First Secretary, who gave him dinner. Charlie's cover came from the Treasury, checking internal embassy accounts. It was the easiest way for quick entry and exit.

'Good,' said the diplomat, whose name was Collins. He was a balding, precise man who cut his food with the delicacy of a surgeon. His attitude reflected that of the ambassador, Charlie guessed.

'There really shouldn't be any trouble,' tried Charlie.

'We sincerely hope not,' said Collins immediately.

He was regarded with the distaste of a sewage worker come to clear blocked drains with his bare hands, decided Charlie. Sod them.

'There is one thing,' said Charlie, remembering the threat made when the CIA presence had been forced upon the department. It seemed rather theatrical now, but it was a precaution he would have to take.

'What's that?'

'I shall want a gun.'

Collins looked at him, incredulously.

'A what?' he echoed.

'Don't be bloody stupid, man,' replied Charlie sharply. 'A gun. And don't say the embassy haven't got one because I had three sent out in the diplomatic pouch a fortnight ago.'

Collins dissected his meat, refusing to look at him.

'The instructions to the embassy were signed personally by the Prime Minister,' threatened Charlie, irritated by the treatment. He was behaving just like Ruttgers, Charlie thought, worriedly.

'I'll ask the ambassador,' undertook Collins.

'*Tell* the ambassador,' instructed Charlie. His anger was ridiculous, he accepted, quite different from his normal behaviour in an overseas embassy. Because of it, the meal became stifled and unfriendly and Charlie drank too much wine. He did it knowingly, anticipating the pain of the following day but needing it to submerge his fear and spurred by irritability. Twice during the dinner, offended at the continued pomposity of the First Secretary, Charlie stopped just short of fermenting a pointless dispute.

He retired immediately after the meal, sitting in the window of the room with a tumbler of duty-free whisky, gazing out over the darkened city. A thousand miles away, he ruminated, an old man for whom he would once have happily died was probably sitting in a window holding a larger amount of whisky, staring out over his rose bushes. The degeneration of Sir Archibald had frightened him, accepted Charlie. He snorted, drunkenly, at the thought. And Berenkov had frightened him and the assignment frightened him.

'Wonder I'm not constantly pissing myself,' he mumbled.

Spittle and whisky dribbled down his chin and he didn't bother to wipe it.

'Got to stop talking to myself,' he said.

He slept badly, rarely losing complete consciousness and always aware of himself through spasmodic, irrational dreams in which first Ruttgers and then Sir Archibald pursued him wielding secateurs and he panted to evade them, burdened by the wheezing Braley slung across his shoulders.

He abandoned the pretence of sleep at dawn, sitting at the window again, watching the sun feel its way over the ochre, picture-painted buildings in the old part of the city immediately below him.

He had the hangover he had expected. His head bulged with pain that extended down to his neck and his mouth was arid. It had been a stupid thing to have done and would affect his meeting with the Russian, he thought.

He breakfasted alone, in his room, uncontacted by anyone. Finally he approached Collins's office, determined to control the annoyance.

'The ambassador has approved the issuing of a revolver,' said the meticulous diplomat.

'Yes,' said Charlie. He felt too ill to compete with the man, anyway.

The weapon lay on the desk and Collins looked at it but refrained from touching it, as if it were contaminated. Charlie picked it up and placed it in the rear waistband of his trousers, at the small of his back, where it would be undetectable to anyone brushing casually against him and not be a visible bulge unless he fastened his jacket.

He was conscious of Collins studying him, critically.

'I don't bloody like it, either,' said Charlie, venting his apprehension.

It was a warm, soft day and if he hadn't felt so unwell Charlie would have enjoyed the walk down the sloping, sometimes cobbled, streets.

The Charles Bridge is one of the ten that cross the Vitava to link both sides of the city but is restricted entirely to pedestrians. Each parapet is sectioned by huge statues of saints.

Charlie approached early from the direction of Hradcany, so he loitered before the shops in the narrow, rising approach to the bridge, stopping for several moments apparently to study the fading, pastel-coloured religious painting adorning the outside of the house at the immediate commencement. He was not being followed, he decided.

The bright sunlight hurt his eyes, increasing the discomfort of the headache. He felt sick and kept belching.

Slowly he began to cross the bridge, professionally glad it had been chosen as a meeting place. It was thronged with tourists and provided excellent cover.

He saw the American first.

Braley had approached from the opposite side of the river and had halted by one of the statues. He was wearing sports clothes and an open shirt, with a camera slung around his neck. It was very clever, conceded Charlie, reminded again of the fat man's expertise. Without creating the slightest suspicion, the American was ideally placed to photograph the meeting between him and Kalenin.

So thick was the midday crowd he almost missed the General. The tiny Russian was standing where they had arranged, wearing a summer Russian raincoat that was predictably too long, staring up towards the sluices. Charlie felt a shudder of fear go through him and he shivered, as if he were cold. He gripped his hands tightly by his side, pushing his knuckles into his thighs.

'Too late to be frightened, Charlie,' he told himself. 'You're committed.'

As he covered the last few yards, he tried to isolate the watchers in addition to Braley but failed. It was to be expected, rationalised Charlie. Those immediately around the KGB chief would be the absolute best; Ruttgers and Cuthbertson would have people there as well, he knew.

Charlie grinned, despite the nervousness and discomfort. There hadn't been a moment for the past three months when he hadn't been under collective surveillance from one service or another, he thought. Presidents didn't get better protection.

He positioned himself alongside the Russian without looking directly at him.

'Sorry I'm late,' he apologised. He was still dehydrated from the alcohol and his voice croaked.

'Not at all,' assured Kalenin. 'I was early.'

Charlie felt the other man examining him.

'Are you all right?' asked the General. 'You don't look well.'

Charlie turned towards him.

'Fine,' he lied.

Kalenin nodded, doubtfully.

'I'm afraid Snare has had a collapse,' announced the General.

Charlie stayed, waiting.

'Apparently couldn't stand solitary confinement,' reported the Russian. 'Our psychiatrists are quite worried.'

'He's in the Serbsky Institute?' predicted Charlie.

'Yes,' agreed Kalenin. 'It's remarkably well equipped.'

'So we've heard in the West from various dissidents who've been brainwashed there,' responded Charlie, sarcastically.

Kalenin frowned at the remark, then shrugged.

'My people will be upset at the news,' said Charlie.

'It was quite unintentional, I assure you,' replied Kalenin. 'In the circumstances, I couldn't let him come into contact with anyone, could I?'

'No,' accepted Charlie. 'I don't suppose you could.'

Kalenin looked back up the river.

'I've always liked Prague,' he said, conversationally. 'I think of it as a gentle city.'

Charlie was perspiring, not just from the heat, and the pain in his head drummed in time with his heartbeat.

'We're not here to admire the city,' he reminded, curtly.

Again Kalenin turned to him.

'Are you *sure* you're all right?'

'Of course.'

'You're recording this meeting?' queried Kalenin, expectantly.

'Yes,' said Charlie, patting his pocket. Kalenin nodded.

'You were very punctilious about the money.' Further along the bridge, Charlie saw Braley manoeuvre for a photograph.

'I see your companion in Vienna and France is a little further along,' continued Kalenin, without turning around. 'Shall I meet him?'

The Russian was smiling, happy at his control of the situation.

'That's a matter for you,' said Charlie, disconcerted.

'I think we should, in a moment,' replied Kalenin. 'I've worked out the crossing with great care and I don't want anything to go wrong; it's best he hears at the same time as you.'

'We've also done a fair amount of planning,' guaranteed Charlie.

Kalenin nodded again. He's patronising me, thought Charlie.

'The money will be in Austria?' demanded Kalenin.

'I've already lodged it at the embassy,' said Charlie.

'Good,' praised Kalenin. 'Good. You really do seem to have put some thought into it.'

The General turned, looking towards the American. 'To avoid repetition, shall we join Mr Braley now?' It would have been relatively easy to compare pictures taken in Austria and France against those of former personnel at the Moscow Embassy, supposed Charlie.

The American saw them approaching and moved against the parapet, gazing fixedly at the view.

'Are there many pictures of our meeting, Mr Braley?' greeted Kalenin.

Braley's chest pumped uncertainly.

'We were photographed as well as seen during the money-changing,' enlightened Charlie, feeling sorry for the CIA man.

Braley swallowed, trying to curb the nervous reaction. 'Good day, sir,' he said to the Russian, awkwardly. It sounded a ridiculous greeting in the circumstances and Charlie wanted to laugh. Nerves, he thought.

Kalenin continued walking, without replying, leading them from the bridge. He appeared very confident, thought Charlie; too confident, even. The man could ruin the whole thing by conceit, thought the Englishman, worriedly.

'There's a very attractive horologue in the old town,' lectured Kalenin, like a tourist guide, as they reached the covered pavement. 'And some pleasant cafés.'

Charlie and Braley exchanged looks, but said nothing. The American was as uncertain as he was, saw Charlie.

Kalenin made a point of showing them the gilded time-piece before courteously seating them at a pavement table and ordering drinks. He and Braley had beer, but Charlie selected coffee.

'I have been thinking very deeply about what is to happen,' said Kalenin slowly. He was speaking, thought Charlie, as Cuthbertson would have addressed a class at staff college.

Kalenin looked directly at both before continuing.

'I have become increasingly aware of the enormous value I have in the West,' said the General. 'Upon reflection a value far in excess of $500,000.'

Braley moved to speak, anticipating a change of mind in the Russian, but Kalenin raised his hand imperiously, stopping the interruption. From somewhere in the square, Charlie knew, there would be cameras recording every moment of the encounter; the admiration of the horologue and selection of the conveniently free café table was very rehearsed.

'I am determined to be properly treated,' continued Kalenin.

He was ill at ease with pomposity, thought Charlie.

'I don't think you need have any doubt about that,' assured the Briton.

Kalenin looked at him, irritably.

'Allow me to finish,' he demanded. 'As I have already indicated, I will cross over on the nineteenth. I've arranged a visit to the border area in such a way as to allay any suspicion. I have selected Jaroslavice as the crossing point...'

The General paused.

'...don't forget that,' he instructed.

'...Jaroslavice isn't on the border,' corrected Charlie, immediately.

Kalenin sighed. 'I know,' he accepted. 'I mention the town for map reference. I shall cross at Laa an der Thaya. I presume you will have people back at Stronsdorf, but that won't be enough...'

Charlie smiled at the man's behaviour. It wasn't natural, he knew. But Kalenin was sustaining it well.

'We won't forget the crossing point,' he promised.

Kalenin looked at him sharply, suspecting mockery. 'I've not the slightest intention of crossing in the vague expectation of a reception committee in Stronsdorf,' announced the General. 'I must know the arrangements that have been made to receive me in the West. And be assured they will be followed.'

Braley looked questioningly at Charlie, who nodded. 'You were quite right, sir,' began the American at last, 'in your assessment of your importance. If it will convince you of our awareness of it, let me say that both the British and American Directors are personally making the trip to Austria to greet you...'

Kalenin beamed.

'Exactly,' he said, apparently not surprised by the news. 'That's at exactly the sort of level I want to conduct the whole affair.'

Charlie began to feel better and waved for more drinks, ordering a beer for himself this time. He stared around the square, trying to identify the watchers. It was hopeless, he decided, abandoning the search.

'What time do you intend to be at Laa?' he asked the Russian.

'Night will be best,' said Kalenin, immediately. 'According to my estimate, if we travel through Ernstbrunn and Korneuburg, we can reach Vienna in little over an hour...'

Charlie nodded, doubtfully. Longer, he would have thought.

'...I want you waiting on the Austrian side of the border promptly at 10.30. But not before. I don't want a caravan of cars attracting attention,' ordered Kalenin.

'It'll hardly be dark,' complained Braley.

'Dark enough,' insisted Kalenin.

'Shouldn't we arrange a contingency situation, in case there is any cause for your being delayed?' asked Charlie.

Kalenin smiled sympathetically at the Englishman.

'Instructing me on trade-craft?' he mocked.

'Trying to guarantee a successful operation, General,' retorted Charlie, tightly.

'Nothing will go wrong,' said Kalenin, confidently. 'Nothing at all.'

He raised his glass, theatrically.

'To a perfect operation,' he toasted.

Feeling uncomfortable, both Charlie and Braley drank.

'And another thing,' said Kalenin. 'I want the money brought to the border. I want to see it…'

'But…' Charlie began.

'I want to see it,' cut off Kalenin, definitely.

He stared at Charlie, alert for any challenge.

Charlie shrugged. 'As you wish,' he said.

'I *wish*,' picked up Kalenin. 'And please inform your people…' He paused. '…on both sides of the Atlantic,' he qualified, 'of my insistence at being accorded the proper reception and continued treatment befitting my position.'

'We'll inform them,' undertook Charlie. It would be interesting to see the reaction of both Directors when the tape was played in London, he thought.

'There need be no further contact between us,' said Kalenin, curtly. 'You know the crossing point and my demands…' he hesitated, looking at Charlie. '…be at Laa,' he instructed the Englishman. 'I shall remain in Czechoslovakia until I'm personally sure you hold the money and the Directors are somewhere in the capital.'

Charlie nodded, frowning.

'You want me to make another crossing into communist territory?' he asked.

'Yes,' smiled Kalenin, easily. 'What possible apprehension need you have? It'll only be a few yards.'

Abruptly the tiny Russian stood up.

'I will leave you,' he said. He turned, then came back to them.

'Until the nineteenth,' he said.

Charlie and Braley watched the tiny figure bustle across the square and disappear along one of the covered pavements.

Braley extended his examination of the square, like Charlie aware they had been placed by design at the particular café table. They paid, rose and without talking, suspicious that listening devices might have been installed, walked into the open.

'Well?' demanded Charlie, as they slowly followed the route the General had taken. Both walked with their heads bent forward, so it would have been impossible for the conversation to have been lip read by their observers.

'It's wrong,' judged Braley. 'We've been set up.'

'That's what I'm afraid of.'

'Incidentally,' side-tracked Braley. 'That gun was visible when you sat down.'

Charlie loosened his jacket, annoyed at the criticism. He hadn't checked its concealment by sitting down; a stupid mistake.

'Did you mean it, Charlie?' asked Braley, interested. 'If there had been any CIA involvement during the meeting, would you have shot me?'

'Yes,' said Charlie, immediately.

Braley paused, then shook his head slightly. It was impossible to discern whether the attitude was one of disbelief or incredulity.

The CIA man jerked his head in the direction in which Kalenin had disappeared.

'What do you think he's going to do?'

Charlie slowed in the shadow of the covered pavement.

'I wish to Christ I knew. I've tried every possible permutation and it still doesn't come out right.'

Braley looked pointedly at his watch.

'He's been gone fifteen minutes,' said the American. 'If we were going to be arrested, it would have happened by now.

Charlie nodded agreement, having already reached the same conclusion.

'The table would have been the best spot,' he enlarged. 'During the conversation, his men could have got so close that we wouldn't have had a chance to blink.'

'So we *aren't* going to be busted?' demanded Braley.

It was a hopeful question, recognised the Briton. He shrugged, unhelpfully. 'How the hell do I know?'

They went through the archway and began to walk towards Wenceslaus Square.

'If they're going to arrest us, it won't really matter,' said Charlie. 'But I think we should immediately part to double the chances of what's been said getting back to London.'

Braley nodded.

'If I manage to reach it, I'm going to remain in the embassy until the last possible moment for the flight,' advised Charlie.

'Right,' agreed Braley, enthusiastically.

'There's a flight at 15.30 tomorrow, BE 693,' listed Charlie. 'Aim for that.'

Charlie's walk back across the Charles Bridge to the embassy was a pleasant, relaxed meander. He ate alone in his room that night, drinking nothing and left the following day with just two hours to reach the airport, knowing the flight would have been called by the time he reached the departure lounge.

Braley was waiting for him aboard the aircraft, the asthma gradually subsiding.

'Well?' queried Charlie. 'Now what do you think?'

'It doesn't make sense,' said Braley. 'It just doesn't make bloody sense.'

'Good trip?' asked Edith.

'All right,' agreed Charlie.

'Surprised you came straight home,' said his wife, accusingly.

Charlie stared back at her, curiously. For several seconds she held his gaze, then looked away.

'There's been a reason every time I've been late home,' he insisted. 'You know that.'

'So you keep telling me,' she said, unconvinced.

'Don't be stupid,' he said.

He snapped his mouth shut. It would be wrong to argue with her, using her to relieve his nervousness, he thought.

She ignored the challenge.

'So it is definitely the nineteenth?' she said.

'Looks like it.'

She looked directly at him again, the hostility gone.

'I'm frightened, Charlie,' she said.

'So am I,' said her husband. 'Bloody frightened.'

Kastanazy paused at the end of his account to the full Praesidium. There was no movement from the other fourteen men.

'And that, Comrades, would appear to be a full summation of the situation thus far,' he said. No one believed him, he saw.

'Are you sure?' demanded the Party Secretary.

Kastanazy nodded.

'Incredible,' judged Zemskov. 'Absolutely incredible.'

16.

Cuthbertson would think of it as a war-room, thought Charlie, watching the British Director move around the office, indicator stick held loosely in his right hand. He had used it like a conductor leading a symphony orchestra all morning.

Charlie yawned, unable to conceal the fatigue. It had been a series of fifteen-hour days since their return from Czechoslovakia. After the combined report from him and Braley, Ruttgers had been withdrawn to Washington for final consultations with the Secretary of State and the President, and two special Cabinet meetings had been called at which Cuthbertson had given the complete details at the personal prompting of the Premier.

There had been a final, direct telephone liaison between the American leader and the Prime Minister and then joint approval given for the crossing plan devised by Cuthbertson and Ruttgers.

One hundred and fifty British and American operatives had already been drafted into Vienna and three tons of mobile electrical equipment flown in and housed at the American embassy. Fifty more men were being moved in that day.

In Cuthbertson's room, the map displacements had been completed. A gold flag marked Kalenin's crossing at Laa and then markers indicated his anticipated journey along the minor roads through Stronsdorf to Ernstbrunn, then to Korneuburg and into Vienna through Lagenzerdorf.

If there were pursuit, then the decoy car was to ignore the Ernstbrunn turning and carry on towards Mistelbach. Separate coloured pins marked this contingency.

If the crossing went unchallenged, Kalenin would be brought to Vienna through a corridor of operatives, all linked by radio, so that they could close in behind, surrounding the Russian general in a circle of safety.

For two hours that morning, Cuthbertson and Ruttgers had stood before the map-table, lecturing on the crossing to the four section heads who were leaving that afternoon for the Austrian capital to co-ordinate the surveillance of the field operatives.

James Cox had already been withdrawn from Moscow and was in Vienna, waiting to be briefed on the decoy manoeuvre he would perform on the Mistelbach road if the necessity arose.

Only the American section head knew about the explosive device and had been briefed in the privacy of the CIA Director's Washington office before the Atlantic flight. The explosive package had been flown to Austria with the electronic equipment.

The section leaders had filed out fifteen minutes before, leaving the five of them in the room.

'All you've got to do,' said Ruttgers, talking to Charlie, 'is get him just one yard across that border; from then on there'll be no way it can go wrong.'

Both he and Cuthbertson were hoarse with talking and it was Wilberforce who took up the discussion.

'Even so,' he said, 'we've been concerned at the conviction of both of you that there's still something wrong with this operation.'

Charlie humped his shoulders, resigned.

'It's not a new feeling with me,' he reminded them. 'I've had doubts from the beginning.'

'Which have so far proven groundless,' rasped Cuthbertson.

'Harrison is dead and Snare insane,' returned Charlie, immediately.

Cuthbertson reddened even more, annoyed at his error. 'It's not good about Snare,' he admitted. 'It'll go badly for him after Kalenin crosses.'

'*If* he crosses,' corrected Charlie. The Director didn't give a damn about Snare, Charlie knew. The whole project had become one of personal aggrandisement of himself and Ruttgers.

Ruttgers sighed, spreading his hands.

'For Christ's sake,' he said, to both operatives. 'What are you trying to say?'

'I agree with Charlie,' offered Braley, helpfully. 'There's not a thing I can prove, not a fact I can show to support the slightest doubt, yet I have the same misgivings.'

Wilberforce looked up from his bony hands.

'But if anything were to have happened, it would have done so by now, surely?' asked the tall man, reasonably. 'You were open, identifiable targets in Prague.'

'I've still got to cross at Laa, to assure him everything is ready,' reminded Charlie.

'That wouldn't make sense, to grab you there,' Wilberforce rejected. 'Why bother to trap one man when he had two in the Czech capital. And he could have had you arrested far easier in Moscow, weeks ago.'

Charlie nodded.

'I know,' he said, defeated.

'I think this is a pointless discussion,' dismissed Cuthbertson. 'Every proposal upon which we've decided has been assessed and analysed for faults. Any illogicality would have been thrown up. The only thing to result from further discussion will he confusion.'

Charlie gestured reluctant agreement.

'So let's get to the last details,' hurried Ruttgers, impatiently.

Again it was Wilberforce who spoke, addressing the two operatives.

'Kalenin said he didn't want a caravan of cars,' he reminded. 'So there'll just be you two in the lead Mercedes. In three other vehicles, about fifty yards back from the border, will be the resistance teams in case there is a pursuit, and the driver of the decoy car.'

'What if Kalenin brings his own car across?' asked Braley.

'Transfer him immediately and leave it for disposal to the back-up team,' instructed Wilberforce. 'A Czech registered car will attract too much attention.'

'There's no courtyard in the Wipplingerstrasse house,' remarked Charlie, looking at a blown-up photograph of where they were going to conceal Kalenin.

'So?' asked Ruttgers.

'What happens if there is pursuit and your contingency plan doesn't work quite as smoothly as you expect it to? Our car could be spotted at the border and then become a marker in Wipplingerstrasse. If the Russians try to get him back, it'll he a blitz.'

'Good point,' praised Cuthbertson, reluctantly. 'Once Kalenin is out of the vehicle in Wipplingerstrasse, move it away... hand it over to one of the back-up groups that will have travelled with you.'

'What about border guards on the Austrian side?' persisted Braley.

'We've realised the importance of the time Kalenin stipulated,' said Wilberforce. 'Both sets of guards change duty at ten. The resistance team will look after the Austrian border officials and maintain the regular telephone liaison to ensure that nobody becomes suspicious until Kalenin is safely aboard the aircraft and on his way to London.'

'How the hell do you avoid a diplomatic incident, immobilising border guards?' queried Charlie.

'We don't try,' lectured Wilberforce. 'The men who take out the Viennese posts will be dressed as Czech soldiers and speak Czech. The protests will involve Czechoslovakia, not us. There's no way we can be caught up.'

'Unless the attack goes wrong.'

'We've checked the border,' insisted Wilberforce, irritated by the persistent argument. 'At that time of night it'll be staffed by three men and nothing has happened at the border since 1968. They've grown sloppy.'

'Will we have a radio link in the Mercedes?' asked Charlie.

'Yes,' took up Cuthbertson, 'obviously you will. But I don't think we should utilise it unless Kalenin needs any assurance that he's being well cared for.'

'What about separation?' asked Braley. Ruttgers smiled, an amateur magician with a favourite trick.

'Kalenin is obviously determined to have the money with him at all times,' he reminded them. 'The bag will have a transmitter concealed in the bottom, allowing us complete monitoring at all times.'

'Seems everything has been considered,' said Braley, sycophantically. Both Cuthbertson and Ruttgers smiled, appreciatively.

'Forty-eight hours from now,' predicted Cuthbertson, 'we'll be sitting in this office, celebrating the biggest intelligence coup of our lives.'

'With Aloxe Corton?' asked Charlie, in soft sarcasm.

'What?' asked Wilberforce.

'Nothing,' said Charlie, standing up and going over to the flagged and pinned map.

'All this, just for one man,' he said, reflectively.

'Not just for any one man,' corrected Cuthbertson. 'A very special man.'

'Yes,' agreed Charlie, after a pause. 'A very special man.'

Charlie lay on his back in the darkness. Beside him he could just discern the smoke of Janet's cigarette.

'I'm sorry,' he said.

'Don't be stupid,' she answered, practically.

'It's never happened before,' he complained.

'Keep on about it and you'll become permanently impotent,' said the girl. 'With what you've got on your mind, what happened tonight is hardly surprising, is it?'

'Didn't happen,' corrected Charlie.

The girl shifted position, annoyed again at the self-pity. 'I don't suppose the Director told you, did he?' she asked, obtusely.

'What?' said Charlie, disinterested.

'Sir Archibald Willoughby,' said the girl. 'He died while you and Braley were in Prague.'

For several moments, there was silence in the room. There was no movement at all from Charlie.

'He was an alcoholic, apparently,' offered the girl. 'Been drinking for years.'

'Not years,' corrected Charlie, quietly. 'Just about eighteen months. That's all.'

'Anyway,' accepted the girl. 'Cause of death was cirrhosis of the liver.'

'He was a very unhappy man,' said Charlie, more to himself than to the girl. 'I'm glad he's dead.'

He felt her turn to him in the darkness.

'What an odd thing to say,' she picked up. 'How can you be glad anyone is dead?'

'I knew him very well,' explained Charlie. 'He really didn't want to live.'

The girl moved, rising on one arm to grind out the cigarette and then twisting, so that she hovered over him. The tips of her breasts were brushing his chest but there was no sexual feeling between them.

'Be careful, Charlie,' she said, worriedly.

'Of course.'

'Don't be glib. I want you to come back.'

It was several minutes before he replied.

'I'll come back,' he guaranteed, finally.

Janet was glad the room was in darkness. She would have been embarrassed for him to see her cry again.

17.

Charlie had protested about the danger of attracting attention, but Ruttgers and Cuthbertson, in complete and unified command now, had insisted on final rehearsals, actually driving to within a mile of the frontier along the winding, tree- and meadow-edged road to the Czech border and then back again, stop-watching the journey and testing the surveillance over every mile.

Satisfied, they had toured first by car and then on foot the streets surrounding the secure CIA house in Wipplingerstrasse, isolating the watchers and ensuring each team had the necessary and prepared back-up group to move on any emergency radio command.

To the safe house the Directors had then summoned the section leaders for a final briefing. An American marine commander, Gordon Marshall, was controller of the resistance team at the crossing point. Another American, named Alton, was responsible for the route security into Vienna and a Briton, Arthur Byrbank, was co-ordinator for the journey to the airport. A British commando, Hubert Jessell, was to supervise the house and grounds.

The Directors agreed the placings were perfect and then took the four men through the entire operation, checking and cross-referring the codes and call signs until they were completely satisfied.

Neither Ruttgers nor Cuthbertson was going to allow the slightest possibility of error reflecting upon their personal involvement, decided Charlie, wryly, sitting near the window while the four section leaders received their final instructions.

It was a perfect house for the operation, apart from the absence of a courtyard in which to conceal the car, thought Charlie. It occupied its own grounds; tree-dotted and easily guarded, and secure behind an electronically controlled gate opened by a command room console switch to a password known to only ten men.

The ground floor was given over to radio communications and staffed by three men. The lounge in which they were now gathered and in which they intended to greet Kalenin was a huge, first-floor room, illuminated by chandeliers that hung from the high, vaulted ceilings. Despite the obvious cleaning, the faint, dusty smell of disuse still clung to the over-padded Viennese furniture which had been arranged in a loose circle around the table.

If the crossing went without incident, there was actually talk of a snack meal before the flight to London, remembered Charlie, amused.

At 6 p.m, the section heads left to get into position and Cuthbertson and Ruttgers were alone with the two operatives. The American Director was chain smoking; the occasional jerk in Cuthbertson's eye and the increased redness of his face were the only indications of his nervousness.

'Well,' asked Cuthbertson, confidently.

'It was a mistake to have gone so completely over the route,' criticised Charlie again, knowing Braley shared his view. 'It created an unnecessary risk.'

Ruttgers sighed. Increasingly, the CIA Director found himself agreeing with the view that Cuthbertson had expressed; the Englishman was losing his nerve.

'It excluded the possibility of an error once the thing starts rolling,' insisted the American.

'Or created it,' argued Charlie.

'Are you frightened?' demanded Ruttgers, aggressively.

'Yes,' came back Charlie. 'Very frightened...' he paused. '...Only a fool wouldn't be frightened,' he added, then concluded, pointedly, 'or a psychopath.'

Ruttgers jerked up at him, sharply, and Charlie answered the challenge. It was Ruttgers who looked away first.

Cuthbertson shifted, embarrassed at the hostility that had grown in the room.

'This isn't going to help the operation,' he complained. 'We're all on edge... bound to be. Let's make allowances, for God's sake...'

He moved to a side table and held up whisky.

'A drink, Charles,' he suggested, immediately turning back. 'Charlie,' he corrected.

He was trying very hard, thought Charlie, sympathetically, watching the British Director pour quickly and then hurry the glasses to each man. The four of them stood embarrassed, like abandoned strangers at a party seeking conversation.

'To everything going well,' toasted Cuthbertson, raising his glass.

Sir Archibald had usually given him a drink before the commencement of any operation, recalled Charlie. The hope had always been 'a safe return'.

He drank self-consciously, then looked pointedly at his watch, wanting to quit the company of men whom he despised.

'I think we should move,' he said. 'We can always stop en route if we make good time, but I don't want to be late.'

Both Directors nodded agreement. It was going to be a diarrhoeic four hours for them, thought Charlie, waiting alone in the lofty room with only sporadic radio messages to tell them what was happening.

Ruttgers stopped them at the door.

'Good luck,' he said.

'Thank you, sir,' said Braley.

'And you, Charlie,' pressed the American, smiling at his acceptance of the other man's affectation.

Charlie nodded, without replying, leading the way from the room.

Unchallenged, Charlie took the driver's seat and began moving the car along the now familiar route towards the Marien Bridge. Within fifteen minutes he had picked up the road to Langenzerdorf and had begun to relax. The traffic was comparatively light and it was a warm, dry evening with clouds, which would reduce the light during the cross-over. Perfect, thought Charlie.

As they passed each monitoring point, Braley depressed the code key on the radio, signalling their progress. Ruttgers and Cuthbertson would be in the control room now, guessed Charlie, charting their route on the map that had been laid out there.

'There's no reason why you should like them,' said the American, after a while. 'But equally there's no reason why you should be so bloody rude.'

'They're fools,' judged Charlie.

'That's ridiculous and you know it,' rejected Braley. 'Fools can't hold down the positions they do.'

Charlie shrugged, unwilling to pursue any argument. As they

approached the border, Braley's breathing became more difficult, he noticed. When they got on the outskirts of Ernstbrunn, their radio clattered briefly as the units in Stockerau and Wolkersdorf identified themselves.

'It's working well,' said Braley, nervously.

'Traps always do until they close around you,' said Charlie, unhelpfully.

There was hardly any traffic on the road and they cleared Ernstbrunn in minutes. At the junction with the road to Mistelbach, Charlie slowed and then halted, knowing he was well ahead of time.

'It's a terrible road for a chase,' he assessed, professionally.

Braley nodded agreement.

'I've been thinking that for miles,' replied the American, miserably. 'Let's hope to Christ we can hold anything sufficiently long to make the decoy work.'

Charlie looked sideways at him, questioningly.

'Just how hard do you think the Russians and the Czechs would go to get Kalenin back?' he demanded, rhetorically. 'There's hardly a man in the Soviet Union more important to them. If they come, they'll cross that border like a steamroller, flattening everything in their path.'

Braley slumped in his seat.

'Let's get going,' he avoided. 'I don't want to be late.'

They reached the back-up cars, parked two miles from the border, at 9 p.m. Braley and Charlie stopped and crossed to the lead car, where Braley stared in momentary amazement at Cox sitting in the front seat.

'Jim,' he exclaimed. 'What the hell are you doing here?'

'Part of the team,' said the athlete, happily. 'Recalled from Moscow a week ago. I'm handling the decoy car. Think it'll work?'

'We hope so,' replied Braley. He wondered what real diversion had been planned to involve Cox; certainly there would be no question of his getting captured. Poor bastard. Still, he wasn't a very good operative.

Marshall, the section leader of the resistance group, was a crew-cut, taut man of sharp, abrupt movements. He sat alongside Cox, flexing and shrugging his shoulders, like a boxer limbering up before a bout. He's hoping there will be a chase, so he can involve himself in a fight, assessed Charlie.

'No last-minute snags?' demanded the Briton.

Marshall grinned sideways at the question, as if the idea were unthinkable.

'No last-minute snags, he echoed. He looked at the heavy Rolex watch that had been part of the élite snobbism of the Green Berets in Vietnam.

'The team are setting off in fifteen minutes to take out the border post,' he reported.

'No one is to be killed,' said Charlie, immediately. Marshall worried him, he decided. The marine was the sort of man who enjoyed killing.

'My men know what to do,' snapped the American, gazing at the unkempt Briton as if he'd trodden in dog droppings.

'They'd better,' reminded Charlie, unperturbed. 'The object is to avoid trouble, not cause it.'

Marshall turned to look at him fully, his face inches away from Charlie's.

'You trying to tell me how to do it?' he demanded.

He would keep his voice very low because he would have read in books that it was how men spoke in such circumstances, thought Charlie. The marine's breath smelt of mint and he wore a heavy cologne, Charlie detected.

'No,' he said, not moving his head away. 'But if it becomes necessary, I shall. And I'll pull rank, gun or whatever other crap is necessary to ensure that my instructions are followed. The war in Asia, commander, is over. And your lot made a balls of it.'

The man's control was remarkable and Charlie was glad of it. There would have been no way he could have physically confronted him, Charlie knew.

The departure of the assault group broke the tension between them. Their faces were cork-blackened and they moved without sound. Complete experts, thought Charlie. And killers.

'I'll be in the lead car, fifty yards from the border,' reported Cox, speaking to Braley.

The fat American nodded.

'If there's no chase, I shan't bother to stop. I'll leave you to follow automatically,' Charlie told the marine commander.

Marshall nodded, tightly.

Charlie turned as Braley nudged him. The man was offering the luminous dial of his wristwatch to him.

'Time to go.'

His breathing was very bad now, Charlie realised.

The Briton let himself quietly out of the car, returned to the Mercedes and sat for several seconds, hands gripping the wheel.

'You all right?' asked Braley, worried.

Charlie released a long sigh, then started the car.

'Yes,' he said. 'I'm fine.'

'That was unnecessary, back there,' said Braley, nodding over his shoulder to the car where Marshall sat.

'I know,' conceded Charlie, embarrassed now.

'Then why do it?'

Charlie shrugged in the darkness.

'You've got to buck everyone, haven't you, Charlie?'

The Briton said nothing. It *had* been bloody stupid.

'You shouldn't do it, Charlie. There's no need for you to keep proving yourself.'

'Forget it,' said Charlie, irritated.

Braley stopped talking, looking sadly at the Englishman, and they made the two-mile drive enclosed in their separate fears. The road bent immediately before the border and Charlie stopped just short, so that the car was hidden. Braley's protest in Prague had been right, thought Charlie. Despite the clouds, it was hardly dark.

'Let's check on foot,' he suggested.

They got carefully from the car, easing the doors open so there was no sound. Charlie led, keeping against the bank where the shadows were deepest. He'd moved like this with Snare he recalled, all those months ago in Berlin. And there'd been a trap for him at the border. And now Snare was mad.

The Austrian border post was completely quiet. Through the window of the tiny office, they could see one of Marshall's assault group. The man sat next to a telephone that kept liaison between the stations. He appeared relaxed and very comfortable.

'Do you think they'll have killed the guards?' asked Charlie.

'Yes,' said Braley, immediately. As if it were justification, he offered, 'It's the only way they're trained.'

Charlie looked beyond the post, across the twenty yards of no-man's-land and into Czechoslovakia. There was no sign of activity from the communist side.

'We'll drive up,' decided Charlie.

He took the car slowly, stopping against the customs office and dowsing the lights.

'It's too quiet,' started Braley, worriedly, staring through the barriers.

'We're three minutes ahead of time,' reminded Charlie. Inside the customs post the telephone rang and one of Marshall's commandos answered, the dialect perfectly modulated. Ruttgers and Cuthbertson had considered every detail, conceded Charlie, listening to the exchange. The telephone call was a routine time check and the receiver was replaced within seconds. Beside him, Braley was dragging breath into his lungs, his shoulders rising and falling with the effort.

'Come on!' demanded the American, gazing over the border, hands clenched against his knees. 'Come on!'

Charlie checked his watch.

'10.35,' he recorded.

'Shall I radio the delay?' enquired Braley, quickly.

'It will have been done already,' soothed Charlie. 'If *we* make contact as well, it will create panic.'

'Where is the bloody man?' asked Braley, irritably.

'There,' responded Charlie, pulling forward in his seat. Two hundred yards across the border, a set of headlights had flashed, once. It was not possible to discern the outline of a car.

'What now?' asked Braley. His voice was uneven, the words jumping from him.

Charlie sat momentarily uncertain. The lights flickered on again, briefly.

'I go across,' said the Briton, simply.

He tried to get quietly from the car, but this time the sound of the door opening seemed to echo in the quiet night. From the back seat he hauled the bugged money-bag, hefted it in his right hand and looked briefly back into the vehicle.

'See you in a few moments,' predicted Charlie.

The American stared back at him, but didn't reply.

The men in the border posts were watching him, Charlie knew, as he began to walk towards the barrier; the signal indicating contact would have already been flashed by one of Marshall's men to the secluded house in Wipplingerstrasse. He wondered what Cuthbertson and Ruttgers were doing.

Around him the sounds of the night chattered and rustled and he started looking into the darkness ahead, trying to detect movement. It was a warm, mellow evening; ideal for walking, reflected Charlie. At the Austrian barrier he paused, then ducked beneath it. He hadn't realised the money would weigh so heavily. He stopped, transferring it to the other hand. It was the unexpected weight of the bag that had made his hand shake, he decided.

'Keep cool, Charlie,' he advised himself. 'Don't ruin it all now.'

He could make out the outline of a car, a small, inconspicuous shape half hidden by the Czech border installation. Barbed wire stretched from either side of the barrier posts and he could just identify the triangular shapes of tank obstructions. There would be mines, guessed Charlie, and electronic sensors. Just like East Berlin.

At the Czech barrier, he stood still, right hand resting on the pole. The shaking had stopped, he saw, gratefully. The impatient light burst from the darkened car, urging him on.

He hesitated several seconds, then ducked beneath it. The Czech border posts were completely deserted, he saw, yellow lights pooling into empty rooms. Beyond the control houses, he walked through a cathedral of tall pines which made it completely dark. It was still and quiet, like a church, he thought, extending his metaphor.

Gradually the whiteness of a face registered through the windscreen of the car he was approaching and when he got nearer he saw the figure move, winding down the driver's window.

'You appear very nervous, Mr Muffin,' greeted Kalenin.

'Yes,' agreed Charlie.

The General got from the car, smiling up at him. He opened his coat, disclosing civilian clothes.

'I had intended to wear my uniform and medals,' he said, calmly. 'But then I decided it might have created difficulties in Vienna.'

'Yes,' said Charlie, 'it might have done.'

Around them the night was wrapped like a blanket. There was no sound from the forest, realised Charlie, suddenly. Which was wrong. There should have been animal movement, as there was on the Austrian side.

'I've a great many medals,' said Kalenin.

'I know,' said Charlie.

The Russian nodded towards the bag.

'Is that the money?'

Charlie lifted it on to the bonnet of the car.

'Yes,' he said.

'I suppose I should examine it?'

'Yes,' said Charlie. 'It was bloody heavy carrying it all this way.'

Kalenin unsnapped the fastenings and ruffled the notes.

'So much money,' he said, whimsically.

'Enough for a lifetime,' assessed Charlie.

Kalenin jerked his head back across the border.

'They'll be watching through infra-red nightglasses,' he guessed.

'Yes,' said Charlie. 'The advance party will have them. The message will have already been sent to Vienna that we've met.'

Kalenin nodded. He seemed reluctant to move, thought Charlie.

'The whole border seems deserted,' pressed Charlie.

'Yes,' said Kalenin, easily. 'I've got very great power in all the satellite countries. Whatever I say is obeyed. It was really very easy.'

Charlie looked back into Austria.

'There's a man back there who hoped you'd be pursued by armed guards,' he reported.

'Sometimes I feel sorry for the Americans,' said Kalenin. 'There's so many who'd like still to go West in covered wagons, shooting Indians.'

The two men stood for several seconds looking at each other.

'Well,' said Kalenin, finally, 'shall we go?'

'Yes,' said Charlie.

'I think I should carry the money,' said Kalenin, reaching out.

'Of course,' agreed Charlie.

Wilberforce remained on duty in the Whitehall office, waiting for the message from Vienna that Kalenin was on his way. He had delayed until late in the evening seeing Janet, hoping a signal would make the encounter impossible, but no contact had been made and now he sat gazing down into his lap, embarrassed by the completeness of the girl's account of the previous night. He'd already listened to the recordings of the tapes of which she was unaware and knew she had omitted nothing. Involving her had been an offensive mistake, decided Wilberforce.

'In many ways,' he said, apologetically, 'I regret the decision to ask you to inform upon the man. It's proved completely unnecessary. And distasteful.'

'I know,' said Janet.

Wilberforce looked up at her and for the first time she realised how pale his eyes were. They gave his face an unreal, frightening expression.

He smiled, kindly.

'You've grown very fond of him, haven't you?' he probed.

'Yes,' admitted Janet, immediately, 'which makes what I've done even worse.'

'You'll have to get over it, you know,' advised the civil servant. 'Nothing can possibly come of any relationship.'

'I know,' accepted the secretary.

She moved forward in her chair.

'Tell me,' she demanded, 'he'll be all right, after this, won't he? I mean the Director won't dump him, like he was planning to, all those months ago.'

Wilberforce took several minutes to reply.

'I don't know,' he lied, finally.

The telephone made them both jump.

'They've met,' reported Wilberforce, replacing the receiver. 'Kalenin and Charlie have met.'

18.

'It's very heavy,' complained Kalenin, as they approached the Austrian border.

'Shall I help?'

'I think I can manage,' said the General, using two hands to hold the case. The tiny Russian paused before the barrier, lowering the bag to the ground.

'The moment of commitment,' he said, turning to Charlie.

'Yes,' agreed the Briton.

Kalenin sighed, then positively shoved the bag beneath the post with his foot. It grated over the road, an irritating, scratching sound.

'Too late to go back now,' he said.

'Yes,' said Charlie. 'I thought that on the way over.'

They bent together beneath the bar and walked easily towards the Mercedes. Braley had turned the car, Charlie saw. He would have expected to have heard the sound of the engine.

Marshall was in the border post now, Charlie noticed, gazing hopefully over their shoulders for pursuit. His men would be deployed on either side of the road, Charlie knew. They were very professional; it was impossible to isolate them against the blackness of the woods.

Charlie escorted the Russian past the point without looking, suddenly anxious to get away from the area. Braley was waiting, the car doors already open.

'I'll travel in the front,' selected Kalenin. He turned to Charlie.

'Are you the driver?'

'Yes,' said Charlie.

The Russian nodded, as if the information were important.

Braley held the door for him and Kalenin seated himself fussily, arranging his coat comfortably about him before lowering the case on to his lap.

Charlie and the American paused briefly, looking at each other. Then Braley closed the door and Charlie hurried to the driver's seat.

He started badly, accelerating too quickly and felt Kalenin's eyes upon him. Charlie gripped the wheel and slowed, staring at the twisting road.

'A pleasant evening,' remarked Kalenin, conversationally.

'Yes,' said Braley, after waiting for Charlie to respond. 'Very pleasant, sir.'

Charlie reached the Ernstbrunn turning and came off the road to Mistelbach. On the highway far behind he could just detect the lights of the cars returning Marshall and his unhappy commandos.

'I'm glad there was no trouble, sir,' tried Braley embarrassed by the silence in the car.

'I was confident there wouldn't be,' said Kalenin, immediately. 'If I decree a border post remain unmanned, then it is unmanned.'

The lights of Korneuburg fireflied in front. The teams at Stockerau and Wolkersdorf would have already been informed that it had been a quiet crossing and be moving in to cover him, Charlie knew. And Marshall's cars were quite close behind now. The protection was complete.

'We're well guarded?' queried Kalenin, presciently.

'Utterly protected,' assured Charlie. 'It would be impossible to stop us now.'

'What about a routine Austrian police patrol?'

'They would only want my driver's documents,' said Charlie. 'And they're in order.'

Langenzerdorf was deserted and they were on the outskirts of Vienna in the time that Ruttgers and Cuthbertson had estimated during their trial run. They crossed the Danube canal and passed the post office, turning right into Fleischmarktstrasse to get into the old part of the city. Over the rooftops, he could see the spire of St Stephen's Cathedral. It looked very peaceful, thought Charlie.

Every unit would be on full alert now; and Ruttgers and Cuthbertson would have quit the first floor lounge and be in the radio room, he guessed, charting their progress street by street.

He turned slowly into Wipplingerstrasse. Marshall's team had stopped at the junction behind him, blocking it until the Russian had entered the house.

'Escort the General in,' said Charlie. 'I'll take the car on.'

The American left the car and opened Kalenin's door. The tiny Russian got out immediately and stopped, waiting for Braley's lead. The secured gate opened the moment the American spoke into the grill. Subserviently, he allowed Kalenin to lead as they went along the darkened pathway. The door was opened by Hubert Jessell as Braley knocked. The American led up the stairway, the breath squeaking from him.

The lounge door was already open, light shafting into the corridor.

Ruttgers and Cuthbertson stood side by side, the table separating them from the Russian. Braley entered and then closed the door, standing directly inside. For several seconds, no one spoke, apparently unable to believe the crossing had gone so well.

Ruttgers recovered first, hurrying around the table, hand outstretched.

'General,' he greeted. 'Welcome! Welcome indeed.'

Kalenin smiled at the greeting, accepting his hand.

'You must be...?' he invited.

'Ruttgers,' identified the CIA Director. 'Garson Ruttgers. And allow me to introduce my English counterpart, General Sir Henry Cuthbertson.'

The Briton had followed him around the table, hand held forward.

'A pleasure, General,' assured Cuthbertson. 'A very great pleasure.'

Kalenin shrugged off his topcoat and held it awkwardly. Immediately Braley was at his arm, taking it.

Ruttgers took the Russian by the elbow, moving him further into the room.

'A perfect crossing,' congratulated Cuthbertson. 'A copy-book operation.'

'I have the necessary power,' reminded Kalenin, modestly.

'A drink,' suggested Cuthbertson. 'I think a celebration is in order.'

'I enjoy your Scotch whisky very much,' accepted Kalenin, hopefully. 'And I agree, we've got something to celebrate.'

Ruttgers and Cuthbertson were tight with excitement, each aware of the incredible prestige of their coup. The Briton over-filled the glasses, only remembering Braley as an afterthought.

'We had taken every precaution to ensure nothing would interfere on this side,' guaranteed Ruttgers, eager to boast.

'A plane is waiting, at Schwechat,' added Cuthbertson, 'we'll be safely in London by dawn tomorrow.'

From the communications centre below, notification of Kalenin's safe arrival had already been sent to Wilberforce and Downing Street. By now, guessed Cuthbertson, a personal telephone call would have been made by the Premier to the American President.

'Your health,' toasted Kalenin, raising his glass.

'And yours,' responded Ruttgers, sincerely.

Kalenin moved to one of the more comfortable chairs arranged around the table.

'It was important that you came personally to greet me,' he said, to both Directors.

'It's unthinkable that we would not come,' replied Ruttgers.

Kalenin sipped the drink, appearing quite relaxed.

'Tell me your plans,' he ordered.

'There is accommodation waiting in England,' reported Cuthbertson. 'Four completely safe houses in each of which you'll live from time to time.'

'It will be a long process,' suggested Kalenin. Apparently reminded of time, he looked at his watch.

'Yes,' agreed Ruttgers. 'But during it you will live in absolute luxury and complete safety. Your security will be a joint American-British responsibility.'

'Of course,' said Kalenin.

'We've taken every step to ensure your comfort,' expanded Cuthbertson. He smiled, a man about to produce the best present at a party.

'You enjoy war-games with tanks, I believe?' he asked.

Kalenin frowned, then nodded.

'They've been provided for you, at every house,' smiled the English Director.

'That was very thoughtful of you,' thanked Kalenin.

'We are anxious that you will be completely happy... we've complied with your every request so far...'

'Indeed,' said Kalenin. 'I've been very grateful.' He looked pointedly at his empty glass and Cuthbertson moved immediately to fill it.

'As soon as you feel sufficiently rested,' said Ruttgers, 'perhaps it would be a good idea if we were to get to the airport.'

Kalenin nodded, without replying, the glass held before his face with both hands.

'You created a remarkable operation,' said the Russian, at last.

'Thank you,' said Ruttgers.

'...the road all the way to Schwechat covered, this entire area from the canal to the city hall and Am Hof Square, right down to the riding school and the Volksgarten...'

Ruttgers nodded, content with the praise. His voice was strained by the smoking and he coughed, frequently.

'...and then the border organisation, with teams at Stockerau and Wolkersdorf, Ernstbrunn and Korneuburg...'

Ruttgers began staring at the Russian, curiously.

'How...' he began, but Kalenin shook his head, imperiously. Again he looked at his watch.

'It's been an hour and thirty minutes since I arrived in Vienna,' the Russian declared, smiling.

Both Directors were looking at him now, baffled.

'Time enough,' completed Kalenin.

'General,' tried Cuthbertson, hopefully, 'I'm sorry, but...'

'...you don't understand,' finished Kalenin. There was a tone in his voice now, a man in control.

Reluctantly he placed his empty glass on the table.

'Excellent whisky,' he praised, turning to them and smiling. 'No, there's no possible way that you could...'

He looked carefully from Cuthbertson to the American and then back again.

'Over a year ago,' he said, addressing Cuthbertson, 'you British broke a Soviet espionage chain... it was remarkable for you to have done so. We thought of it as a brilliant installation, virtually undetectable. That you did uncover it was extremely damaging for us... and personally embarrassing to me...'

Both Directors were quite still; Cuthbertson had his head bent to one side, as if he had difficulty in hearing. His face was deepening in colour and his eye was fluttering.

'Moscow regarded the system created by Alexei Berenkov as the best in Europe since the war...'

From where Braley stood there was an uncomfortable movement of scuffing feet.

'...Now Berenkov is in jail. And you both know that Russia does not allow its operatives, particularly one as highly regarded as Berenkov, to remain in captivity longer than is absolutely essential...'

'Are you telling us...' attempted Ruttgers, but again Kalenin cut him off.

'I'm telling you that the Soviet government, which has already, incidentally, established a service to replace that which was broken, decided to repatriate Berenkov as soon as possible and deal to the espionage services of the West as damaging a blow as possible, to compensate for the destruction of Berenkov's network.'

He stopped, waiting, but now neither Ruttgers nor Cuthbertson spoke.

'Within the last ninety minutes,' recounted the Russian General, 'my men have seized, I sincerely hope without any fighting, the 200 operatives that you had positioned to guard my crossing...'

'But that's impossible!' protested Cuthbertson.

'Oh no, not at all,' disagreed Kalenin. 'All you need is organisation and the right information, and I've got both. But I anticipated you would find it difficult to accept. I'm now in complete charge of this house. No doubt you've a method for summoning your people. Try it...'

Cuthbertson jabbed at a button set into the table, prodding it impatiently for response. They remained waiting for several minutes, but no one came.

'Oh my God,' muttered Cuthbertson.

'But that means...' realised Ruttgers, unwilling to complete the fear.

'That, as well as your operatives, I intend taking back to the Soviet Union for barter the English and American security Directors,' confirmed Kalenin, happily.

'As I explained,' he enlarged, 'we decided to make it as damaging as possible. Of course, we'll release you both, in exchange for Berenkov. And all your operatives, too. They will be useless, unfortunately, photographed, fingerprinted and identified. But at least you'll have them back...'

He hesitated, preparing the blow.

'And you'll both be utterly discredited,' he added. 'The whole operation will set your services back years.'

'What you've outlined would be impossible,' insisted Cuthbertson, laughing nervously. 'So few people knew the complete operation...'

His voice broke away and he looked beyond Kalenin to where only Braley stood.

'Yes,' concurred the Russian, seeing the gradual realisation. 'There was no way I could have evolved the thing by myself.'

'Jesus!' exclaimed Ruttgers.

'You really were incredibly stupid, Sir Henry. Charlie Muffin was one of the few real operatives in your service. Yet you set him up to be shot in Berlin, vilified him for his handling of the Berenkov affair when it was he who originated and coordinated the capture and then announced he was being downgraded...'

Kalenin spread his hands, in mock exasperation.

'How can you expect loyalty when you treat a man like that?' he demanded.

'The bastard,' shouted Ruttgers.

'Yes,' agreed Kalenin. 'But he never made the pretence of being anything else, did he?'

'You don't think we'll let you get out of this room alive?' demanded Ruttgers, desperately defiant.

The Russian frowned, irritated.

'Mr Ruttgers,' he protested, mildly, 'this room is the only one in the house not occupied by my men, all of whom are armed. Not that their weapons really matter. They'll be through that door exactly two seconds after I give the command. I agree you could probably shoot me in that time, but to what point? At the moment, my country is prepared to deal with this matter in the utmost secrecy. But if I die, every detail will be leaked to the West, before your repatriation. That wouldn't make for a very pleasant homecoming to Washington would it?'

'We'll still be laughing-stocks,' said Ruttgers, deflated.

'I'm afraid so,' accepted the Russian. 'But only to a few people in your governments. And you'll be alive.'

'What about the money?' demanded Cuthbertson, suddenly.

'Oh yes,' said Kalenin, reminded. 'That's Charlie's. Don't forget he's got a long retirement and he's forfeited his pension rights.'

'I'll get him,' vowed Ruttgers. 'If it takes me until the day I die, I'll get him.'

'He expects you might try,' said Kalenin. 'I don't think he's too worried.'

He felt in his pocket.

'He thought you might want this back,' he said to Ruttgers, extending the device the American had installed in the bottom of the money bag.

'Not that it would really have mattered,' added the Russian. 'You've no one for a hundred miles you could have employed to trace it.'

Kalenin stood, shouting a command as he rose. Braley remained stolidly in front of the door, awaiting instructions.

Ruttgers tensed, then sighed, his shoulders drooping. He shook his head impatiently and the fat American unlocked it.

'Shall we go?' invited Kalenin.

19.

Charlie and Edith sat cross-legged on the floor, the money piled neatly before them. Charlie held the list of numbered notes he and Braley had created and was carefully removing those that were a danger to them. Edith sat nearer the fire, feeding the money into the flames.

'Fifty thousand,' she moaned. 'It seems such a waste!'

Would she ever lose her concern for money? wondered Charlie.

'We'll have to be very careful,' he warned. 'Both Ruttgers and Cuthbertson are vindictive sods. It'll all have to go.'

'Are you really worried, darling?' asked his wife.

Charlie paused in his selection, considering the question.

'Properly aware of the dangers,' he said, firmly.

'You've got more money than me now, Charlie,' said the woman, in sudden realisation. The barrier would be down between them, at last. She was glad, she decided.

Charlie smiled at her, content with her admission.

'I know,' he said. The satisfaction was very obvious in his voice.

'Why don't we spend mine first? I cashed all the shares and drew the money out, as you asked. Let's get rid of my damned inheritance.'

Charlie looked at her, aware of the sacrifice. Edith was embarking completely upon a new life, he thought. He hadn't known she'd appreciated so fully the resentment he had always felt about her wealth.

'Yes,' he agreed. 'That would keep us going for several years, without having to touch this.' He patted the bricks of money lying on the floor, then stood up, stretching the cramp from his legs.

'I never thought it would work, Charlie, when you told me why we were going on holiday after East Berlin and the Berenkov trial. I really didn't,' she said.

'No,' agreed Charlie, gazing through the window and watching the incoming tide throw pebbles up on to the beach. 'There were times when I was doubtful.'

'I'm amazed you and Kalenin were able to cover every eventuality from that one set of meetings in Austria.'

'Kalenin is brilliant,' praised Charlie. 'It was his idea to bring in the Americans, knowing that Washington's presence would occupy Cuthbertson so much initially that any flaws we hadn't covered would have more chance of going unnoticed. Kalenin had a personality file on Ruttgers and guessed exactly how the American would behave. He and Cuthbertson were too worried thinking about each other to properly consider what I was doing...'

'Didn't you ever make a mistake?' asked his wife, admiringly.

'Not really a mistake,' conceded Charlie. 'Kalenin was anxious Berenkov should know he'd not been forgotten and that efforts were being made to get him out. So during a meeting with Berenkov in Wormwood Scrubs, months ago, I had to mention Kalenin's name before I was supposed to have known about it. I sweated for days that it would be spotted on analysis, but it wasn't.'

He stopped, reflecting Edith's question.

'And then,' he continued, 'during the first meeting with Cuthbertson, I got worried at one stage that I was being too convincing with the doubts about Kalenin's defection. I got away with it, though. They might have doubted my courage, but never my loyalty.'

'*Don't* you feel guilty?' seized the woman.

'No,' he insisted, positively. 'There was hardly a meeting when I didn't warn them there was something wrong. I repeated it until they were tired of hearing it...'

'...which was the entire psychology of doing it,' rejected Edith, '...and to salve your own conscience...'

'Perhaps,' said Charlie. 'But I'm not sorry to have disgraced Cuthbertson. He'll have to retire, which means another Director. And that can only result in good for the service. Wilberforce will still be there to ensure continuity. I don't like him, but at least he understands the system!'

'I can't believe you don't feel any guilt,' persisted Edith. 'You betrayed your country.'

'I rid the service of a man who was bound to lead it to disaster.'

'That's a personal justification.'

'And exposed to every Western intelligence system the identity of Kalenin, who had been a mystery for thirty years.

'And got a fortune in return,' she said.

'The service had abandoned me,' insisted Charlie. 'It's better than growing roses on a Grade IV pension and being pissed by three o'clock every afternoon.'

Edith shook her head. He would feel ashamed, in the future, she knew. Would it create another barrier? she thought, worriedly. They only had each other, now.

'I'm going to enjoy being able to afford good clothes,' reflected Charlie. 'And keeping a decent wine bin.'

He looked down at his scuffed Hush Puppies. He'd keep them as a souvenir, he decided.

'You always were a snob, Charlie,' protested his wife, laughing at him.

'But honest about it,' he defended. 'Always honest.'

'Why *did* you have to be so scruffy?'

'Psychology,' avoided Charlie. 'It made them contemptuous of me. People never suspect a person of whom they're contemptuous.'

And it would have meant using even more of your money, he added, mentally.

'Don't you feel sorry about Harrison and Snare?'

He frowned. Why was Edith so determined there should be some contrition? he wondered.

'Those two bastards stood on a viewing platform in Berlin, watching for me either to get captured or shot. When I got to the Kempinski, they were celebrating my death. Why should I feel sorry for them?'

Edith shuddered, very slightly.

'You don't forget, do you, Charlie? Ever?'

'No,' he accepted. 'Never.'

His wife stared at him for several minutes, uncertain whether to raise the question. Then she said, hurriedly:

'Was it really necessary to have an affair with that secretary?'

'Essential,' said Charlie. 'It deflected their interest away from you completely... made it possible for you finally to draw all the money out without their thinking of checking your account. When they bugged her apartment, which I didn't expect, it gave me a channel to feed Cuthbertson any attitude I wished. And from Janet I got everything I wanted to know about their thinking.'

She sat, unconvinced.

'With Janet,' persisted Charlie, 'they thought they had a tap on every unguarded moment. Through her and the recorders, I was able to prove myself and allay any suspicion before it had time to arise.'

'Poor Janet,' said Edith, sadly.

'Forget it,' advised Charlie. 'There was no feeling. It was a game for her, like backgammon or Scrabble. And I bet she made some money, as well.'

'It seems a daft thing to say in the circumstances, Charlie, but I hope you're right. I don't like to think of you being cruel.'

'It was a necessary part of survival,' said Charlie.

'Promise me you never loved her?'

'I promise,' said Charlie, looking up and smiling directly at his wife.

'Will they be searching for us now, Charlie?'

The man nodded.

'Bound to be,' he said. 'But knowing their minds they will think of the Mediterranean. Or perhaps the Far East. Certainly not here, in Brighton.'

'I do hope it's a nice summer,' said Edith, going to the window. 'I did so much like to travel.'

'I gave you a holiday of a lifetime before contacting Kalenin,' reminded Charlie. 'And we'll do it again, in a few years' time.'

'Kiss me, Charlie,' said Edith, urgently. 'Kiss me and say you love me.'

He crawled across the floor, dislodging the money from the orderly piles, and embraced his wife.

'I *do* love you, Edith,' he said.

'And I love you, Charlie. I was very worried, you know.'

'Worried?'

'That you'd leave me for her.'

Charlie frowned, his face inches from hers.

'But why should I have done that?'

'It's just that sometimes you frighten me, Charlie... we've been married fifteen years and there are times when I think of you as a stranger.'

'That's a point,' he said, pulling away and wanting to lighten the mood. 'I'll have to get another name.'

'But Charlie is so... I don't know. It just seems to fit,' she protested.

'Not any more,' insisted the man. He squatted, reflectively. He would take the Christian name of the old Director, he decided.

'It will be Archibald,' he announced, grandly. 'I'll keep the first name, but from now on it will be Charles.'

What a pity that Cuthbertson would never know, he thought. He rolled the words uncomfortably in his mouth.

'Charles Archibald,' he declared. 'With a very definite accent on the "Charles". Charlie Muffin is dead.'

The Home Office car drove directly on to the airstrip, ten minutes after the rest of the passengers had boarded BE 602 to Moscow.

Berenkov got unsteadily from the vehicle and stood for several minutes, supported by one of the officials, gazing for the last time at the Heathrow complex. Finally he turned and shuffled with difficulty up the steps and into the specially curtained first class section.

The steward approached him after they had cleared the airport and the seat-belt sign had been turned off.

'A drink, sir?' he suggested.

Berenkov looked up, whey-faced, considering the invitation.

'It's been so long,' he said, quietly. 'So very long.'

The steward waited.

'You'd only have claret in those little bottles, of course,' said the Russian, professionally. 'And that wouldn't be what I'd enjoy. I'll have a miniature champagne.'

He watched apprehensively as the drink foamed in the glass, then waited for the bubbles to settle.

Finally he lifted it, then paused, glass almost to his lips.

'Your health, Charlie Muffin,' he said.

'Sir?' enquired the steward, half turning.

'Nothing,' said Berenkov. 'Nothing at all.'

Clap Hands, Here Comes Charlie

'Oh well, this is a can of worms as you know a lot of the stuff that went on. And the people who worked this way are awfully embarrassed... but the way you have handled all this seems to me has been very skilful, putting your fingers in the leaks that have sprung here and sprung there.'

Former President Richard Nixon to John Dean, his then counsel, September 15, 1972, from the submission of recorded Presidential conversations to the Committee of Judiciary of the House of Commons.

1.

The third turning would mean he would be going back the way he had come. He took it as a test and when they kept in step Charlie Muffin knew they were following. The fear belched up, sour in the back of his throat, like the brandy sickness every morning.

'Oh, Christ,' he said, desperately.

So it was to be disguised as a backstreet brawl. Scuffling, grunting men, fighting expertly. Back against a slimy wall. No escape. Clawing for the knife-hand, stomach bunched and tight against the first searing burst of pain. No sound. Not words, anyway. Only in the end, perhaps. Before they fled. Traitor, they'd say. So he would know they'd got him. At last.

The road was narrow, hardly more than an alley, leading back towards the Sacré Coeur he could see outlined blackly on top of the Montmartre hill. High, anonymous buildings either side. No people. And dark. Jesus, it was dark.

He'd actually made it easy for them. Careless again. Like Edith kept saying.

Behind, the footsteps quickened, as they recognised the opportunity. He tried to move faster, too, but it was difficult. The road had begun to steepen, with the final gradient before the steps up to the massive Paris landmark; handrails were set into the walls for support. He snatched out, hauling himself along. Shoulders heaving, he stopped, winded and panting, looking back. About fifty yards, he guessed. Surprised they were so far away. Moving steadily, though. Sure of themselves. No hurry now. After all these months, they'd found him.

The break in the wall actually alarmed him, so that he pulled away from it, whimpering. If it led into an enclosed courtyard, he would be trapped. Charlie could hear them now, much closer. More noise than he would have expected. He pushed into the opening, the relief moaning from him when he saw the narrow rectangle of light at the far end from a parallel road. It was one that the tourists climbed to the cathedral, lined with bars and souvenir shops. And with people.

At last the neglected training, so deeply instilled it was almost instinct, began to take over from the initial terror. So he didn't run.

Why the fifty-yard gap? And the unnecessary noise? And this, a passageway to safety? It meant they weren't professionals. And that he'd panicked. So he wasn't professional. Not any more.

At the entry to the broader street he paused, letting himself be silhouetted, then went right, at the sound of their suddenly scurrying footsteps. He was already inside the bar when they thrust out, looking wildly in both directions. Itinerant North Africans, he identified immediately. Knitted headpieces, pulled down over their ears, secondhand westernised clothes, threadbare and greasy. Muggers, he guessed. Frightened, nervous illiterates trying to catch an unsuspecting tourist in a back alley and grab enough money for a cockroach-infested blanket or maybe a roll of kif.

And Charlie Muffin, who had fought and defeated the intelligence systems of England and America, had collapsed. No, he certainly wasn't professional any more.

Angrily he swilled the rest of the cognac into his mouth, gagging slightly as it caught at the back of his throat. He could still taste the sourness of his fear.

Outside, the two men shrugged, looked around uncertainly and finally moved into an opposite bar.

Charlie gestured and when the waiter came, asked for a *jeton* for the telephone. He waited until his glass was refilled and then moved to the corner booth, jiggling the coin between his fingers.

He'd already started on his third drink by the time the police responded to his anonymous call and swept into the café opposite He'd reported the men as drug pedlars, guessing one of them would be carrying kif. If not, then it was a reasonable bet their papers wouldn't be in order. Either way, it didn't matter. By the time they were released, they would have been as frightened as he had been an hour earlier.

He snorted at his own reflection in the mirror behind the zinc-topped bar. Some victory. But it had been even more instinctive than the training. Anyone who attacked Charlie Muffin had to be attacked in response. And hurt more.

It was time to move on, he decided abruptly. Edith wouldn't mind leaving Paris. Welcome it, in fact. She had always preferred Zürich.

'Another cognac?' enquired the barman.

'Why not?' said Charlie.

Because he got drunk and made mistakes, he answered himself. It didn't seem to matter. Whatever he did, it wouldn't be as disastrous as the mistake he'd already made. And from which he could never recover.

It was a rotten existence, thought Charlie.

2.

Alexei Berenkov preferred the dacha in the autumn evenings, about an hour before it got truly dark. Then he could look down from the Moscow hills and see the Soviet capital swaddled in its smoky, protective mist, like a Matisse painting. He wondered what had happened to the one he had had in the lounge of the Belgravia house. Sold, probably. The British government would have made money, he knew. It had been a bargain when he bought it. The furniture would have gone up in value, too. Certainly the French Empire.

He heard movement and turned expectantly, smiling at Valentina. His wife was a plump, comfortable woman, warm to be next to on a winter's night. Wouldn't have been quite the same near the Mediterranean. Or in Africa, perhaps. But then, he thought, he wasn't near the Mediterranean. Or Africa. Nor would he be, ever again.

'Happy?' she asked.

'Completely.'

'I never thought it would end like this. So perfectly, I mean.'

Berenkov didn't reply immediately.

'Were you very frightened?' he asked.

'Always,' she replied. 'I expected it to get better, when you'd established yourself with a good cover. But it didn't. It got worse. When I heard you'd been arrested, it was almost a relief... the news I'd expected for so long.'

He nodded.

'I was getting very nervous, too, towards the end,' he admitted.

'Was prison very bad?'

He nodded again.

'I knew I'd never serve the full sentence, of course,' he said. 'I thought, in the beginning, that I would be able to withstand it easily enough, waiting for the exchange that we always arrange... but it had a strange, destructive effect.'

Valentina looked at the man she had seen so rarely in the past twenty years. The furtive, cowed look had gone at last, she realised. Now the only legacy was the hair, completely white. Once it had been so black, she remembered nostalgically. My Georgian bear, she had called him. She reached out, feeling for his arm, looking down with him over the faraway city.

'What was Charlie Muffin like?' she asked unexpectedly.

He considered her question.

'A very unusual man,' he said firmly. 'Very unusual indeed.'

'I owe him so much,' said the woman. 'And I'll never be able to thank him.'

'Neither will I,' said Berenkov.

'It would be nice to show my gratitude.'

'Yes,' agreed the man.

'Did you like him?'

'Very much,' he said, distantly. Then he added: 'And now I feel sorry for him.'

'Sorry?'

'He was very clever, doing what he did. But I'm sure he never completely realised what it would be like afterwards.'

He shivered, a man suddenly exposed to the cold.

'...More terrible than prison,' he said. 'Far more terrible.'

It had been stupid to begin the conversation, she decided, irritated with herself. It had led to needless reminiscence and they had been getting away from that in the last few months.

'It's all over now,' she said briskly. 'And we can forget about it.'

'I'll never be able to do that,' he said. 'Nor want to.'

'Just prison, then,' she accepted. 'The worst part.'

He looked down at the woman, smiling at her misunderstanding.

'Prison wasn't the worst part,' he said.

She frowned up into his face.

'Not knowing was the worst part,' he tried to explain, with difficulty. 'Being aware, as I was, for almost a year that I was being hunted yet not knowing what they were doing or how to fight back...'

He paused, back among the memories.

'Not knowing is like being aware that you're dying and unable to do anything about it,' he said.

For several moments, neither spoke. Then Berenkov said, 'And Charlie's got to live like that forever.'

'Unless he's caught,' she reminded him.

'Unless he becomes careless and is caught,' he agreed.

3.

It was an unfortunate coincidence, each event detracting from the other. On balance, there was far more ceremony and pomp about the inauguration of the American President so the coverage from Washington unquestionably overshadowed the election victory of the British Premier.

Comparison was inevitable, of course. Radio and television commentators maintained a constant interchange of fact and fallacy to make their points and from the grave that provided complete surveillance of the cemetery the man sighed irritably, knowing there would be no other subject covered that day.

He had never before switched the softly tuned transistor lodged against the headstone to anything but continuous news coverage or talk programmes. He looked around and saw some genuine mourners only yards away; they'd be bound to hear any pop music. Damn it.

Still, remembered the man, it had been worse in the early days. He hadn't thought of bringing the radio then, even for boring current affairs debates. Or evolved the method he now employed to pass the time. Other shifts had copied him and there wasn't a better-kept burial spot in the graveyard. He felt quite proud. No one had said anything officially, though. Hadn't really expected them to; civil servants were a miserable lot.

His jacket lay neatly folded and far enough away to avoid it being splashed by water from his bucket or scrubbing brushes. He knelt on a specially padded piece of blanket and cleaned to a slow rhythm, a regular metronome movement, forward and back, forward and back.

'... bright new future from the gloom of the past...' intoned the American President, Henry Austin, and the undertaking was relayed instantly by satellite from the podium on Pennsylvania Avenue to the churchyard in Sussex.

What sort of future did he have? wondered the grave-cleaner. Damn all, he decided. His gloom of the past would be the gloom of the future.

Some clumsy so-and-so had chipped the bordering granite near the headstone, he saw.

'Sorry; love,' he said.

He frequently wondered about Harriet Jamieson, spinster, who had died on the 13th of October, 1932, aged 61 years and been buried in the hope of eternal peace. Probably a relation of someone in the department, he had decided. Otherwise there might have been a query about all the care being expended on the grave.

'Bet you didn't have so many men sweating over you when you were alive, Harriet my girl,' he said.

The radio programme switched to the BBC's Westminster studio. The new Premier had made a brief Commons appearance, said the reporter, his voice urgent to make the event sound more exciting than it had really been.

'...time to bind our wounds...' said the commentator, quoting Arthur Smallwood's message verbatim.

'Good grief,' quietly muttered the man in the cemetery.

He heard the church clock strike and rose gratefully. There was a telephone just outside the lychgate and he was connected immediately.

'Nothing, as always,' he reported.

'Thank you,' replied the duty clerk.

'Someone's chipped the surround, near the headstone.'

'I'll make a note of it.'

'I don't want to be held responsible.'

'I said I'd record it.'

'How much longer are we going to keep this up, for Christ's sake?'

'Until we're instructed otherwise,' said the clerk.

Prissy bastard, thought the man, as he went off duty.

In Washington, Henry Austin gazed over the crowds that lined the avenue right up to the White House, happy in the politician's knowledge that the inaugural address had caught just the right note.

'I come to office,' said the new President, 'intending to honour the pledge I have made several times during this campaign to the American people. The mistakes of the past will be corrected... when necessary with the utmost vigour. And I will do my best to ensure that fewer are committed in the...'

And from the specially equipped room at Downing Street, Arthur Smallwood stared into the television cameras and out at the watching British people, his face grave with sincerity.

'...overcome accepted and difficult problems,' he said, coming to the conclusion of his address to the nation. 'They are inherited from the past. My government and I are confident that we can do better than that which we succeed. We are determined in that resolve. And prepared to be judged by you, the people, on our efforts...

'My God!' protested the grave-cleaner in familiar exasperation, leaning forward to snap off the television set on which he'd watched both events. 'That's all I've heard, all day. Empty politicians making empty bloody promises. And they haven't a clue what's going on. Not a clue.'

'Chops,' announced his wife, through the kitchen hatch of their semi-detached house in Dulwich. 'I've got pork chops. Is that all right?'

The man didn't answer. He'd get the blame for that damaged grave, he knew. Charlie Muffin was a bloody nuisance.

Henry Austin enjoyed it all, the speech and the triumphal drive to the mansion that was to be his home for the next four years and the photographic session and the reception and the grand ball.

'Brilliant speech, Mr President,' Willard Keys, the Secretary of State, congratulated him.

'I meant what I said,' replied Austin seriously. They were in the corner of the ballroom, momentarily away from most of the guests.

'Mr President?'

'About mistakes. I want this administration squeaky clean. And I want everyone to understand that. Everyone.'

'I'll see to it.'

'And Willard.'

'Mr President?'

'I mean the past as well. I don't want any embarrassments that we're not prepared for. Make that clear, too. Everything tidied up... no loose ends.'

'Why don't we make it the first policy memorandum from the Oval Office?'

'Yes,' agreed the President. 'Why don't we?'

Four thousand miles away, Arthur Smallwood stared across the first-floor study at Downing Street, inviting the Foreign Secretary's assessment.

'Good,' judged William Heyden. Feeling he should say more he added: 'Pity about the American inauguration.'

'Couldn't be helped,' said Smallwood, philosophically.

The two men sipped their whisky.

'It isn't going to be easy,' admitted Smallwood, suddenly. 'I made a number of promises because I had to. There will be a lot of people waiting for the first slip.'

'Yes,' agreed Heyden, who thought the Premier had overcommitted them but didn't know the man well enough to suggest criticism. 'We'll have to watch ourselves.'

'We must let the departments and ministries know the new feeling,' said Smallwood 'Particularly the permanent people who think they can ignore us and make their own policy.'

'A gentle hint?' said Heyden carelessly.
'No,' Smallwood corrected him. 'A positive directive.'

4.

The mid-Channel passport check was always the most dangerous part, the moment when, despite the previous occasions, there could be a sudden challenge and they would be trapped aboard the ship, unable to run.

They had learned to time the public announcement about the immigration office and in the last few minutes preceding it Edith became increasingly nervous, sitting tense and upright and abandoning any attempt at conversation. There were no outward signs from Charlie, except perhaps in the way he drank the habitual brandy, not in spaced-out, even sips, but in deep swallows, so that the barman had already recognised him as a drinker and was standing close at hand, waiting for the nod.

They made an odd couple, she restrained, carefully coiffured and with the discreet but expensively maintained elegance of a Continental woman unafraid of obvious middle age, he baggy and shapeless in a nondescript suit, like a dustcover thrown over a piece of anonymous furniture about which nobody cared very much.

Edith started up at the metallic-voice broadcast, coming immediately to Charlie for guidance. Unspeaking, he led the way out into the purser's square, then paused by the perfume and souvenir shop.

'Don't worry,' he encouraged her.

She appeared not to hear.

What he wanted appeared almost immediately and he smiled at Edith. She looked back, without expression.

The smaller child was already crying, overtired and demanding to be carried. The mother, face throbbing red and split by sunburn, tried to push it away and by mistake hit the other girl, who started crying too, and immediately an argument began between the woman and her husband.

'Perfect,' judged Charlie.

He moved quickly now, his hand cupping Edith's elbow. He could feel the nervousness tighten within her as they wedged themselves behind the squabbling family and began edging closer to the immigration office.

'It'll be all right,' he assured her emptily. She remained stiff by his side, staring straight ahead.

The children caused the expected distraction, filling the tiny room with noise. The parents' row spilled over to the immigration officer at a query about the children being entered on both passports and Charlie and Edith passed through in the wake of the official's anticipated anxiety to regain order in the file of people.

'Works every time,' said Charlie, still holding Edith's arm and leading her back towards the bar. She was still very frightened, he knew.

In recent months she had shown her concern at his drinking by almost total abstinence, but she accepted the brandy now, gulping at it.

'It's been too long,' he said. 'They will have abandoned the blanket scrutiny long ago. And there's nothing wrong with the passports.'

She shook her head, refusing the lie.

'That's nonsense and you know it. They'll never give up. Not until you're dead.'

'This is the fifth time we've crossed from the Continent without any trouble.'

She shrugged, still not accepting the reassurance.

'Thank God we won't have to go through it again.'

'We're safe, I tell you.'

With his empty glass, he gestured to the attentive barman, waving away the change.

'If you're so safe, why are you drunk every night by ten o'clock?' she demanded. It was an unfair question, Edith realised. Fear wasn't the only reason. But she wanted to hurt him, desperate for any reaction that would cause him to stop. She was very worried at the growing carelessness. She should be grateful, she supposed, that he'd finally agreed to abandon England. It had taken enough arguments.

He smiled, a lopsided expression.

'Nothing else to do,' he said, answering her question. Edith shook her head, sadly.

'You know something, Charlie?' she said.

He drank awkwardly, spilling some of the liquor down his suit. It was already stained, she saw.

'What?'

'I never thought I would feel sorry for you. Almost every other emotion, probably. But never pity. And that's nearly all there is now, Charlie. Pity.'

Another attempt to hurt, she recognised. Because it wasn't true. 'What about love?'

'You're making it difficult,' she persisted. 'Very difficult.'

He tried to straighten, to conceal the extent of his drunkenness, then discarded the pretence, slumping round-shouldered in the chair.

'Thank you for agreeing to leave England,' she said sincerely. The gesture was for her, she accepted.

Charlie shrugged, knowing the words would jam if he tried to speak. She had been right in persuading him, he knew. They were both much happier in Zürich, and having dispensed with Paris there wasn't much point in retaining the Brighton house either. That was the trouble, he decided, extending the thought; there didn't seem much point in anything any more.

'We've still got to get nearly £300,000 out of England,' he said. 'Won't you be frightened?'

'Yes,' she said. It would be wrong to suggest he just left it and lived on the money she had, she knew. 'Won't you be?' she asked.

He humped his shoulders, an uncaring gesture.

'Perhaps,' he said. He nodded and the refilled glass dutifully appeared.

He probably wouldn't recall the conversation in the morning, decided Edith. It was already long past remembering... long past many things.

Charlie was bored, she recognised. Bored and uninterested. For someone who had led a life as unique as Charlie's, it was like an illness, gradually weakening him. Now he had nothing. Except guilt. There was a lot of that, she knew.

'Promise me something else,' she tried, hopefully, as the ferry began to move alongside the Southampton quayside.

His eyes were filmed, she saw, and his face was quite unresponsive.

'Don't go to the grave,' she pleaded. 'It's a stupid, sentimental pilgrimage. He wouldn't have expected you to do it.'

'Want to,' said Charlie, stubbornly.

'It's ridiculous, Charlie. There's absolutely no point And you know it.'

'We're coming here for the last time,' he reminded her. 'So I'm going, just once. I've waited long enough. It'll be safe now.'

She sighed, accepting defeat. 'Oh Charlie,' she said. 'Why does it all have to be such an awful mess?'

The office of George Wilberforce, Director of British Intelligence, was on the corner of the Whitehall building that gave views over both the Cenotaph and Parliament Square.

It was a darkly warm, reassuring room, in which the oil paintings of bewigged and satined statesmen adorning the panelled walls seemed an unnecessary reminder of an Empire.

The modern innovation of double glazing excluded noise from outside and deep pile carpet succeeded within. The books were in hand-tooled leather and the massive desk at which Wilberforce sat had been salvaged in 1947 aboard the same vessel that brought home the Queen's throne from an independent India. Wilberforce considered he had the more comfortable piece of furniture.

The Director appeared as tailored for the room as the antique furniture and the unread first editions. He was a fine-featured, elegantly gangling man who affected pastel coloured shirts with matching socks and a languid diffidence that concealed the fervent need for acceptance in a job he had coveted for fifteen years and seen go to two other men before him.

The only intrusive mannerism was the habit, during acrimonious or difficult discussions, of using a briar pipe, which he was never seen to light, like worry-beads, revolving it between his peculiarly long fingers and constantly exploring the bowl with a set of tiny tools that retreated into a gold container.

'It's good to see you again,' greeted Wilberforce formally. Always before the meetings had been in Washington; he couldn't recall an American Director of the CIA making a visit like this to his predecessors, he thought.

Onslow Smith responded with one of the open-faced, boyish smiles that Wilberforce recalled from the sports photographs that littered the man's office.

'Seemed a good idea to hitch a ride on the same aircraft taking the new Vice-President on his tour of Europe,' said the CIA director.

Wilberforce looked doubtful and the other man's smile became apologetic.

'And there was another reason,' he conceded.

'What?'

Smith hesitated, arranging the words.

'The President has a new broom complex,' he said. 'Just like your guy.'

He cleared his throat, to make the quote obvious.

'"... loose ends neatly tied... mistakes vigorously rectified where necessary."'

Already, recalled Wilberforce, political cartoonists were featuring Austin and Smallwood taking turns at being each other's ventriloquist's dummies.

'So I hear,' said the Briton, waiting.

'There's been an official policy document,' said Smith.

'We've had something like that here,' admitted Wilberforce.

'Which means we have the same old problem,' said Onslow Smith.

Wilberforce nodded, reaching out for a worry pipe.

'Charlie Muffin,' he agreed. 'The bastard.'

5.

It wasn't until he got into the churchyard and felt the damp, cold wind that always seems to blow in English cemeteries in November that Charlie Muffin sobered sufficiently to realise completely what he had done. And that the stupidity could kill him, like so many stupidities before it.

The trained instinct surfaced through the swamp of alcohol and he pulled away from one of the main pathways, using a straggled yew tree for cover. About ten yards away, a black knot of people huddled speechless around a grave still cheerfully bright from funeral flowers. Nearer, a practised mourner, shirt-sleeved despite the cold, knelt over a green-pebbled rectangle on a padded cloth, scrubbing the headstone and surround into its original whiteness, lips moving in familiar conversation with someone who couldn't reply any more. Charlie turned, widening his vision. At least twenty people spread throughout the churchyard. Too many.

'You're a prick,' Charlie told himself. 'A right prick.'

He frowned, surprised at the emergence of the habit. He'd always talked to himself, unashamedly, when he was under stress or afraid. It had been a long time since he had done it; like welcoming back an old friend, he thought.

The drunkenness was gone now, but the pain was banded around his head and his throat was dehydrated. For a man apparently seeking a momentarily forgotten grave, he'd stood long enough beneath the tree, Charlie decided, groping for the professionalism of which he had once been so confident. He swallowed, forcing back the desire to flee, to run back along the wider pathway to the car he could still see, over the low wall.

'Never run,' he murmured. 'Never ever run.'

One of the basic lessons. Often ignored, though. Sometimes by people who should know better. And invariably by amateurs. Günther Bayer had been an amateur. No, Charlie corrected, not an amateur. An innocent. A trusting, manipulated innocent who had believed Charlie was sincere in trying to help him escape across the Wall. And so he'd run when he got caught in the East German ambush that had been intended for Charlie. He'd been dead before the flames had engulfed the Volkswagen, Charlie assured himself Had to be, in that cross-fire.

He pushed away from the tree, rejoining the main path, alert for the attention the movement would have caused even an untrained watcher. Nothing. Perhaps he was all right, after all. Perhaps, after so long, there was no observation. Or perhaps they were too well trained.

The pathway along which he was walking ran parallel with the perimeter wall, Charlie realised. But there was a linking lane, built like a spoke through the middle. He could turn on to that and regain the entrance. Four hundred yards, he estimated. It seemed a very long way.

The hesitation was hardly perceptible when, suddenly, he saw the tomb. In his earlier drunkenness he had imagined that Sir Archibald Willoughby's grave would be marked in an ordinary, traditional way, like that tended by the shirt-sleeved man near the yew tree. The family vault was an ornate, castellated affair, protected by an iron fence and reached through a low, locked gate. Plaques were set into the wall, recording the names of the occupants.

Charlie was confident his reaction to the vault had been completely covered; to stop, pause, even, would be all the confirmation they would need.

He was past, actually on the straight path leading to the exit, when the challenge came.

'Charlie! Charlie Muffin!'

Afterwards Charlie remembered with satisfaction the smoothness of his reactions. The gateway was still too far away to consider walking on, as if the name meant nothing. He couldn't run, of course. But they could. They'd get him before he'd gone twenty yards. They? It had been a single voice. Just one man, after so long? Probably. Fight then. Feign bewilderment, to gain the moment of uncertainty. Then fight to kill. Quickly, before anyone in the cemetery realised what was happening. Go for the throat, the carotid artery, smashing the voice box with the same blow. Sir Archibald's tomb would give him the concealment. He'd only need minutes to get to the car.

He tensed, to make the turn, then stopped. There'd been all the training, certainly. Poncing about in canvas suits, waving his arms about and yelling 'aargh' like a bloody idiot. But he'd never killed anyone – not body to body, feeling the warmth of their skin and possibly seeing the terror in their faces. That had always been done by proxy, by others.

He completed the turn, head held curiously, keeping the movement purposely slow.

'I'm sorry...' he frowned, the confusion perfectly balanced.

It was a tall man habitually stooped in an effort to reduce his size. Beaked nose too large for his face. A clipped, military moustache, a darker brown than the swept-back, short-cropped hair. Familiar, decided Charlie. Someone from the old department then. The man smiled and began coming forward.

"It *is* Charlie Muffin, isn't it?'

He wasn't professional, judged Charlie. Couldn't be. What properly trained man openly challenged a victim? And then walked forward, both arms held out, losing any chance of surprise in producing a weapon? He wouldn't make another juvenile mistake like Paris, Charlie decided.

Who then?

'Willoughby,' the man identified himself, as if in answer to Charlie's question. 'Rupert Willoughby.'

Charlie's eyes flickered for a moment to the name on the tomb plaques, then back to the man who was now offering his hand, recognising the similarity. The handshake was firm, without the usual ridiculous tendency to turn it into a form of Indian palm wrestling, and the brown eyes held Charlie's in a direct, almost unblinking gaze. Just like the old man's, remembered Charlie. Until the end, that was.

'What an incredible coincidence,' said Willoughby.

'Yes,' agreed Charlie, the confusion genuine now.

Immediately fear swept it aside. If the graveyard were still under surveillance, then now he had been positively identified, he realised. Sir Archibald's son would be known, to all of them. And they were standing immediately outside the vault, the marker he'd managed to avoid only minutes earlier. He still had a little time, he decided. Not much. But still enough to use.

He tried to withdraw his hand, turning back to the gate.

'...decided to pay my respects,' he stumbled, badly. 'Haven't been able to, before... in a hurry, though. Really must go.'

'No, please, wait.' protested Willoughby. 'There's a great deal for us to discuss... a business matter...'

'Perhaps another time... sorry, I'm very late...'

Willoughby was walking with him, frowning at the rudeness. He reached into his pocket and Charlie edged away, apprehensively. The man produced a small wallet and offered Charlie a card.

'We must meet again,' he said. 'It's most important... to do with my father...'

'Call you,' promised Charlie, thrusting the pasteboard into his pocket. He was almost at the exit now. The obvious place, he decided; the lychgate would certainly provide some cover and they could get him away in a car before anyone in the cemetery realised the attack had happened. Charlie paused, examining it. There was no one there.

'Promise?' demanded Willoughby.

Charlie turned to the man, realising the need to recover.

'I really am very sorry,' he said, stopping with his back to the support pole for the gate roof, positioning himself where he could see the beginning of any approach. 'It must seem very rude.'

Willoughby didn't reply, confirming the assessment.

'Like to spend more time... believe me.'

'Call me then?'

'Of course.'

'When?'

'Soon,' promised Charlie hurriedly, turning through the gate. The mourners he had seen around the fresh grave were dispersing, heads bowed, into various cars. A woman was crying. The man who had been scrubbing the surround had finished, too, he saw. Carefully the man had packed the brush, cloths and bucket into the boot of an old Morris and was walking slowly towards the telephone.

'I'll be waiting,' called Willoughby, after him.

Charlie drove alert for the slightest danger, eyes constantly scanning the rearview mirror. Purposely he went north-west, choosing Tunbridge Wells because it was the first town of any size, twisting and turning through the streets and then continuing north, to London, to repeat the evasion.

'You're a prick, Charlie,' he accused himself again, as he took the car over Vauxhall Bridge. 'A careless, idiot prick who deserves to die.'

He'd arranged to clear out the bank the following morning. But that didn't matter now. Only survival mattered.

'Prick,' he said.

The London home and elegant, sophisticated refuge of George Wilberforce was a second-floor apartment overlooking Eaton Square. Here, from Monday to Friday, he lived, returning only at the weekends to a nagging, condescending wife who refused him the respect that everyone seemed to find so difficult, and from whom he would have welcomed divorce but for the admittedly remote but nevertheless possible harm such an event might have caused his career. Those responsible for appointments in the permanent civil service were known sometimes to possess strong religious views and it was wise not to take chances.

Particularly not now. Because now his career was more assured than it had ever been.

Delius, he decided, would suit his mood.

Apart from the habit with never-smoked pipes, the Director was a man who rarely betrayed any emotion, but now after standing for several movements by the stereo unit he suddenly moved away in a halting, stiff-jointed attempt at what appeared to be a waltz. He stopped, embarrassed by his efforts.

'I've got you, Charlie Muffin,' he said. 'And now you're going to suffer for what you did. Christ, you're going to suffer.'

6.

George Wilberforce blinked at the gritty sensation behind his eyes, knowing he should have allowed more time after the flight from London before this conference in the CIA complex in the Virginia countryside. But this time he had wanted the meeting in America; to arrive the courier of news for which they had waited so long and sense the approbation, even if there were no open praise.

'You're quite sure?' demanded Onslow Smith urgently. The American Director, whom he had had to tell in advance of the meeting, was a large open-faced man who seemed constantly restricted within the confines of an office chair, business suit and subdued tie. As if in apologetic explanation for his build, the wall behind his desk was patterned with sports pennants, shields and group pictures of the Yale rowing and boxing teams. The Onslow Smith smile was featured in all.

'Quite sure,' said Wilberforce, keeping the exhilaration from his voice. 'We've caught Charlie Muffin.'

'Thank God for that,' said Smith distantly. 'It's about goddam time.'

Appearing suddenly aware that the remark could be construed as criticism, he added quickly: 'Congratulations.'

Wilberforce's shrug of uncaring dismissal was perfect.

'And now can we kill him?' demanded Garson Ruttgers. Wilberforce came up from the pipe at which he had already begun probing, staring at the diminutive, frail-seeming American whose ambition to become, as chief of the CIA, what Edgar Hoover had been to the FBI, had been destroyed by Charlie Muffin. Ruttgers was an unsettling feature of the group, thought Wilberforce, watching the man light a cigarette from the stump of that which had preceded it, never once breaking the staring-eyed gaze across the table through clerk-like, half-lens spectacles. About Ruttgers there was an aura of unpredictability, thought the Briton. And something else. The man physically frightened him, Wilberforce realised, surprised.

'It's not quite as easy as that,' he said guardedly.

'Why not?' demanded Ruttgers.

The constant inhalation of nicotine had turned the man's false teeth yellow. Why, wondered Wilberforce, didn't the American soak the dentures in stain remover? His breath must smell appallingly.

'Yes, why?'

The repeated question in the unpleasantly recognisable, phlegmy tone, came from Wilberforce's right and he turned to Sir Henry Cuthbertson. The baronet was a bulky, cumbersome man proud of family links that went back to the service of James I, who had conferred the original baronetcy. He'd earned the DSO in the Second World War and been seconded from the Chief of Staff council to revitalise Britain's intelligence system after the fading, twenty-five-year directorship of Sir Archibald Willoughby. And lost the job in less than a year. Four hundred years of honour wrecked in a few short months by a scruffy ex-grammar school boy with an irritating Mancunian accent and the distressing tendency not to change his shirt every day, reflected Wilberforce.

It was hardly surprising Cuthbertson and Ruttgers wanted Charlie Muffin's immediate assassination, thought Wilberforce. But neither had operated under the new governments. Or knew – because nobody knew – of Wilberforce's determination to make Charlie Muffin's capture a personal triumph.

'Because there mustn't be any mistake,' said the British Director simply.

'No,' agreed Onslow Smith hurriedly. 'No mistakes.'

To be convinced, the feelings of the two older men would have to be bruised, realised Wilberforce.

'Let's not forget,' he said, 'that the errors made with Charlie Muffin in the past were absolutely horrifying.'

Ruttgers and Sir Henry shifted, both discomforted at the prospect of being reminded.

'Four years ago,' said Wilberforce, 'the British uncovered in Europe the most successful Russian infiltration of NATO since the Second World War. The man who led their operation, Alexei Berenkov, was jailed for forty years. It was one of the worst disasters ever suffered by the Russians – so grave, in fact, that it came as little surprise to either America or Britain to learn, as they did within a year, that Valery Kalenin, operational chief of the KGB, wanted to flee for asylum to the West…'

'We're all aware of the history,' said Ruttgers, in an attempt to halt the other man.

'And now we must put it in proper perspective,' insisted Wilberforce. 'It was a deceit. A deceit conceived and operated by Charlie Muffin, working not for the British intelligence organisation that employed him, but with Kalenin. A deceit to expose not just ordinary agents, but the British and American Directors; for them to be seized and offered in exchange for the repatriation of Alexei Berenkov.'

The embarrassment, recalled Wilberforce, had been incredible after that numbing evening in the CIA 'safe' house in Vienna when Kalenin had arrived not nervous and alone, as they had expected, but followed by a Russian commando team who had carried Ruttgers and Cuthbertson back across the Czechoslovakian border. Charlie Muffin had shown a surprising knowledge of psychology, judging the ambition of both men would drive them to such close involvement. Upon reflection, it seemed lunacy. He hadn't thought so at the time, though. That was something else no one was ever going to learn.

'The man is a traitor,' insisted Ruttgers. 'So he should be shot.'

'A traitor,' agreed Wilberforce. Legally so, he qualified. But aware as he was – and as Charlie Muffin had certainly been – that Cuthbertson had decided he could be abandoned at the East German border in the final stages of the Berenkov seizure, Wilberforce found the accusation difficult. Another reservation, never admitted to anyone. Any more than it had ever been admitted that it had been Charlie who had coordinated Berenkov's capture, fitting together the disparate jigsaw so cleverly that not only Berenkov but nearly everyone in the European cell was caught, Charlie, who had deserved first praise and then acceptance within the reorganised department Sir Henry was establishing. And who instead had realised that he had been selected for sacrifice in the final stages. Sir Henry would never concede he had decided Charlie should die, of course. Convenient amnesia wasn't a new affliction in the department.

'But a traitor who should not be allowed to cause further embarrassments to either government,' Wilberforce added.

The irritation of Ruttgers and Cuthbertson was increasing, Wilberforce saw. The American fussily lighted yet another cigarette and the British baron twisted the family-crested ring on the little finger of his left hand as if seeking solace in a talisman of his family's greatness.

'That's vitally important,' said Onslow Smith, once more in immediate agreement.

'And we couldn't guarantee that by a simple elimination,' declared Wilberforce. The American Director was definitely deferring to him, he decided.

'Why not?' demanded an unconvinced Ruttgers.

'To start with,' said Wilberforce, 'because he isn't in England. He was, very briefly. That's where we picked him up and from where we followed him back to Zürich.'

'I don't see the problem,' argued Cuthbertson. 'What's wrong with killing the man in Switzerland?'

The British Director sighed. They were very obtuse, he thought. But then, they hadn't considered the long-term advantages as he had.

'Initially,' he said, 'the problem is risking an assassination in a country other than our own, where we could not ensure complete co-operation of the civil authorities.'

'We've done it dozens of times before,' disputed Ruttgers.

'Maybe so,' agreed Wilberforce. 'But not so soon after your President and my Prime Minister have pledged, publicly, that theirs are going to be open governments, free from unnecessary criticism.'

He paused. They still weren't accepting the reasoning, he knew.

'But more importantly,' he started again, 'we can't kill Charlie Muffin without knowing whether he has established any automatic release of information from, say, a bank vault that would compound the difficulties he has already caused. Don't forget how devious the damned man is.'

'There's no way we could do that, for Christ's sake,' objected Ruttgers.

'Oh, yes there is,' said Wilberforce, smiling. 'And it's the way to ensure that Charlie Muffin comes back to England like an obedient dog answering a whistle.'

He was going to enjoy himself, decided Wilberforce. Enjoy himself very much indeed.

Johnny Packer, who was never to learn the real reason for his good fortune or how closely his life was so very briefly to become linked with a man called Charlie Muffin, decided that the party to celebrate his release from Parkhurst was exactly right. Far better than he could have expected, in fact. He'd ruled there wouldn't be any rubbish, no amateur tearaways in their flash suits and cannonballs of money where the other sort should have been, to impress whatever slag they were trying to pull that night. But he hadn't been able to guarantee who *would* come. And that was the value of the party, showing how well he was regarded. Everyone was there, he saw. Everyone who mattered, anyway. Harry Rich, the soft-voiced Irishman, who'd personally put two people into the supports of the M4 flyover while the concrete was still wet and was now the undisputed controller of the East End as far west as Farringdon Street; Herbie Pie, who had wept – though from pleasure, not remorse – carving the faces and the Achilles tendons during the last confrontation in Soho and now giggled at the rehearsed joke and said he had the whole place stitched up; even Andie

Smythe, who rarely came this far east, silk-suited, smooth-haired and shiny-faced, looking always as if he'd been polished all over with a soft cloth before setting out for the nightly tours of the Mayfair casinos to receive what was rightfully his for ensuring that the unloading of the innocent was never violently interrupted.

Like an actor in a long-running play aware of his spot on stage at any one moment, Johnny stood stiffly in his two-day-old suit, away from the bar that had been erected in the upstairs room of The Thistle, nodding and smiling to everyone but getting involved in no prolonged conversation.

The positioning was decreed by the rules of such gatherings, as formalised as the steps of a medieval dance or the mating rituals of some species of African birds.

It was Herbie who broke away from the group, the appointed spokesman.

'Good to see you out, Johnny.'

'Thank you, Mr Pie. Nice of everyone to come.'

'Always happy to come to such functions. Specially when it's kept to the right people.'

Johnny sighed at the reminder of why he had served five years in Parkhurst.

'No more amateurs who can't stop boasting about what they've done,' he promised.

'Hope not, Johnny,' said Pie. 'Craftsmen like you shouldn't take risks.'

And he wouldn't, any more, thought Johnny. If he were caught again through not taking sufficient care about the people he was working with, he'd go down for ten. Maybe longer.

'Any plans, Johnny?' enquired the other man.

'I'm in no hurry, Mr Pie. Got to get myself together first.'

The man nodded.

'Still got the little house in Wimbledon?'

'Yes,' said Johnny. 'Neighbours think I've been working on a five-year contract in Saudi Arabia.'

Pie nodded again, the encounter concluded. Everything was to a formula, even the apparent small talk.

'So, should anyone want you they could contact you there?'

'Any time,' Johnny assured him, keeping the hope from his voice. 'Any time.'

'And no amateurs this time?'

'No amateurs,' promised Johnny.

A clear enough warning, Johnny decided. The repeated criticism meant they still doubted him. So no one would be visiting Wimbledon until he'd proved himself again, no matter if he were one of the three top safecrackers in London. He'd have to do something pretty remarkable to recover, he decided.

'I think you'll like it,' said Onslow Smith.

Wilberforce sipped the wine, nodding appreciatively. The other man was unquestionably accepting his leadership, he decided, gratified.

'Not French,' he judged.

'Californian,' agreed the American Director.

'Excellent,' said Wilberforce. Surrounding himself with sports mementoes was all part of a carefully maintained affectation on Smith's part, decided the other Director generously, an invitation for people to imagine his thinking and intelligence as muscled as his body. Which would have been a mistake. Smith's decision to involve Ruttgers in the meeting that morning, just as he had included Cuthbertson, showed they were both aware of the dangers of the operation upon which they were embarking. And were taking out insurance. Both he and Smith could afford to be magnanimous in the vengeance hunt; if it were successful, then both would gain sufficient credit because of their association, while the two men worst affected would salvage something of their reputations. But if anything went wrong, then the fault could be hopefully offloaded on to those already disgraced. Perhaps that was why Smith was letting him take the lead, he thought fleetingly.

'It *is* a bank, isn't it?' guessed the American, suddenly.

Wilberforce smiled. Definitely very intelligent.

'What made you realise that?'

'When Charlie Muffin walked out of the house in Vienna, leaving Ruttgers and Cuthbertson to be grabbed, he took with him $500,000 we'd provided in the belief it was what Kalenin wanted to cross over. But you didn't mention the money this morning. So you must know where he's hiding it...along with anything else that might embarrass us.'

'Yes,' admitted Wilberforce. 'It's a bank. And I know which one.'

'How?'

'We picked him up in a cemetery. Eventually he went to a house in Brighton, where he collected a woman we've since identified as his wife. It was obviously a house they'd had for some time. From the voters' register we got the name they had assumed. From then on, it was merely a routine job of having a team of men posing as credit inspectors calling up all the banks in the area until we found an account. We didn't expect a safe deposit, though... that's what has made me worry he might have tried to protect himself with some documents.'

Wilberforce paused. Just like the drunken sot of a previous Director, Sir Archibald Willoughby, had tried to do, he thought. He hadn't succeeded, though; they'd sealed up that difficulty just as they'd erase this if it existed.

The American added more wine to both their glasses.

'You know something that surprises me?'

'What?' asked Wilberforce.

'That Charlie Muffin didn't go to Russia. He'd have been welcome enough there, for God's sake.'

Wilberforce sighed. It was increasingly obvious, he thought, why it would have to be he who initiated everything in this operation.

'But Russia is the last place he would have gone,' he tried to explain. 'Charlie Muffin wouldn't have regarded what he did as helping Russia. Any more than he would think of it, initially anyway, of being traitorous to Britain or America.'

Onslow Smith frowned curiously at the other man.

'What the hell was it then?'

'Charlie Muffin fighting back,' said Wilberforce. 'When he realised we were prepared to let him die.'

'This isn't going to be easy, is it?' said Smith thoughtfully.

'No,' said Wilberforce. 'But it's the only way we can guarantee there won't be problems.'

'And it's necessary for us to be personally involved, potentially dangerous as it is?'

He seemed to be seeking reassurances, thought Wilberforce.

'There's no one else we could trust with it.'

Onslow Smith nodded, slowly.

'You're right, of course,' he accepted.

He smiled uncertainly.

'I bet the President never had this in mind when he promised to correct mistakes with the utmost vigour,' mused the American.

'But that's exactly what we're doing,' encouraged Wilberforce. 'But neither he nor the Prime Minister will ever appreciate it.'

'If they did know,' said Smith, 'they'd be damned scared. Tell me, George, are you frightened?'

'Properly apprehensive,' answered Wilberforce evasively.

Somehow, he had decided, the British Premier would learn what had been done for him. When it was all safely concluded, of course.

The CIA Director smiled across the table.

'I'm scared,' he admitted. 'I'm damned scared.'

7.

He wasn't asleep, Edith knew. Any more than he had been the previous night at this time, just before dawn. Or the night before that. Any night, in fact, since the cemetery incident. She breathed deeply, hoping Charlie wouldn't realise she was awake and start talking. If they talked, they'd row. It was too late for rows. And anyway, Charlie's response would be to fight back. Survival, he called it. She sighed, maintaining the pretence of sleep. The need to survive; Charlie's panacea for anything unpalatable.

She became annoyed with herself, recognising the criticism. She had no right to think like that, she thought. No right at all. They *had* decided that Charlie was a disposable embarrassment, someone who could be dumped because he didn't have the right accent or public school tie and was a remnant from another, discredited era. So he had had every justification for what he had done. Justification on the filthy terms within which they operated, anyway.

If only Charlie hadn't stopped believing that. Poor Charlie. No matter what explanation or reasoning he advanced, he could never lose the feeling of remorse that had grown during the last year. Misplaced remorse, she thought. Because Charlie Muffin wasn't a traitor. An opportunist, she accepted. Amoral, too. Worryingly so. But no traitor. He couldn't dislodge the doubt, though. Perhaps he never would. And from that uncertainty, all the others had grown. And the drinking. Perhaps the drinking most of all. The churchyard mistake had certainly been through booze.

And all the others, before. At least that had stopped, after the latest scare. Odd how real fear made him abandon alcohol. Survival again, she supposed.

'How long have you been awake?'

She turned at his question, discarding the charade of sleep.

'Quite a while. You?'

'Quite a while.'

'I still wish you wouldn't go.'

'I've got to.'

'They couldn't find us now.'

He didn't reply and she demanded urgently, 'Could they?'

'If I don't meet Rupert Willoughby, he might contact the department,' he said. 'Don't forget how closely his father involved him... he wouldn't have the hesitation of anyone else. And if he were to telephone them, he'd give them the lead they need.'

'You said it was safe here,' she accused him. 'We moved back the same day, for heaven's sake.'

'I overlooked it,' he admitted. Like so many other things, he thought.

'You could be exposing yourself completely,' she warned, frowning at the repetition of a previous argument.

'I'll be careful,' he said. 'Very careful.'

'Will you bother about the money?'

'I don't know.'

So he *did* think he had been identified. If she hadn't kept on about quitting England completely, they wouldn't have gone back for the confounded money, she thought bitterly. The fact that she was a rich woman had always been a barrier between them.

Frightened that he might detect her tears in the growing half-light, Edith turned towards the window. Lake Zürich was already visible, dull and flat like a thrown-away silver dish.

'What happens if he has contacted them?' she asked, bringing the fear into the open. 'It would be a trap.'

Again there was a pause. Then he said: 'I won't know. Not until I get there.'

They'd move on, she knew. Again. Away from the hideout where she felt most safe, just a five minute walk from the Swiss Bank Corporation building in the Paradeplatz where her money was held in its numbered account, together with the false passports and forged documents, another identity to be donned, like new clothes, if that under which they had existed for the past two years were discovered because of that bloody graveyard idiocy.

Move on to where? At least not back to the small, greasy apartment in the Pigalle area of Paris, she thought gratefully; smelly and anonymous rooms among the no-questions-asked hotels in which the transient workers from North Africa and Turkey lived out their frightened existence, without the proper entry or work permits. So where? God knows.

'I wish you hadn't done it, Charlie.'

'I've apologised, haven't I? Don't you think I regret it, every bit as much as you?'

She held back the response, recognising the defiance in his voice. She *wouldn't* argue, she determined. There was no purpose in holding an inquest. She gnawed at the inside of her cheek, caught by the word. Inquests were for people who had died. Usually violently.

'I'll go by myself; of course,' he said.

'Of course,' she agreed. Quickly, the feeling clogging her voice, Edith added: 'Be careful.'

He laughed.

'I'm a survivor, remember?'

'I'm very frightened, Charlie. It's different now. You're completely on your own. And everything seems to be going wrong.'

'That's how I've always been, on my own.'

She moved her head, a rustling gesture of rejection against the pillow.

'I love you, Charlie,' she said. 'I couldn't bear to live without you.'

'You won't have to.'

'I wish I could believe that.'

She waited for the reassurance to be repeated, but Charlie said nothing. The tears she had so far managed to hold back began feeling their way across her face and she turned farther towards the window, away from him.

'You haven't said you loved me for a long time,' he remarked and she started crying even more.

In Moscow, the British ambassador, Sir Robert Black, accepted the sheaf of papers from the Soviet Minister of Culture and affixed his signature. The signing of the outline agreement completed, both men rose from the table. Immediately the waiters approached with the trays of drinks for the regulation toasts. Despite the regeneration of the British economy, it was sherry, not champagne. The Russian, Boris Navetsky, hesitated, looking disdainfully at the amber liquid. Bloody mean, he thought.

'My country is eagerly looking forward to the exhibition,' said the ambassador.

Navetsky nodded.

'A pity, perhaps,' ventured the Briton, 'that it was not possible for the actual Romanov jewellery to be displayed.'

'It is only the Fabergé replicas that have ever been allowed to leave the country on exhibition,' Navetsky reminded him stiffly. He'd refuse a second drink, he decided.

'Surely you don't imagine my country would expose such works of art to any risk?' said the ambassador.

'Of course not,' Navetsky assured him.

In London, a report on the exhibition of the Russian royal jewellery was despatched, as a matter of routine, from the Foreign Office to Wilberforce. It was to be several days before he read it.

The protection would never be necessary, Johnny Packer knew. But like Herbie Pie had said, he was a craftsman. And craftsmen always did things properly. So at the back of the shed, where the more volatile explosives were stored, Johnny had constructed a double-thickness brick wall, to cushion any accidental blast. Each was housed in its carefully partitioned section, with metal sheets forming an inner lining. The P-4 plastic, the easiest and least dangerous to use, was most readily to hand. Then the cordite, which he disliked because of the difficulty of control in certain circumstances. And in front of it all, the sacks of sodium chlorate, to be mixed with the sugar in the kitchen if the sudden need arose. Which he hoped it wouldn't. Sodium chlorate and sugar was all right for the killers of Belfast, but Johnny Packer was a craftsman.

Away from the explosive material but still within the reinforced area the fuses and detonators were packed carefully into their boxes and in a third case were the clocks and pressure mechanisms.

He locked the shed and began walking round to the house. With equipment like that, there wasn't an explosive device he couldn't construct, decided Johnny. But when? Six weeks and there'd been nothing. It was a test, Johnny knew. The trade... the real, no-fucking-about trade... had to be sure he'd learned his lesson. Trouble was, the only way to prove that was to do a job. And without help, how the hell was he going to do that?

8.

Charlie had allowed himself three days before the London meeting. The first two had been taken up travelling to England by as confused a route as possible, going by train from Zürich to Lyons, from there to Paris, backtracking to Auxerre and then returning to Paris to catch the night sleeper to Victoria.

The remaining day had been devoted entirely to watching Rupert Willoughby, following him from his house off Sloane Street to his City office, occupying the secluded table at Sweetings during the man's business lunch, checking his firm to uncover any possible links to dummy or cover companies the names and addresses of which he might have recognised and then, finally, trailing him in his trendy, smoked-glass mini back from the City to Knightsbridge in the evening. Just like old times, reflected Charlie, welcoming the activity.

It would have needed a team of men to have established absolutely that the man was not under deep surveillance, Charlie accepted. And as Edith had warned, now he was completely on his own.

And so he would always be now, he reflected, content with the protection of the rush-hour crowd in the middle of which he spilled from the Bank underground station on the morning of the appointment.

'So far, so good,' he assured himself.

'Yes,' agreed a commuter beside him. 'Much better this morning, wasn't it? Extra trains at London Bridge, you know.'

'About time,' answered Charlie. He'd have to control the habit, he decided. It was embarrassing.

The office of the Lloyd's underwriters of which, from enquiries he'd already made through the Company Register, Charlie knew Willoughby to be the senior partner, was off Leadenhall Street, high in a converted block with a view of the Bank of England.

Willoughby was already standing when Charlie entered the spacious, oak-panelled office. Immediately he came forward, hands held out like that Sunday in the churchyard. Remarkably like his father, decided Charlie. Even more so than he had realised from their initial encounter.

'At last,' greeted the underwriter, leading Charlie to a leather, button-backed chair immediately alongside the desk.

'At last?'

Willoughby smiled at the quickness of the question, looking down at the man. Thinning, strawish hair, perhaps a hint of blood pressure or even alcohol from the slight purpling around the face and nose and a hunched, maybe apprehensive way of sitting. A very ordinary sort of man; the 8 a.m. traveller on every bus and train. Which proved, decided Willoughby, how deceptive appearances could be.

'I always hoped you would make contact,' he said. 'If you could, that was. My father did, too.'

Very direct, assessed Charlie. Almost as if the man had some knowledge of what had happened.

'I've cancelled everything for today,' said Willoughby. 'There'll be no interruptions.'

Charlie remained silent, sitting forward in the chair. How could Willoughby know? It was impossible. Unless he were involved in the pursuit. And if he were involved, then he wouldn't be so direct, arousing suspicion. It was a circle of doubt, Charlie recognised, without a beginning or an end.

'So we, finally meet,' said Willoughby again, as if he couldn't believe it.

'There was a previous occasion,' Charlie reminded him. Willoughby had been at Cambridge, Charlie recalled. Sir Archibald had brought him into the Whitehall office on his way for his first visit to the House of Commons. The boy had acne and seemed disappointed nobody carried a gun.

'I'm sorry,' apologised Willoughby. 'I don't remember meeting you with my father. But he didn't take me into the office very often.'

'No,' agreed Charlie.

'Do you know,' continued Willoughby, leaning back in his chair and looking away from Charlie, 'in the end those bastards Cuthbertson and Wilberforce actually tried to use something as ridiculous as that against him.'

'What?' demanded Charlie, very attentive. The continued openness was disconcerting; almost the professional use of honesty that he had employed to gain a person's confidence.

'His taking me into the office,' explained the underwriter. 'Claimed it was a breach of security.'

Charlie felt the tension recede. It would be wrong to formulate impressions too soon. But perhaps it hadn't been a mistake to come, after all.

'It's the sort of thing they would have done,' accepted Charlie. And been right, he thought honestly. But Sir Archibald had always made his own rules; that was one of the reasons why he and Charlie had established such a rapport. And why, in the end, Cuthbertson and Wilberforce had manoeuvred his replacement.

'You realise he committed suicide, don't you?' said Willoughby.

Charlie shook his head.

'No,' he said. 'I didn't. I was away when he died. It was never directly mentioned, but I inferred it was natural causes...'

Charlie paused.

'Well...' he started again, but Willoughby talked over him.

'Cirrhosis of the liver?' anticipated the man. 'Yes, that too. They made him into an alcoholic by the way they treated him. And when he realised what had happened to him, he hoarded some barbiturates and took the whole lot with a bottle of whisky.'

'I'm sorry,' Charlie began, then stopped, irritated by the emptiness of the expression. But he *was* sorry, he thought. There were few people to whom he had ever been close. And Sir Archibald had been one of them.

'There was a note,' continued Willoughby, appearing unaware of Charlie's attempt at sympathy. 'Several, in fact. The one he left for the police put the fear of Christ up everyone. Spelled everything out... not just what shits Cuthbertson and Wilberforce were in the way they got him fired, but the mistakes they had made as well. He did it quite deliberately because he believed that if they weren't moved, they'd make a major, serious blunder.'

His feelings, remembered Charlie.

'The department took the whole thing over,' continued Willoughby. 'They have the power, apparently, under the Official Secrets Act. Allows them to do practically anything to protect the national interest. Squashed the inquest, everything. That's how the natural causes account got spread about.'

Sir Archibald's death could only have been a matter of weeks before he had exposed their stupidity and got them captured in Vienna by the Russian commandos, Charlie calculated. What, he wondered, had happened to Cuthbertson? Back where he belonged, probably, fighting long forgotten battles over the brandy and cigars at Boodles. Wilberforce would have survived, he guessed. Wilberforce, with his poofy socks and shirts and that daft habit of breaking pipes into little pieces. Always had been a sneaky bugger, even under Sir Archibald's controL Yes, he would certainly have hung on, shifting all the blame on to Cuthbertson. Would he still be the second in-command? Or had he finally got the Directorship for which he had schemed for so long? Always an ambitious man; but without the ability to go with it. If he had remained, then the danger of which Sir Archibald had warned still existed.

'He asked me to tell you the truth, if ever you contacted me,' said Willoughby.

'I don't...' frowned Charlie.

'I told you he wrote several letters. To avoid them being seized by the police, he posted them, on the night he killed himself. He really planned it very carefully. The one to me talked about his fears for the department... he felt very strongly about it, after all those years, and didn't want it destroyed because incapable men had managed to reach positions of power. And another was devoted almost entirely to you.'

'Oh.'

'He told me you'd visited... just before going away to do something about which you were frightened.'

So he'd realised it, thought Charlie. He'd imagined Sir Archibald too drunk that day he had gone down to Rye and sat in the darkened room and felt the sadness lump in his throat at the collapse of the old man.

'He appreciated it very much... the fact that you regarded him as a friend.'

It was true, reflected Charlie. That was always how he'd thought of the man under whom he had spent all his operational life.

'He often talked about you when... when he was Director and we were living together, in London. Boasted about you, in fact. Said you were the best operative he had ever created... that there was practically nothing you couldn't do...'

The man's forthrightness was not assumed, decided Charlie,

unembarrassed at the flattery. Willoughby would have made a mistake by now, had he had to force the effect.

'There were times when I was almost jealous of you.' Willoughby added.

'I don't think he'd be very proud now,' said Charlie, regretting the admission as he spoke. Carelessness again.

Willoughby raised his hands in a halting movement. 'I don't think I should know,' he said, quickly. He paused, then added bluntly, 'The guilt was pretty obvious in the cemetery.'

Justified criticism, accepted Charlie. He wouldn't have stood a chance if the graveyard had been covered that day.

'I've known for a long time they've been looking for you,' announced Willoughby.

Charlie came forward on his seat again and Willoughby tried to reduce the sudden awkwardness by smiling and leaning back in his own chair.

'You've no need to be concerned,' he said. He dropped the smile, reinforcing the assurance.

'How?' asked Charlie. His feet were beneath the chair, ready to take the weight when he jerked up.

'They remembered the relationship between you and my father,' recounted Willoughby. 'I had several visits from their people, about four months after he died...'

'They would have asked you to have told them, if ever I made contact with you,' predicted Charlie, the apprehension growing.

'That's right,' agreed Willoughby. 'They did.'

'Well?' Charlie demanded. He'd buggered it, he thought immediately. Edith had been right; he was wrong again.

'Charlie,' said Willoughby, coming forward again so that there was less than a yard between them. 'They reduced my father to a shambling, disgusting old drunk who went to sleep every night puddled in his own urine. And then, effectively, they killed him. I don't know what you did, but I know it hurt. Is it likely I'm going to turn in someone who did what I'd have given my eye-teeth to have done?'

Charlie was hunched in the chair, still uncertain.

'It's been five weeks since your telephone call,' Willoughby reminded him, realising Charlie's doubt. He waved his hand towards the window.

'In five weeks,' said the underwriter, 'they would have made plans that guaranteed that once inside this office you'd never be able to get out again. Go on, look out of the window, By now the roads would have been sealed and all the traffic halted.'

Willoughby was right, Charlie realised. He got up, going behind the other man's chair. Far below, the street was thronged with people and cars.

'The outer office would have been cleared, too,' invited the underwriter.

Without replying, Charlie opened the door. The secretary who had greeted him looked up, enquiringly, then smiled.

'Satisfied?' asked Willoughby.

Charlie nodded.

'Tell me something,' said Willoughby, in sudden curiosity. 'What would you have done if it had been a trap?'

'Probably tried to kill you,' said Charlie. And more than likely failed, he added to himself, remembering his hesitation at personal violence in the cemetery.

Willoughby pulled his lips over his teeth, a nervous gesture.

'What good would that have done, if you'd been bottled up here?'

'Kept me alive,' suggested Charlie. 'They couldn't have eliminated me, if I'd committed a public murder.'

Why, wondered Charlie, was he talking like this? It was ridiculous. He waited for the other man to laugh at him.

Willoughby remained blank-faced.

'And do they want to eliminate you?'

'I would imagine so.'

Willoughby shook his head in distaste.

'God, it's obscene,' he said.

Charlie frowned. That wasn't a sincere remark, he judged. The man still thought of it as he had as a boy that day in the office, a sort of game for grown-ups.

'Consider it,' Willoughby went on. 'Two men, sitting here in the middle of London, calmly using words like eliminate instead of planned, premeditated murder.'

'Yes,' agreed Charlie. 'Sometimes it has to happen. Though not as much as you might think...'

He looked at the other man, to see if he were appreciating the words.

'...thank God,' he concluded.

'That was one thing about the service over which my father could never lose his disgust,' recalled Willoughby. 'He talked to me a great deal...'

He smiled over the hesitation. 'Cuthbertson and Wilberforce would say too much – another breach of security. My father believed very strongly in what he did... the need for such a department. But he was always horrified that people occasionally had to die.'

'I know,' said Charlie. The remaining doubts were being swept away by the reminiscence. Willoughby would have had to be very close to his father – as close as he had been to him in the department – to know so well the old man's feelings.

Willoughby sighed, shedding the past.

'And now I know about you,' he said, gravely. 'Whether I wanted to or not.'

'Only their possible verdict,' qualified Charlie. 'Not the cause.'

'It must have been serious?'

'It was.'

For a moment, neither spoke. Then Willoughby said: 'My father often remarked about your honesty. Considered it unusual, in a business so involved in deceit.'

'You seem to have the same tendency.'

'My father preferred it.'

'Yes,' remembered Charlie. 'He did.'

It was strange, thought Charlie, what effect the old man had had upon both of them.

The intercom burped and Willoughby nodded briefly into the receiver, smiling up at Charlie when he replaced the earpiece.

'From your reaction in the cemetery, I thought you'd prefer lunch here, in the seclusion of the office,' he said. 'Now I'm sure you would.'

Charlie detected movement behind him and turned to see two waiters setting up a gatelegged table. There were oysters, duck in aspic, cheese, chablis and port. Underwriters lived well, he thought.

Willoughby waited until they had seated themselves at the table and begun to eat before he spoke again.

'I must satisfy myself about one thing, Charlie,' he said.

'What?'

'Whatever you did... was it illegal?'

Charlie examined the question. There couldn't be a completely honest answer, he decided.

'Nothing for which I would appear in any English court of law,' he said. 'I was just trying to achieve, although in a different way, the sort of changes that your father believed necessary.'

And survive, he thought.

Willoughby smiled.

'Then you've nothing to fear from me,' he said. 'The opposite in fact.'

'Opposite?'

'In the letter,' explained Willoughby, 'the one in which he mentioned you so much, my father said he thought they were trying to do to you what they had done to him. He asked that if the opportunity or necessity arose that I should help you in any way I could.'

Charlie finished the oysters and sat fingering his glass, staring down into the wine he had scarcely touched. Trying to do to him what they'd done to Sir Archibald; certainly the drinking had become bad. He'd never considered suicide, though. And didn't think he ever would.

'You've already helped,' he said, 'by saying nothing.'

'There was something else,' continued the underwriter.

'What?'

'My father was a very rich man,' said Willoughby. 'Even after the settlement of the estate and the payment in full of death duties, there was still over three-quarters of a million pounds. He left you £50,000.'

'Good God!'

Willoughby laughed openly at the astonishment.

Charlie sat shaking his head. Three years ago, he reflected, he was saving the taxi fares from the Wormwood Scrubs debriefings with Alexei Berenkov by walking in the rain with holes in his shoes. Now he had more money than he knew what to do with. Why then, he wondered, did he feel so bloody miserable?

'I've had it for two years on long-term deposit at fourteen per cent,' added Willoughby. 'It'll have increased by quite a few thousand.'

'I don't really need it,' shrugged Charlie.

'It's legally yours,' said Willoughby.

And fairly his, added Charlie. Better even than the American money. He had more than Edith now. The thought lodged in his mind, to become an idea.

The meal over, Willoughby poured the port and leaned back in his chair.

'Why did you go to the cemetery, Charlie?' he asked. 'Surely, it was a dangerous thing to do?'

Charlie nodded.

'Absolutely insane,' he agreed.

Willoughby waited.

'I'd drunk too much,' Charlie admitted. 'It was becoming a habit. And I had intended it to be my last visit to England. So I wanted to make just one visit.'

'They *did* watch the grave,' offered Willoughby.

Charlie's eyes came up, questioningly.

'Must have been for almost six months,' expanded the underwriter. 'I go there about twice a month... learned to recognise them, in the end. They were quite obvious, even to an amateur like me...'

So he'd been lucky, decided Charlie. Bloody lucky.

'It wasn't just drink,' Charlie tried to explain. 'I'd always wanted to... just couldn't take the risk, earlier...'

He stopped, looking at Willoughby in sudden realisation.

'I came here to guarantee my own safety,' he said. 'You know, of course, that I could have compromised you...'

There was no artifice in the gesture of dismissal, assessed Charlie. The underwriter definitely regarded it as a game for adults, he decided. But then, how would any outsider regard it otherwise?

'My distaste for them, Charlie, is far greater than yours. I loved my father.' Willoughby spoke without any embarrassment.

'I think we both did.'

'Are we going to meet again?' asked Willoughby.

Charlie sat, considering the question. For two years, he thought, he and Edith had been imprisoned, bound together in a bizarre form of solitary confinement by the knowledge of what he had done, able to trust no one. Being able to talk, comparatively freely, to Willoughby, was like having the dungeon door thrown open.

'It would hardly be fair to you,' said Charlie.

'You know how I feel about that.'

The unexpected inheritance intruded into his mind again, the ill-formed idea hardening. He'd got away from the cemetery. And Willoughby was sincere. He was safe. So now he had to do something to fill the vacuum that had been destroying him. The inheritance and Willoughby's occupation presented an opportunity from which he couldn't turn away. It would mean leaving a reserve of money in the Brighton bank, but he'd only agreed to move it because of Edith's insistence. She'd understand why he'd changed his mind; be glad he'd found something to interest him.

He cleared his throat. Willoughby could always reject it, he decided. And should do, if he had any sense. He was using the other man, Charlie realised. Just as he'd used Günther Bayer for the ambushed crossing. It didn't lessen the guilt to admit to himself that he was sometimes a shit, Charlie decided.

'I'm thinking of asking you to do something that might offend you,' he warned. 'Professionally, I mean.'

'What?'

The question was immediate, without the gap that would have indicated reluctance. The man thought he was being invited to play.

'The money your father left me... the money I don't really need.'

'What about it?'

'Use it for me.'

'Use it?'

Charlie nodded.

'Part of the problem, the drinking I mean, was the absolute boredom,' he confessed. 'For almost two years, I've done nothing. Atrophied, almost. Can't I invest that money... more, if it's not enough, through you?'

Willoughby poured himself some more port.

'There couldn't be anything in writing,' he said, thinking aloud.

'That doesn't worry me.'

Willoughby looked up, smiling at the trust.

'A very silent Lloyd's underwriter,' he identified. 'Breaking every rule in the profession.'

'So I'd be embarrassing you,' said Charlie.

Willoughby made an uncaring motion with his hand.

'I can't see how,' he said. 'The money would be in my name... nothing traceable to you... I was executor of my father's estate, so it can be transferred without any problem.'

Again the underwriter smiled.

'And it would create the need for us to meet from time to time, wouldn't it?' he said presciently.

'Yes,' admitted Charlie. He waited several moments, then added: 'I'm asking you to take a very big risk.'

'I know,' said Willoughby.

'Greater than I've really any right to ask, despite the request of your father.'

'Yes.'

'It would be right for you to refuse... sensible to do so, in fact,' advised Charlie.

'Yes, it would,' said Willoughby. After a moment's pause, he added: 'But we both know I won't refuse, don't we?'

Yes, thought Charlie.

The underwriter stood, proffering his hand.

'This is the only way we'll have of binding the agreement,' he said.

'It's sufficient for me,' said, Charlie, shaking the offered hand.

'Underwriting is sometimes dangerous,' warned Willoughby.

'Any more dangerous than what I've done so far?' Willoughby laughed at the sarcasm.

'Sorry,' he said. 'I live a normal life and it's easy to forget.'

'Perhaps,' said Charlie, 'going to the cemetery wasn't the mistake I believed it might be.'

'No,' reflected Willoughby. 'I don't think it was.'

The ambassador turned away from the window and its view of the Moscow skyline, smeared grey by the sleeting rain. Next week, when it snowed, Moscow would look beautiful again, he thought.

Idly, Sir Robert picked up the inventory that had arrived that morning from the Hermitage in Leningrad, comparing it to the list from the Moscow Armoury. The Russians were making available far less of the regalia than he had expected from the agreement he had signed with the Minister of Culture, he saw. Still, at least they were letting some out. He supposed he should be grateful for that.

In London, a man whose hatred of Charlie Muffin was absolute sat in an office adjoining that of George Wilberforce, carefully examining the files obtained through the combined but unsuspecting channels of the Special Branch, Scotland Yard records, the Inland Revenue and the Bank of England and Clearing Houses security sections. A vivid scar disfigured the left side of his face and as he worked his fingers kept straying to it, an habitual movement.

Tonight he was concentrating upon the Special Branch and Scotland Yard dossiers and after two hours one folder remained for detailed consideration on the left of the desk.

'John Packer,' he identified, slowly, opening the cover.

He read for a further hour, then pushed it away.

'From now on,' he said, staring down at the official police photographs, 'it's the big time for you, John Packer...'

He paused.

'...for a while, anyway,' he added.

9.

Edith looked away from the view from the Baur au Lac balcony, coming back to her husband. It had been a long time, she thought, since she had seen him as relaxed and as happy as this. Almost two years, in fact. She'd never know him completely, she accepted. He was a strange man.

'You're fun again, Charlie,' she said gratefully.

He responded seriously to the remark. 'I'm sorry,' he said.

'It's been ages,' she said.

'It'll be better now,' he promised.

'It's a lot of money,' she protested cautiously, reverting to the conversation in which they'd been engaged throughout the dinner.

'Two hundred thousand, added to what Sir Archibald left me,' recounted Charlie. 'Still less than half of what I've got. And that's not an unusual amount for underwriters to deposit. To be admitted simply as a member of Lloyd's needs assets of £75,000.'

He saw it as even greater independence from her money, she realised. Not moving the remainder from the Brighton bank worried her.

'You're not a normal underwriter. I'm amazed the man agreed.'

'So am I,' admitted Charlie. 'He shouldn't have done.'

'You're quite sure it's safe?' she asked, a frequent question since he had returned from London three weeks earlier.

Charlie sighed patiently.

'I've checked the firm thoroughly,' he reminded her. 'There's no trace with any of the standby companies the department use for links with outside businesses. And for three days after I made the arrangement with Rupert Willoughby I watched him, from morning to night. There was no contact whatsoever.'

'You still can't be one hundred per cent sure.'

'Ninety-nine is good enough.'

'It used not to be.'

Charlie frowned at her concern.

'Edith,' he lectured her, 'it's now over six weeks since the cemetery... almost a month since I went to London, by an appointment they would have known about had he been in any way connected with them. And here we are having a pleasant dinner in one of the best restaurants in Zürich. If Rupert Willoughby weren't genuine, then I wouldn't be alive. We both know that.'

She nodded, in reluctant agreement. His involvement with Willoughby would provide the interest he had lacked, she decided. And it was wonderful to see him laugh again.

'I suppose you're right,' she said.

'I always have been.'

That was another thing that had been absent for too long – Charlie's confidence. It had been one of the first things to attract her, she remembered. It had been at a party at the Paris embassy, where Charlie had been on secondment and she had been the guest of the ambassador. The diplomat had apologised for Charlie afterwards, she recalled. Described him as an upstart. When she'd told Charlie, he'd nodded quite seriously and said 'bloody right': and two weeks later established that the ambassador's mistress had links with Soviet intelligence.

'What are you smiling about?' asked Charlie.

'Just thinking,' said Edith.

'What about?'

'You.'

He smiled back at her.

'It's going to be all right, Edith,' he promised.

'Tell me something, Charlie,' she said, leaning over the table to enforce the question. 'Honestly, I mean.'

'What?'

'You regret it, don't you?'

He took his time over the answer.

'Some things,' he admitted. 'People died, which is always wrong. But I'm not sorry I exposed Cuthbertson and his band of idiots.'

He stopped, smiling sadly.

'I tried to do it and Sir Archibald tried to do it,' he recalled. 'And I wouldn't mind betting that people like Wilberforce have still clung on. Bureaucracy is a comfort blanket to people like that.'

'The killing wasn't your fault,' she said.

'Some was,' he insisted. Günther Bayer had had a fiancée in West Berlin, he remembered. Gretel. She'd been preparing a celebration dinner on the night of the crossing and Günther had wanted him to go.

'Not all.'

'But for me, it wouldn't have happened.'

'No one would be feeling regrets if you'd died,' she said. 'And God knows, they tried hard enough.'

'Only you,' he said.

'Yes,' she agreed, 'I'd still be regretting it.'

Did Charlie have the love for her that she felt for him? wondered Edith. She wished he'd tell her so, more often.

'And the money was a mistake,' he conceded. 'It was necessary, to make the Kalenin crossing seem absolutely genuine. But to take it was wrong…'

Because it put a price on his betrayal, decided Edith. Money – his lack of it and her inheritance – had always been a problem for Charlie. He'd accepted the house beyond that which he could have afforded on his Grade IV salary. And the furnishing. But he had always adamantly refused any for his personal needs, keeping shoes until they were worn through and suits until they were shiny at the seat and elbows. He'd actually tried to change in the early months after the Kalenin affair. He'd bought Yves St Laurent and Gucci and looked as comfortable as Cinderella at five minutes to midnight. The seat and elbows weren't shiny, but the suit still came from a department store. And the shoes were still Hush Puppies even though they weren't down at heel any more. Charlie would always be the sort of person to wear a string vest with a see-through shirt, she thought fondly.

'Let's stop living in the past,' she said.

He nodded, brightening.

'Right,' he accepted. 'At last we've got something to consider in the future… I'm going into high finance, Edith.'

She laughed with him, trying to match his enthusiasm. Please God, she thought, make it last. She hadn't liked Charlie Muffin very much in the last two years.

'John Packer?'

The safebreaker looked up from his drink, gazing steadily at the man standing at the other side of the table.

'Yes,' continued the man, as if satisfying some private question. 'You're John Packer.'

Packer sat back, waiting. The man pulled out a chair and sat down, smiling. Smart, decided Packer. But not flash. Good voice; air of breeding, too, so he could make everyone else feel a turd. Confidence trickster, maybe. Nasty scar on his face. Perhaps a job had gone wrong.

'What do you want?' asked Packer.

'Want?' echoed the man, as if it were an amusing demand. 'I want to put you into the major league, John Packer.'

10.

George Wilberforce sat easily at his desk, moving a pipe between his long fingers, letting everyone else settle in the Whitehall office. They'd all come to him, he thought. And that was how it was going to be, until the end of the operation. He was going to be in command.

'We're ready to move against Charlie Muffin,' he announced. 'Tonight.'

'Still think it's a waste of time,' said Ruttgers defiantly.

'Not if it makes Charlie Muffin suffer.'

Everyone turned to the speaker, one of the two men whom Wilberforce had accepted for the final planning session. It had taken almost a year for Brian Snare to recover physically from his Moscow imprisonment, Wilberforce remembered. He looked at the man. Perhaps, in other ways, he never would. Snare's hand had gone automatically to the jagged, star-shaped scar where the skin had burst, rather than been cut, on the left side of his face. A warder's boot in Lubyanka had caused that, Wilberforce knew. But at least he was still alive. Douglas Harrison had been shot down by East German Grenzschutztruppen.

Wilberforce moved to speak, then paused, halted by a sudden thought. It had been Snare and Harrison, following Cuthbertson's instructions, who had actually set up Charlie Muffin for sacrifice in East Berlin. And Charlie's retribution had been planned as carefully as that which he himself was now evolving to destroy the man, decided Wilberforce. In many ways, he thought, he and Charlie were very similar. He was just a little cleverer, determined the Director. As he was going to prove.

'It would be a mistake to let personal feelings overly affect our judgment on this,' warned the other newcomer. William Braley had been the CIA Resident in the American embassy in Moscow specially appointed to work with Charlie on the last stages of Kalenin's supposed crossing. Few people knew Charlie better, which was why Braley was being included in the discussion.

Reminded of the association, Wilberforce said: 'Do you think there's any undue risk in what has been proposed?'

The man squinted nervously at the direct question. Braley was a man fattened by a glandular malfunction and given to asthma in moments of tension. Predictably, his breathing became jerky and he wondered if he would be able to use his inhaler.

'There's always a danger with Charlie Muffin,' he pointed out. 'We should never forget that.'

'But can he react any other way than that which we expect?'

Again Braley delayed replying, feeling his chest tighten further.

'No,' he said at last. 'I've thought about it, putting myself in his place. And I don't think he can.'

Wilberforce smiled, turning to the others in the room, patting as he did so the thick file that lay before him on the desk.

'You've all read the dossier,' he said. 'There hasn't been a moment since we picked him up at the cemetery when Charlie Muffin has not been under detailed surveillance. There's not a thing we don't know about him. And we've planned against every eventuality.'

'He seems to have found a friend in Rupert Willoughby,' remarked Cuthbertson.

'For the moment, that doesn't affect what we are going to do,' said Wilberforce. But it might, later on, he thought, remembering the report of the Russian exhibition. He was beginning to enjoy the idea of Charlie Muffin dancing in whatever direction he dictated; and if tonight went as he expected, that was all the man would be able to do from now on – perform as ordered.

'So we go ahead?' demanded Snare anxiously.

Wilberforce came back to the man who was going to be most dangerously involved in manipulating Charlie Muffin. He seemed desperate for them to agree, thought the Director. Which was out of character, for what he was being expected to do. But then, he'd suffered probably more than any of them. So his need for revenge was stronger.

'Well?' queried Wilberforce, taking the question to the Americans. He still had to give them the impression of consultation, he thought, even if it were really he who was making the decisions.

'You're still sure that what you propose will bring Charlie Muffin back to England?' said Onslow Smith.

'He won't be able to do anything else.'

'What if you're wrong?' said Ruttgers.

It was time, realised the British Director, to make concessions. Hardly a concession; if Charlie didn't respond as he expected, then it would have to be done anyway, despite the risk of any incriminating documents Charlie might have prepared.

'If Charlie Muffin isn't back in Brighton within three days,' said Wilberforce, 'then I agree he should be immediately killed.'

He smiled, deciding to extend the offer.

'Why not send an assassination squad to Switzerland, just in case?' he suggested. 'That way there would be absolutely no risk.'

Onslow Smith shrugged, an almost embarrassed gesture.

'We already have,' he admitted.

'And I'm going there tonight,' added Ruttgers, smiling to expose his yellow teeth.

Wilberforce frowned. Ruttgers was determined to be present when it happened, he thought. And the unexpected independence of Onslow was irritating.

'So we go ahead,' he announced.

11.

A professional, judged Johnny Packer. A bloody good professional, too. The knowledge tightened inside him, a comforting feeling. Which meant he was regarded in the same way. So this was going to be proof. No one would doubt him, after this.

'Drill.'

Johnny looked up at the order. The other man was breathing heavily through the exertion of crawling along the confined space and the jagged, star-shaped scar on the left side of his face had reddened into an ugly blotch. Appearing suddenly aware of the disfigurement, he put his hand up, covering it. He often made the gesture, Johnny realised. When they'd got to know each other better, he'd have to ask him how it had happened. They would become friends in time, he hoped. Proper friends.

Johnny passed the tool along the narrow air-conditioning duct to the other man, wondering what his real name was. If he hadn't been such an obvious expert, Johnny would have sniggered at the man's insistence on Brown. But he hadn't. It wouldn't have been right. He wasn't the sort of person you laughed at. Or with, even. If he wanted to play around with names, that was all right with Johnny. Another indication of how good he was, really; neither knew the other, so there couldn't be any risk of grassing if one were caught. Not quite true, corrected the safebreaker. The other man knew his name. And his record. And that he'd only been out for four months. The knowledge didn't disturb Johnny. He regarded it as another indication of professionalism.

The drill, rubber-cushioned, began eating into the ducting at the spot the other man had selected, working from a set of draughtsman's plans. Johnny leaned against the cold metal, experiencing another surge of admiration. Plans not just of the adjoining buildings and central heating and air conditioning systems, but every alarm installation in the place. And all the tools they were likely to need, brand new and bought with cash, one at each town along the south coast in an undetectable preparation that had taken over a week. They'd spent at least £4,000, guessed Johnny. He'd even queried the figure.

The man had smiled and said: 'You've got to speculate to accumulate,' and made it sound original.

Bloody professional.

'Cutters.'

The snips went along the narrow passageway and Snare enlarged the hole, then drilled into the mortar. Johnny started back at the sudden eruption of dust, lacking the protection of the face mask that Snare had put on.

'Vacuum.'

The more subdued whine of the cleaner came as a relief after the harsher bite of the drill.

'There!'

Johnny strained forward, narrowing his eyes at the brightness of the extension lamp which Snare had erected over the hole he had begun to mark. The blue and green wires of the alarm system embedded into the concrete stood out like veins in an old man's hand.

Snare reached back and Johnny gave him the bypass leads. Snare clamped them at either end of the exposed alarms, scraping his way through the plastic covering with a surgeon's scalpel, then cut through the middle of the wire. They had made long connections, maybe five feet, giving themselves room for a big entry hole. Snare taped the surplus wire against the metal sides of the ducting so there would be no risk of dislodging it, and then began drilling again, enlarging the hole.

It took almost an hour, with two stops to vacuum away the debris before Snare stopped.

'Enough,' he announced. He turned, gesturing Johnny back. Dutifully, the safebreaker turned and crawled along the shaft until he reached their carefully reinforced entry point, then dropped down into the basement of the building adjoining the bank in Brighton's North Street.

'What's the matter?' he asked worriedly, as the other man dropped through immediately behind him.

'Coffee break,' announced Snare.

He went to one of the four haversacks they'd brought in, took out a Thermos and poured the drinks. His hands were shaking, Johnny realised, embarrassed, as he cupped the plastic beaker to his lips. And the heat of the drink was making the surgical gloves he wore wet and sticky.

'We're thirty minutes ahead of schedule,' he said.

'You mustn't worry about time.'

Johnny smiled, knowing the other man had seen his nervousness.

'It's not yet midnight. Tomorrow's Sunday, so you've got all the time in the world,' the man assured him.

Johnny nodded.

'Shan't need it,' he said, trying to sound confident. 'Couple of hours and there won't be a lock still in place.'

Snare smiled tolerantly, hand up to his scarred face. It wasn't proving as difficult as he had feared, he decided, feeling the well-concealed apprehension ebbing away. He found a strange comfort in having so many plans to work from: it was always easier, having properly prepared diagrams to follow.

'Just don't worry,' he advised the other man.

It was ten minutes before they went back into the air-conditioning system and this time Johnny led, hauling the light with him. There was a hole about three feet in diameter cut into the bank wall. Careful to avoid the clamped arms, Johnny eased through, wedging the light on top of a filing cabinet.

'Storeroom,' Snare identified it, a fresh set of plans in his hand now. He felt out for a switch and the neon light flickered into life. Filing cabinets lined the walls and in one corner files were heaped, one on top of the other.

They went out of the room, Johnny still in front.

'Manager's office first,' instructed Snare.

The door at the top of the steps was secured from the far side, but by squinting through Johnny saw the key was still in the lock.

'Easy,' he smiled, looking for some reaction. Snare gazed back, unimpressed.

From the attaché case, new like everything else, Johnny took the long-spined dentist's pliers, poked through to grip the key shank and unlocked the door.

On the main floor of the bank they relied upon shielded torches, moving slowly between furniture towards the office which Snare had designated. That, too, was locked and this time the key was missing.

Johnny smeared thick grease on to a sliver of plastic, pushed it into the lock and then gently twisted, as if it were a key. He withdrew it and the tumbler edges were imprinted clearly into the grease. He lay the coated plastic along a matching piece of metal, plugged a dentist's electric drill into a table lamp socket and within five minutes had cut the basic shape of the key from the impression he had made. It took a further ten minutes to file away the mistakes and open the door. As he moved to do so, Snare touched his shoulder, pushing the light around the surround. The alarm breaker was near the top of the jamb. They used another bypass, magnetised this time, putting wedges either side of the door so that it wouldn't swing and pull the wire free.

'The first safe,' said Snare.'
'Standard Chubb.'
'Difficult?'
'Course it's difficult,'
'But not impossible?'
'Not impossible,' said Johnny.

He worked with a stethoscope, hearing the tumblers into place. Twice, in his nervousness, he over-adjusted, missing the combination.

'What about the key?' asked Snare, reaching out to the second lock.

'Drill it out,' decided Johnny. 'Can't work the same trick as with the door.'

He used the dentist's drill again, first driving out the rivets and securing screws and then, when there was sufficient looseness in the lock to pull it back, revealing the securing arm, inserted the blade of the electric saw and cut through it.

Johnny pulled the door back and then stood away, for Snare to get to it. Files and documents were neatly stacked on the shelves and at the bottom there was a small cash box.

Snare worked through the documents in complete concentration. Anything he didn't want he replaced tidily within the file and then put the file back upon the shelf from which he'd removed it.

'Ah!'

Snare turned, smiling.

'Here it is.'

The man moved away from the safe with a sheaf of papers.

'What about the cash box?'

Snare turned to the safebreaker, the pain etched into his face.

'Let's leave them their tea money, shall we?'

Johnny trailed the man from the office, face burning with regret at his first mistake. At Snare's insistence, he relocked the manager's door, then went back down the stairs, turning off at the first landing towards the barred safety deposit room.

The opening was like a huge safe door, set into metal barriers within the protection of the wall. Johnny felt another jump of excitement. He'd done one before, he recognised. So it wouldn't be difficult; he'd pass the test.

He used the stethoscope again, more controlled this time, so he didn't over-adjust the combination control. After the third tumbler, he allowed himself the conceit, counting aloud as each combination clicked home.

'No alarms,' declared Snare, bent over another blue-print.

The man hadn't noticed the expertise, realised Johnny, annoyed. Irritably he pulled open the entrance to the vault.

The gates that formed the secondary barrier were ceiling to floor, protected by a wire alarm system and then by an electrified beam which triggered a signal when it was broken by any interruption between the 'eyes'. Snare bypassed the first as he had the other wired precautions, then placed immediately in front of the door two wire cages used in hospitals to keep the pressure of bedclothes off patients suffering from broken limbs. Securing holes had been bored in the frames and he quickly bolted them to the floor. The beam played unbroken beneath the cages. To get into the deposit room, they would have to step over but even if their feet hit the protection, the bolts prevented it sliding into the beam.

Johnny stooped before the lock, then shook his head.

'Have to blow it.'

Snare nodded, accepting the judgment.

From the attaché case, Johnny took his favourite, the P-4 plastic and a detonator, pressing it around the lock. Briefly in command now, he sent Snare to an office to get cushions and these he wired around the explosives, legs straddling the invalid hoops.

The explosion, decided Johnny, made up for the mistake over the petty cash box. He'd wedged the door, in case it swung too hard against the cages, but so well had he primed it that the caution wasn't necessary. The lock blew with a muffled, crackling sound, hardly displacing the cushions.

'Very good,' Snare praised him. The department's detailed training in use and construction of explosive devices would have been more than sufficient, decided Snare. But then, the real purpose of Packer's involvement came later.

Johnny smiled, grateful for the remark.

Inside the safety deposit room, Johnny worked again from impressions, operating to Snare's quiet instructions from the list of box holders. They took only cash and jewellery. Documents were replaced and then the boxes locked again. Snare stood in the middle of the room, packing the cash into stiff-sided cases and the jewellery into a leather holdall.

'What do you reckon?' demanded Johnny, unable to control the excited question. 'How much?'

The other man looked at him, as if he found the query curious.

'Maybe a million,' he said, casually.

It wasn't normal, thought Johnny, for someone to be as calm as this bugger was.

They worked for another hour, the only conversation Snare's commands to the other man.

Suddenly, Snare said, 'Try 216.'

It took Johnny fifteen minutes to get the key right. He moved the lock, tugging at the deep metal tray as he did so and then stopped in amazement.

'Jesus!' he said softly.

Snare made no response, calmly reaching over his shoulder and extracting the dollars, banded together in tight bricks. He abandoned the suitcases, counting the money out on a small table in the corner of the room.

'Two hundred thousand,' he announced. 'And some insurance policies.'

Christ, he was cool, admired Johnny. Still not showing the slightest excitement. His own stomach was in turmoil and he knew he'd have diarrhoea in the morning.

Snare packed the money into a holdall he kept separate from the containers in which he'd stored the rest of the property.

'What about the policies?' asked Johnny.

The other man hesitated, then laughed.

'Leave the policies,' he said. 'The bastard is going to need all the insurance he can get.'

There were no incriminating documents anywhere. Charlie Muffin had been too conceited. Always had been. So now there wasn't a thing he could do to prevent his own destruction.

Johnny frowned.

'You know him, then?'

Again the hand came up to the disfigurement.

'Oh yes,' said the man. 'I know him.'

It had been worth it, decided Snare. Every gut-churning minute had been worth it.

The Aeroflot freight carrier touched down precisely on schedule and taxied to the north side of London airport, where maximum security could be guaranteed. Ignoring the rain, the diplomats from the Russian embassy insisted on standing next to the ramp, ticking the numbered boxes against the manifest as they were unloaded on to the ground and then into armoured cars.

'These sort of jobs frighten the piss out of me,' said a Special Branch inspector, huddled in the doorway for protection.

His sergeant looked at him quizzically.

'It's only jewellery,' he said. 'And copies at that.'

'Fabergé copies,' corrected the inspector. 'Lose sight of one piece of this and our feet won't touch the bloody ground.'

12.

Because two film actors and an MP were named among the victims, a single-column story on the bank robbery was even carried in the *Neue Zürcher Zeitung*, where Charlie read it first. From the international newsstand in the foyer of the Dolder Hotel, he managed to buy that day's *Daily Telegraph* and *The Times*. Both led their front pages with it; the *Telegraph* even had a diagram, showing the thieves' entry. The work of complete professionals, a police spokesman was quoted as saying. Until all the safe-deposit box holders were contacted, no positive assessment could be made of the value.

'The bastards,' said Charlie. 'The cunning bastards.'

He paused on the Kurhausstrasse outside the hotel. He was trapped, he recognised objectively. In a way he'd never foreseen. He prolonged the hesitation, then made his way to a pavement café to consider it fully before going home to Edith. She'd panic, he knew. Especially so soon after the cemetery business. And panic was the last thing he could afford. Not any more. So what could he afford? Very little.

'Charlie,' he said. 'You've made a balls of it, like everything else. And now they've got you.'

The waiter who had served his coffee turned enquiringly and Charlie shook his head.

The involvement of the civil police – and the restrictions it would impose upon him – had been the one thing he had never envisaged, he realised. The one simple, obvious thing that took away his freedom to react in anything but a predictable way. So who was it? Wilberforce? He was devious enough. Or just bad luck, the chance-in-a-million he could never insure against? And why this way? To let him know he'd been found, and then watch him scrabbling for escape, like an animal in a trap of which they had the key? More than that, he decided. What then? He didn't know. He'd need more clues.

And they'd be sure to prevent that.

'Never run,' he reminded himself. 'Basic rule never to run.'

He put some francs on the table and began walking back to Edith. He went directly to the apartment, making no effort to evade any possible surveillance. If they knew enough to have learned about the Brighton bank account, they would know about his Zürich home.

Edith looked up, smiling, as he entered. The expression faltered when she saw Charlie's face.

'What is it?'

'The Brighton bank has been robbed,' he reported. 'The safe-deposit room.'

The fear was immediate. She rose up, without thought, then remained standing in the lounge like a rabbit caught in a poacher's torch, not knowing which way to flee.

'So it's all over,' she said, very softly.

'It could just be coincidence,' he tried, hopefully.

'Don't be damned stupid,' she said. 'You can't believe that.'

She moved at last, going towards the bedroom.

'What are you doing?'

She stopped at the question.

'I'm going to pack, of course.'

'What for, Edith?' he said. He spoke calmly, trying to reduce her apprehension.

She sniggered, control slipping again.

'To get out… run… what else?'

'We can't run anywhere, Edith.'

She turned fully to face him.

'What do you mean, we can't go anywhere?'

'Just that.'

'Don't be ridiculous, Charlie.'

'That's exactly what I'm not being. I've got to go back to Brighton, today.'

'Charlie! For God's sake!'

He went forward, taking both her hands in his. Fear was vibrating through her. Poor Edith, he thought, studying her. Poor frightened, abused, trusting, faithful Edith. She'd suffered a great deal because of him, Charlie realised. And never once complained, not even during their most bitter rows. The evidence wasn't overly visible, not physically. Her body was still firm enough to be exciting; the figure of a woman ten years younger, he often assured her. And meant it, quite sincerely. It was in her face that the anxiety had settled, defying the efforts of successive and increasingly more expensive beauticians, lining the pale blue eyes and around her mouth and furrowing the forehead that had once been so smooth and unworried. It would have shown in the greyness of her hair, too, if she hadn't constantly had it disguised during those weekly visits to the beauty salons.

'Edith,' he said, his voice even and deepened by the sadness. 'The one thing we could never sustain is any detailed investigation by a civilian police force...'

'But...'

'Listen to me, Edith. There's been a robbery estimated at upwards of a million pounds. What would happen if I don't go back, the one box-holder they can't locate? I'll be the prime suspect, the man who rented the facility to obtain access to the deposit room, to plan the robbery.'

'But it's an assumed name,' protested Edith, desperately.

'Which would unquestionably establish the guilt,' he insisted. 'A box-holder who fails to turn up and is then discovered to have taken out the rental under a phoney name...'

He paused, waiting for the acceptance to register. Her face remained blank.

'...an assumed name,' he resumed. 'That we are currently using on the passports legitimately obtained on forged birth certificates. It would be normal police routine to check for passports, if I don't show up. From the application forms, they would get our pictures...'

She went to speak again, but he raised his fingers to her lips, stopping her.

'I know we've got other passports, in your vault here. But the photographs are the one thing we can't alter. If I don't return to Brighton, our pictures will be circulated by Interpol distribution within forty-eight hours and there won't be a passport control through which we could pass without identification...'

She sagged, like a puppet whose strings had been cut.

'Oh, God,' she said. The lines on her face seemed to deepen.

He led her back to the chair, sitting her down.

'I'm taking no risks, going to the police,' he attempted to reassure her. 'I'm not wanted for anything... not by them, anyway...'

She shook her head.

'I'm confused, Charlie.'

To a degree, so was he, he thought. How soon would he be able to understand completely what was happening?

'It's quite simple,' he said. 'All I have to do is return to Brighton and answer whatever questions the police will want to ask.'

'But the money...'

'...will be gone,' he cut in. He hoped, he thought. If it had been left, it would need some explanation.

'So all I have to do is name the insurance policies, admit to a small sum they will expect me to have had lodged there and that'll be the end of it...'

The dullness had gone from her face, he saw.

'You're forgetting something, Charlie,' she accused him. 'Or perhaps trying to make me forget something.'

'What?'

'That would be all right if we thought the robbery were a coincidence...'

'We can't be sure...'

'If we thought it were a coincidence,' she repeated, refusing the interruption. 'And we both know it isn't. We both know that you've been found, Charlie. Not just found, either. They've discovered everything about you, Charlie – everything – we're not discussing the end of anything. We're talking about the beginning.'

'There's no proof of that. Not yet.'

'Do you need proof, for heaven's sake?'

'I certainly need more than we've got so far before I abandon something it's taken us so long to establish.'

She shook her head.

'You're walking right back to them, Charlie... right back to where they can do whatever they like.'

She was right, Charlie accepted. And too intelligent to be persuaded otherwise. And there was not a thing he could do about it. Not a bloody thing. Bastards.

'The problem is, darling,' he said, feeling the first surges of real fear, 'that I've got no choice. At least this way I gain time to fight back.'

'Fight back!'

She spat the words out, face twisted in disgust. She was very frightened, Charlie accepted.

'Stop it, Charlie,' she demanded. 'Stop all this rubbish about fighting back and survival. Do you realise what you're facing this time?'

'Edith,' he said, avoiding the question, 'we both knew, no matter how much we tried to avoid admitting it, that it could happen, one day.'

Her anger died as quickly as it had erupted.

'Oh, Charlie,' she said, 'I'm so frightened.'

'I'll find a way out,' he promised.

It had been a fatuous thing to say, he realised, seeing the look on her face.

Charlie caught the evening flight to London. He travelled with only hand baggage and was one of the first Swissair passengers through passport control. It was 7.15 p.m.

At 7.35, George Wilberforce received a telephone call at his London flat, confirming the arrival for which he had been alerted by the earlier message from Zürich. He began to hum in time with the stereo and then smiled, in recognition. Delius. He'd played that the night he'd first located Charlie Muffin. And now he'd trapped him. He'd enjoy the satisfaction of the following day's meeting with the Americans, he decided.

Onslow Smith was waiting at the Albemarle Street hotel in which they were both staying when Ruttgers returned from Zürich.

'Everything according to plan?' he greeted the ex-Director.

Ruttgers frowned at the assessment.

'No,' he disagreed. 'He's still alive.'

13.

Charlie had identified the unmarked police car about twenty yards from the house, so he was waiting for the doorbell when it sounded. He paused, briefly, preparing himself and when he opened the door the expectant smile was carefully in place.

'Yes?'

'Police,' identified the taller of the two men. He produced a warrant card, holding it steadily for Charlie to examine it. 'We…'

'Of course,' broke off Charlie. 'Come in.'

He stood back for them to enter. They were both smart but unobtrusive men, grey-suited, muted ties, polished black shoes. Hendon, guessed Charlie.

'Why of course?' demanded the first man, unmoving.

Aggressive, too, decided Charlie. But properly so.

'The robbery,' he said. 'What else?'

'Ah,' said the man. Then waited. It was a practised reaction, realised Charlie, leading them into the lounge. So the older man prided himself on his interrogation technique. He had once, remembered Charlie. He'd been damned good. He hoped it hadn't been too long ago; he felt the tingle of apprehension.

The policeman looked at Charlie and Charlie smiled back.

'So you know about the robbery?' queried the man. 'I didn't get your name?' replied Charlie. The detective frowned, off-balanced by the response. Then he smiled.

'Law,' he said. 'Superintendent Harry Law.' He stared at Charlie, expectantly. Charlie gazed back. 'Law,' said the man, again.

Still Charlie said nothing.

'Unusual name for a policeman,' offered the detective, at last. 'Law... police...'

It was a prepared charade, the clumsy joke at his own expense to put an interviewee falsely at ease, decided Charlie.

'Very unusual,' he allowed, hardly intruding the condescension. On the flight to London, he'd rehearsed the inevitable meeting, deciding on the vague impatience of a rich man.

The superintendent detected the attitude. The smile slipped away, irritably.

Law was an almost peculiar figure, thought Charlie. Smooth, shining-pink cheeks, glistening oiled hair, perfectly combed and in place, eyes wetly bright and attentive. A disconcerting man, Charlie labelled him. Because he chose to be. He would have to be careful. It was not going to be as easy as he had imagined. Perhaps nothing was.

'You knew about the robbery?' Law repeated. There was a hardness to his voice now. The man had almost lost his temper, guessed Charlie. Maybe he wasn't as good an interrogator as he thought he was.

'It's the main item in every newspaper,' pointed out Charlie. 'It would be difficult not to know about it.'

'But you didn't bother to contact the bank?' criticised Law.

The reason for the waiting police car and the visit from such a senior officer within thirty minutes, realised Charlie. It would have been sensible to have telephoned from Switzerland. And even more sensible to have picked upon an alternative reaction to the police approach. He'd never be able to play the rich man as long as he had a hole in his ass. It was too late now to change it; it would increase rather than allay suspicion.

'No,' he admitted. It would be as wrong now to hurry an explanation.

'Why?'

The question thrust from the man, the voice even harder.

'Please sit down,' deflected Charlie. He gestured Law and the other man to a couch in the middle of the room.

'I didn't catch your name, either,' he said, to the younger man, aware as he spoke of the anger stiffening the superintendent's body.

'Hardiman, sir,' responded the young policeman. 'Sergeant John Hardiman.'

'Why?' repeated Law.

Charlie turned back to the man. Very soon, Charlie guessed, the superintendent would become openly rude.

'Didn't I contact the bank?'

Law nodded, breathing deeply. The temper was the man's failing, thought Charlie.

'I didn't want to be a nuisance,' explained Charlie simply.

Law frowned.

'Forgive me, sir,' he said. 'I don't follow.'

A clever recovery, assessed Charlie. Seize the apparent conceit of the person you're interviewing and convey the impression they're far more intelligent than you, so they'll over-reach themselves.

'The newspapers talked of the value being in the region of a million pounds,' said Charlie.

'Could be,' agreed Law. 'Once we establish the contents of the deposit boxes.'

'Quite,' said Charlie, as if that were sufficient explanation. 'So I didn't want to be a bother.'

There was another sigh from the older detective.

'You're still not making yourself clear.'

'Can I offer you a drink?' Charlie slipped away again. He gestured towards the drinks tray. Law had begun to perspire, he saw. Charlie decided he wasn't doing too badly.

'Whisky would be very nice, sir,' accepted Law. The man fitted a smile into place, the protective mask behind which he was determined to operate.

Charlie went to the bottles and poured Scotch for himself and the superintendent. Hardiman hesitated, then shook his head in refusal.

'You were telling me you didn't want to be a nuisance,' encouraged the superintendent.

'Yes,' said Charlie. 'I imagined that people who had had valuables in their boxes would be inundating the bank with telephone calls and visits and I thought my enquiries could wait until tomorrow.'

Slowly Law placed the glass on a side table that Charlie had positioned close to him and nodded to Hardiman. The younger man took a notebook from his pocket.

'I see,' said Law, slowly. 'So there was nothing valuable in your box?'

'Not valuable in the terms of the robbery,' said Charlie. 'Some insurance policies... the lease to this house and the conveyancing documents... that sort of thing.'

'Just papers?' demanded Law.

'And a little money... perhaps £500...' The superintendent sipped his drink again. 'You don't know the actual amount?'

He let the disbelief leak into the question.

'I travel a great deal,' said Charlie. 'The odd bits of currency and travellers' cheques I don't spend I normally put into the box for use another time. So I can't give you the precise figure, no.'

'But it certainly wouldn't be more than £500?'

'Certainly not,' said Charlie.

He waited, disguising the apprehension. If the money had been left, as Sir Archibald would have decreed it should if he had organised the operation, then this would be the moment when he lost the encounter, Charlie knew. A formal accusation of lying, maybe even the official warning under Judges' Rules and then the request to accompany them to the police station for further questioning.

Law was nodding, disclosing nothing. Hardiman was busily writing in the notebook.

'Isn't that rather expensive?' asked the superintendent, ending the pause.

'Expensive?' asked Charlie. His voice almost broke, showing anxiety. Had the money been there, they would have challenged him immediately, he knew. He felt the first bubble of hope.

'Hiring a safe-deposit box for the sort of stuff most people keep in a cupboard drawer?' enlarged the detective.

Charlie forced the smile.

'Ironic, isn't it?' he said. 'I'm the sort of person who likes to know everything is safe... so I put it in a bank because I thought there was less chance of a robbery than here, in the house.'

'Ironic,' agreed Law.

But it wasn't agreement, guessed Charlie. There was still doubt.

The superintendent emptied his glass and shook his head in refusal when Charlie gestured towards the bottle.

'You wouldn't mind if I checked with your insurance companies about the policies?'

'Of course not,' said Charlie. 'The Sun Life of Canada and the Royal Assurance.'

Hardiman noted the names.

'Hope I haven't caused difficulties,' said Charlie.

'Difficulties?' queried Law.

'By not bothering to contact the bank... you seemed to attach some importance to it.'

'It appeared odd,' allowed Law.

'And I was just trying to be helpful,' repeated Charlie.

'Yes, sir.'

Law paused, then demanded again: 'There was nothing more than the policies, documents concerning this house and the small amount of money?'

'Nothing,' Charlie assured him. The insurance had been Edith's idea, he remembered; being normal, she'd called it.

Both men were staring at him, he realised. A silence settled into the room. Charlie stayed perched on the edge of the armchair, curbing any indication of nervousness.

'Then you're lucky,' said Law, at last.

'Lucky?'

'The policies weren't even taken... so you won't have to bother with duplicates.'

Charlie nodded. He'd got away with it, he thought. The realisation swept through him.

The two detectives still didn't seem completely satisfied.

'That's very fortunate,' said Charlie.

'Yes,' said Law. 'Very fortunate.'

'The money's gone, I suppose?' asked Charlie.

'Yes,' confirmed the superintendent. 'All five hundred pounds of it.'

Again the policeman waited, letting the sarcasm settle. So it was the smallness of the amount they couldn't accept. Another mistake, like the artificial attitude.

'So I'm lucky all the way around,' said Charlie.

'Sir?' questioned the superintendent.

'That it was only £500,' expanded Charlie. 'It's enough, but not as much as the other people seem to have lost.'

'No, sir,' accepted Law. There was still doubt, Charlie gauged.

'You say you travel a great deal, sir?' pressed Law.

'I have a home in Switzerland as well as here,' said Charlie. 'I move between the two very frequently.'

'That must be nice,' said Law.

He managed always to convey the impression that he expected more from any sentence, decided Charlie. It was an interesting technique.

'It is,' he said. 'Very nice.'

'How long do you plan to be here this time, sir?' asked the superintendent.

Charlie delayed answering, guessing some point to the question.

'I don't know,' he shrugged. 'A week... maybe two... depends on business.'

'What business?'

The query was abrupt again, cutting across Charlie's generalisation. Charlie grew cautious again, recognising the danger.

'Investment,' he said. 'Finance... that sort of thing.'

Both detectives stared, waiting for more.

When he didn't continue, Law prompted: 'You're a financier?'

'My passport describes me as a clerk. But I suppose financier is a better description,' smiled Charlie.

'Any particular firm?'

'Predominantly Willoughby, Price and Rowledge,' responded Charlie easily. 'I deal with Mr Willoughby.'

'A financier,' picked up the superintendent. 'Yet you only kept £500 in a safe-deposit box?'

'Exactly,' retorted Charlie. 'Money that isn't working for you is dead... useless. No one who's interested in making money leaves it laying around in safe-deposit boxes.'

'And you are interested in making money, sir?' asked Law, unperturbed.

'Isn't everyone?' asked Charlie.

Law didn't reply immediately, appearing to consider the question.

'And where will you be going, after one or two weeks?' he demanded, changing direction.

'Back to Switzerland,' said Charlie.

'You could let us have an address, of course?'

'Of course,' agreed Charlie. 'But why should you need it?'

The superintendent smiled apologetically.

'Never know, sir. Things come up that you can't anticipate. Always handy to be able to contact people.'

Charlie nodded.

'And I'd like a formal statement,' continued Law. 'Could you come to the station tomorrow?'

Charlie hesitated, a busy man remembering other appointments.

'I suppose so,' he said, at last.

'We'd appreciate that,' said Law.

The approach had changed, realised Charlie.

'Naturally I'll come.'

'You know,' said Law, extending the apparent friendliness. 'Of all the people we've interviewed, you're probably the most fortunate.'

'How's that, superintendent?'

'Apart from the money... and as you say, that's not a great deal... you've lost practically nothing.'

'Except my faith in the safety of British banks,' suggested Charlie, trying to lighten the mood.

Law didn't smile.

'In every other box there was more money... jewellery... stuff like that. Really you are very lucky,' insisted the superintendent.

'Very lucky,' concurred Charlie.

Law looked hopeful, as if expecting Charlie to say more.

'Is there anything else I can do to help?' asked Charlie. He shouldn't seem too eager to end the meeting, he knew. But equally it would be a mistake to abandon the attitude with which he'd begun the encounter, wrong though he now knew it to be. It was the sort of change Law would recognise.

The superintendent gazed directly at him. Then he shook his head.

'Not at the moment, sir. Just make the statement, tomorrow, if you wouldn't mind.'

'Of course not.'

'And let us know if you're thinking of going anywhere,' the detective continued.

Charlie allowed just the right amount of time to elapse.

'All right,' he said.

'And perhaps tomorrow you could let my sergeant have the Swiss address?'

Charlie nodded.

'Tomorrow, then,' said Law, standing. Immediately Hardiman followed.

'Good-night, sir,' said Law.

'Good-night, superintendent. Don't hesitate to contact me if I can do anything further to help.'

'Oh we won't, sir,' Law assured him. 'We won't hesitate for a moment.'

Charlie stood at the doorway until he saw them enter their car and then returned to the lounge. He'd just got away with it, he judged, pouring himself a second whisky.

But only just. Not good enough, in fact. He'd lost his edge, in two years. So he'd better find it again, bloody quickly.

'Otherwise, Charlie, your bollocks are going to be on the hook,' he warned himself.

He looked curiously at the whisky, putting the glass down untouched.

'And that's how they got there last time,' he added into the empty room.

For several minutes the policemen sat silently in the car. The lights of Palace Pier were appearing on the left before Law spoke.

'What do you think?' he asked Hardiman.

'Cocky,' replied the sergeant, immediately. He'd been waiting for the question.

'But involved?'

Hardiman shook his head.

'Would you rent a box to discover the layout practically next door to your own house? And having pulled off a million-pound robbery, risk coming back and being questioned, even if you had been that stupid in the first place?'

Law moved his head, in agreement.

'Hardly,' he said. 'They're big points in his favour.' The car entered the town, pulling away from the seafront.

'There was something though, wasn't there?' said Hardiman.

Law smiled at the other man's reservations.

'Couldn't lose the feeling that he was used to interrogation... didn't have the uncertainty that most people have... the natural nervousness that causes them to make silly mistakes,' he confirmed.

'Yet he *was* nervous,' expanded Hardiman.

'Know something else that struck me as odd?' continued Law.

'What?'

'For a financier, he was a scruffy bastard.'

'Yes,' agreed the sergeant. 'Still, don't they say that only the truly rich can afford to dress like tramps?'

'And can you really believe,' went on the superintendent, ignoring the sergeant's remark, 'that a financier with a house like he's got here and who openly admits to another home in Switzerland would only have five hundred quid in a safe-deposit box?'

'No,' agreed Hardiman, as the car entered the police station compound. 'But he's not the first one we've encountered on this job who's lied about the amount. That's just tax avoidance, surely?'

'Probably,' said Law. He started to get out of the car, then turned back into the vehicle, towards the other man.

'Let's just keep an eye on him,' he said. 'Don't want to waste any men on full-time observation, but I want some sort of check kept.'

'Good idea,' agreed Hardiman. 'Who knows what we might come up with?'

'Who knows?' echoed the superintendent.

Despite a friendship that stretched back more than two decades, there had been few meetings with Berenkov since his repatriation to Moscow from British imprisonment, General Valery Kalenin accepted. Too few in fact. He enjoyed the company of the burly, flamboyant Georgian. The KGB chief smiled across the table, offering the bottle. Berenkov took the wine, topping up his glass.

'French is still best,' he said, professionally. 'More body.' During his twenty years in London, Berenkov had developed the cover as a wine importer, which had allowed him frequent trips to Europe for contact meetings, into an enormously successful business.

'Not the sort of remark a loyal Russian should make,' said Kalenin, in mock rebuke. 'You'll have to get used to Russian products from now on.'

'That won't be difficult,' said Berenkov, sincerely.

Kalenin pushed aside the remains of the meal he had cooked for them both in his bachelor apartment on Kutuzovsky Prospect. Berenkov had enjoyed the food, the other Russian knew.

'Glad to be back?' Kalenin asked, caught by the tone in the man's voice.

Berenkov nodded.

'I'd had enough,' he admitted. 'My nerve was beginning to go.'

Kalenin nodded. Now Berenkov could lead a pampered life in the Russian capital, he thought, teaching at the spy college to justify the large salary to which he was entitled after the success of such a long operational life, spending the weekends at the dacha and the vacations in the sunshine of Sochi.

'You did very well,' Kalenin praised him. 'You were one of the best.'

Berenkov smiled at the flattery, sipping his wine.

'But I got caught in the end,' he said. 'There was someone better than me.'

'Law of averages,' said Kalenin. Should he tell Berenkov? he wondered. The man had developed a strong feeling for Charlie Muffin, he knew. A friendship, almost.

'Charlie has been trapped,' he announced bluntly, making the decision.

Berenkov stared down into his wine, his head moving slowly, a man getting confirmation of long-expected bad news.

'How?' he asked.

Kalenin gestured vaguely.

'I don't know,' he said. 'But from the amount of leakage it's obvious the British want it recognised they intend creating an example out of him.'

'Charlie would have expected it, of course,' said Berenkov distantly.

Kalenin said nothing.

The former spymaster looked up at him.

'No chance of your intervening, I suppose? To give him any help?'

Kalenin frowned at the suggestion.

'Of course not,' he said, in genuine surprise. 'Why ever should I?'

'No, of course not,' accepted Berenkov. 'Stupid of me to have mentioned it.'

'He's still alive, apparently,' volunteered Kalenin. 'It's not at all clear what they are going to do.'

'Charlie was very good,' said Berenkov. 'Very good indeed.'

'Yes,' agreed Kalenin. 'He was.'

'Poor Charlie,' said Berenkov.

'More wine?' invited Kalenin.

'Thank you.'

14.

Perhaps, thought Wilberforce, arranging the money on the desk for everyone to see had been too theatrical. Onslow Smith was openly smirking he saw, annoyed. That would stop, soon enough. The time had passed when people laughed at George Wilberforce and from today they would begin to realise it.

'Just over two hundred thousand dollars,' said the British Director, indicating the money. 'About half of what was stolen from you... and no affidavits that might have caused problems.'

'So now we kill him,' Ruttgers interrupted impatiently.

'No,' said Wilberforce simply.

For several moments there was no sound from any of the men in the room. It was Sir Henry Cuthbertson who broke the silence.

'What do you mean, no?' he demanded. 'We've achieved what we set out to do. Let's get the whole stupid business over.'

'No,' repeated Wilberforce. 'There are other things to do first.'

'Director,' said Onslow Smith, trying with obvious difficulty to control himself, 'this affair began with the intention of correcting past problems. We've put ourselves in a position of being able to do so. Let's not risk making any more.'

'I intend teaching the Russians a lesson,' announced Wilberforce.

'You're going to do *what*?'

Onslow Smith's control snapped and he looked at the other Director in horror. The damned man was on an ego trip, he realised.

'For almost two years they've mocked and laughed... *I've* been ridiculed. Now I'm going to balance the whole thing.'

'Now wait a minute,' said Onslow Smith urgently. He stood up, nervously pacing the room. 'We agreed, not a month ago, that what we were attempting to do was dangerous...'

He looked intently at the Briton for reaction. Wilberforce nodded.

'But it worked,' continued Smith. 'Charlie Muffin is now back in England. We can do anything we like with him. So now we just complete the operation as planned and invite no more problems.'

'There will be no problems,' insisted Wilberforce, quietly. They were all very scared, he decided.

'With Charlie Muffin, there's always risk,' said Braley breathily, risking the impertinence. Surreptitiously he slipped an asthma pill beneath his tongue.

'How do you intend teaching the Russians a lesson?' asked Cuthbertson.

From the rack on his desk, Wilberforce selected a pipe and began revolving it between his fingers. Sometimes, he thought, he felt like a kindergarten teacher trying to instil elementary common sense. It would be pleasant hearing them apologise for their reluctance in a few days' time.

'I've already seen to it that the Russians know we've located the man,' he admitted.

'Oh, Christ!' blurted Onslow Smith, exasperated. Already, he thought, it might be too late.

Wilberforce shook his head sadly at the reaction.

'And tonight, for a little while at least, we are going to borrow the Fabergé collection that has just arrived from Russia for exhibition here.'

'You're going to do *what*?'

Onslow Smith appeared in a permanent state of shocked surprise.

'Take the Fabergé collection,' repeated Wilberforce.

'The Russians will go mad,' predicted Braley.

'Of course they will,' agreed Wilberforce. 'That is exactly what I intend they should do. And what will they find, when we leak the hint about one of the insurers of the collection? What we found, by elementary surveillance and checking the company accounts after the churchyard encounter with Rupert Willoughby – that their precious Charlie Muffin is a silent partner in the firm.'

'It's lunacy,' said Smith, fighting against the anger. 'Absolute and utter lunacy.'

'No it's not,' insisted Wilberforce. 'It is as guaranteed against fault as the method I devised to get Charlie Muffin back to England.'

'But we can't go around stealing jewellery,' protested Cuthbertson.

'And I'm not interested in settling imagined grievances with Russia. It's over, for Christ's sake. It has been, for years,' said Smith.

'Not with me, it hasn't,' said Wilberforce. He turned to the former Director. 'And I've no intention that we should permanently steal it. The Fabergé collection is priceless, right?'

Cuthbertson nodded, doubtfully.

'But valueless to any thief,' continued Wilberforce. 'He'd never be able to fence it.'

'So why steal it in the first place?' asked Ruttgers.

'For the same reason that such identifiable jewellery is always stolen,' explained Wilberforce. 'Not to sell or to break up. Merely to negotiate, through intermediaries, its sale back to the insurers who would otherwise be faced with an enormous settlement.'

They still hadn't understood, realised Wilberforce. Perhaps they would, after it had all worked as perfectly as he intended.

'With something as big as this, the insurers are guaranteed to co-operate and buy it back,' he tried to convince them. 'Every piece, apart from those which are absolutely necessary to achieve what I intend, will be back in Leningrad or Moscow within two months. And the only sufferers will be Willoughby's insurance firm who have had to pay up on the missing items. And Charlie Muffin, who will lose the other half of what he stole from you... paying America back for something stolen from Russia. Can't you see the irony of it? Charlie Muffin will. That's why I'm letting him stay alive, to see it happen. There's no hurry to kill him now... he can't go anywhere and he knows it.'

When there was still no response, Wilberforce pressed on: 'We'll have put the Russians in their place and there won't be a service, either in the West or the East, who won't know about it... because I've already made damned sure it's being spelled out, move by move...'

'It's very involved,' said Cuthbertson reluctantly.

'And foolproof,' said Wilberforce. 'No risk. No danger.'

'There are too many things over which we haven't any control,' said Ruttgers, through a tobacco cloud. 'Charlie Muffin has only got to do one thing we don't expect and the whole thing is thrown on its ass.'

'But it won't be,' said Wilberforce. 'The jewellery is being taken tonight. Once that goes, everything else follows naturally. It hardly matters what Charlie Muffin does. He's helpless to affect it, in any way. In fact, that's exactly what he is – helpless.'

'What about the civil police?' protested Smith. 'They're already involved in the bank robbery. There's a risk there.'

'We employed a petty crook on that... the same one who will be used tonight. We'll arrange his arrest, so that most of the stuff taken from the Brighton bank can be recovered and returned to its owners – those not too frightened of any tax investigation to claim it, anyway.'

'He'll talk,' said Smith.

'About what?' enquired Wilberforce. 'A mystery man called Brown who seems to have an enormous amount of inside information and knowledge?'

He nodded towards Snare, whose reluctance at the instructions he had been given that night was growing with the objections from the other people in the room.

'The meetings are always arranged by telephone. They've only ever met at crowded railway stations. And they'll part immediately after the Fabergé robbery, just as they separated directly after the

Brighton bank robbery. Packer can talk for as long as he likes and it won't matter a damn. He's a villain, with a list of previous convictions. Which is exactly why we chose him. We've even ensured that during the bank robbery he drank from a mug which was left behind, so there will be saliva contrasts for blood type identification. He'll be sufficient for the police, especially when they'll be able to return most of the property. Why can't you accept that there is nothing that can go wrong?'

'Because I'm not convinced it's that easy,' said Smith. He hesitated, then added quietly: 'So I won't agree with it.'

Wilberforce stared back expressionlessly at the other Director. He hadn't expected an outright refusal.

Smith stood up, feeling he had to emphasise his reasons. 'Not only is it dangerous,' he said, 'it's stupid. Because it's unnecessary.'

'I don't really see that there's a great deal you can do to stop it,' pointed out Wilberforce objectively. It was unfortunate he had to be quite so direct, he thought. In many ways, Smith's growing condescension reminded him of his wife. At least, he decided, he'd be able to make Smith express his regret, later on.

For several moments, the two Directors stared at each other and Wilberforce imagined the American was going to argue further. Then Onslow Smith jerked his head towards Ruttgers.

'Let's go,' he said.

As the men walked to the door of the huge office, Wilberforce called out: 'I do hope that you're not severing our co-operation on this matter.'

Smith halted, looking back.

'It was not I who ended the co-operation,' he said.

Neither American spoke until they had settled in the back of the waiting limousine and were heading towards Grosvenor Square.

'We going ahead by ourselves?' asked Ruttgers, expectantly.

'We bring men in,' agreed Smith. 'A lot more than were with you in Zürich.'

'Why?'

Smith didn't answer immediately.

'Wilberforce is a sneaky son of a bitch,' he said, after several minutes' thought. 'I'm not going to get our asses in any snare he's laying for us.'

'I don't understand.'

'Even when you can control the civil police, as Wilberforce can within limitations on a thing like this, a killing is still a killing. I'm not making a move against Charlie Muffin until I'm convinced that Wilberforce isn't setting us up.'

'More delays,' moaned Ruttgers bitterly. 'We're giving the bastard a chance.'

'But we're not making any mistakes,' said Smith. He'd already made too many, imagining there was safety in letting Wilberforce take the lead. It was time, thought Smith, that he started looking after himself. And that was what he was going to do.

Back in the Whitehall office, Cuthbertson stared at the Director's desk he had once occupied.

'They forgot to take the money with them,' he said.

'They'll be back,' said Wilberforce confidently.

Contacting Rupert Willoughby by telephone, instead of going personally either to his flat or City office, was probably a useless precaution, decided Charlie. But it might just reduce the danger to the younger man. So it was worthwhile. It was right he should feel guilt at compromising Sir Archibald's son, he knew.

'Warn me?' queried the underwriter.

'The robbery must mean they've found me,' said Charlie. 'It's very easy for the department to gain access to bank account details. If they're aware of the meetings between us, they'll know the £50,000 inheritance has been moved from deposit. And probably guessed the other money came from me, as well.'

'Couldn't the robbery just be a coincidence?'

'No.'

'Why not?'

'It's a guaranteed way to get me back here... where they can do what they like, when they like and in circumstances over which they'll have most control.'

'Christ,' said Willoughby softly.

Very soon, thought Charlie, the man would appreciate it really wasn't a game.

'I've already had to involve you,' apologised Charlie. 'I've had to make a statement to the police and I gave you as a business reference.'

'They've already contacted me,' confirmed Willoughby. 'I think I satisfied them.'

Law was very thorough, Charlie decided.

'Thank you,' he said.

'I had little choice, did I?' said Willoughby.

The attitude was changing, recognised Charlie.

'What are you going to do?' asked the underwriter.

'I don't understand enough to do anything yet,' said Charlie. He stopped, halted by a thought. If Wilberforce were the planner, he'd get perverse enjoyment moving against the son of the man he considered had impeded his promotion in the department.

'Has anything happened to you in the last few weeks that you regard as strange?' Charlie continued. 'Any unusual business activity?'

There was a delay at the other end of the line, while the man searched his memory.

'No,' said Willoughby finally.

'Sure?'

'Positive. Whatever could happen?'

'I don't know.'

'You're not very encouraging,' protested Willoughby.

'I'm not trying to be. I'm trying to be objective.'

'What should I do?' asked the underwriter.

'Just be careful,' said Charlie. 'They're bastards.'

'Shouldn't you be the one taking care?'

Charlie grimaced at the question. Wilberforce was using him like a laboratory animal, he thought suddenly, goading and prodding to achieve an anticipated reaction. When laboratory tests were over, the animal was usually killed. When, he wondered, would Wilberforce's experiment end?

'I am,' promised Charlie, emptily.

'When are we going to meet?'

'We're not,' said Charlie definitely.

'Let's keep in touch daily, at least.'

The concern was discernible in the man's voice.

'If I can.'

'My father always said there was one thing particularly unusual about you, Charlie. He said you were an incredible survivor,' recalled Willoughby.

But usually he'd known from which way the attack was coming, thought Charlie. Willoughby had meant the remark as encouragement, he recognised. To which of them? he wondered.

'I still am,' he said.

'I hope so,' said the underwriter.

'So do I,' said Charlie. 'So do I.'

15.

Because the northern extension of the Tate Gallery had once been the Queen Alexandra Hospital, occupied by hundreds of people, the sewer complex immediately beneath it was much larger than the other outlets that served the area. They had gone in through a manhole in Islip Street, Snare leading. He was still ahead, guiding the safebreaker, the miner's lamp he wore perfectly illuminating the huge cylindrical passageways.

'What a bloody smell!' protested Johnny. He moved clumsily, feet either side of the central channel, trying to avoid going into the water.

'In Paris, visiting the sewers is considered a tourist attraction,' said Snare. The man was right; it did stink.

'So's eating frogs,' sneered Johnny. Like Snare, he was wearing a hiker's rucksack, bulging with material it had again taken over a week to purchase. In addition, he hauled a collapsible sledge upon which was strapped the drilling motor and heavier equipment. The light from Snare's lamp was sufficient for them both, so Johnny hadn't bothered to turn his on. There was a sudden sound of scurried scratching, and Johnny grabbed out for Snare.

'Rats,' the larger man identified the noise, shrugging the hand away.

Johnny snapped on his light and in his anxiety went in up to his ankle in the water. Snare smiled at the outraged gasp.

'Can't stand rats,' said the safebreaker. He shivered 'Let's hurry up and get out of here.'

Snare ignored the other man, trying to play his light on to the Department of the Environment plan he'd taken from the sidepocket of his bulging pack. The gallery extension had meant there had been a lot of plans available, he thought gratefully. The sewer route had been marked on the chart in red, with notes on the alarm system and precautions installed overhead.

He heard another splash, an immediate curse and then felt Johnny pressing close to him.

Snare pulled away, recalling a medical record he had studied in one of the police files and the assessment of why Packer's downfalls invariably involved burly young men of limited intelligence.

'Jesus,' said Johnny, looking over his shoulder. 'Never worked with anyone who managed to get hold of the stuff you do... it's like a bloody guide-book.'

'Got a friend,' said Snare. It was the sort of remark the man would remember when he'd been arrested. Might even cause further embarrassment to Willoughby's firm if the man talked about drawings of the sort that insurers might possess.

The tunnel surround began to get smaller and they had to proceed at a crouch.

'Now we're right beneath the original building,' said Snare.

Positioning Packer where the narrowing began, Snare carefully measured along the slimy wall, making a mark where he had to begin digging and then insisted on measuring again, to avoid any miscalculation.

He brought out another plan from the rucksack, a detailed diagram of all the alarm installations and wiring.

'Where the hell did you get that?' exclaimed Packer.

'Same friend,' said Snare. Confidently he traced their entry hole on to the sewer wall.

'We'll have to work cautiously,' he said, almost to himself. 'There are some vibration alarms in the flooring.'

Snare operated the drill, as he had in Brighton. Again the tool was rubber cushioned, reducing both the noise and the recoil. The man worked very gently, discarding the bits the moment he thought they were becoming blunt and needed a sharper edge to cut into the concrete and brickwork. Frequently he referred to the wiring plan, using a rule to measure the depth of his hole. After about thirty minutes, he put aside the drill, chipping instead with a chisel and rubber-headed hammer, constantly feeling in and scraping away rubble and plaster by hand.

He found the first cluster of wires after an hour. Then he rejected even the hammer, scratching an inch at a time with just the chisel head When sufficient room had been made, he clamped the carefully prepared bypass leads, with their alligator clips, at either side of the wire cluster and then cut through.

Johnny sighed.

'No sound,' he said.

'There wouldn't have been,' Snare answered. 'This alarm only operates in the Scotland Yard control room.'

Because the adhesive tape they had used for the purpose at Brighton would not have stuck to the slime of the sewer walls, Snare knocked securing hooks into the bricks to hold the bypass leads out of the way.

He used the drill again now, still stopping every few minutes for measurement. It was a further hour before he turned the drill off and began gently prodding at the hole. Suddenly there was a clattering fall of bricks and concrete different from the rest and Snare turned, smiling at the other man.

'The floor,' he said. 'We're through.'

It took thirty minutes before the hole was big enough for them to clamber up, hauling the equipment behind them.

'Thank Christ we're out of there,' said Johnny sincerely. The revulsion shook his body.

Snare motioned him to silence, then checked his watch. 'An hour and forty minutes before there's any guard tour,' he whispered. 'But I don't want any unnecessary sound.'

He'd turned off his miner's headset, using now a large hand-torch with an adjustable cowl, so that the light beam could be accurately controlled. Another plan came from the rucksack.

'The Duneven room is above us and in that direction,' indicated Snare, to his left. 'The photographic room and restaurant is to the right and the stairs up to the ground floor should be immediately behind you.'

Johnny turned, using his own torch, but Snare stopped him.

'Don't forget the bags,' he said.

From the sledge they were leaving near the hole, Johnny took a number of plastic containers, then walked towards the stairway.

At the bottom he paused, awaiting Snare's lead.

'The first six are pressure activated,' said Snare.

He reached past the other man, laying a retractable plank stiffened at either edge by steel rods up to the eighth step.

'Be careful,' he warned.

Hand lightly against the handrail for balance, Johnny inched up the ramp. The door at the top was locked and Johnny knelt before it, torch only inches away.

'Piece of cake,' he declared. From his pack he took the dentist's pliers which he had modified since the Brighton robbery, so that the jaws could be locked. Into them he clamped a key blank and impressed it into the lock. Against the impressions he sketched a skeleton and within minutes had shaped a key from steel wire. The lock clicked back on his second attempt.

'Alarm at the top,' cautioned Snare. He pushed past, the magnetised bypass already in his hand. He slipped it over the break and then eased the door open. From his pack he took a wooden wedge, driving it beneath the door edge to prevent it accidentally slamming and disturbing the leads.

Just inside the main hall, Snare went to a panel set into the wall, gesturing for Johnny to follow.

'The first of the two alarm consoles,' he said. 'Open it.'

Johnny used a wire probe this time, easing the tumblers back one by one.

Snare had a plan devoted entirely to the wiring system that suddenly cobwebbed in front of them. He made Johnny hold it, freeing both his hands, and for fifteen minutes worked intently, muttering to himself, fixing jump leads and clamps.

'There,' he said, finally. 'Castrated.'

'You said two?' queried Johnny.

'This is the obvious one,' said Snare. 'The other one is identical but independently wired and concealed.'

It was a floor panel, just inside the cloakroom.

'Clever,' said Johnny, admiringly.

'Unless you know the secrets,' smiled Snare. Practised now, it didn't take him as long to neutralise the second system.

'What now?' asked Johnny.

'Now,' said Snare. 'We just help ourselves if not to the actual crown jewels, as near as makes no difference.'

He paused, checking the time.

'And there's still forty minutes before the attendant patrol.'

The Russian collection was in the main exhibition room, every piece under glass. They stopped, as the torches picked out the jewels of the Fabergé reproductions.

'What's that?' demanded Johnny.

'A miniature jewelled train,' said Snare. 'It's usually kept in the Armoury, in Moscow, along with those Easter egg ornaments in the next case…'

'Imagine those in a necklace,' said Johnny, wistfully.

'Beautiful,' agreed Snare. Pity you'd never have a chance to wear it, he thought, cruelly.

'What sort of people have jewelled trains and Easter eggs?' mused Johnny.

'Rich people,' said Snare. 'Very rich people.'

'Didn't they all get killed though?' queried Johnny.

Snare frowned at the qualification.

'Only because they were too stupid to realise the mistakes they were making,' he said.

He moved forward, gesturing to Johnny for the bags he had taken from the sledge. Against the side of each exhibition case he affixed a handle, with adhesive suckers at either tip, then sectioned the glass with a diamond-headed cutter. Gently, to avoid noise, he placed each piece of glass alongside the stand, put each exhibit into a protective chamois leather holder and then, finally, into a bigger container.

Apart from the eggs and the train, Snare took the copies of the Imperial Crown surmounted by the Balas ruby, the Imperial Orb, topped by its sapphire and the Russian-eagle-headed Imperial Sceptre, complete with its miniature of the Orloff diamond.

Snare lifted the bags, testing their weight. 'Enough,' he decided.

He turned, looking at Johnny. 'You know what you've just done?' he demanded.

'What?'

'Carried out the jewel robbery of the century,' said Snare, simply.

'Now all we've got to do is sell them back,' said Johnny. And then let Herbie Pie and all those other doubting bastards know. But discreetly, so they wouldn't think he was boasting.

'That'll be no trouble,' said Snare, confidently. He was glad there wouldn't he any more burglaries, he decided. From now on he could sit back and watch all the others do the work, enjoy the sport of watching Charlie squirm. Johnny humped the straps of the bags comfortably on to his shoulders, then followed Snare's lead down the stairs. Neither spoke until they reached the entry hole in the basement floor. Johnny stood, gazing apprehensively into the blackness.

'I'd very happily give back one of those funny eggs to avoid having to go back down there,' he said plaintively. Snare dropped through first, turning on the beam of his helmet to provide some light. Johnny lowered the jewellery first, then wriggled through, hanging for a moment before letting himself go. He misjudged the drop, stumbling up to his knees in the drainage channel.

'Shit,' he said.

'That's right,' agreed Snare.

They had almost finished the meal in their Moscow apartment when Berenkov apologised, explaining the cause of his silence to Valentina.

'There couldn't be any doubt?' asked the woman.

Berenkov shook his head, positively.

'Comrade General Kalenin was very sure – they've definitely found Charlie.'

She shook her head sadly.

'Poor man.'

'Yes,' he agreed. 'Poor man.'

'Why torture him?'

'I don't know,' he said.

'Just like children... cruel children.'

'Yes,' he accepted. 'It's often very childlike.'

'But in the end they'll kill him?'

'Yes,' he said, saddened by the question. 'They will have to do that.'

Valentina didn't speak for several minutes. Then she said, 'Is he married?'

'I think so.'

'It's her I feel sorry for,' said the woman. 'Perhaps more than for him. He knew the risks, after all.'

'Yes,' said Berenkov 'I suppose he did.'

'I wonder what she'll do?' said Valentina, reflectively.

'You should know, perhaps more than anybody,' Berenkov reminded her impulsively.

His wife looked at him sorrowfully.

'I'd just weep,' she said. She lingered, unsure of the admission.

Then she added, 'Because I wouldn't be brave enough to kill myself.'

16.

Onslow Smith had taken over the larger conference chamber in the American embassy in London's Grosvenor Square. He stood on a dais at one end of the room, a projection screen tight against the wall behind him. While he waited for everyone to become seated, he fingered the control button connected to the screening machine that would beam the pictures through the tiny square cut into the far wall.

The diminutive figure of Garson Ruttgers bustled into the room, moving towards the seat which Smith had positioned just off the raised area but still in a spot separating him from the other operatives, a considerate recognition of the importance he had once enjoyed.

Immediately behind sat Braley, clipboard on his knee. It was a great pity, decided the Director, that the Vienna episode had marked the end of any promotional prospects for the man. Braley appeared to have a fine analytical mind and worked without panic, despite the obvious nervous reaction to stress. He'd arranged everything for that day's meeting and done it brilliantly; one of the few people affected by Charlie Muffin who would easily make the transition to a planner's desk.

One of the few people, he repeated to himself, staring out into the room. Eighty men, he counted. Eighty operatives who had been trained to Grade 1 effectiveness; men from whom the Agency could have expected ten, maybe fifteen years of top-class service. All wiped out by Charlie Muffin. And Wilberforce expected him to sit back and do damn all except be the cheerleader. The apparent success of the early part of the entrapment had gone to the British Director's head, he decided.

'Shall we begin?'

The room quietened at the invitation. Smith stood with his hand against the back of the chair, looking down at them.

'Some of you,' he said, 'may have guessed already the point of drafting you all to London…'

He waited, unsure at the harshness of the next part of the prepared text. It was necessary, he decided. It would remind them of what they had lost and bring to the surface the proper feelings about the man responsible.

'…because you all, unfortunately, shared in the operation that ended your active field careers.'

Ruttgers, who had been initially grateful for the seating arrangement, moved uncomfortably in front of the men he had personally led to disaster, realising too late its drawbacks. Needing the activity, he lighted the predictable cigarette.

'Because of this man…' announced Smith, dramatically. He pressed the control button. A greatly enlarged picture, several times bigger than life, of Charlie Muffin appeared on the screen. It had been taken in the churchyard. Several times Smith pressed the button, throwing a kaleidoscope of photographs on the wall, shots of Charlie Muffin in Zürich, coming through passport control at London airport, outside his Brighton house and entering and leaving the offices of Rupert Willoughby.

'Taken,' said Smith, 'by the British.'

He paused to let the murmur which went through the room settle into silence. It was like baiting animals, bringing them to the point where their only desire was to fight, thought the Director.

'Charlie Muffin has been found,' he declared.

He waited again for the announcement to be assimilated. 'Found,' he picked up, 'by a very painstaking but rewarding operation conducted by the British…'

There was complete silence in the room, realised Smith. The concentration upon what he was saying was absolute. He sighed, shuffling the prepared speech in his hand.

'I wish to make it quite clear at the outset that since the discovery of the man, the handling of the affair has been jointly handled by the British and ourselves.'

He appeared to lose a sheet of notes, then stared up at them.

'At very high level,' he emphasised.

He waited for them to assess the importance, then went on: 'A certain course has been decided upon, a course of which you've no need to be aware…'

Harsh again, recognised Smith. But necessary, a reminder of just how far down they'd all been relegated. After this they'd be clerks at Langley until retirement, with only the Virginia countryside to relieve the boredom.

'It is sufficient for you to know that no immediate action – open action, anyway – is being taken against Charlie Muffin.'

The noise started again, the sound of surprise this time.

'Which does, of course,' continued the CIA chief, 'create a danger.'

He stopped once more. He'd really fucked it up, he decided honestly.

The response from the room was growing louder and several men were trying to catch his attention, to ask questions.

'And that is why I have gathered you here,' said Smith quickly, trying to subdue the clamour. 'The British consider the surveillance they have established is sufficient and certainly, thus far, it has proven to be. But I have no intention whatsoever of this Agency taking a subservient role in the continuing operation envisaged by the British.'

Smith sipped from a glass of water and in the gap a man at the front blurted: 'You mean we are going to stop working with the British?'

Smith smiled, the timing of the question over-riding any annoyance at the interruption.

'I intend giving the impression of continued cooperation,' he said. 'Before this meeting is over, you will all be given dossiers containing every item of information about Charlie Muffin that the British have so far been able to assemble... it is quite extensive. With the benefit of that information, we are going to establish our own, independent operation. When the shit hits the fan, I still want us wearing clean white suits.'

The persistent questioner in the front row pulled forward again.

'He will be eliminated, sir, won't he? Charlie Muffin will be eliminated?'

It was almost a plea, thought Smith. He moved to speak, but Ruttgers responded ahead of him, emotion momentarily washing away his awareness of his reduced role.

'Oh, yes,' said the ex-Director, fervently. 'He'll be eliminated. I promise you that.'

'But not until I've given the explicit order,' instructed Smith.

Charlie stood at the lounge window of the Brighton house, gazing out at the tree-lined avenue. The uniformed policeman who had passed twice was standing at the corner now, stamping his feet against the early evening chill. Where, wondered Charlie, were the others?

He turned into the room, staring at the bottles grouped on the table by the far wall. No, he decided easily. He didn't need it. Not any more.

'What I need,' he told himself, 'is for them to over-reach themselves. Just once.'

And Edith, he thought. He wanted her by him very much. But not yet. He had to get a clearer indication of what was happening before putting her to any more risk than she already faced. Poor Edith.

17.

Charlie arrived in Rupert Willoughby's office an hour after making the telephone call for the confirmation he scarcely needed. The underwriter greeted him with an attitude that swung between nervousness and anger. At last, thought Charlie. He hoped the growing awareness wouldn't affect the man's memory of his father.

'You knew we'd covered the exhibition?' challenged Willoughby immediately.

Anger first, Charlie accepted.

'It was obvious,' said Charlie. 'Once I heard of the robbery. And more particularly, what was stolen and from whom.'

'What does it mean?'

'That the department has known from the very beginning of our meeting. That they know I've put money into your firm. That they had you under permanent observation for as long as they've been watching me. And that in one operation they intend hitting back at everyone.'

Willoughby nodded, as if agreeing some private thought. His throat was moving, jerkily.

'No wonder my father was so frightened in the last year,' he said.

'I warned you,' Charlie reminded him.

Willoughby looked at him, but said nothing.

'Tell me about the cover,' said Charlie.

Willoughby pulled a file towards him, running his hand through the papers.

'Completely ordinary,' he said. 'For an exhibition of this value, the government always goes on to the London market, through Lloyd's. For us, it's usually a copper-bottomed profit. Security is absolute but because of the value and alleged risk, we can impose a high premium.'

'How much cover did you offer?'

'Two and a half million,' said Willoughby.

'What happens now?'

'Claim to be filed. And then the squabbling begins, to gain time.'

'You expect a sell back?'

Willoughby looked surprised.

'Of course,' he said. 'That's what always happens in a case like this.'

'What percentage?'

'Varies. Usually ten.'

Charlie laughed, appearing genuinely amused.

'Two hundred and fifty thousand,' he said. 'Exactly what I put in. They don't mean me to misunderstand for a moment, do they?'

'Is it significant?' asked Willoughby.

'Very,' said Charlie. To continue would mean admitting he was a thief. The man deserved the honesty, he decided.

'They want to recover $500,000 from me. Plus interest,' he said. 'They got almost half from the Brighton robbery. This would be the remainder.'

Willoughby sat, waiting. It was impossible to judge from the expression on his face whether there was any criticism.

'You told me once you hadn't done anything criminal,' he accused Charlie.

The anger was on the ascendancy, Charlie decided.

'They set out, quite deliberately, to kill me,' said Charlie. 'That was the penalty I imposed upon them for being abandoned... abandoned like your father was. He tried to fight back against them as well, remember. We just chose different ways of doing it. Mine worked better than his. They lost more than money.'

'What happens next?' asked the underwriter.

'I don't know,' confessed Charlie. 'I'd guess they're getting ready to kill me now.'

'You're not worried enough,' said the younger man in sudden awareness. 'Boxed in like this, you should be terrified. Like I am.'

'I'm not,' confirmed Charlie easily. 'The Russian robbery was the error... the one I was waiting for them to make...'

Willoughby shook his head.

'Your father was very good at this sort of thing,' said Charlie. 'He'd do it to get someone whom he suspected to disclose themselves completely.'

'You're not making yourself clear,' complained the underwriter.

'I *know* the pattern,' said Charlie. 'It must be either Wilberforce or Cuthbertson or both. And I learned from your father a bloody sight better than they did.'

Willoughby gazed back, unconvinced. It was the first time the confidence, almost bordering on conceit, had been obvious, he realised. Another thought came, with frightening clarity. He'd been a fool to become involved, no matter what his feelings for the men who had destroyed his father.

'You've got to get out,' he said.

'Oh, no,' answered Charlie. 'You don't survive looking constantly over your shoulder. I've tried for the past two years and it's almost driven me mad.'

'You don't have an alternative.'

'I have,' said Charlie. He considered what he needed to say but still began badly, speaking as the thoughts came to him.

'I told you at our first meeting there was a risk of your being compromised,' he said. 'And you have been...'

'And I said then that I was prepared to accept that,' interrupted the underwriter in a vain attempt at bravery.

'Because you didn't really know what it was going to be like,' argued Charlie. 'Now it's different. The robbery was directed against you and your firm. And because of it, other underwriters could be out of pocket, coming to a buy-back settlement. From this firm all that is at risk at the moment is the money I've deposited. So this time you've been let off with a warning...'

'What do you want?' Willoughby interrupted.

'The sort of help which, if it goes wrong, could mean that next time there won't be any warning,' said Charlie bluntly.

'I'll hear you out,' said Willoughby guardedly.

Charlie stood and began pacing the office, talking as he moved.

'The misjudgment they've made is one that your father never allowed,' lectured Charlie. 'They've given me the opportunity to react.'

'I still don't think you've got any choice,' said Willoughby.

'That's it,' agreed Charlie. 'And that is what Wilberforce and whoever else is working with him will be thinking.'

Charlie stopped walking, thoughts moving sideways.

'Buying back the proceeds of unusual or large robberies isn't particularly uncommon, is it?' he asked suddenly.

'Not really,' said Willoughby. 'Although obviously we don't make a point of announcing it. There's usually some token police objection, as well. Although for political reasons, I don't think that will be very strong in this case.'

'So there are people in this office who wouldn't regard it as odd if they were asked to behave in a somewhat bizarre way?' Charlie hurried on. 'They'd accept it could be part of some such arrangement?'

'I don't think we've the right to put other people to the sort of danger you seem to think exists.'

'It's not dangerous – not this part,' Charlie assured him. 'I just want them as decoys.'

'I have your promise on that?'

'Absolutely,' said Charlie.

'Then yes,' agreed Willoughby. 'There are people who wouldn't think it at all strange. They might even enjoy it.'

'And what about you?'

'I'm not enjoying any of it any more,' admitted Willoughby, with his customary honesty.

'Well?' asked Charlie nervously.

The underwriter considered the invitation to withdraw. 'Are you going to ask me to do anything illegal? Or involve the firm in any illegality?' he asked, repeating his paramount concern.

'Definitely not.'

'I must have your solemn undertaking.'

'You have it.'

'Then I'll help,' said Willoughby. Quickly, he added, 'With a great deal of reluctance.'

With the number of friends he had, decided Charlie, he could hold a party in a telephone box. And still have room for the band.

'Excellent,' he said enthusiastically. 'Now I think we should celebrate.'

'Celebrate?' questioned Willoughby, bewildered.

'As publicly as possible.'

'I wish I knew what was going on,' protested the underwriter.

'It's called survival,' said Charlie, cheerfully.

It was a tense, hostile encounter, different – although for opposing reasons – from what either the Americans or Wilberforce had anticipated when Smith and Ruttgers had stormed from the office less than twenty-four hours before.

'Well?' insisted Smith.

'It isn't what I expected,' conceded Wilberforce, reluctantly.

'Isn't what you expected!' echoed Smith, etching the disgust into his voice. 'At this moment, Charlie Muffin should be trying to disappear into the woodwork!'

He stood up, moving to a sidetable where copies of the photographs had been laid out. He picked them up, one by one, as he spoke.

'Instead of which,' he said, displaying them to everyone in the room, 'he's practically advertising his presence from the rooftops, drinking champagne at the Savoy until he can hardly stand and then occupying the centre table at the river-view restaurant for a lunch that took almost three hours!'

'He's very clever,' said Cuthbertson, in his wet, sticky voice. 'We shouldn't forget he's very clever.'

'We *shouldn't* forget anything,' agreed Smith. 'Any more than we should have forgotten the point of this operation.'

'It's not been forgotten,' said Wilberforce stiffly.

'Just endangered,' hit back the American Director. 'God knows how badly.'

The Russian robbery had been in England, he thought suddenly. At the moment there was nothing to prove any American involvement. That was how it was going to stay.

'We can't eliminate him, not now,' said Cuthbertson. 'Not until we discover the reason for his extraordinary behaviour.'

'Of course we can't kill him,' accepted Smith, careless of his irritation.

'What do you think it means?' demanded Wilberforce of Braley.

Braley considered the question with his customary discomfort.

'That there's something we don't know about... despite all the checks and investigations, there's obviously something we overlooked... something that makes Charlie confident enough to act as he's doing.'

Braley blinked at his superiors, worried at the open criticism.

'I've always warned of that possibility,' Wilberforce tried to recover. 'That was the point of the bank entry in the first place, don't forget.'

Smith looked at the other Director in open contempt.

'It could just be a bluff,' said Snare.

'It could be anything,' said Smith. 'That's the whole damned trouble. We just don't know.'

'The Russians are upset,' said Cuthbertson, mildly. The first time anything had gone wrong and Wilberforce was unsettled, he saw. Practically gouging the pipe in half. He smiled, uncaring that the other man detected the expression. Always had thought he could do the job better than anybody else.

'What's happened?' asked Smith.

Wilberforce looked sourly at his one-time chief before replying.

'Formal note of protest to our ambassador in Moscow,' he reported. 'The Russian ambassador here calling at his own request upon the Foreign Secretary and two questions tabled in the House of Commons by some publicity-conscious MPs.'

'Hardly more than you expected,' retorted Smith. No one seemed to realise how serious it was, he thought.

'We decided upon a course of action,' said Wilberforce, pushing the calmness into his voice. 'So far every single thing has proceeded exactly as it was planned. Certainly what the man did today was surprising. But that's all it is, a surprise. We mustn't risk everything by attempting ill-considered improvisations.'

'You know, of course,' said Smith, 'that after that lunch he booked into the Savoy?'

'Yes,' said Wilberforce, the irritation returning.

'Another assumed name?' asked Cuthbertson.

Damn the man, thought Wilberforce. The former Director knew the answer as well as any of them.

'No,' he admitted. 'He seemed to take great care to register as Charles Muffin.'

18.

Charlie knew he had registered at the hotel at exactly 3.45 in the afternoon. That concluding act of a flamboyant performance, using his real name, would have confused them sufficiently for at least a two-hour discussion, he estimated. Barely evening then. And it would have taken more than twenty-four hours from the moment of decision, even if it had been made in the daytime when people were available, for the necessary warrants and authorisations and then the installation of engineers to put any listening device on the telephone in his hotel room.

Even so, he still went immediately after breakfast to the Savoy foyer to book the call to his Zürich apartment from the small exchange by the lounge stairs, then insisted on taking it in one of the booths from which he could watch the operator.

The first conversation with Edith was abrupt, lasting little more than a minute. Charlie allowed her half an hour to reach the Zürich telephone exchange. She was waiting by one of the incoming booths when he made the second call.

'So you think the apartment here will be monitored?' she said immediately.

'Probably.'

'The robbery wasn't a coincidence, then?'

He smiled to himself at her insistence on an admission. She never liked losing arguments.

'No,' he said. 'Of course not. I was trying to stop you becoming too frightened.'

'You really thought that possible?'

He could detect how strident her voice was. He didn't answer, refusing to argue.

'What else happened?' she demanded.

Briefly, Charlie outlined the details of the Russian robbery and the effect any settlement would have upon Willoughby's firm.

'They know everything about you, Charlie. Everything. You're going to get killed.'

The assertion blurted from her and he heard her voice catch at the other end.

'Edith,' he said patiently, 'I know a way out.'

'There isn't a way out, Charlie,' she said. 'Stop being such a bloody fool.'

He sighed, fighting against the irritation in his voice.

'Did you call to say goodbye, just like you said goodbye to Sir Archibald before you left for Vienna to begin this fucking mess?' she said desperately.

She'd been too long alone, Charlie realised. Now all the fears and doubts were firmly embedded in her mind and refusing to leave. And Edith shouldn't swear, he thought. She paraded the words artificially, like a child trying to shock a new schoolteacher.

'I called to say I loved you,' said Charlie.

The tirade stopped, with the abruptness of a slammed door.

'Oh, Christ, Charlie,' she moaned.

He winced at the pain in her voice. She would be crying, he knew.

'I mean it,' he said.

'I know you do.'

'I love you and I'm going to get us out of all this. We'll find another place...'

'... to hide?' she accused him.

'Has it been that bad?'

'It's been terrible, Charlie. And you know it And you'd never be able to make it any different, even if you got away from it now.'

He had no argument to put against that, Charlie realised.

'You should have told me how you felt... before now,' he said.

'What good would it have done?'

None, he accepted. She was right. As she had been about the drinking and the damned cemetery and everything else.

'I'm sorry, Edith,' he said.

'So am I, Charlie,' she said, unhelpfully.

'I need your help,' said Charlie. At least, he thought, she'd have something more than fear to occupy her mind.

'Of course,' she said. Depression flattened her voice. 'We'll need the other passports,' he said. 'Now that they know our identity the ones we've got aren't any good, not any more.'

He heard her laugh, an empty sound.

'For when you've beaten them all, Charlie?' she asked sadly.

'We're going to try, for God's sake,' he said. The shout would carry beyond the box, but he knew he had to break through the lassitude of defeat.

'Yes,' she agreed, trying to force a briskness into her voice. 'At least we must try.'

The effort failed; she was convinced of failure, he realised.

'Do you have a pen and paper?'

'Of course.'

'I want you to draw the passports from your bank and then travel, by ferry, to England.'

He paused.

'Yes?' she prompted. The dullness was still evident. 'Hire a car,' he continued. 'Then set out at your own pace, touring around the countryside.'

'Charlie...?' she began, but he stopped her.

'Wait,' he said. 'But I want you every third night to be at these hotels...'

Patiently he recited from an AA guide book the first listing and then the hotel once removed in case the initial choice was full in towns selected from a carefully calculated, sixty-mile radius of London. It took a long time because Charlie insisted she read them back to him, to ensure there was no mistake.

'Start from Oxford,' he concluded, 'the day after tomorrow and go in order of the towns as I've given them to you.'

'And just wait until you contact me at any one of the hotels, always on the third day?' she anticipated.

'That's right.'

'Sounds very simple,' she said and he started to smile, hoping at last for a change in her attitude.

'There's just one thing, Charlie,' she added.

'Yes?'

'What happens after a month, when I've gone around and around and you haven't contacted me... haven't contacted me because you're lying dead in some ditch somewhere?'

Her voice switchbacked and she struggled to a halt.

'I don't expect to be lying dead somewhere,' he said.

'But what if you *are*, Charlie,' she insisted. 'I've got to know, for Christ's sake!'

Very soon she would be crying, he knew. He hoped she was in one of the end boxes at the Zürich exchange where there would be some concealment from the high wall.

'Then it will be Rupert who calls you,' he admitted, reluctantly.

For several minutes there was complete silence.

'It would mean we'd never see each other again, Charlie.' She was fighting against the emotion, he realised, carefully choosing the words before she spoke.

'Yes,' he said.

'Funny, isn't it,' she went on, straining to keep her voice even. 'That never really registered with me, the day you left to go to London. But that could be it; the last time. And you didn't kiss me, when you left.'

'I said I don't expect to be lying dead somewhere,' he repeated, desperately.

'What would I do, Charlie?' she pleaded. 'I've always had you.'

Now it was his voice that was flat, without expression. It wouldn't be the answer she wanted, he knew.

'You haven't done anything wrong,' he said. 'Not to them, I mean. So they wouldn't try to hurt you.'

'So I could come safely back here, to an apartment where you'd never be again and to a bed in which you'd never sleep or touch me and...'

Grief washed over the bitterness.

'...and live happily ever after,' she finished badly, through the sobs.

'Please, Edith,' he said.

He waited, wincing at her attempts to recover.

'I'm sorry,' she said, finally. 'I can't help blaming you and I know all the time that it's not your fault... not in the beginning, anyway.'

'We can still win,' he insisted.

'You really believe that, don't you?' she challenged. 'You can't lose that bloody conceit, no matter what happens to you.'

If I did, thought Charlie, then I'd be slumped weeping in a telephone box.

'I mean it,' he tried again, avoiding another confrontation.

'I'll be at Oxford,' she sighed, resigned to the plan.

'I love you, Edith,' he said again.

'Charlie.'

'What?'

'If... if you're right... if you manage it... promise me something.'

'What?'

'You'll tell me that more often.'

'Every day,' he said, too eagerly.

'Not every day,' she qualified. 'Just more than you have in the past.'

The telephone operator looked up at him, eyebrows raised, when Charlie left the box. It had been very hot in the tiny cubicle, he realised. His shirt was wet against his back.

'Thirty-five minutes,' said the man. 'It would have been far more comfortable in your room.'

'Probably,' agreed Charlie.

Edith wouldn't have left the booth in Zürich yet, he knew. She'd be crying.

The pipe stem snapped, a sudden cracking sound in the silent room.

'Sure?' asked Cuthbertson.

'Positive,' said Wilberforce.

'Why would the Americans impose their own surveillance?'

'Because they don't trust ours. Probably don't trust us, either. No reason why they should.'

'They won't kill him?' demanded Cuthbertson, worriedly.

'No,' Wilberforce assured him. 'Not until they've found out why he's doing these things.'

'So what are we going to do?'.

'Nothing,' said the British Director. 'It might be a useful safeguard.'

The man was bewildered by Charlie Muffin's attitude, Cuthbertson knew. Served him right; always had been too conceited by half. He coughed, clearing the permanently congested throat.

'Not going quite as we expected,' suggested Cuthbertson.

'No,' admitted Wilberforce.

Upon whom, wondered Cuthbertson, would the man try to put the responsibility this time?

19.

The lunch with Willoughby was as open as that of the previous day, but kept to a much tighter schedule. For that reason they ate at the Ritz, because the bank Charlie had carefully chosen was a private one less than five hundred yards away in Mayfair and he wanted to begin on foot.

They left at three o'clock. Charlie paused outside, handing Willoughby the document case while he struggled into a Burberry, turning the collar up under the dark brown trilby hat.

'You look rather odd,' said Willoughby.

'Glad to hear it,' said Charlie. 'Let's hope others think so too.'

'I'd hate to think we're wasting our time,' said the underwriter.

'We're not,' Charlie assured him. 'Believe me, we're not.'

I hope, he thought.

He led the way through the traffic stop-starting along Piccadilly and up Stratton Street.

An assistant manager was waiting for the appointment that Charlie had made by telephone, one of several calls he had made after speaking to Edith. The formalities were very brief, but Charlie lingered all alone in the safe-deposit vault, keeping strictly to the timing that had been rehearsed with the others in Willoughby's office. Edith would have already decided her route and timetable, thought Charlie, sighing. Maybe even packed. She always liked doing things well in advance.

He and Willoughby left the bank at three-fifty, turning up Curzon Street towards Park Lane.

'We're running to the minute,' said Charlie.

'Are you *sure* we're being followed?' asked Willoughby.

'Stake my life on it,' said Charlie, smiling at the unintended irony. 'In fact, I am,' he added.

'I feel rather ridiculous,' said Willoughby.

'You're supposed to feel scared,' said Charlie.

Four o'clock was striking as they emerged in front of the park. For several seconds they remained on the pavement, looking either way, as if seeking a taxi.

'Here we go,' said Charlie, seeing a break in the traffic stream and hurrying across towards the underground car park. The limousine came up the ramp as they reached the exit and the chauffeur hardly braked as Charlie and Willoughby entered. It slotted easily into the stream of vehicles heading north towards Marble Arch.

'Now I feel scared,' confessed Willoughby.

'There's nothing illegal,' Charlie said.

The halt outside the Marble Arch underground station was purposely sudden, causing a protest of brakes from the line of cars behind, but before the first horn blast Charlie and Willoughby were descending the stairs. They caught the train immediately, an unexpected advantage. As he sat down, Charlie looked at his watch. They were two minutes ahead of schedule, he saw.

'Only another ten minutes and we'll see the beginning of the rush hour,' he said.

Willoughby nodded, without replying. He was staring straight ahead, tight-lipped. The man *was* scared Charlie realised.

They jerked away from the train at Oxford Circus almost as the doors were closing, going up the escalator on the left and walking swiftly. The car pulled smoothly into the kerb as they emerged, turned quickly left through the one-way system into Soho and then regained Regent Street.

'I wish we could go faster,' muttered Willoughby.

'Speed isn't important,' said Charlie.

There was no need for the braking manoeuvre at Piccadilly station because there was a traffic jam. Charlie led again, bustling down the stairs. This time they sat without speaking until they reached Green Park. As they came up beneath the shadow of the hotel in which they'd eaten, one of Willoughby's clerks, wearing a Burberry, trilby, and carrying a document case fell into step with them and the three of them entered the vehicle.

'There's still a car with us,' volunteered the driver, taking a traffic light at amber and accelerating into the underpass on the way to Knightsbridge.

They got out at Knightsbridge station and as they descended the stairway a second clerk, dressed identically to the first and also carrying a matching case, joined the group. They travelled only as far as South Kensington, but when they emerged for the car this time, one of the raincoated men turned away, walking quickly into Gloucester Road. There was another clerk at Victoria and this time they went on for two stations, getting off at the height of the rush hour at Embankment. The throng of people covered the delay of the car reaching them. They travelled north again, to Leicester Square, and when they got out this time, the man who had left them in Kensington was waiting, joining without any greeting until Holborn. They crowded into the car, sped down Southampton Row and then boarded a District Line train at Temple. The car turned, going back along the Strand, circling Trafalgar Square, then pulled in for petrol in St Martin's Lane.

On the underground, the group changed at Monument station, caught a Northern line train and disembarked unhurriedly at Bank. According to the prearranged plan, they waited outside the underwriter's office for the car. It took five minutes to arrive.

'Let's go inside, shall we?' said Willoughby, to the three clerks.

'So where's the Fabergé collection?' quietly complained one of the three men. 'Lot of stupid bloody rubbish.'

He'd missed the 6.30 to Sevenoaks and now his wife would be late for her pottery classes.

'You got a new raincoat out of it,' reminded the man next to him.

'Bought one last week,' said the clerk. 'Sod it.'

To the others in the room, it seemed like blind, irrational rage, but Wilberforce's emotion was really fear, matched almost equally with self-pity. Now the Director sat hunched forward at his desk, even the pipes temporarily forgotten.

'How could it have happened?' he demanded, wearily. 'How the hell could it have possibly happened?'

A sob jerked his voice and he coughed quickly, to disguise it from the others in the room.

'We never considered he would be able to get that much help,' said Snare. 'We just couldn't adjust quickly enough.'

'It was a brilliant manoeuvre,' added Cuthbertson.

'We should do something to Willoughby,' said Snare vehemently.

'What?' demanded Wilberforce. 'There's no law against playing silly buggers on an underground train. And we've already ensured his firm is going to lose money.'

'Frighten him, at least,' maintained Snare.

'Aren't there more important things to worry about?' asked Cuthbertson.

'Christ,' moaned Wilberforce, in another surge of self-pity. 'Oh, Christ.'

A secretary tried to announce the arrival of the Americans, but Smith and Ruttgers followed her almost immediately into the room. Braley's entry was more apologetic.

'Lost him!' challenged the American Director. It was a prepared accusation the outrage too false.

'And what happened to your men?' retorted Wilberforce instantly.

Smith hesitated, disconcerted that his separate operation had been discovered.

'Just a precaution,' he tried to recover.

'Which didn't work. So it was a stupid waste of time and effort,' said Wilberforce, refusing to be intimidated. 'We've both made a mess of it and squabbling among ourselves isn't going to help. Recovery is all that matters now.'

'How, for God's sake?' asked Smith. 'By now Charlie Muffin could be a million miles away.'

'I had men at every port and airport within an hour,' said Wilberforce, anxious to disclose some degree of expertise. 'He's still here, somewhere.'

'But just where, exactly?' asked Cuthbertson. The other man hadn't offered any sympathy after the Vienna débâcle, remembered the ex-soldier. At one enquiry he'd even sat openly smiling.

Wilberforce shook his head, impatient with the older man's enjoyment of what was happening.

'He's shown us how,' said Wilberforce, quietly. They could still recover, he determined. Recover and win.

'You surely don't mean...' Snare began to protest, but the Director spoke over him.

'He went into the bank with a document case,' said Wilberforce. 'And we know he opened a safe-deposit because we've already checked.'

'No,' tried Snare again, anticipating his superior's thoughts.

'We haven't got anything else,' said the British Director.

'We've carried out two robberies!' protested Snare, looking to the others in the room for support. 'We can't risk another one. It's ludicrous. We're practically turning ourselves into a crime factory.'

'What risk?' argued Wilberforce. 'You've gone in knowing the details of every alarm system and with every architect's drawing. There's never been any danger.'

'We're breaking the law... over and over again.'

'For a justifiable reason,' said Wilberforce, disconcerted by the strength of the other man's argument.

'I think it's unnecessarily dangerous,' said Snare, aware he had no support in the room. 'What Charlie did was nothing more than an exercise to lose us... a trick to get us interested, like staying overnight in the Savoy – nothing more than that.'

'But we've got to *know*,' insisted Wilberforce.

'Why can't somebody else do it?' asked Snare, truculently, looking at the Americans. He'd taken all the chances, he realised. It was somebody else's turn.

'How can it be someone else?' replied Smith, impatiently. 'You're the only one who can operate with Packer.'

'Too dangerous,' repeated Snare, defeated.

'It's not the only lead,' Ruttgers said quietly.

Everyone turned to him, waiting.

'You've forgotten the wife,' continued the former Director. 'Eventually he'll establish contact with her... she's the key.'

Both Directors nodded. Cuthbertson shuffled through some papers, finally holding up that morning's report from the Savoy Hotel.

'There was a thirty-five minute telephone call to Zürich,' he said.

'To a number on the main exchange... a number upon which we could not have installed any device,' enlarged Ruttgers.

Wilberforce's smile broadened and he reached out for an unfortunate pipe.

'It's getting better,' he said.

'I'll go,' said Ruttgers, quickly. 'I went before... know the apartment and the woman.'

He looked up, alert for any opposition.

'All right,' agreed Wilberforce immediately. He couldn't remain in complete control any longer, he decided. Didn't want to, either. Finding Charlie Muffin again was the only consideration now. That and spreading some of the blame if anything went wrong.

'Yes,' accepted Smith, doubtfully. It was going to be a difficult tightrope, he thought. So it was right that someone of Ruttger's seniority should be in charge.

The American Director looked back to Snare.

'It's still vital to find out what's in that bank,' he said. 'Even though the idea of a third entry offends me as much as it does you.'

'I've already got men obtaining detailed drawings of the houses on either side from the architects involved and all the protection systems from the insurance companies,' said Wilberforce.

So it had been a pointless objection anyway, Snare realised. They were bastards, all of them.

'Could we be ready tomorrow night?' asked Smith.

'It would mean hurrying,' said Wilberforce.

The American looked at him, letting the criticism register.

'Isn't that exactly what it *does* mean?' he said.

When it became completely dark in the office garage, Charlie eased himself up gratefully from the floor, stretching out more comfortably on the back seat of the car. He cat-napped for three hours, aware he would need the rest later, then finally got out, easing the cramp from his shoulders and legs. His chest hurt from being wedged so long over the transmission tunnel, he realised. And his new raincoat had become very creased. It seemed more comfortable that way. Using the key that Willoughby had given him that morning, he let himself cautiously out of the garage side door, standing for a long time in the deep shadows, seeking any movement. The city slept its midnight sleep.

He walked quickly through the side streets, always keeping near the buildings, where the concealment was better. He'd used the cover like this in the Friedrichstrasse and Leipzigerstrasse all those years ago, he remembered, when they'd tried to kill him before. They'd failed that time, too.

The mini, with its smoked windows, was parked where Willoughby had guaranteed the chauffeur would leave it.

The heater was operating by the time Charlie drove up the Strand. Gradually he ceased shivering. It was 12.15 when Charlie positioned the car in the alley which made the private bank so attractive to his purpose, aware before he checked that it would be completely invisible to anyone in the main thoroughfare.

Quietly he re-entered the vehicle, glad of its warmth. It probably wouldn't be tonight, he accepted. But the watch was necessary. Would they be stupid? he wondered.

'If they are, then it'll be your game, Charlie,' he said, quietly. 'So be careful you don't fuck it up, like you have everything else so far.'

20.

Superintendent Law accepted completely the futility of the review when a detective sergeant from the Regional Crime Squad seriously suggested that the bank robbery had been Mafia inspired.

He sighed, allowing the meeting that had already lasted two hours to extend for a further fifteen minutes and then rose, ending it. He thanked them for their attendance, promised another discussion if there had been no break in the case within a fortnight and walked out of the room with Sergeant Hardiman.

'Waste of bloody time, that was,' he said, back in his office.

Hardiman waited at the door, accepting tea from the woman with the trolley.

'Bread pudding or Dundee cake?' asked the sergeant.

'Neither,' said Law.

Hardiman came carefully into the room, his pudding balanced on top of one of the cups.

'Mafia,' he echoed. 'Jesus Christ!'

'Funny though,' said Hardiman. He pushed an escaping crumb into his mouth.

'What is?'

'The dead end,' said the sergeant. 'We get the biggest job we've had in this manor for years. Indications of a professional safebreaker are everywhere and after almost a month, we've got nothing. No whispers, no gossip, no nothing.'

'So it was someone from outside. We decided that days ago,' Law reminded him. He had spoken too sharply, he realised.

'So who?' asked Hardiman, unoffended. 'Who, a stranger to the area, could set up a job like this?'

Law threw up his hands, wishing he'd accepted the bread pudding. It looked very good and he'd only had a pickled egg and a pork pie for lunch, he remembered.

'It's in there, somewhere,' he said, gesturing towards the files stacked up against the wall. 'All we've got to do is find it.'

Hardiman carefully wiped the sugar from his lips and hands.

'That was nice; you should have had some,' said the sergeant. He looked towards the manila folders. 'It might be in there, but we're going to need help to see it.'

'One hundred and twenty boxes,' reflected Law. 'And carefully hidden in one of them was something that would make it all so clear to us.'

'But which one?' said Hardiman. 'We've interviewed the owners and they're all lying buggers.'

'Crime is not solved by brilliant intuition or startling intellect,' started Law, and Hardiman looked at him warily. The superintendent had a tendency to lecture, he thought.

'...it's solved by straightforward, routine police work,' completed Law. He looked expectantly at the other man.

When Hardiman said nothing, Law prompted. 'And what, sergeant, is the basis of routine police work?'

Hardiman still said nothing, aware of the other man's unhappiness at the lack of progress and unwilling to increase his anger with the wrong answer.

'Statements?' he tried at last.

Law smiled.

'Statements,' he agreed. 'Good, old-fashioned, copper-on-a-bike statements.'

Hardiman waited.

'So,' decided Law, 'we will start all over again. We'll turn out those bright sods who spend all their time watching television and admiring the Mafia and we'll go to every box-holder and we'll take a completely fresh statement, saying there are some additional points we want covered. And then we'll practise straightforward, routine police work and compare everything they said first time with everything they say the second time. And where the difference is too great we'll go back again and take a third statement and if necessary a fourth and we'll keep on until we shake the bloody clue out of the woodwork.'

'It'll take a while,' warned Hardiman, doubtfully. 'That scruffy bloke with the home in Switzerland, for instance. The one we saw last? Telephoned yesterday to say he'd be in London for at least a week, on business.'

'Don't care how long it takes,' said Law positively. 'I want it done. If he's not back in a week contact that firm he gave us and get him back. I want everyone seen again. Everyone.'

'Right,' said Hardiman, moving to leave the room.

Law called out, stopping him at the door, 'If you pass the tealady and she's still got some of that bread pudding, send her back with some, will you?'

'Certainly,' said the sergeant. There wouldn't be, he knew. He'd had the last piece. But the superintendent was annoyed enough as it was, so it was better not to tell him.

Edith left the Zürich apartment early, changing trains at Berne to catch the express. She crossed from Calais to Dover and hired a Jaguar, deciding the need for comfort during the amount of driving she might have to do justified the expense.

It was a bright, sharp day, the February sunshine too weak to take the overnight whiteness from the fields and hedges of Kent. She drove unhurriedly, cocooned in the warmth of the car, missing the worst of the traffic by skirting London to the west.

She got a room without difficulty at the Randolph and by eight o'clock was in the bar, with a sherry she didn't want, selecting a meal she knew she wouldn't enjoy.

'Scotch,' ordered Ruttgers, at the other end of the bar. 'Plenty of ice.'

21.

The man was irritable, decided Johnny. And for the first time he did not appear completely sure of himself. Nervous, almost. The bigger surprise, determined the safebreaker. Because there definitely wasn't any cause for uncertainty. It had all gone like clockwork, just like the other two. Easier, in fact. Far easier. No dusty, gritty air-conditioning tubes. Or shitty drains. Just a simple entry through the back of the adjoining premises, a quick walk through the antique furniture all marked up at three times its price for the oil-rich Arabs and a neat little hole by the fireplace to bring them right into the main working area.

'Never been into a private bank before,' said Johnny, chattily. 'Very posh.'

'Doesn't seem as if they expected anyone to. Not at night, anyway,' said Snare, straightening up from the alarm system. He hadn't believed the plans Wilberforce had given him three hours before.

'What do you mean?' said Johnny.

Snare reached into the bag, bringing up the aerosol tube of tile fixative and squirting it liberally into the control box, sealing the hammers of the alarms.

'Must be fifteen years old,' he judged. 'They probably still count with an abacus.'

'Probably,' concurred Johnny, who didn't know what an abacus was. The other man was definitely friendlier, he decided happily.

They found a pressure pad beneath the carpet in the manager's office, three more behind junior executive desks and an electrical eye circuit, triggered when the beam was interrupted, in front of the strongroom and the safety deposit vault.

They were all governed by a control box it took them fifteen minutes to locate in the basement.

'Kid's stuff?' ventured Johnny hopefully.

'Kid's stuff,' agreed Snare.

'Can't beat a sock or a biscuit tin in the garden, can you?' continued Johnny, as the man immobilised the second system.

Snare grunted, without replying. He'd enjoy seeing this cocky little sod in the dock of the Old Bailey, he decided, trying to talk his way out of a fifteen-year sentence. Where, he wondered, would all the bombast and the boasting be then? Where his brains were, he decided. In his silk jock-strap, as useless as everything else.

'At this rate,' said Johnny, 'we'll be able to retire by the end of the year.'

'Maybe sooner,' said Snare, with feeling. Whatever happened, he determined, positively, this would be the last time. No matter how easy they made it for him, with all the plans and wiring systems drawings, it was still dangerous. And he'd suffered enough. Too much. Didn't he still need special pills, for the headaches? And they'd become more frequent in the last month. Like everything else, something that Wilberforce found easy to forget, in his anxiety to get his head off the block. He wasn't any more considerate than Cuthbertson. Worse even.

'Let's get started,' he said.

It took Johnny longer than they expected to open the safe in the manager's office and then Snare wasn't satisfied with the list of safe-deposit box numbers he got from the top shelf.

'Nothing entered since last week,' he said almost to himself.

'What does that matter?'

'Try the desk.'

That was easier and it was there that Snare found the listing for Charlie.

'Conceited bastard,' he said, again a private remark. 'The conceited bastard.'

'What?'

Things were very different tonight, decided Johnny. Odd, in fact. It was making him feel uncomfortable.

'Nothing,' said Snare. As he had at the Savoy, Charlie had opened an account under his own name.

To get into the safety deposit vault, Johnny drilled out the lock on the protective gate and then filled three holes bored around the safe handle with P-4 to blow a hole big enough to reach inside and manually bring the time clock forward twelve hours, to open the door.

Inside the deposit room, Johnny worked with his steel wire, fashioning the skeleton keys as he worked, giving a little laugh at his own cleverness every time a tray snapped clear and came out on its runners.

'Lot of documents,' complained the crook.

'Perhaps that's why they don't bother too much with alarms.'

Snare allowed twelve boxes to be opened before he said, 'Now 48.'

Obediently Johnny hunched over the container, probing and poking. As the lock clicked back, Snare announced, 'I'll do this one.'

Johnny stepped aside, frowning. Definitely unsure of himself, judged Johnny again. He'd built up a conviction about the other man's infallibility, like a child believing the perfection of a sand sculpture. Now the tide was coming in and Johnny didn't like to see his imagery crumbling.

Snare was standing up in front of the box, staring down fixedly at a single piece of paper he'd taken from the tray.

'Any good?' enquired Johnny.

The other man looked at him unseeingly.

'Any good?' repeated the safebreaker.

Snare blinked, like a man awakening.

'Let's get out,' he said.

Johnny stared at him, his own doubts hardening.

'But we've only just begun... there's dozens more... thousands of pounds...'

'Finished,' ruled Snare, abrupt now but completely recovered. 'We've got enough.'

He mirrored Johnny's look, challengingly.

The safebreaker moved from foot to foot, unsure whether to argue. Finally he spread his hands, overly dismissive.

'Whatever you say,' he agreed. Stupid to spoil the arrangement by appearing greedy. They still hadn't agreed a price with the insurers yet on the Russian stuff and he didn't want to risk that.

Snare went first through the hole, leading back into the antique shop.

'You know what?' said Johnny, trying to reduce the strain and at the same time build up the relationship he was sure he could establish.

'What?'

'I don't know where your information comes from,' said Johnny. 'Don't want to, not necessarily. But I don't reckon we can ever lose. No way.'

Snare's apprehensive anger at everything spilled over and he rounded on the safebreaker, face tight so that the scar was etched out vividly.

'Sometimes,' he said, 'you piss me off.'

'What?' tried Johnny, backing away from the assault.

'Because you're full of piss,' shouted Snare wildly, finding release in the role of the bully. 'Full of piss.'

'You're fucking mad,' said Johnny, trying to match the obscenity. 'Absolutely fucking mad.'

Snare stopped the attack, taking the other man's words. 'You could be right,' he said, quietly now. 'That's the trouble; you could well be right.'

'Wanker,' said Johnny, made miserable by the collapse of yet another relationship.

Charlie, to whom the isolation of detail was automatic, had recognised Snare from his walk the moment the man had left the car and made his way towards the rear of the antique shop. And there he was again, he saw, as Snare left the rear of the building and approached the carefully parked station wagon. Still the same shoulder-jogging lilt he'd had when he'd strode away in East Berlin, to set the tripwire for the ambush.

'Like a duck with a frozen bum,' Charlie told himself inside the darkened car. The cold had occupied Charlie's mind for the last two nights. It was going to be a bad winter, he had decided.

Unspeaking, the two men entered Snare's car. There was a momentary pause and in the darkness Charlie could see Snare putting on his safety belt. Probably too late for that, thought Charlie. Snare's presence had surprised him.

Snare started the car and moved away slowly and almost immediately Charlie pulled out, holding back until they came out alongside the Playboy Club and two cars had intruded themselves between him and the station wagon, a barrier of protection.

'As Wilberforce might say, the hunted becomes the hunter,' he muttered, trying to mock the man's speech. 'Now all you've got to do is to catch the bloody fox.'

'They've been very smart,' said Berenkov, admiringly.

'Yes,' agreed Kalenin. 'Very smart indeed.' He smiled across the table at Valentina. 'After meals like that, I know I'm a fool to have remained a bachelor,' he praised her.

The plump woman flushed at the compliment and continued clearing the table.

'What can you do?'

Kalenin jerked his shoulders.

'Nothing,' he said. 'To make anything more than diplomatic protests would show them we've discovered Charlie's association with one of the insurers and allow the satisfaction of knowing we won't be laughing at them any more.'

'They'll know that anyway,' argued Berenkov. 'That's what it's all about.'

'We still can't admit it,' said Kalenin.

'What about Charlie?'

Again the KGB chief moved uncertainly.

'Wouldn't it be marvellous if Charlie were to win?' suggested Berenkov, expansively.

'Marvellous,' agreed Kalenin, wondering at the amount of wine his friend had consumed. 'But quite unlikely.'

22.

Charlie drove quite relaxed, allowing another vehicle to come between him and the car he was pursuing, so that when it turned unexpectedly to go down Constitution Hill he was able to follow quite naturally, without any sudden braking which might have sounded to attract the attention of Snare.

Only after they had gone around the Victoria monument in front of Buckingham Palace did Charlie close up, not wanting to be left behind at the traffic lights in Parliament Square. The second set were red. Through the glass of the one separating car, Charlie could see Snare and the other man stiffly upright and apparently not talking.

'Always an unfriendly sod,' remembered Charlie.

They went across Westminster Bridge and entered the one-way system. The sudden turn beneath the railway arch, to go into Waterloo station, almost took Charlie by surprise. He only just managed to swerve without tyre squeal, continuing slowly up the long approach and trying to keep a taxi between them. He stopped before the corner, for more taxis to overtake and provide a barrier, so that when he drove into the better-lighted part of the concourse, Snare was already moving off.

Charlie didn't hurry, wanting to see the car to which the second man went. Parked as it was, the vehicle was obviously not stolen but belonged to him. So he could get the man's name from the registration.

He went slowly by, memorising the number as he passed, finally speeding up to get into position behind Snare again.

Snare was driving very precisely, Charlie saw, giving every signal and keeping within the speed limit. Rules and regulations, recalled Charlie, the dictum of Snare's life. Without guidelines to keep within and precedents to follow, Snare had always been uncomfortable. Robbing banks, an open criminal activity, would have been difficult for him, even with the back-up and assistance provided by the department. On the occasions when he'd had to do it himself, he'd rather enjoyed it, thought Charlie. It was like playing roulette and knowing the ball would always fall on your number. But Snare would have hated it. The word stayed in Charlie's mind; the emotion that would have provided the necessary incentive, he supposed.

'He really can't have liked me very much,' Charlie smiled to himself. The expression left his face. There couldn't have been anything very amusing about Snare's Moscow imprisonment, admitted Charlie. Immediately he balanced the self-criticism. Just as there wasn't anything amusing at being chosen for assassination at a border crossing; he had no reason to feel guilt over the man in front. Snare's inability to adjust to the unexpected intruded into his mind. It made the outcome of tonight's journey almost predictable, he thought; Snare was an advantage he hadn't expected.

They went around Parliament Square but Snare kept to the south side of Buckingham Palace this time, heading into Pimlico. Traffic thinned as they entered the residential area and Charlie pulled back, losing his cover.

He stopped completely when he saw the tail lights in front disappear to the left, into an enclosed square. He walked unhurriedly to the side road. The car was halfway along, neatly positioned in its residents' parking area, the permit prominently displayed. Snare was the sort of man to keep a cinema ticket in his pocket, in case he was challenged coming back from a pee during the interval, thought Charlie.

He waited until he saw the ground-floor lights go on, then returned to the car. He drove into the side road, but continued past Snare's home, going almost around the tiny park upon which the tall Regency buildings fronted. He stopped opposite Snare's house, but with the park between them, knowing he was completely concealed.

'How long?' wondered Charlie aloud.

It was nearly an hour. Charlie was beginning to fear he had miscalculated Snare's reaction when the light at which he was staring fixedly suddenly went out and then, seconds later, the door of the house opened. There was the delay while Snare fixed the safety belt and then the car moved off, circling behind to pass within feet of where Charlie waited. He gazed openly through the shaded glass, knowing he would be invisible to the other man. Snare drove bent slightly forward, away from the seat. His back would ache after long journeys, decided Charlie, allowing the man to turn out on to the main road before restarting the engine and pulling out to follow. Even in the darkened car, he had been able to see the scar disfiguring Snare's face. Charlie wondered how it had happened.

They went directly south, crossing the river over Chelsea Bridge and then, gradually, began taking the roads that would give them a route eastwards.

'So it *is* Wilberforce,' said Charlie. 'And he still lives at Tenterden.'

He had been to the man's country home once, Charlie remembered. It had been within a month of Cuthbertson's appointment and Wilberforce, asshole crawling as always, had thrown a party. His own role had been that of the jester, recalled Charlie, paraded as a reminder of the stupid anachronisms that Cuthbertson and his team of bright young university-educated, army-trained recruits were going to revitalise. He'd got drunk and told Wilberforce's wife an obscene story about a short-sighted showgirl and a donkey, expecting her to be shocked. Instead she had started to squeeze his hand and kept asking him to open bottles of a rather inferior Piesporter Goldtropfchen for her, in the kitchen. Should have given her a quick knee-trembler, over they draining board, decided Charlie, in belated regret. She'd worn corsets, though, with little dangly things to support her stockings. And Wilberforce had kept appearing, as if he'd realised the danger.

Even on an open road and as confused as Charlie expected him to be, Snare wasn't exceeding fifty miles an hour. A fact to remember, decided Charlie. Timing the other man was going to be important tonight.

Because Snare was establishing the speed, it took them almost two hours to reach the Kent village. Impatient now and quite sure of the other man's destination, Charlie didn't bother to see him actually enter the drive of Wilberforce's house.

Instead he made a wide loop at the crossroads, hurrying through the gears to pick up speed and rejoin the road to London.

Three hours to achieve what he wanted, Charlie estimated, smiling at the burbling of the widened exhaust. Sounded like Cuthbertson, he thought, just before one of those filthy coughs he was always making. Charlie laughed aloud, extending the thought.

Christ, how Cuthbertson would have choked if he had been in a position to know what was going to happen.

Ruttgers sprawled full length on the coverlet of the hotel bedroom, telephone cupped loosely to his ear, enjoying the admission from the man who had replaced him.

'Quite obvious,' Onslow Smith repeated. 'A meeting between them can be the only point.'

'And we're handling it this time,' Ruttgers reminded him. 'No more foul-ups by the British.'

He'd made a dirty mark on the counterpane, he saw; he should have taken his shoes off.

'I'm thinking of discussing the whole thing with the Secretary of State,' announced Smith.

'He won't like it.'

'He'll like it less if something happens and he's not been warned.'

'Why not wait? We could have the whole thing buttoned up in a day or two.'

'Maybe,' conceded Smith. Thank God he had his own people in Ruttger's support team, to warn him the moment there was any sign of Charlie Muffin. Increasingly Smith was coming to think that Ruttgers saw the whole thing as a personal vendetta, like some Western shoot-out at high noon. He suspected the man didn't give a damn about the Agency any more.

'I want you to be careful, Garson,' he warned. 'Very careful indeed.'

'I will be.'

It was too quick, judged Smith. Dismissive almost.

'I mean it,' insisted the Director. 'There must be no chance of our being identified.'

'Don't worry,' said Ruttgers.

'I *do* worry,' said Smith. 'This whole thing is coming unglued.'

'I'll keep in touch,' promised Ruttgers, swinging his legs off the bed to search for a replacement cigarette. 'Nothing will go wrong.'

'That's what Wilberforce was saying, a week ago.'

'What was in the private bank, by the way?' enquired Ruttgers, locating a fresh pack of cigarettes.

'Snare only went in tonight,' Smith replied. 'I haven't heard yet.'

Wilberforce's dressing gown was very long and full-skirted and made swishing sounds as he strode about the study. Snare sat uneasily on the edge of the chair by the desk, eager for some guidance from his superior.

'I thought you should see it, right away,' he said, almost in apology.

'Quite right,' said Wilberforce absently. 'Quite right.'

He paused before a small side table on which drinks were arranged, then appeared to change his mind, returning to the desk.

'What does it mean?' asked Snare.

Wilberforce picked up a piece of paper that Snare had taken from the Mayfair safe-deposit box and stared down at it, shaking his head.

'God knows,' he said. Concern was marked in his voice. He threw it aside, and Snare retrieved it, examining it with the same intensity as the other man. 'Clap hands, here comes Charlie,' he recited. He looked back to Wilberforce.

'It's like some sort of challenge, isn't it?' he said.

'Yes,' agreed Wilberforce miserably, 'it's a challenge.'

At that moment, fifty miles farther north, Charlie Muffin eased a plastic credit card through a basement window, prodded the catch up and two minutes later was standing in the darkened kitchen of Snare's Pimlico home. Funny, decided Charlie, after all that Snare had been up to in the last few weeks and there wasn't the slightest attempt at security in his own house. Still, he reflected, the attitude was typical. People always expected misfortune to occur to someone else, never themselves. Carefully he refastened the window and began walking towards the stairs leading upwards. He sniffed, appreciatively. Remains of the last meal still smelt good. Curry, he decided. He wouldn't have imagined Snare had had time to cook. Probably out of a packet. Remarkable, the value available in supermarkets these days.

23.

Charlie worked expertly and very quickly. He had been diligently trained by a housebreaker who earned the wartime amnesty for past misdeeds by being parachuted on three separate occasions into Nazi-occupied France and Holland and then stayed on Home Office attachment in peacetime, lecturing on the finer points of his craft to police forces throughout the country.

On the ground floor he moved immediately to the rear, where a door opened on to a small, paved patio and the darkened garden beyond. He opened it, testing to ensure it would not close by its own weight. Satisfied that he had an escape route if the need suddenly arose, he went back into the house, swiftly checking each room in turn, then slowly climbed the stairs, listening for any faint sound of occupation and more carefully now examined the bedrooms. Each was empty. From his examination of the outside, while he had been waiting for Snare earlier in the evening, he knew there was a third storey. He located the stairway at the back of the house and carried out the same precautions in the rooms there. Empty again.

'Charlie,' he said, 'the stars shine upon you.'

And it was about bloody time, he thought.

On the ground floor he began making a detailed search of every room. It was a neat, antiseptically clean house, the furniture and pictures and ornaments arranged more as if for a photograph in a good housekeeping magazine than for living amongst and enjoying. Making constant reference to the time and alert for any sound outside the house that might warn of Snare's return, Charlie still handled everything cautiously, returning every picture and the contents of every drawer or cupboard to exactly the position he had found it, so his entry would not be instantly apparent.

The study was at the back of the house, overlooking the patio, and Charlie checked all the pictures or wall-covering pieces of furniture intently, seeking the safe. After fifteen minutes, he perched contemplatively on the edge of the desk, frowning. Surely Snare would have a safe? Perhaps the stars weren't as bright as he had imagined. He re-checked, still found nothing, and even probed beneath the carpet, in case it were floor mounted.

Finally accepting there was no such installation in the room, Charlie turned to the desk. The working place of an orderly, rules-and-regulations man, Charlie decided. The bills in the top drawer were arranged and catalogued for dates of payment. Letters awaiting reply were in the drawer below, also catalogued, and those answered filed with their carbon copies in the one below that. The files were in the deepest shelf, at the very bottom. Charlie started expectantly, but immediately realised there were just household records; Snare actually kept a detailed account book for the car, he saw. Even the amount spent on petrol was carefully listed.

'Mean bugger,' judged Charlie.

He found the keys in the left-hand top drawer in which there was a partitioned shelf with small containers. Charlie stared down at them. A man as neat as Snare would arrange them in order of importance, he decided. There were duplicates of house, car and Automobile Association keys and in another tray were what appeared to be spare sets for luggage or a briefcase. That left four for which there was no obvious identification. They were in the first container.

Charlie quickly tried the remaining drawers, expecting to find at least one of them locked, but all opened smoothly to his touch.

Charlie left the room and started the search of the first floor. It was easier here, because there was less furniture. In two of the bedrooms, it was actually protected by dust-sheets. Snare's bedroom was as neat as the study, the shoes not only in racks but enclosed in tiny plastic bags and the clothes carefully arranged in a wardrobe like a colour chart, running from pale, summer-weight material through to the darker, heavier suits.

'Housemaster would be very proud of you,' said Charlie. He found the locked cupboard on the floor above and sighed, relieved. It was specially made, he saw, the doors flush and with two locks, top and bottom. He pulled at the handle. There was no movement. So it was rigid-frame, too. Probably steel.

It took less than a minute to return from the study with the unidentifiable keys. The second fitted the bottom lock and when he retried the first, the top clicked back into place.

Charlie edged away, pulling open the door, and then sighed in open astonishment.

'Oh, the fools,' he said. 'The bloody fools.'

The Fabergé collection was laid out almost as if for inspection, arranged on three shelves. On the floor beneath were the plastic bags in which Snare and Johnny had carried it from the gallery.

The whole point of the entry had been to find something – anything – with which he might have been able to incriminate Snare; a plan of the Brighton bank, for instance. Or maybe some connection with the Tate. But not this. Not the single most damning thing there could possibly be.

Of course the proceeds of the robbery could not have been openly taken into the department, accepted Charlie. But Snare should and could have made his own security arrangements; he'd been inside enough banks in the last month to be a bloody expert. His judgment of those who had taken over the department from Sir Archibald and even survived the Kalenin affair wasn't, as Edith suspected and of which she had accused him, the biased sniping of someone who had been dismissed as unnecessary, thought Charlie. They *were* amateurs, like the men who could not accept that Kim Philby was a spy because he'd been to the right school or that there was a risk in Guy Burgess, boozing and male-whoring in every embassy to which he'd been attached.

He packed the jewellery, relocked the cupboard and returned the keys to the desk. He spent fifteen minutes assuring himself that he had replaced everything in the position from which it had originally been moved, then a further ten in one of the spare, unused bedrooms.

Finally he went out the back door, quietly pulling it closed after him, climbed easily over the separating fence at the bottom of the garden and then out through the front gate of the neighbouring house on to the road parallel to that in which Snare lived.

The car was still warm from the drive back from Kent, he found, pausing gratefully before starting the engine.

'You're a lucky sod, Charlie,' he told himself.

'What about the safebreaker?' suggested Cuthbertson, matching everyone else's desperation. 'Perhaps he followed Snare home?'

Onslow Smith sighed at the confusion that had grown in Wilberforce's office since his entry.

'Oh come on!' he said, rejecting the idea. 'This is stupid, panic thinking.'

And there was damned good reason to panic, he thought. If he weren't very careful, this would make the Bay of Pigs and the Allende overthrow in Chile look like a training exercise for Boy Scouts. Which, upon examination, seemed about its right level.

'It's a possibility,' Cuthbertson said defensively, his thick voice showing he knew it was nothing of the sort.

The American picked up the note that had been taken from the Mayfair bank.

'That's rubbish and you know it,' he said, waving the paper towards the ex-Director. 'We've been suckered. Well and truly suckered.'

'Personal animosity isn't going to help,' said Wilberforce, trying to reduce the tension. It had been impossible to sleep after Snare's visit the previous night and the hollow feeling that had gouged out his stomach at the man's breakfast telephone call, reporting that the collection was missing, had developed into positive nausea. He'd even tried to be sick, thrusting his finger down his throat in the bathroom adjoining his office, and merely made himself feel worse.

'I don't know what will,' said Smith. 'I can't believe it. I just can't believe that you didn't take any precautions. Jesus!'

'Would you have stored it in the American embassy?' threw back Wilberforce.

'No,' admitted Smith immediately. 'I'd have certainly put it in Snare's house. And then I'd have made damned sure that there were so many people watching that house that a kitchen mouse couldn't have taken a pee without someone knowing it.'

He was going to get out, decided Smith, suddenly. He was going to withdraw all his men and get to hell out of it, before the smell really started to rise. From now on, Wilberforce was where he'd always wanted to be. On his own.

'I made a mistake,' conceded Wilberforce, reluctantly. 'I'm very sorry.'

The other Director looked crushed, thought Smith, without any pity.

'Does anyone in your government know what's been going on?' he asked.

'No,' said Wilberforce. 'And yours?'

'No.'

'It'll be a miracle if it remains a secret,' said Wilberforce.

'It is quite obvious that Charlie has taken it,' said Braley.

'To return to the insurers?' queried Cuthbertson.

Wilberforce nodded at the question. 'Equally obvious,' he said. 'It's the only way he could ensure that Rupert Willoughby wouldn't be damaged by association. Don't forget how close he was to Sir Archibald.'

Wilberforce laid aside his worry pipe, looking across the desk encouragingly.

'The Fabergé collection was always intended to be returned to the Russians, which is now what will undoubtedly happen. So the damage at the moment is still minimal.'

'But we don't know where the hell Charlie Muffin is,' said Snare.

'But we know *how* to re-locate him,' said Wilberforce. 'There's got to be some sort of pattern in the woman's tour. The moment there is any contact, we'll have him again.'

Smith decided he'd wait until he organised the removal of his own men before letting Wilberforce know what he was doing. Then the son of a bitch could do what he wanted about watching Edith.

'I'd like to think so,' said Snare. He felt revulsed that Charlie Muffin had entered his home and actually touched things that he owned. Quite often, he recalled, the man hadn't bathed every day.

'Where's the flaw?' demanded Wilberforce. No one guessed the depths of his uncertainty, he knew.

Smith shook his head at the other man's stupidity.

'The flaw,' he said, patiently, 'is what it's always been – Charlie Muffin.'

24.

Quite irrationally, which she even recognised but still could not prevent, Edith had developed a conviction that despite the lengthy list of cities and hotels that Charlie had given, he would have contacted her almost immediately. She'd actually invoked ridiculous, childlike rituals. If the waiter at dinner were Spanish, then Charlie would telephone before midnight. If the winter coldness broke, turning to rain, then that would be the day she would walk into the car park and find Charlie waiting for her.

The desperation had grown with each day until that morning, just before leaving her Cambridge hotel and starting the drive southward to Crawley, the next town designated, she had had to hold herself rigidly at the bedroom door, fighting against the overwhelming impulse to cry.

That it should happen there, today, was understandable, she supposed. She had read history at Girton and the memories had soaked through her. She had driven along the Huntingdon Road and gazed in, trying to locate her old room. And walked past King's Chapel, so that she could stand on the tiny, humped bridge to stare down into the icy water of the Backs, too cold even for the ducks, and remember the summer punting of so long ago. And smiled reminiscently at the couples, encompassed in their scarves and undergraduate romances, and envied them their happiness.

And now she was going back to Sussex, which she had already come to hate, even before Charlie had made the drunken mistake there that had begun all the agony. Then again, she thought, her mind slipping away on a familiar path, perhaps it was an omen; perhaps it would be here that it would end, where it had begun. That was it; had to be. Charlie would appear today, with the shy yet cocky I-told-you-so smile that always came when he'd proved himself right, and explain how he'd fooled everyone and they could clear out forever, burying themselves in Switzerland again.

She felt the panic building up and gripped the wheel. Just like the Spanish waiters and the weather, she thought, angrily. Damned ridiculous. Why couldn't she accept it? Charlie wouldn't come. Today. Or any other day. It would be a month of aimless journeyings to towns she didn't want to see until one day there would be a telephone call from Rupert Willoughby, a man she'd never met and probably never would, trying to infuse the proper melancholy into his voice to tell her that Charlie, who had forgotten to kiss her when he left that day in Zürich, hadn't been clever enough this time and was dead.

She pulled the car into a lay-by, trying to blink the emotion away. She had to stop it, she knew. She was collapsing under the weight of her own self-induced fear. And Charlie wanted her help, not her collapse. She found it so difficult.

Recovered, she felt her way back into the traffic and reached the timbered George Hotel just before lunch. Despite the determination in the lay-by, she still searched hopefully around the car park as she pulled in, then again in the foyer as she registered. With difficulty, she focused on the receptionist, realising the girl was repeating a question.

'I wondered if you would want lunch?'

'No,' said Edith, too sharply. 'No thank you,' she repeated, embarrassed at her own rudeness.

'Is anything the matter, madam?'

'Long drive,' stumbled Edith. 'Rather tired.'

She didn't bother to unpack the suitcases. Instead she stood at the window of her room, staring down unseeingly into Crawley High Street.

'Hurry up, Charlie,' she said softly. 'I need you so very much.'

In the lobby below, the polite receptionist was dealing with an unexpected influx of guests. It was fortunate, she thought, that it was so early in the season, otherwise she would have had difficulty in finding accommodation for them all. There were no wives, so it must be a business conference, she decided. Unusual that she hadn't heard about it. Probably in Brighton.

And in that town, just twenty miles to the south, Superintendent Law was summoning the sergeant for the second conference of the day.

'Well?' demanded the superintendent.

Hardiman shook his head, indicating the files banked up against the wall.

'Still got about twenty more statements to repeat,' he said. 'But so far there's nothing.'

'It must be there somewhere,' said Law, refusing to admit his idea was wrong.

Then you're the best bugger to find it, thought the sergeant.

'Odd overnight report,' he said, trying to move the superintendent past his fixation with the statements.

'What?'

'You know we asked the uniformed branch to keep an eye on that financier's house?'

Law nodded.

'Copper on last night hadn't done it before,' continued Hardiman. 'Got the impression that there was some sort of separate observation being carried out... mentioned it to his superintendent in case there had been some confusion and we were duplicating...'

'What about the other policemen, before him?' demanded Law instantly.

'I've checked,' said the sergeant, glad he'd anticipated the request. 'Two others got the same impression. Didn't mention it because they thought we *were* doubling up.'

'Stupid bastards,' said Law. 'Have we interviewed him again?'

Hardiman shook his head.

'Away on business,' he reminded him. 'Took the trouble to telephone us.'

He picked up Charlie's file and the superintendent took it from him, staring down as if he expected a clue he hadn't appreciated from the statement suddenly to present itself.

'It's not much,' said the sergeant, concerned at the other man's interest. He hoped Law wouldn't get too worked up. The constable's report hadn't been made overnight. It had been lying around for two days, but Hardiman had forgotten to mention it.

'Willoughby, Price and Rowledge,' Law read from the file.

'They've confirmed his association with them,' said Hardiman. 'Shall I contact them again?'

Hurriedly Law shook his head.

'Mustn't frighten the rabbit,' he said.

'What then?' asked Hardiman. It was almost impossible to guess which way the superintendent's mind would jump, he thought, annoyed.

'Let's try to find out a bit more about him first,' suggested Law. He paused and the sergeant waited, knowing he hadn't finished.

'Remember what he said that first night, when we went to his house?' prompted Law.

Hardiman looked doubtful.

'Made some remark about being a financier, even though his passport described him as a clerk.'

'Why should that be odd?' asked Hardiman.

'I don't know, laddie. I don't know,' said the superintendent, patronisingly. 'Why don't we check the passport office, to discover if it is?'

Why did Law have to conduct everything like it was a sodding quiz game? wondered Hardiman, walking towards his own office. Sometimes the man really pissed him off.

Involvement had been thrust upon Willoughby and Charlie had anticipated the reluctance that was becoming obvious. He hadn't expected the underwriter's argument against the stupidity of vindictiveness. That had surprised him.

To Willoughby, of course, the two were so interlinked as to be practically the same. But to Charlie, they were quite separate. To beat them, as he knew he now had, as well as surviving, had more than justified any risk. And there hadn't been any; not much, anyway. Almost like rigged roulette, again. Now it was over. And he'd got away with it.

Momentarily he looked away from his search for the turning off Wimbledon Hill Road that Willoughby had named during their argumentative conversation, checking the time. Almost midnight; everything would have happened by this time tomorrow, he thought.

He'd been very fortunate, Charlie thought. The confidence bubbled up. But he'd been clever enough to seize that good fortune and utilise it. Christ, how he'd utilised it.

Despite the force of a Lloyd's insurers behind it, he had still been surprised at the speed with which Willoughby had obtained John Packer's address from the car registration. The house was at the bottom of a cul-de-sac, a horseshoe indentation between two major roads. Charlie didn't stop, driving out on to the avenue that backed on to Packer's property, counting along until he isolated the house between him and the one he was seeking. He parked the car, entered through a tree-lined drive, skirted the darkened building and then smiled, with growing awareness, at the lowness of the fence between it and Packer's home. The separation between the other adjoining property, from which it would be possible to reach the alternative main road, would be similarly low, he guessed.

Charlie realised almost immediately that he would not be able easily to enter the house. Inside each of the lower windows there was actually a reinforced mesh clamped into a separate frame to form a positive barrier, in addition to the special window locks and the small steel bolts that had been fitted in each corner. With such precautions, it was pointless trying the doors, Charlie decided.

'Pity a few other people hadn't been as cautious as you, Mr Packer,' muttered Charlie.

At first Charlie thought the shed might have been built over an old coal-chute, by which he might still have been able to get in, through the cellar. Obedient to his training, he remained unmoving immediately inside the door, first feeling out for any obstruction and then, careful to avoid the reflection showing through the side windows, probing with the pencil-beam torch.

It wasn't until he'd shifted the sodium chlorate aside, thinking first of its gardening use, and discovered what lay behind that he appreciated its proper significance, squatting before it and all the other explosives, then moving up to the shelves to feel through the detonators and fuses and finally examining the box containing the timing and pressure devices. There were even clocks, to activate them.

'A regular little bomb factory,' mused Charlie. 'So you're the professional, Mr Packer? The one who's necessary to make it look right.'

It was the confirmation of the impression that had come to him climbing over the garden fence; the house was ideally positioned, with three easy escape routes against arrest.

Charlie extinguished the torch, re-locked the outhouse and left the garden by the route he had entered. The man had been manipulated enough, he decided.

25.

The arrests on the day that George Wilberforce was later to regard as the worst in his life should have been perfectly coordinated, but inevitably there was a mistake. The information had identified the Kent house and the assumption of the Flying Squad and the Regional Crime Squad was that Wilberforce would be there as well. But it was a weekday and so he was staying in the Eaton Square apartment.

The superintendent who had liaised between the two forces and organised the raid went with just two cars to London, leaving the main police contingent at Tenterden, with instructions to the women police officers that the woman bordering on hysteria should in no circumstances be allowed near a telephone.

During the drive through the early morning traffic they heard by radio that the seizure of Brian Snare had gone perfectly. The man had answered the door in his dressing gown, eyes widening in surprise at the number of police cars effectively sealing the Pimlico square, and was still spluttering his protests when they had found some jewelled eggs and the orb from the Fabergé collection hidden in the spare bedroom of the house.

Wilberforce was dressed when the squad arrived and his reaction was more controlled than they had expected. They refused his demand to use a telephone and when he had tried to insist upon his legal rights, an inspector said 'Bollocks' and the superintendent nodded in agreement.

They had left London before Wilberforce spoke again.

'This is a very big mistake,' he said.

The superintendent sighed. 'I'd like ten pounds for every time I've been told that as I've got my hand on a collar,' he said. He spoke across Wilberforce, as though the man were quite unimportant.

'Me too,' said the inspector.

'I'll want your names,' blustered Wilberforce.

'Here we go,' said the inspector. 'Bet he knows the commander.'

'I do,' insisted Wilberforce.

'The names,' said the superintendent, bored with the familiar charade, 'are Superintendent Hebson and Inspector Burt. We do have warrant cards, if you'd care to see them.'

'I shall hold you personally responsible if the men you've left behind at my flat cause any damage,' said Wilberforce.

'Of course,' agreed the superintendent. He was staring through the window, appearing more interested in the countryside.

'I'm still waiting for a satisfactory explanation,' said Wilberforce.

The superintendent remained gazing out of the window, so Inspector Burt turned, smiling over the back of the seat

'We have reason to believe that you might have information to help us in our enquiries into the theft of the Fabergé collection which was on show at the Tate,' he said formally.

'Oh, my God,' said Wilberforce.

Hebson turned back into the car at the remark.

'And it's still a big mistake, is it?' he said sarcastically.

'You don't understand,' said Wilberforce.

'Perhaps you'd like to explain it to me.'

The Director shook his head.

'You can't know,' he said, his voice still clouded. 'Oh, my God!'

The two policemen exchanged looks.

'We're going to, eventually,' Hebson assured him. Again Wilberforce shook his head, but this time he turned to the policeman, struggling to compose himself.

'There must be no announcement about the recovery,' he said urgently. He gestured to the front of the car. 'Get on to the radio and say you want a complete publicity blackout.'

'There's to be no announcement, until we're sure we've got everything nicely stitched up,' guaranteed the superintendent, intrigued by the man's demeanour.

'Repeat it,' urged Wilberforce, reaching out and seizing the man's arm in his anxiety. 'I insist that you do.'

'At the moment,' Hebson reminded him, 'you're not in a position to insist upon anything, Mr Wilberforce.'

The policeman had allowed Wilberforce's wife to dress but she hadn't applied any make-up. She giggled when she saw her husband enter between the two officers, looking at him hopefully.

'What is it, George?' she demanded, shrilly. 'Where did all that jewellery come from?'

Hebson looked enquiringly at the inspector he had left in charge of the Tenterden house.

'In the cellar, sir,' reported the inspector. He nodded towards Wilberforce's wife. 'Says she knows nothing about it.'

'Where?' asked Wilberforce, dully.

He had expected the inspector to answer, but instead his wife replied, giggling as if inviting him to be as amused as she was.

'I'd even forgotten we had it,' she said. 'Do you remember that rather cheap Piesporter Geldtropfchen we got... must be years ago. It was behind there.'

'Shall we see?' invited Hebson.

Wilberforce led the way, shoulders sagged at the complete acceptance of what had happened At the bottom of the cellar steps he stopped, uncertainly, so it was his wife who guided the party the last few yards towards an archway at the rear of the dank-smelling basement.

'There!' she announced. In her bewilderment she sounded proud.

The collection had been taken out of the plastic containers and laid out, almost for inspection. In the dull light from the unshaded bulbs, the diamonds, rubies and pearls glittered up, like the bright eyes of limp, unmoving animals.

The woman sniggered.

'Look,' she said, to her husband. 'Look at the way the long coach of that train has been arranged between those two Easter eggs...'

The laughter became more nervous.

'...it looks like... well, it's positively rude...'

Hebson looked painfully to the back of the group, to a policewoman. 'I think we're going to need a doctor soon,' he warned. He came back to Wilberforce. 'Well sir?' he said.

Wilberforce turned abruptly, trying to regain some command. He pointed to Hebson and Burt.

'My study,' he said.

He walked hurriedly back to the cellar steps, leaving his wife to the care of the policewoman.

'No doubt,' said Wilberforce, when the three of them had entered the room off the main hallway, 'you found similar jewellery in the home of a man called Brian Snare!'

'We did,' said Hebson, imagining the beginning of a confession.

'The bastard,' said Wilberforce, softly.

'Sir?' said Burt. He'd taken a notebook from his pocket. Wilberforce straightened, fingers against the desk. Instinctively, he groped out, picking up a pipe but when he felt into his waistcoat he discovered that in the flurry from the Eaton Square apartment, he'd forgotten to take the tiny container of tools from the dressing table. He stared down at the pipe, as if it were important, then sadly replaced it in the rack.

'My name,' he announced, looking back to the men, 'is George Wilberforce...'

'We know that, sir,' said Hebson.

'And I am the Director of British Intelligence,' Wilberforce completed.

The confidence fell away from the two detectives like wind suddenly emptying from a sail.

'Oh,' said Hebson.

Wilberforce jerked his head towards the telephone.

'Call your commander,' he instructed. He took an address book from a desk drawer, selected a page and then offered it to the superintendent. 'And then the Prime Minister's office,' he added. 'That's the private number which will get you by the Downing Street exchange. I want his Personal Private Secretary, no one else.'

Hebson hesitated, finally taking the book. He began moving towards the telephone, but then turned to the inspector.

'Get on to one of the radios,' he ordered, indicating the driveway outside. 'For Christ's sake screw the lid on this.'

Burt began moving.

'...and make sure we get a doctor for poor Mrs Wilberforce,' Hebson shouted after him.

The meeting with the Prime Minister took place the same day. It was originally scheduled for the afternoon, but Smallwood postponed it twice, first for assurances from the Chief Constable of Kent and the Metropolitan Police Commissioner that the information could be suppressed and then because of an interview which the Russian ambassador suddenly requested with the Foreign Secretary. It was not until late into the evening that Wilberforce was finally shown into the study overlooking St James's Park. Smallwood sat behind the desk, stiff formality concealing his apprehension, well trained in the brutality of politics and moving quite calculatingly.

'There seems little point in saying how sorry I am,' said Wilberforce.

'None,' agreed the Premier.

'There were some miscalculations,' admitted the Director.

'About which I do not want to hear,' cut in Smallwood. 'You've been made to look ridiculous... utterly ridiculous.'

'I realise that,' said Wilberforce.

'Over fifty policemen were involved in the raids upon you and that other damned man. Fifty policemen! Can you imagine that we're going to be able to stop something like this leaking out, with that many mouths involved?'

'We've still got the chance of locating him,' said Wilberforce, unthinkingly. 'The man responsible, I mean.'

'Mr Wilberforce,' said Smallwood, leaning forward on the desk and spacing the words for effect. 'I don't think you fully understand me. Or the point of this meeting. From this moment... right at this moment... the whole preposterous matter is concluded. There is to be no further action whatsoever. By anyone. Is that clear?'

The Director did not reply immediately and Smallwood thought he was going to argue.

At last he said: 'Quite clear.'

'Nothing,' reiterated Smallwood. 'By anyone.'

'I see,' Wilberforce answered.

Silence came down like a partition between them.

'No,' said the Prime Minister. 'I still don't think you do.'

'Sir?' enquired Wilberforce.

Smallwood looked expectantly at him.

'Don't you have something to say to me?' he encouraged.

'Say to...' started Wilberforce and then stopped, swallowing.

'Oh,' he said, comprehending.

'There can be no other course, surely?' said Smallwood. He wanted a scapegoat trussed and oven-ready. Several, in fact.

'I wish to offer my resignation,' said Wilberforce. He spoke mechanically, as if he were reading the words from a prepared speech. His hands moved, anxious for activity. He clasped them tightly in his lap.

'Thank you,' bustled the Premier. 'I accept. With regret, of course.'

'Of course.'

'It will have to be in writing,' said Smallwood.

'You'll have it by noon tomorrow,' promised Wilberforce.

'I'd like it earlier,' said Smallwood. 'Tonight'

'But that's...' Wilberforce began to protest, then saw the paper that the other man was offering. He scrawled his signature at the bottom of the already typed letter, not bothering to read it.

'Goodbye, Prime Minister,' said Wilberforce, striving for dignity.

'Goodbye,' said Smallwood.

He suddenly became occupied with some document on his desk and did not bother to look up as the man left the room.

'Every piece?' enquired Berenkov.

'Everything,' said Kalenin. 'All returned.'

The burly, white-haired Russian stood up and went to the window of Kalenin's office. The central heating was keeping the windows free from ice, but the snow was pouched on the roof-tops, like dirty white caps.

'That would mean they've finished with Charlie, then?'

'Yes,' agreed the KGB officer.

'There haven't been any more leaks?'

'Not yet.'

'There would have been, surely?' said Berenkov, hopefully.

'Alexei,' said Kalenin, kindly. 'He *must* be dead.'

'Yes,' Berenkov agreed. 'He must be.' He turned into the room. 'At least the agony will be over for him,' he said.

26.

Before assuming overall command of the Agency, Onslow Smith had been administrative director and it was with organisation that he felt happiest. He worked quickly and incisively in the room that had been set aside for him in the American embassy, the master set of papers immediately before him and the subsidiary files in an orderly arrangement at the top of the desk. Braley had arranged it all and done it well, considered Smith. If he could, he'd salvage Braley, he decided. He'd just have to be circumspect about it. And that was exactly what he was going to be about everything, thought Smith. Circumspect. Within twenty-four hours, every single operative involved in the Charlie Muffin fiasco would have been safely airlifted back to the protective anonymity of the CIA headquarters in Virginia.

He looked up from the papers, stopped by a thought. And not one of them compromised. He looked back at the list of names before him, frowning at the number of operatives. All those men operating in the field, he thought. Damned near a miracle, he accepted. He extended the reflection, leaning back in his chair. One lucky; another one unlucky. Poor Wilberforce. He'd been so sure of himself.

And in the beginning, the idea had looked pretty good, conceded the American honestly. Dangerous, but still good. They'd just underestimated the victim.

He reached out, pulling a file nearer and then opened it at a picture of Charlie Muffin. He stared down at the image, running his finger along the edge of the photograph. Once, he remembered, the idea had been half-formed in his mind that perhaps he might possibly meet the man who had caused so much damage. But now it would never happen; Charlie would always remain a slightly out of focus impression and a bad memory. A very bad memory.

The telephone jarred into the room. The American Air Force transporter had arrived at London airport from Mildenhall; as they were being processed under diplomatic passports, bypassing completely the main passenger section and all the usual formalities, departure for Washington was scheduled within three hours.

Smith sighed, replacing the receiver. With a flourish betraying his rising confidence, he drew a line through the main list of operatives. Perfect, he decided. Like everything he organised.

Smith watched the seconds flicker by on the digital clock on the desk, waiting for ten o'clock to register. When it did, he put another line through the team that had been operating Zürich. Because there were only five men, he'd felt it safe for them to fly direct from Switzerland to America on a scheduled flight: it was leaving on time, he knew from the confirmation he'd already received. So, too, were the couriers he had sent by road to ensure the withdrawal from the Brighton house and the Crawley hotel.

Charlie, who had been watching the George since just after dawn and had actually caught sight of Edith's drawn, unsmiling face through the breakfast room window, saw the messenger arrive and the trained attention to detail marked the significance.

'How many Ivy League suits are there in Crawley at this time of the year?' Charlie asked himself.

Quite a few, he thought, watching the sudden exodus of men. The newcomer urged them into various cars, then pushed towards the driver of each an apparent written sheet of instructions. The newcomer left first, heading north. The other cars followed at five-minute intervals, to avoid attracting attention. Charlie waited until the last vehicle pulled out and then started his own engine.

'Better make sure,' he advised himself.

Once clear of the town, the cars had slowed, so by the time they reached the motorway, they were travelling in loose convoy. Charlie kept them comfortably in sight, glad of the flow of traffic he knew would conceal his pursuit.

It was not until they had continued past Gatwick airport, but then looped off, on to the Leatherhead road, to avoid the congestion of

London to join the M4, that Charlie realised they were heading for London airport, not the city. So the clothes *had* identified them as Americans. It had been a joint operation, he guessed, an operation being abandoned with all the panic that Willoughby had inferred at the strained meeting between the Russians and the government officials when the Fabergé collection had been returned. Now it was all over, the underwriter's attitude was changing again to friendship, he reflected.

Because of the increased volume of cars as they neared London airport, Charlie had to move closer than he really wanted, but it meant he was close enough not to be confused when, instead of becoming part of the crocodile slowly funnelling beneath the tunnel into the airport complex, the cavalcade swung off the roundabout and picked up one of the roads skirting the airport.

In a greater hurry than he had imagined, decided Charlie, slowing in recognition. They were going towards the north side of the airport, to the private section. The arrival had obviously been communicated ahead by radio in one of the cars. From the buildings swarmed not only airport security men, but American marines as well. They patterned out, sealing the area for a radius of three hundred yards.

Charlie pulled quickly into a car park reserved for the airport staff, then got out of the car, straining to focus the aircraft in the distance. He got final confirmation of the thoughts that had begun when he had seen the men move out of the hotel from the US military plane drawn up close to one of the VIP buildings, its dirty-khaki colouring merging with the surroundings.

He saw the cars stop and the occupants start to emerge, filing into one of the buildings. American military staff began loading the baggage directly into the aircraft hold.

'Complete diplomatic clearance,' mused Charlie, then stopped, identifying the figure in apparent command of the aircraft boarding.

So William Braley had been involved, as well as Snare. He smiled at the realisation; everyone who had had reason to hate him most. Good motivation, Charlie accepted.

He'd admired Braley, Charlie remembered. A complete and thorough professional. He was one of the people about whom Charlie felt most regret at what had happened in Vienna.

He sighed. A necessary casualty of survival, he decided. But still sad.

He got back into the mini and started back towards the roundabout from which he could rejoin the motorway.

'You did it, Charlie,' he congratulated himself. 'You beat them.'

Superintendent Law would seize the credit, realised Hardiman. And it had really been his idea. But when the time came for the commendations and the celebration drinks, the poor sod who'd had all the work would be forgotten.

Law looked up enquiringly as the sergeant entered the room.

'Well?' he asked.

Hardiman smiled down at the seated man.

'Remember you told me to check that financier's passport?'

'Of course.'

'Nothing wrong with it... at first glance.'

'Then what?'

'So I looked further. Checked out the birth certificate, with government records...'

Law began to smile, in anticipation.

'According to them, no such person exists,' concluded the sergeant. 'So I put the certificate through to forensic. It's a forgery.'

'Well done, laddie,' praised the superintendent. 'Well done.'

He stood up, taking Charlie's file from those stacked against the wall.

'Routine,' he said softly. 'That's what does it, every time.'

It had taken long enough, thought Hardiman.

'Still not back at the house yet?' Law enquired, expectantly.

'Not yet.'

Law frowned at a sudden thought.

'What about that report from uniformed, their belief there was some sort of observation?'

'Checked on my way here,' said Hardiman. 'Not there any more.'

'Which leaves us with the London firm of underwriters,' said Law. 'I think it's time we checked to see how deeply they investigate their people.'

Onslow Smith looked down contentedly at the file lying before him. Through everything now there was a curt red ink mark: every entry erased. He deserved the comfort of the separate military aircraft that he had arranged for himself he decided. And it would have been quite wrong anyway to have travelled back with the rest of the team.

He put the documents into the briefcase with the combination lock and placed it alongside the other sealed file holders that would all be taken by courier to the airport for transportation back to America and then oblivion in the CIA archives. In a separate container was the money Wilberforce had insisted on returning. The money would probably upset their computer, he thought; it had already been written off. Just like Wilberforce. Poor bugger.

The telephone surprised him and he stared at it, hesitating before lifting the receiver. He smiled, immediately recognising Braley's voice.

'All aboard?' enquired Smith, cheerily.

'Not quite,' said the man and for the first time Smith realised the apprehension from the other end.

'What do you mean, not quite?'

'I'm sorry I've left it so late,' said Braley. 'I wanted to be sure, so I carried out a complete check…'

'For Christ's sake, what is it?' demanded Smith.

'Ruttgers isn't here.'

27.

Edith opened the door without interest, looking dully out into the corridor. Then she saw Charlie and started back. She couldn't make the words and so she just stood there, shaking her head in disbelief.

'Hello,' he said.

'Oh, Charlie… Charlie,' she said and all the feelings of the previous days overflowed and she burst into tears.

He came into the room, holding his arms out to her and she clung to him so desperately that he could feel her fingers bruising into his back. He held her as tightly, stroking her hair and her shoulders, trying to calm her, but she couldn't stop, huge sobs racking through her.

Her face muffled into his shoulder, she just kept repeating 'Charlie, oh, Charlie' and he felt her groping at him, needing the physical reassurance of his body.

'It's all right, Edith,' he said, soothingly. 'It's over. All over.'

She wept on and Charlie let her cry, knowing she had to wash the fear and anxiety out of herself. She'd suffered far more than he had, he realised. But he'd make her forget, eventually. Certainly she'd never suffer again, he determined. Never.

Gently he moved her sideways, so they could both sit on the edge of the bed. The crying was becoming less hysterical, he recognised.

'Over, Edith,' he repeated. 'All over.'

It still seemed a long time before she had recovered sufficiently to pull away from him. Her eyes were red and sore and her nose had run. Lovingly, he dried her face. The breath was still jumping unevenly through her, so that her shoulders kept shaking.

'Please kiss me,' she said.

Gently he leaned forward, putting his lips to hers, but when she tried to pull close to him, dragging his mouth towards her in a sudden frenzy, her breath caught again and she had to jerk away, gasping a mixture of laughter and fresh tears.

He put his hands out, holding her face, so she wouldn't collapse.

'Stop it,' he said curtly. 'Stop it, Edith.'

She bit against the emotion, lips tightly closed.

'I'm all right now,' she said, after a while. Still he held her, bringing her forward and lightly kissing her forehead.

'I love you, Edith,' he said.

She smiled up at him, remembering the promise.

'I was so frightened, Charlie,' she said. 'I thought I'd lost you.'

He shook his head.

'They made too many mistakes,' he said.

'You were lucky.'

'Yes,' he agreed seriously. 'They reacted exactly as I thought they would.'

'Let's hide somewhere, Charlie. Somewhere they will never find us.'

'We'll hide,' he said. 'They'll never get this close again.'

'Charlie.'

'What?'

'Make love to me, Charlie. It's been so long.'

Her breath didn't catch and they kissed open-mouthed, trying at the same time to pull the clothes away from each other in urgent tugging movements. They couldn't do it, so they patted briefly, clawing the covering away and then snatched, one for the other, falling back on to the dishevelled bed. The fear that Charlie had kept so tightly controlled surged through him, so that he shuddered as deeply as Edith had done when she'd first seen him and he clung desperately to her, needing the comfort of her body that she'd felt for his earlier. But not sexually, he realised, in sudden, horrified awareness. He crouched over her, flaccid and unresponsive, head buried into her shoulder.

'I *want* to, Edith. I really want to.'

'It doesn't matter.'

'Help me to do it.'

'It won't work, Charlie. Not now.'

'Please.'

'Later, Charlie. It will be better later.'

He toppled sideways, head still into her shoulder so that he couldn't look at her.

'Oh, God, I'm sorry,' he said.

She lay, gently stroking his back. Conscious of how cold he was, she tugged the blanket over them. Because of the confused way they were lying, their legs protruded from the bottom.

'I'm glad,' she said.

He pulled slightly away, still not looking at her.

'Glad?' he said.

'Glad to know you were as scared as me.'

He burrowed into the blanket.

'I was scared,' he admitted, quietly. 'Very scared.'

'And now it's over. For both of us,' she reminded him.

He laughed, an uncertain sound.

'What?' she asked.

'It was supposed to be me, comforting you,' he said.

She pulled his head closer to her, so that his lips were near her breast.

'We need each other very much, don't we, Charlie?' she said, happily.

'Yes,' he said.

'I'm glad you love me, Charlie.'

'Even though I can't prove it?'

'Don't be silly.'

It was growing warm beneath the blanket, 'Your trousers are puddled on the floor,' she said. 'They're going to be very creased.'

'They usually are,' he said, sleepily.

'Yes,' she remembered, 'they usually are. Don't ever alter, will you, Charlie?'

He grunted and she felt his breath deepening against her.

'I love you so much,' she said softly, knowing he couldn't hear her. 'I love you so much.'

She trailed a finger over his cheek, smiling as he twitched at the irritation. It was so good to have him back, she thought. Completely.

It was an hour before he awakened and because he was clinging to her she felt the momentary tightening of his body, until the awareness of where he was registered.

'Hello again,' he said, relaxing.

'Hello.'

'Forgiven me?'

'I told you not to be silly.'

He pulled himself close to the warmth of her body.

'It's good to be with you,' he said.

'Don't ever go away again?'

'Never,' he said.

'Can we leave, straightaway?'

He shook his head.

'Get dressed and while we have a celebration meal I'll tell you what else has to be done.'

'Shall we eat here?'

'Too early,' he decided. 'Let's drive somewhere and then take pot luck.'

'All right,' she agreed immediately. He was like a schoolboy on the first day of a summer vacation with a five-pound note in his pocket, she thought, rising from the bed and spreading the blanket more fully over him. She knew he was watching her through the bathroom door and turned, smiling.

'You're beautiful, Edith,' he said.

She grew serious, coming to the linking door.

'It is going to be all right, from now on, isn't it, Charlie? No more mistakes... no more running?'

'No more mistakes,' he guaranteed.

'I don't think I could go through it again,' she said gravely.

'I promise.'

As if suddenly reminded, Edith stopped, towel in hand, by a travelling bag. It was a large, soft leather case with a shoulder strap and sufficient space to carry anything a person might need on a long journey.

'You'd better have these,' she said, passing over the passports she had drawn from the Zürich bank.

She looked at him expectantly, but Charlie just leaned across the bed, putting them into his jacket pocket. Any conversation about new identities would only rekindle her fear, he decided.

'Hurry,' he urged her. 'It's going to be a great evening.'

Because the car was pointing in that direction, Charlie drove westwards.

'You know,' said Edith, 'for the first time in weeks I feel safe.'

She reached across the tiny car, squeezing his hand.

'So do I,' said Charlie.

It was an hour after they had left that Braley and the American team despatched by Onslow Smith arrived at the hotel, seeking Ruttgers. The man was still registered, agreed the receptionist. But he'd left the hotel. About an hour before. Why didn't they wait?

Superintendent Law and the sergeant had risen to go, pausing in the hallway of Willoughby's apartment.

'It was good of you to see us at home, sir,' said the superintendent.

'You said it was urgent,' Willoughby reminded them.

'And you've no idea why there should be this strange business about the passport?'

Willoughby spread his hands at the question that had been asked already. He was beginning to perspire, he knew.

'Absolutely none,' he said. 'We don't actually check on a person's birth certificate when they become associated with us.'

'Perhaps you should, sir,' said Law. 'You couldn't suggest where we might locate him?'

Again the underwriter made the gesture of helplessness. Another repeated question.

'There was an address abroad... Switzerland...'

'The Zürich police have already checked, on our behalf,' said Hardiman. 'There hasn't been anyone at the apartment for several days.'

'Then sorry, no,' said Willoughby. So far, he knew he'd kept the concern from his voice. But it was becoming increasingly difficult.

'You will tell us, the moment there is any contact, won't you?' said Law.

'Of course,' Willoughby agreed. 'And I'd appreciate any news that you might get. I don't like the thought of my being involved in something that could be questionable.'

'We will,' said Law, finally opening the door. He paused, looking back at the underwriter.

'The *moment* there is any contact,' he reiterated.

'I understand,' said Willoughby.

'Well?' demanded the superintendent, as they settled into the back of the car that had brought them from Brighton.

'I don't know,' said Hardiman, reflectively. 'According to the checks we asked the Fraud Squad to make, the firm is so straight you could draw lines by it.'

Law nodded.

'Exactly the sort of screen you'd try to hide behind if you were a villain,' said Law.

'Exactly,' agreed Hardiman. 'But without the principals being aware of it.'

'So we're not much farther forward,' said the superintendent. 'What are we going to do?'

Law considered the question.

'Request a meeting with the Chief Constable and if he's agreeable, tomorrow call as big a press conference as possible and name our mystery man as someone to help in our inquiries. It will be the only way to bring him out.'

'The only way,' concurred Hardiman, dutifully.

John Packer was always ready to move at short notice; regarded it as part of being a professional. He'd been late learning of the Fabergé recovery, getting the first hint from a newspaper poster about a jewel haul and then confirming it from the car radio.

He'd approached the house cautiously, alert for any signs that the police were waiting for him. Satisfied, he hadn't bothered to turn off the ignition while he collected his share of the Brighton and Mayfair bank robbery money from the concealed floor-mounted safe in the basement and packed a case.

He'd go north, he decided. He wasn't known in Manchester and it was a big enough place in which to get lost. He was surprised that none of the reports had referred to arrests; he'd have to watch the newspapers closely for the next few days, to establish if he were safe, before attempting a quick flight to the Continent. Amsterdam, he decided. Nice people in Amsterdam.

What had happened to the man with the star-shaped scar? he wondered. He *must* have been nicked. Pity. He'd been bloody good. Odd. But still good.

28.

The meal had been unexciting, but neither Charlie nor Edith had noticed. There had been long periods without conversation, when they'd just stared at each other and twice, aware of the waiter's amused attention, Edith had looked away embarrassed, telling Charlie to stop.

There was still wine left in the half-bottle that he had ordered as the meal began and when the waiter enquired about brandy with the coffee, Charlie refused.

Edith smiled, gratefully.

'Seems like everything has turned out all right,' she said.

'Yes,' agreed Charlie, holding the glass in front of him. 'That's over too.'

'You are sure, aren't you, Charlie?' she asked, expanding the question with sudden urgency. 'Nothing can go wrong now, can it?'

Charlie reached across, squeezing her hand. She was still frightened, he decided, remembering the doubt with which she had given him the passports at the hotel.

'Willoughby's firm was one of the major Lloyd's insurers,' he said. 'So he was able to be present when the collection was returned to the Russians... to ask questions without the interest appearing strange. He's never known such official embarrassment.'

'But...?' she started.

'And I personally saw the surveillance lifted from you.'

She gazed at him, coffee suspended before her.

'What?' she said. Her voice was hollowed out with nervousness.

'There was a team of men assigned to you,' he said gently. 'American. I followed them back to the airport.... they'll be gone by now.'

'I never knew.'

'You weren't supposed to.'

Edith shivered.

'Let's get away from here, Charlie.'

'There's still the Brighton robbery,' he said, calmly. 'And Mayfair, too, although I'm not linked with that as far as the police are concerned.'

'What does that mean?'

'That we can't get out, not immediately. I know who did them, apart from Snare. We can leak the man's name to the police through Willoughby's insurance outlets, like we did that of Wilberforce and Snare with the Fabergé collection.'

'It won't be long, will it, Charlie?'

'Just days, that's all,' he said. 'A week at the most.'

'Then what?'

'Anywhere you choose,' he said. He put the wine glass down, feeling for her hand again.

'Let's go home to bed,' he said.

She answered the pressure of his fingers.

'And I won't fail you there, either,' he added. 'Not this time.'

'That's not important,' said the woman. 'Having you safely back with me, that's important.'

His training had been never to leave a vehicle in a car park, where there was a risk of being boxed in and trapped and Charlie had responded automatically, putting the mini on the edge of an annexe area, immediately adjoining the main road.

He had had to wait at the exit of the restaurant, to receive his change and tip the waiter and so Edith was about five yards ahead of him, walking towards the car, when he left the hotel.

She turned for him to catch up and because it was darker than in the main parking area he didn't at first see the terror spreading over her face. Fear drained the strength from her voice, so the warning came out as little more than a gasp, hardly reaching him at first.

'Charlie,' she said. 'Please God, no, Charlie.'

She came towards him, arms thrown out pleadingly and it was the movement that completely alerted him. She was staring beyond him, eyes bulged, Charlie realised. He turned back towards the hotel as the woman reached him and saw perfectly in the brighter light Garson Ruttgers spread over the bonnet of the car, his whole body supported, arms triangled out in the officially taught shooting position, left hand clamped against the right wrist to minimise the recoil from the gun.

It took seconds but seemed to unfold in an agonisingly slow motion. The need to snatch up Edith and run fixed itself firmly in his mind and stayed there, isolated, and he wondered why he couldn't react and do such a simple thing.

Then Edith collided with him from behind and he reached out to support her, recognising as he did so that Ruttgers was going to shoot.

The lined, sharp face that Charlie remembered so well from the Kalenin affair tightened against the expected noise and the gun moved up slightly and Charlie even identified it as a heavy weapon, a .375 Magnum.

The explosion and the shock of the impact appeared simultaneous and almost immediately there was the roar of a second shot. Charlie tried to breathe, but couldn't because of the biting pain which numbed his lungs from smashing backwards against the bordering stones of the forecourt. Edith was lying on top of him and he didn't see Ruttgers move. He heard the sound of the car engine, though, and tried to get out from beneath the woman's body and it was then he realised that she was quite motionless and stopped pushing at her.

The crushed breath groaned into him and then wailed up into an anguished moan. The action of supporting Edith had pulled her between them at the moment that Ruttgers had fired and she had taken the full impact of both shots and when Charlie felt up he discovered she didn't have a back any more.

He rolled her away, very gently, crouching over her. The horror had gone from her face. Instead, in death, there was a pleading look, the sort of expression she had had asking him not to go to the cemetery, all those weeks ago.

'Not you, Edith,' he sobbed. 'It shouldn't have been you.' A shoe had fallen half off her foot, he saw. As if it were important, he reached down and replaced it. And then tried to wipe away a smudge of dirt that had somehow got on to her cheek.

A scream came from the hotel, breaking through to him. He cradled her head against him, very quickly, then carefully lowered her to the ground.

'I've got to run, Edith,' he said. 'Now I've got to.'

Largely governed by instinct, he went low to the car, doubled against recognition. He held the door shut, to avoid any noise, and as he started the engine, he saw just one man walking hesitantly towards the woman's body.

He kept the lights off, so the registration would not be visible, accelerating the car out on to the road in a scurry of gravel. It was difficult to be sure because of the darkened windows of the vehicle, but the man's reactions had been too slow to get anything more than a vague description, Charlie decided.

Which way, he wondered, had Edith's killer gone? It hardly mattered. Ruttgers would have been part of the Crawley hotel surveillance. The part, in his carelessness, he had missed. He'd need a weapon, he decided. It was fortunate he had bothered to examine John Packer's house. Why, he wondered, in the first flood of self-pity, hadn't he shown such detailed caution about everything?

Twenty miles away, on the outskirts of the Sussex village of Cuckfield, Garson Ruttgers stared curiously at the Magnum revolver lying beside him on the passenger seat, then blinked out of the car. Condensation from the exhaust billowed whitely around him, making it difficult to see. A lay-by, he realised. With a telephone. That was it, a telephone; that's why he'd stopped. He looked back to the gun. He'd done it. Now he had to let those bastards in London know. They'd have to admit he was right, decided Ruttgers, getting unsteadily from the vehicle. Succeeded where Onslow Smith and his team had failed. Get the Directorship back, after this, he thought. Be good, hearing everyone admit how wrong they'd been.

Superintendent Law answered the telephone on the third ring, stretching the sleep from his eyes. Beside him his wife tugged at the bedclothes, showing her annoyance. Irritable cow, he thought.

'Knew you'd want to be told immediately,' said the equally tired voice of Hardiman.

'What?'

'Woman's been shot outside of an hotel on the outskirts of Guildford... same name as our financier...'

'Dead?'

'Dead.'

Law swung out of bed, ignoring the growing protests of his wife.

'I'll be waiting when you get here,' said the detective.

'I won't be able to sleep again now, not without a pill,' complained the woman, but Law had already closed the bathroom door.

'Damn it,' she said, miserably, dragging the covers over her.

29.

Apart from Ruttgers, oblivious in his private reverie, everyone sat silently awaiting Onslow Smith's lead.

'Damn,' said the Director. 'Damn, damn, damn.' With the repetition of every word, he punched hard at the desk, needing physical movement to show his rage and there were isolated shifts of embarrassment from the men watching.

Since they'd arrived at the embassy, Smith had done little but vent his temper in irascible, theatrical gestures, his mind blocked by what had happened.

Apparently aware of the impression he was creating, the Director straightened. 'Right,' he said, as if calling a meeting to order.

The shuffling stopped.

'You're *positive* he hasn't been identified?' demanded Onslow Smith.

'Of course I can't be positive,' said Braley, uncomfortable with the question he had already answered.

He'd been so near, thought Smith, in a sudden flush of remorse. So damn near. And then the fucking paranoid had to go and screw everything up. It would be wrong to let Washington know yet.

'You must have some idea,' he said irritably.

'When we got to the lay-by,' Braley continued, recounting the familiar story, 'Mr Ruttgers was just sitting in the car...'

'Just sitting?'

'Yes, sir. Staring straight ahead and doing nothing, except smiling. The engine was still running. And the telephone he'd used to call you was hanging off the hook, where he'd let it drop.'

'The engine still running and there hadn't been a police check?' queried the Director.

'Cuckfield is quite a way from the shooting,' said Braley. 'But it only took us about fifteen minutes from the Crawley hotel.'

'Where the hell was he trying to go?' wondered Smith. He spoke to a bespectacled man on his right.

'Probably never know that,' replied the embassy doctor. 'Perhaps back to the hotel... perhaps nowhere. Just the urge to get away.'

'How long will he be like that?' asked Smith, nodding towards the immobile figure of the former Director.

'Not long, I shouldn't imagine,' said the doctor. 'I don't think it's anything much more than shock. Could be over in a few hours.'

As if conscious of the attention, Ruttgers suddenly stirred into life, smiling over at Smith and leaning forward to reinforce the words.

'Killed him,' gloated Ruttgers. 'Shot the bastard, like we should have done weeks ago. Saw him fall. Dead. Charlie Muffin is dead. No need to worry any more... dead...'

'But...' began Braley, who had already had an enquiry made to the police. Smith waved him to silence. Christ knows what mental switchback the correction would make, he thought.

'It could be days before we're able to establish definitely whether Mr Ruttgers was seen sufficiently to be identified,' offered Braley. He'd impressed the Director on this job, he knew. And wanted to go on doing so.

'And we don't have days,' said the Director distantly.

But they still had luck, he decided. Only just. But enough to matter; enough to avoid a humiliation as embarrassing as Vienna. Providing he handled it properly. Thank God that even mentally confused, the bloody man had wanted to boast, to prove how much better he was than the rest of them. Without that wild, incoherent contact it wouldn't have been possible to have snatched him off the streets and brought him back to the safety and security of Grosvenor Square.

So he still had the advantage, determined the Director.

Now he had to capitalise upon it. Which meant Ruttgers had to be got out, immediately. And then buried as deeply as possible within some psychiatric clinic.

Smith realised he himself would have to remain in England, and attempt to establish some sort of relationship with whoever was going to succeed George Wilberforce to agree an approach which would satisfy the civilian police.

There would be arguments, Smith anticipated. Bad ones. Maybe even a break between the two services as severe as that which followed the Vienna débâcle. But whatever happened, it would be less embarrassing to America than having a former Director of the CIA arraigned in a British court of law on a charge of murder. That's all he had to consider; keeping America out of it.

He looked up at a movement in front of him and saw the doctor leaning forward, to take a smouldering cigarette from Ruttgers' fingers before it burned low enough to blister him. Ruttgers stirred at the approach, looking around for a replacement. Gently the doctor lit one for him.

'I did it,' suddenly declared Ruttgers, with the bright pride of a child announcing a school prize. 'Everyone else fouled it up, but I did it.'

'Yes,' soothed the doctor. 'You did it.'

'He couldn't have managed it,' said Ruttgers, pointing a nicotine-stained finger at Onslow Smith. 'Not him.'

'Can't you shut him up?' demanded the Director, exasperated.

The doctor turned to him, not bothering to disguise the criticism. 'Is it really doing any harm?' he said.

Smith snorted, twisting the question.

'You wouldn't believe it,' he said, bitterly. 'In a million years, you wouldn't believe it.'

He turned back to Braley, positive again.

'We've got blanket diplomatic clearance,' he said. He indicated the former Director. 'And his name was on the list approved by the Foreign Office. So he leaves. Tonight.'

Seeing the doctor move to speak, Smith hurried on, 'There's an aircraft already laid on... for me. He can go instead.'

'I think he still might need some medical help,' warned the doctor.

'I'll fix it with the ambassador for you to go as well,' said Smith, anxious to move now he had reached a decision. He'd have to speak to the Secretary of State, he knew. Very soon.

'You will go, of course,' he ordered Braley.

The man nodded in immediate agreement. 'Of course,' he said.

'By this time tomorrow I want nothing to associate us in any way with this,' announced the Director.

'Oh, Christ,' said Braley, softly.

'What's the matter?' demanded Smith, the alarm flaring.

'The hotel at Crawley,' remembered Braley. 'The one in which we were waiting for Mr Ruttgers to return when you called us...'

'What about it?'

'The woman stayed there... and Mr Ruttgers is registered. With his luggage.'

Beneath the desk, where they couldn't see the tension, Smith gripped and ungripped his hands, fighting against the desire to scream at them for their stupidity. They had had no idea two hours before why he was panicking them from the place and couldn't then have anticipated the danger of not collecting the cases, he remembered. And he'd lost control in front of them sufficiently for one evening, he decided.

'Get your asses back there,' he said, his voice unnaturally soft in his anxiety to contain his anger. 'Get down there and explain that Mr Ruttgers has had to leave, in a hurry. Pay his bill and collect his bags and then get out. And hurry. For God's sake hurry.'

The police would unquestionably uncover the link, he accepted. But by then Ruttgers would be over three thousand miles away and he would have begun negotiations.

'Can we get Ruttgers to London airport by ourselves?' queried

Smith, to the doctor.

The bespectacled man nodded, pausing at the doorway. The unexpected flight to Washington upset a lot of arrangements, he realised, annoyed.

'You guys lead an asshole of a life, don't you?' he said.

'Yes,' agreed Smith dully. The hotel was an awkward complication, he thought.

'Then why the hell do you do it?' persisted the doctor.

The Director concentrated upon him, fully.

'Sometimes,' he said, 'it seems important.'

But this hadn't been, he decided. Apart from a few inflated egos and a questionable argument about teaching the Russians a lesson, this hadn't been important at all. Quite worthless, in fact.

'How often do you get it right?' asked the doctor.

'Not often enough,' admitted Smith honestly. Suddenly annoyed at the interrogation, he started up and said, curtly, 'Let's get Ruttgers to the airport, shall we?'

Road blocks would have been established within an hour of the murder, Charlie knew, sealing a wide area. It had meant he had had to drive in a circuitous route, impatient at the amount of time it was taking him to do all that was necessary.

Purposely he was crowding the thoughts into his mind, trying to blot out the memory of Edith's collapsed, pulped body.

The Wimbledon house had seemed deserted, he decided. Where, he wondered, was John Packer? Certainly not arrested; the garden shed would have been empty after a police search.

The jewellery recovery had been publicised everywhere. Panicked then. Panicked and run. The word stayed in his mind, linking the next thought.

Perhaps, in their panic, they would forget Ruttgers' luggage. No, he assured himself, in immediate contradiction. The connection was too important. Braley wouldn't overlook something as vital as that. And he'd certainly appeared in a position of authority at the airport, someone involved in the final planning. No, Braley would think of the luggage; it was that sort of professionalism that made him so good.

Charlie lost the fight against recollection and knuckled his eyes, trying to clear the blur.

'Shouldn't have been you, Edith,' he said. 'I won't fail... even if this goes wrong, I won't fail.'

30.

The improvement in Garson Ruttgers' condition began almost immediately they left the American embassy and started through the quiet, early dawn streets of London. By the time they had cleared the city, he was lighting his own cigarettes and as they neared the airport, he turned to the doctor and asked, quite rationally, if they were going back to America.

When he nodded, Ruttgers turned to Onslow Smith.

'You coming?'

The Director shook his head.

'Then I'll let them know how well it all went,' said Ruttgers.

Smith looked sharply at the man but was stopped by the doctor's warning look.

'Sure,' he said, dismissively. 'You tell them.'

It would take seven hours for the aircraft to reach Washington, calculated Smith. Sufficient time for him to sleep away the fatigue that was gripping his body, before attempting to meet with British officials. It wouldn't be easy, now Wilberforce was gone. Perhaps, he thought, it would be better to arrange through the American ambassador an appointment with somebody in the government. Perhaps, he thought, the Secretary of State would insist upon taking control. There'd be a lot of anxiety in Washington when he told them.

He swayed at the sudden movement of the car and realised they had turned off the motorway.

'I hardly think there's any need for me to go,' said the doctor, in hopeful protest.

Smith looked at Ruttgers before replying.

'I think there is,' he insisted. 'It's a long flight.'

The internal injury would be intensive, Smith knew. And he was going to make damned sure that he closed every avenue of criticism that he could, even down to something as minor as having the man accompanied back to Washington by a physician.

'I really don't think there's much wrong with him,' said the doctor.

'You can be back here by tomorrow,' said Smith, closing the conversation. He had more to worry about than the feelings of an embassy doctor, decided Smith. It was his future career he was trying to save.

They looped off before the tunnel, taking the peripheral road to the private section. Soon, thought Onslow Smith. It would all be over very soon.

Because of the twenty-four-hour activity at the airport there were several cars in the staff park and the darkened mini was quite inconspicuous as the limousine swept by.

Despite the growing daylight, lights still held the building in a yellow glow. The driver had already spoken into the radio and as they pulled in front of the embarkation lounge, marines and airport security men moved out into a prearranged position, closing off the area. Others arranged themselves loosely around the aircraft, an inner protection for the people boarding.

'I missed the announcement,' said the doctor, uncaring now in his anger. 'What time did the war start?'

Smith looked at him, shaking his head.

The chauffeur opened the door and Smith got out, leaving the doctor to help Ruttgers.

'Anything more?' enquired the driver.

'Wait for me,' instructed Smith. 'We'll see the plane away.'

The chauffeur re-entered the car, moving it to the designated parking area alongside the buildings and Smith smiled mechanically at the customs and immigration officials who approached.

Smith had arranged the papers in his briefcase during the journey and produced the authorisations as they were requested.

'Seems a lot of activity,' suggested the customs officer.

'Yes,' agreed Smith.

'No need for me to see anything, is there?' asked the man.

'No,' agreed Smith. 'No need at all. Just personal belongings, nothing more.'

They turned at the hurried arrival of the second car. Braley misjudged the last corner, actually scuffing stones and dust against the barrier wall.

Braley took the vehicle almost to where his superior was talking to the officials.

'The baggage,' Smith identified it, as Braley got out of the car.

'Fine,' said the customs man.

'No need for me to delay you either,' said the immigration official. 'Thank you.'

'Thank you,' responded Smith, politely.

The men who had gone with Braley were already unloading the luggage, he saw, turning to the car.

He waited until the British officials were sufficiently far away, then demanded urgently: 'Well?'

'Absolutely no trouble,' Braley assured him.

'The police hadn't got there then?'

'No.'

Breath was rasping into the man. He'd made a complete recovery, decided Braley.

The Director turned to where Ruttgers and the doctor were waiting.

'Let's get him away,' he said. It was still going to be all right, he thought, in a sudden burst of euphoria.

Ruttgers followed a military steward up the steps, taking without question the wide, double seat that the man indicated to the left side of the aisle. The doctor belted himself into the seat immediately to the right and then looked up at Onslow Smith.

'Call me at the embassy, from Washington,' ordered the Director.

'There'll be nothing to report,' said the doctor, truculently. Behaving like a lot of kids, he thought, irritably.

'Call me anyway. I want to know he got there safely.'

'OK.'

Smith turned back to where Braley and his men were coming aboard, stacking the luggage they had collected from the Crawley hotel into seats at the rear and then spreading themselves around the aircraft.

'Thank you,' said Smith to Braley. 'You did very well.'

The man smiled at the praise. His breathing was easier. 'Want me to stay with him all the way?' he enquired, nodding towards Ruttgers.

'All the way,' confirmed the Director. 'You're being routed through to the Andrews Air Base. There'll be an ambulance waiting when you arrive, to take over from the doctor.'

The man nodded.

'And Braley?'

'Yes, sir.'

'I've been impressed with the way you work. Very impressed. I think we can establish a working relationship when all this is over.'

'Thank you,' said Braley.

There was movement from the front of the aircraft and Smith looked up to see the co-pilot nodding.

'I'll see you in a few days,' said Smith, automatically.

'Good luck,' responded Braley.

'I'll need it,' said Smith, caught by the expression.

Men were standing by the ramp as he descended, to wheel it away. He hurried to the doorway of the building, where the chauffeur was waiting with a coat. Smith pulled it on and they both turned to watch the aircraft start its take-off manoeuvre, taxiing out on to the slip runway.

Inside the plane, the steward ensured that Ruttgers had his seat-belt secured and then sat down for take-off in the seat immediately in front.

'I'm hungry,' Ruttgers announced.

The steward turned, smiling politely at the man he'd been told was a government official of high rank who was suffering a mental collapse.

'There's food on board,' he said. 'I'll be serving it once we've taken off.'

At the rear, Braley's team were already sprawled out, eyes closed. Only Braley remained awake, staring up the aircraft at Ruttgers. It was a pity, the man decided. A damned pity. Ruttgers had his faults, but he'd once been a very good Director. He didn't deserve a back-door hustle to some sanatorium, just because a few people in Washington needed protection. Braley closed his eyes, reflectively. So Charlie had escaped for the second time. But not as cleanly as in Vienna. How badly would he be affected by his wife's death? he wondered. Probably, thought Braley, he was one of the few people caught up in the Vienna operation who didn't hate Charlie Muffin. Perhaps because he had known him so well. He smiled at the sudden thought. Actually, he decided, he was quite glad Charlie had slipped away again.

The plane began its take-off run and then snatched up. Braley opened his eyes and looked out at the fast-disappearing ground. The sodium lights still stretched away from the airport like yellow strands of a spider's web. It looked very peaceful and calm, he thought.

As the aircraft's climb flattened out, the steward unclipped his belt and stood up, smiling down again at Ruttgers.

'I'll get you something to eat,' he said.

The man was staring up at the light forbidding smoking and the moment it was extinguished began groping into his pocket. Gratefully, he flipped open the top and then turned, frowning at the doctor, holding out the empty packet like a spoiled child showing an exhausted sweet bag.

'Don't smoke,' apologised the doctor.

'In my grip,' said Ruttgers. 'There's a carton in my grip.'

The steward was even farther back, in the galley, the doctor realised. He unfastened his belt and walked down to Ruttgers' luggage. An armrest had been removed and the seat-belts from two places adjusted through the straps for take-off safety. The doctor disentangled them, then stood frowning. Finally he picked up two shoulder bags and walked back up the aisle, holding them stretched out before him.

'We're still climbing. Do you mind sitting down,' the steward called out, from behind.

The doctor smiled, apologetically, then looked back to Ruttgers.

'Which one?' he asked Ruttgers.

The former Director hesitated, frowning his confusion and the doctor immediately wondered at a relapse. Curiously, Ruttgers reached out for the soft black leather bag that Edith had used during her trip from Zürich and over which Charlie, hands shaking with emotion and urgency, had worked upon five hours before in the Crawley hotel, after returning from the Wimbledon home of John Packer.

'Don't understand,' mumbled Ruttgers.

The doctor realised the difficulty the man was having assembling his thoughts and turned towards his own bag, on the adjoining seat There was some Valium, he knew. That's all the man needed, he was sure. Just a tranquilliser.

Ruttgers scraped back the zip and looked inside. Lodged on top of the dirty clothing was a hard, black rectangle. Ruttgers turned it, then opened the passport that Charlie had used for the two years since the Vienna disaster.

'Him!' shouted Ruttgers, loud enough to awaken the sleeping men behind, thrusting the passport towards the startled doctor and trying to snatch the clothes out of the bag.

At that moment, the pilot levelled further, at one thousand feet sufficiently away from the noise restrictions of the airport, and the first of the pressure devices that Charlie had taken from Packer's home and triggered for that height detonated the plastic explosive.

The jet jumped and momentarily appeared to those watching on the ground to hang suspended. Then it sagged, where the explosion had shattered the fuselage in half and as the two sections fell away the full cargo of fuel erupted in a huge ball of yellow and blue flame.

Charlie was already out of the car park, needing the initial confusion to avoid detection from the people statued four hundred yards away, gazing open-mouthed into the sky.

The movement of the small car was quite undetected.

As he headed eastwards along the M4 towards London, fire engines from Hounslow and Feltham blared in the opposite direction, sirens at full volume, blue lights flashing.

It was too much to think that Ruttgers might have looked into the bag, decided Charlie.

31.

Superintendent Law had telephoned from London, so when he swept white-faced into the office, Hardiman had all the files from the Brighton robbery carefully parcelled and waiting on the tables against the wall.

The sergeant stood uncertainly, frowning at the men who followed the superintendent into the room.

'There they are,' said Law, sweeping his hand towards them.

'What...?' questioned Hardiman, but Law waved the hand again, stopping him.

The strangers began carrying the files from the office. They didn't speak to each other and Superintendent Law didn't speak to them. It took a very short time.

'You'll want a receipt?' said one of the men.

'Yes,' said Law.

Quickly the man scribbled on to a pad and handed it over.

'Thank you for your cooperation,' he said.

Law didn't reply.

'What the hell has happened?' demanded the sergeant, as the room emptied.

Law slammed the door, turning to stand immediately in front of it.

'That,' he said, a vein throbbing at his temple in his anger, 'was the beginning of the big cover-up.'

'I don't understand,' said Hardiman.

'Neither do I, not completely,' admitted the superintendent. 'Nor am I being allowed to.'

'But what *happened*?' repeated Hardiman.

Law walked away from the door, seating himself with elaborate care behind the desk and then staring down at it, assembling the words.

'In Whitehall,' he started. 'There were separate meetings. First the Chief Constables of Surrey, Sussex and Kent were taken into an office and addressed by God knows who. Then we were taken into another room and told that the whole thing had been taken over by a government department and that as far as we were concerned, the cases were closed.'

The vein increased its vibrations.

'Cases?'

'The Brighton robbery. And the shooting.'

'But you can't just close a million pounds robbery. And a murder,' protested Hardiman. 'That's ridiculous.'

'Yes,' agreed Law. 'It is, isn't it? But you can, apparently, if it's felt sufficiently important for national security. And that's the bullshit we've been fed, all day… a question of national security and official secrets.'

'But what about… what about the money?' floundered the sergeant, with too many questions to ask.

'Everyone who suffered a loss will be compensated by the Clearing Houses… who I suppose will receive their instructions like we received ours today.'

'But how shall we mark the files?'

Law snorted, waving towards the door.

'What files?'

'I don't believe it,' said Hardiman, slumping down.

'No,' said Law. 'Neither do I. Incidentally, because of your close involvement, you're to see the Chief Constable at four this afternoon.'

'What for?'

'To be told, presumably, that if you disclose anything of what happened to anyone, you'll be transgressing the Official Secrets Act.

'But what about that damned man's passport… the one that was found with all that other stuff after the crash? It was a direct link. It was all tidied up: the robbery, the murder, the air crash…'

Law shook his head. 'We are told that no explanation could be made, other than that it was part of an attempt… an attempt which failed… to discredit Britain. I don't think that a complete account was even given to the Chief Constables.'

Hardiman laughed, suspiciously.

'Attempt to discredit Britain by whom?'

Law made an irritable movement.

'Ask the Chief Constable this afternoon, perhaps he knows.'

'Does it mean the bloody man is dead?'

'I presume so,' said Law. 'Perhaps he was being taken to America in the aircraft. I don't really know. We weren't allowed to ask questions.'

The superintendent's annoyance thrust him from the chair and he began walking around the office without direction.

'What are you going to do?' asked Hardiman.

Law smiled at him, a crooked expression.

'Resign, you mean?' he queried. He shook his head. 'In another two years I'll have got my thirty in. Do you think I'm going to chuck up a pension, just for this?'

'No,' accepted Hardiman. 'I suppose not.'

'But I'd like to,' added the superintendent, softly. 'Christ, I'd like to. Can you imagine how frightened they'd be by that?'

He looked up at the sergeant, throwing his arms out helplessly.

'The way they use people!' he protested. 'What gives them the right to use people like... like they didn't matter?'

'Power,' said Hardiman, cynically. 'Just power.'

'Wouldn't it be nice,' reflected the detective, 'to know that just occasionally it all gets cocked up?'

'For them it never does,' said Hardiman. 'Not enough, anyway. There's usually too many people between them and personal disaster.'

'Yes,' said Law. 'People like us.'

'So,' said Hardiman, positively, 'what do we do now?'

'The official orders,' recited the superintendent, 'are to conclude the matter, bringing to an immediate close any outstanding parts of the investigation.'

The sergeant glanced over at the empty file tables.

'Are there any outstanding parts?'

'The underwriter, Willoughby, is probably wondering where his mysterious investor is... he's obviously been used, like everybody else....'

He moved towards his coat.

'And the journey will do me good. I don't want to stay around a police station any more today. I might be reminded about justice and stupid things like that.'

'What are you going to tell Willoughby?'

Law turned at the door.

'The way I feel at the moment,' he said, 'I feel like telling him everything I know.'

'But you won't,' anticipated the sergeant.

'No,' agreed Law. 'I won't. I'll do what I'm told and wait another two years to collect a pension. Don't forget that four o'clock appointment.'

The tiredness dragged at Smallwood's face and occasionally the hand that lay along the arm of the chair gave a tiny, convulsive twitch.

'Well?' demanded the Foreign Secretary.

The Premier made a dismissive movement.

'There's an enormous amount of police annoyance,' he said. 'But that was to be expected.'

'Will they obey the instructions?'

'They'll have to,' said Smallwood. 'The Official Secrets Act is a useful document. Thank God none of them knows the complete story.'

'What about America?'

Smallwood shifted in his chair.

'They made the bigger mistakes this time. We agreed to cover for them.'

'So, hopefully not too much damage has been caused?' said Heyden.

'Not too much,' agreed Smallwood.

32.

The grief would always be there, Willoughby knew. In time, he supposed, Charlie would learn to build a shell around it, a screen behind which he would be able completely to hide. It wouldn't happen yet though. Not for months; maybe more. The amount of time, perhaps, that it would take his own feelings to subside.

'I was wrong,' announced the underwriter. It seemed so long, he thought, since he had practised the honesty upon which Charlie had once commented.

Charlie looked up, the concentration obviously difficult.

'In thinking I would do anything to help you,' expanded Willoughby. 'Even though we talked about it, on that first day here in this office. I still didn't believe it would result in that sort of slaughter.'

When Charlie said nothing, the underwriter demanded, 'Do you realise there were twelve people on that plane... a total of twelve people killed?'

'Thirteen,' reminded Charlie. 'Don't forget Edith died.'

'An eye for an eye, a tooth for a tooth,' quoted Willoughby. 'I can't accept that biblical equation, Charlie. Can you?'

'Yes,' said Charlie, simply. 'I can. I don't expect you to. But I can.'

'With no regrets at all?'

William Braley had been on the plane, remembered Charlie.

'I would have preferred to kill just one man... the man responsible,' he said. 'But that wasn't possible.'

He straightened, sloughing off the apathy.

'Your father disliked killing, too,' he went on, staring directly at

Willoughby. 'And avoided it, whenever it was possible, just as he taught me to avoid it. But sometimes it isn't possible. We didn't make the rules...'

'Rules,' exclaimed Willoughby infusing the word with disgust and refusing Charlie's defence. 'Is that what it was, Charlie? Some sort of obscene game? Do you imagine Edith would have wanted that sort of revenge?'

Charlie looked evenly across the desk at the outraged man. It was proper that Willoughby should feel like this, he decided. There was no point in trying to convince him. At least he fully understood it now.

'No,' he replied softly, abandoning the explanation. 'Edith wouldn't have wanted it. But I did.'

Willoughby shook his head, exasperated.

'The police found your passport, you know. Just slightly charred. Superintendent Law told me. They've closed the case, incidentally. I inferred the civil police believe you were on board... you're probably freer now than you've been since Vienna.'

'Oh,' said Charlie, uninterested.

'Why *did* you do that?' asked Willoughby. 'If they'd found your passport, in a bag that shouldn't have been aboard, then Ruttgers would have lived.'

'No,' said Charlie, definitely. 'That's why the passport and Edith's bag *were* important.'

Willoughby sat, waiting. It would only increase the man's disgust, realised Charlie. It didn't seem to matter.

Sighing, he went on: 'The bomb that destroyed the aircraft wasn't in Edith's bag. There were two other bombs, both in separate pieces of Ruttger's own luggage. I wasn't able to get near enough to the aircraft to see what sort of baggage checks were being conducted. So I had to create a dummy... something that could have been discarded, if there had been any sort of examination. In fact, there wasn't.'

'That's horrifying,' said Willoughby. He seemed to have difficulty in continuing, then said at last: 'Did my father teach you to think like that, as well?'

'Yes,' confirmed Charlie simply.

'And I thought I knew him,' said Willoughby sadly.

'I'm sorry that you became so deeply involved,' Charlie apologised. 'It was wrong of me to endanger you as much as I did.'

'I would have refused, had I known it was going to turn out like this,' said the underwriter.

'Of course you would,' said Charlie.

'What are you going to do now?'

'It's over a month since the headstone went up on Edith's grave,' he said. 'Those laburnum trees are very near and they stain...'

'I didn't mean that,' corrected Willoughby.

'I know,' said Charlie. 'But that's as far ahead as I want to think, at the moment.'

He rose, moving towards the door.

'I saw a man working on a grave when we met that day near your father's tomb. He'd maintained it in a beautiful condition. I want to keep Edith's just like that.'

'Charlie,' said Willoughby.

He turned.

'Keep in touch?' asked the underwriter.

'Maybe.'

'I was wrong to criticise,' admitted Willoughby. 'I know they weren't your rules...'

Charlie ignored the attempted reconciliation. It might come later, he supposed.

'They won, you know,' he said. 'Wilberforce and Ruttgers and God knows who else were involved. They really won.'

'Yes, Charlie,' said Willoughby. 'I know they did.'

'We were damned lucky, Willard.'

'Yes, Mr President. Damned lucky.'

Henry Austin pushed the chair back and stretched his feet out on to the Oval Office desk.

'Can you imagine what the Russians would have done if they'd found the stuff that fell out of the plane?'

'It's too frightening to think about.'

'Thank Christ the British were so helpful.'

'I think they were as embarrassed as we were.'

The telephone of the appointments secretary lit up on the President's console.

'The new CIA Director is here, Mr President,' said the secretary.

'Send him in,' ordered Austin.

33.

Although the last snows of winter had thawed and it was officially spring, few other people had opened their dachas yet, preferring still the central heating of Moscow. Berenkov had lit a fire and stood, with the warmth on his back, in his favourite position overlooking the capital.

He heard the sound of glasses and turned as Valentina came towards him.

'It was kind of Comrade Kalenin to give you this French wine,' said the woman.

'He knows how much I like it,' said Berenkov. He sipped, appreciatively.

'Excellent,' he judged.

His wife smiled at his enjoyment, joining him at the window.

'So she died, as well?' said Valentina, suddenly. Berenkov nodded. The woman's interest in the Charlie Muffin affair had equalled his, he realised.

'We've positive confirmation that it was her,' he said.

'But not about him?'

'Enough,' said Berenkov. 'There's really little doubt.' Neither spoke for several moments and then Valentina said: 'That's good.'

'Good?'

'Now there won't be the sort of suffering that you and I would understand,' explained the woman.

'No,' agreed Berenkov. 'There won't be any suffering.'

One thousand five hundred miles away, in a cemetery on the outskirts of Guildford, Charlie Muffin scrubbed methodically back and forth, pausing occasionally to pick the red and yellow laburnum pods from among the green stone chips.

The Inscrutable Charlie Muffin

1.

The fire boats had been placed so that their sprays created a paper-chain of rainbows for the *Pride of America* to sail through when she left New York for the last time. Every vessel in the harbour set up a cacophony of farewell sirens and the streamers hung, like just-washed hair, over the ship's side and from Pier 90 and several other jetties by which she slowly passed.

Lights in the twin towers of the Trade Center windows had been specially illuminated, so that the message read 'Farewell', matching the word spelled out over the Manhattan skyline by the skywriting plane which arced and circled above, its purple smoke streaming behind.

The waterside was jammed with people and the Circle Line boats had arranged special ferry trips to remain alongside until the liner reached the Statue of Liberty, a vantage point crowded with more sightseers.

It was here that Mr L.W. Lu called the major press conference on board the ship, to enable the film and television crews and journalists who would not be remaining for the entire voyage to Hong Kong to be conveniently air-lifted back to La Guardia in helicopters waiting on the cleared observation deck.

There had been press flights from England and every major European country and over two hundred people crowded into the former observation bar. Not since Onassis had there been a ship-owner more internationally known, so the press-kit was hardly necessary. But Lu was a consummate publicist. As each of the press-men had entered the room, they had been handed a bulging file setting out the already familiar history of an orphan boy born into poverty who had risen from junior shipping-office clerk to speculative investor on the Hong Kong stock market to tanker magnate, Asian oil millionaire, free enterprise entrepreneur and benefactor of three fully supported orphanages and two hospitals.

He sat on a raised dais, the panoramic view from the ship behind him, patiently waiting amid the chaos that precedes any such gathering. By his side, as always, sat his son. There was a remarkable physical resemblance between the two men. The father was a Buddha-plump, benign-looking man, the harsh klieg lights of the cameras glistening against his polished face and silk suit and occasionally, when he extended his almost constant smile, picking up the gold in his teeth. John Lu was slightly thinner and, unlike his father, wore spectacles. He had no gold in his teeth either, but that was difficult to establish because John Lu was a man who hardly ever smiled.

It was the younger man who stood first, holding out his hands for silence.

'My name is John Lu,' he said. 'I would like you to welcome my father, who wishes to begin this conference with a statement.'

There was a surprising but isolated burst of applause from the Asian journalists present and Lu smiled in appreciation. He didn't stand. He merely leant forward upon the table that had been set with microphones and radio equipment, tapped the mouthpiece to ensure he had selected the right amplifier and said, in an ordinary conversational tone, 'Thank you all for coming.'

The microphone picked up the sibilant blur in his voice and there was an immediate response, the room quietening within seconds. Lu's smile widened slightly at the reaction.

'There has been, I know, much speculation about my reasons for purchasing this still magnificent liner...' The man was very aware of the seating arrangements for the conference and turned fractionally towards the section he knew to be occupied by Americans.

'I have always felt it a tragedy that a vessel like the *Pride of America*, still the holder of the Blue Riband for the fastest crossing of the Atlantic, should, because of a change in world travelling preference, be mothballed and left to lie almost forgotten, if not abandoned, off the coast of Virginia...'

He paused. Imperceptibly, a glass of water appeared at his elbow from the attentive son. The Chinese sipped at it, smiling out at people he could no longer see because of the fierceness of the lights. He made almost an affectation of politeness.

'And so,' he resumed, 'I have found for it a function that will maintain the liner not only in its former glory, but put it to a purpose that will make it perhaps more famous than it ever was as a sea link between Europe and America...'

The millionaire paused again, to achieve effect.

'We are bound, as you know, for Hong Kong. Once there, it will be necessary to carry out some alterations and modifications for that role, a role best explained by the new name which will appear on its hull – the *University of Freedom*.'

There was another pause, this time forced upon him by the sudden burst of noise from the assembled journalists. Lu raised his hand, silencing the room again, then gestured to a bank of seats upon which a group of people had assembled minutes before the opening of the conference.

'You see behind me,' he announced, 'professors who have agreed to take chairs at this university and who have joined me from the Sorbonne, Heidelberg, Oxford, Yale and Harvard...'

There was a fresh outburst of noise from the journalists and a slight shift in the lighting at the sudden demand for identification.

Lu gestured again. 'Some of you may recognise Professor James Northcote, from Harvard, recipient of last year's Nobel Prize in Physics...'

The lights and cameras wavered and a bonily thin, balding man shuffled awkwardly into a half-standing position and nodded his head.

'...an indication,' took up Lu, bringing the attention back to himself, 'of the level of teaching which will be available at my university.'

He indicated the man who had opened the conference. 'Under the personal control and organisation of my son, I intend to provide perhaps the best education in the world for students of any nationality.'

He made a deprecatory gesture with his hands.

'There are some of you who may already know a little about me,' he said, pausing for the laughter that came from the room and smiling with it. 'Those that do will be aware of the steadfast conviction and belief that I have advanced whenever possible... a conviction and belief that the free, democratic world is growing increasingly blind to the dangers of communism...'

He sipped from his water glass.

'I believe there is a need for that warning to be repeated, over and over again, until people at last begin to take proper notice. So upon the *University of Freedom* I will provide something more than a superior education. Every undergraduate, no matter what subject he reads, will compulsorily attend daily lectures at which will be fully debated and explained the dangers of the evil, pernicious regime which exists upon the mainland of China...'

Lu rose for the first time, waving his hands to quell the clamour.

'A pernicious regime,' he repeated, the hiss in his voice more obvious because he had to shout, 'which, because of its growing acceptance by the free world, endangers the very existence of democracy.'

Lu remained standing, very aware of his stance and the sound of the cameras recording it, refusing any questions. At last the sound died.

'The *University of Freedom* will be permanently anchored off a small island in the Hong Kong archipelago,' he enlarged. 'We will be less than five miles from the Chinese mainland, a constant and visible reminder to Peking of the truth it tries so hard to suppress...'

Lu sat, nodding to his son. It took fifteen minutes to achieve adherence to the system of questioning upon which Lu insisted, receiving queries first from the American section and then from the European press. Two hours had been set aside for the conference, but it overran by a further two, so that the liner had to slow and finally turn back in a meandering arc upon itself to enable the helicopters to get away, just before nightfall.

The discussions with the assembled academics had been purposely shortened, to guarantee coverage from the journalists travelling in the liner down the east coast to the Panama Canal. The *Pride of America* stopped at Hawaii during its crossing of the Pacific and Lu chartered another plane to fly in journalists demanding access as the result of the concerted publicity during the voyage.

The arrival in Hong Kong was even more dramatic than the departure from New York. Lu had instructed his tanker and liner fleet to assemble and the *Pride of America* sailed along a five-mile avenue of welcoming, hooting vessels. All the time, it was preceded by two helicopters, between which was supported a massive pennant spelling out its new name, and on the final mile it had to negotiate fire boats which had introduced dye into their water tanks, creating technicolour fountains of greeting.

It was mid-morning before the Chinese millionaire and son reached their house on the far side of the Peak. Immediately they entered the sunken lounge a servant brought in tea, but it was John Lu who solicitously poured it for his father, standing back and waiting for an indication of approval.

'Very nice,' said the older man.

John smiled gratefully, the attitude one of constant deference.

'The publicity has been fantastic,' he said. He spoke hopefully, anxious his father would agree with the opinion.

Lu nodded. 'It's a matter of organisation.'

'Surely you didn't expect this amount of coverage?'

'No,' admitted Lu. 'Not even I had expected it to go so well.'

'Let's hope everything else is as successful,' said the younger man.

His father frowned at the doubt. Without an audience, Lu rarely smiled.

'Surely that's been even more carefully organised?' It was a reminder, not a question.

'Yes,' said John hurriedly. 'Of course.'

'Then we've nothing to worry about.'

'I hope not.'

'So do I,' said Lu. 'I hope that very much...'

John's nervousness increased at the tone of his father's voice.

'You mustn't forget,' continued Lu, 'that the whole thing is being done for you.'

'I won't forget,' said the son. Or be allowed to, he knew.

Jenny Lin Lee had become quiet as the car moved up the winding roads through Hong Kong Heights, actually passing the Lu mansion, and she had realised their destination.

By the time Robert Nelson parked outside the Repulse Bay Hotel, she was sitting upright in the passenger seat, staring directly ahead.

'Not here.'

'Why not?'

'You know why not.'

'Everyone comes here on Sunday.'

'Exactly.'

'So why shouldn't we?'

'Chinese whores aren't welcome, that's why.'

Nelson gripped the wheel, not looking at her.

'You know I don't like that word.'

'Because it's the correct one.'

'Not any more.'

'They don't know that,' she said, moving her head towards the open, bougainvillaea-hedged verandah and the restaurant beyond.

'Who gives a damn what they know?'

'I do.'

'Why?'

'Because I don't want to shame you in their eyes.'

He reached across for her hand, but she kept it rigidly against her knee. She was shaking, he realised.

'I love you, Jenny,' he said. 'I know what you were and it doesn't offend me. Doesn't even interest me. Any more than what they think interests me.'

She gestured towards the hotel again, an angry movement. He wasn't a very good liar, she decided.

'The rules don't allow it,' she said.

'What rules?' he demanded, trying to curb the anger.

'The rules by which the British expatriates live,' she said.

He laughed, trying to relax her. She remained stiff in the seat beside him.

'Don't be silly,' he pleaded.

'I know them,' she insisted. 'Had them sweating over me at night and shoving past me in the street with their wives the following morning, contemptuous that I exist.'

'Come on,' he said, determinedly getting out of the vehicle.

He walked around to the passenger side, opening her door.

She stayed staring ahead.

'Come on,' he repeated.

She didn't move.

'Please,' he said. He had begun to enunciate clearly, a man intending to show his words and judgment were unaffected by the midmorning whisky back at the apartment.

She looked up at him, still unable to gauge the effect of drink upon him, but with a professional awareness of its dangers.

'It's a mistake,' she warned him.

'No it's not,' he said, reaching out for her.

Reluctantly she got out of the car. He took her arm, leading her to the verandah, gazing around defiantly for seats. There were two at the end, with a poor view of the sun-silvered bay and the township of Aberdeen beyond, but he hurried to them, ahead of another couple who emerged from inside the hotel.

The waiter was not slow in approaching them but Nelson began waving his hands, clapping them together for attention, and when the drinks were finally served Jenny spilled some of hers in the contagious nervousness and then used too much water trying to remove the stain. It meant there was a large damp patch on her skirt when they finally walked to the buffet line and then to the table he had reserved. Conscious of it, she walked awkwardly. At the table, she ate with her head bent over her plate, rarely looking up when he tried to speak to her.

'They know,' she said. 'It's like a smell to them.'

'No one has even looked at us,' he tried to reassure her.

'Of course not,' she said. 'They know. But to them I do not exist.'

The man whose job it had been to prevent Jenny Lin Lee setting up home with Robert Nelson and who had failed to frighten her was tied that night beneath the Red Star ferry that crosses the harbour from Kowloon to Hong Kong island in such a way that by straining upwards he could just keep his mouth free of the water, but not far enough for his shouts for help to be heard above the noise of the engine. It took several hours before he became completely exhausted and collapsed back into the water, to drown. And several days before the ropes slackened, releasing the body.

Some time later, already partially decomposed and attacked by fish, it surfaced against the sampans and junks that cling like seaweed to the island side of the harbour.

Knowing it not to be one of them, because sampan people never fall into the water, and with the gypsies' suspicion of the official enquiries it would cause, they poled the corpse along from craft to craft, until it caught in the currents of the open water, near Kai Tak airport, and disappeared out to sea.

The man's disappearance was never questioned. Nor wondered at. Nor reported, either.

2.

Seven thousand miles and eight hours apart, there was another lunch that Sunday, as unsuccessful as that of Jenny Lin Lee and Robert Nelson. Charlie Muffin drove carefully, habitually watchful for any car that remained too long behind. He was unused to the road, too, and was looking for the pub accorded three stars in the guide book. He hoped to Christ it was better than the one the previous week: cottage pie made from Saturday's meat scraps, overwarm beer, a bill for £5 and indigestion until Wednesday. At least it had given him something to think about. He sighed, annoyed at the increasingly familiar self-pity. Last time it had almost killed him.

He glanced behind at the thought, checking again, and nearly missed what he was looking for. The Saxon Warrior lay back from the road, an instant antique of sculpted thatch over mock-Tudor beams. Inside he knew there would be mahoganied plastic, fruit machines in every bar and men wearing blazers and cravats solving Britain's economic ills while they felt the milled edges of the coins in their pockets to decide if they could buy the next round of drinks.

'Shit,' said Charlie fervently. He pulled into the car park and looked at his watch. He hadn't time to find an alternative. Not if he wanted to eat. All he had at the flat was cold beef.

Few people saw Charlie enter, because he didn't want them to and had long ago perfected being unobtrusive. He reached the bar between a group of men to his left reallocating Britain's oil wealth and a circle to his right undermining communist influence in Africa. The fruit machine was by the toilets. The people around had formed a kitty, in an effort to recover their money before closing time.

The barmaid was a blonde, tightly corseted woman with the bright smile that barmaids share with politicians. Charlie estimated she was about twenty years older than the pub.

'Whisky,' said Charlie, unwilling to risk the beer. There would be no danger, provided he restricted himself to two.

'And lunch,' he said, when the woman returned with the drink.

'There's mince,' she offered doubtfully, looking behind her to the serving hatch.

'No,' said Charlie. At least last week they'd disguised it with instant mashed potato.

'Bread and cheese?'

'No.'

'Beef salad?'

'The guide book said three stars.'

'Trouble in the kitchen.'

'Bad day, then?'

'Afraid so.'

'Beef salad,' said Charlie, resigned. He'd overcooked the meat at home anyway.

The barmaid retreated to the kitchen hatch and Charlie looked around the bar, sipping his drink. There were pictures of men in flying gear standing alongside Battle of Britain aircraft, a propeller mounted over the bar and near the counter-flap a man who was obviously the landlord stood frequently touching the tips of a moustache that spread like wings across his face. Mechanic, guessed Charlie. He'd never met a World War II pilot who wore a moustache like that; something to do with the oxygen mask.

Professional as the barmaid, the landlord isolated a new face and detached himself from the African group, moving down the bar. As the man approached, Charlie was aware of the critical examination; the man kept any expression of distaste from his face. Charlie resolved to get his suit pressed. And perhaps a new shirt.

'Afternoon.'

'Afternoon.'

'Sorry about the food. Fire in the kitchen.'

'Can't be helped,' said Charlie.

'Repaired by next weekend.'

'Afraid I won't be here then,' said Charlie.

'Didn't think I recognised you. Just passing through?'

'Just passing through,' agreed Charlie. As always. Never the same place twice, always polite but distant in any conversation.

'Nice part of the country.'

'Very attractive.'

'Been here since '48,' said the landlord, hand moving automatically to his moustache.

'Straight after the war, then?' said Charlie, joining in the performance. Why not? he thought.

'More or less. You serve?'

'Bit too young,' said Charlie. 'Berlin airlift was around my time.'

'Not the same,' dismissed the man.

'So I've heard.'

'Had a good war,' said the landlord. 'Bloody good war.'

Charlie avoided any reaction to the cliché. It sounded as obscene now as it had when he first heard it. The bastard who had taken over the department had had a good war. And tried to continue it, by setting him up to be killed.

'There were a lot who didn't,' said Charlie.

The landlord looked at him curiously, alert for mockery then relaxed.

'Sorry for them,' he said insincerely. 'I enjoyed my time.'

His glass was empty, Charlie saw. He pushed it across to halt the reminiscence.

'Could I have another? Large.'

'Certainly.'

Charlie knew the man would expect to be bought a drink. But he decided against it, even though it was the first conversation he had had for more than twenty-four hours. He wondered how the man would react to know he was serving whisky to someone technically a traitor to his country.

The landlord returned with the drink and waited expectantly.

'Thank you,' said Charlie.

There was an almost imperceptible shrug as the man took the money and returned Charlie his change.

'What line of business are you in, then?' he asked, lapsing into the pub formula.

'Traveller,' said Charlie. It seemed the best description of the aimless life he now led. Even before Edith had been killed they had done little else but move nervously from one place to another.

'Interesting,' said the publican, as automatically as he fingered the moustache.

'Sometimes,' agreed Charlie.

The woman returned with the salad. The meat had been carefully cut to conceal the dried edges.

'Looks very nice,' said Charlie. Insincerity appeared to be infectious. Then again, it was always dangerous to draw attention to himself, even over something as trivial as complaining about a bad meal in a country pub. He manoeuvred himself on to a bar-stool and the landlord nodded and walked back to his group. Charlie sawed resolutely at the meat, examining his attitude. What right had he to criticise a man for whom the war had been the biggest experience of his life? Or feel contempt for opinionated Sunday lunchtime drinkers? Charlie was always honest with himself, because now there was no one else with whom he could share the trait. And he knew bloody well that he would have gladly handed over the fortune he possessed to change places with any one of them, walking stiff-kneed back to their detached, white-painted, executive-style homes to worry about their mortgages and their school fees and their secretaries becoming pregnant. His attitude wasn't really contempt, he recognised. It was envy; envy for people who had wives and mistresses and friends. There was only one person whom Charlie could even think of as a friend. And there had been no contact from Rupert Willoughby for over a year. So perhaps he was even exaggerating that association.

He pushed away the meal half-eaten and immediately the barmaid took his plate.

'Like that?' she said.

'Very nice,' said Charlie. It was nearly closing time. She would be in a hurry to get away. He hesitated, decided against another drink and paid his bill. Another £5. And he was regarded as someone who had stolen money!

Back in the car, he sat for a moment undecided. If he took the B roads and drove slowly, it would be at least seven before he got back to London.

On the balcony of his apartment high on the island's Middle Level, Robert Nelson stood, glass in hand.

'Fantastic,' he said, looking down at the *Pride of America*. The liner was an open jewel-case of glittering lights. Because it was late, the slur was more noticeable in his voice.

Beside him, Jenny Lin Lee said nothing.

'I've taken six million of the cover,' he announced, suddenly.

'What?' she asked, turning to him.

He smiled at her, wanting to boast.

'Lu put the insurance out on the open market. Christ, you should have seen the scramble.'

'But you got £6,000,000 of it?'

'Yes,' he said, missing the urgency in her voice. 'Beat the bloody lot of them.'

He frowned at her lack of reaction.

'I thought you'd be pleased,' he complained, petulant in his drunkenness. 'No one else got anything like that much. There's already been a cable of congratulation from London, signed by Willoughby himself. Even promised a bonus on top of the commission...'

'If it's important for you, then I'm pleased,' she said, turning away from the balcony and the view of the floodlit ship, shifting slowly at anchor.

He followed her into the room.

'Sometimes,' he said, 'I find it completely impossible to understand you.'

She stood in the middle of the room, a slim, almost frail figure, the hair which she constantly used for dramatic effect cascading to her waist because she knew he liked it worn that way and it was inherent in her to please the man she was with.

She walked to him, smiling for the first time, cupping his head and pulling his face to hers.

'I love you, Robert,' she said. 'Really love you.'

He held her at arm's length, looking at her.

'Why tell me that?' he asked.

'Because I wanted you to know.'

The noise of the explosion woke Nelson and the girl four nights later, as it woke nearly everyone on the island and the Kowloon waterfront. By the time Nelson got to the balcony, the flames were already spurting from the stem and as he watched there was a noise like a belch and the blaze gushed through the main funnels of the *Pride of America*.

A gradual glow in the stern was the first indication that there was fire there too, then one of the plates split and huge orange gouts burst out, like a giant exhaust.

'Oh my God,' said Nelson softly. He was very sober.

Beside him, the girl remained silent.

Because it was dark, neither could see that the water with which the fire boats were already attacking the blaze was still stained with the welcoming dye. It looked like blood.

3.

Lu had wanted to hold his press conference on the *Pride of America*. But the engine-room explosions had blown away plates below the waterline, settling the liner to top-deck level in the water, and the harbour surveyors forbade the meeting as too dangerous. Instead the shipowner led a small flotilla of boats out to the still smoking, blackened hull, wheeling around and around in constant focus for the cameras, the customary silk suit concealed beneath protective oilskins and the hard-hat defiantly inscribed 'The University of Freedom'. John Lu was by his side.

The millionaire waited four days after the fire for the maximum number of journalists to gather and then took over the main conference room in the Mandarin Hotel to accommodate them. He entered still carrying the hat and put it down on the table so that the title would show in any photographs.

He was more impatient than at previous conferences, striding up and down the specially installed platform, calling almost angrily into the microphone for the room to settle.

Finally, disregarding the noise, he began to talk.

'Not a fortnight ago,' he said, 'I welcomed many of you aboard that destroyed liner out there…'

He swept his hand towards the windows, through which the outline of the ship was visible.

'And I announced the purpose to which I was going to put it.'

The room was quiet now, the only movement from radio reporters adjusting their sound levels properly to record what Lu was saying.

'This morning,' he started again, 'you have accompanied me into the harbour to see what remains of a once beautiful and proud liner…'

He turned to the table, taking a sheet of paper from a waiting aide.

'This,' he declared, 'is the surveyor's preliminary report. Copies will be made available to you individually as you leave this room. But I can sum it up for you in just two words – "totally destroyed".'

He turned again, throwing the paper on to the table and taking another held out in readiness for him, this timer by John Lu.

'This is another report, that of investigators who have for the past four days examined the ship to discover the cause of the fire,' continued Lu. 'This will also be made available. But again I will summarise it…'

He indicated behind him, to where two men in uniform sat, files on their knees.

'And I have asked the men who prepared the report to attend with me today, should there later at this conference be any questions you might like to put to them. Their findings are quite simple. The *Pride of America* has been totally destroyed as the result of carefully planned, carefully instigated acts of arson.'

He raised his hand, ahead of the reaction to the announcement.

'Arson,' he went on, 'devised so that it guaranteed the *Pride of America* would never be put to the use which I intended.'

He referred to the report in his hand.

'"A large quantity of inflammable material spread throughout cabins in the forward section,"' he quoted, '"…sprinkler system disconnected and inoperative and fire doors jammed to prevent closure… debris of two explosive devices in the engine room, together with more inflammable material, ensuring immediate and possibly uncontrollable fire… kerosene introduced into the sprinkler system at the rear of the vessel, so that the fire would actually be fed by those attempting to extinguish it…"'

He looked up, for what he was saying to be assimilated.

'Provable, incontrovertible facts,' he said. 'As provable and as incontrovertible as this—'

Again the aide was waiting, handing to Lu a length of twisted, apparently partially melted metal about a foot long. The millionaire held it before him, turning to the photographers' shouted requests.

'There is some lettering upon the side,' he said, indicating it with his finger and once more holding the metal for the benefit of the cameramen. 'A translation will be made available, together with all the other documents to which I've referred today. But again I will summarise it for you. This is part of the outer casing of an incendiary device. It was found, together with other evidence still in the possession of the Hong Kong police, in the engine room. The lettering positively identifies it as manufactured in the People's Republic of China...'

Lu returned the casing to the table behind him, happy now for the noise to build up.

'Arson,' he shouted, above the clamour. 'Arson committed by a country frightened of having the free world constantly reminded of the evils of its doctrine.'

He snatched again for the incendiary casing.

'Their former leader, Mao Tse-tung, once preached that power comes from the barrel of a gun. This is the proof of that doctrine.'

He slumped back against the table, reaching out for the instantly available glass of water and throughout the room more aides began moving with microphones so that questions would be heard by everyone.

'Do you feel fully justified in making the accusations that you have today?' was the first, from an unseen woman at the back.

Lu led the mocking laughter that broke out.

'I've rarely felt so justified in doing anything in my life,' he said. 'Is it possible for a country to sue someone for defamation of character? If it is, then I shall be happy to accept any writ from the People's Republic of China.'

'Will you attempt to buy another vessel to create another University of Freedom?' asked the *New York Times* correspondent.

'And have it burned out within days? That blackened hulk out there can speak as eloquently as any political lecturer of the dangers I publicise.'

'What about the professors whom you had already engaged?' demanded the same questioner.

'They were employed upon a year's contract. In every case, that contract has been honoured in full and first-class air fares made available to return them to whichever country they choose.'

'How much has all this cost?'

'I have never made any secret of the fact that I purchased the *Pride of America* for $20,000,000.'

'Does that mean you've lost that amount of money?' queried an Englishman representing the *Far East Economic Review*.

'Of course not. International maritime regulations insist that all vessels be properly insured.'

'So the $20,000,000 is recoverable?'

'Certainly I shall eventually be reimbursed for the purchase of the vessel. But that, gentlemen, isn't important. What is important is for the world to recognise the flagrant reaction of a country terrified of the truth, and the lengths to which it is prepared to go to prevent that truth…'

'Who were the insurers?' asked the Englishman.

'The cover was spread amongst a syndicate of Lloyd's of London.'

'Is the claim already submitted?'

'Probably,' said Lu dismissively. 'I've left the matter in the hands of my lawyers.'

Two days after Lu's heavily publicised conference, an announcement was made in the name of Chief Superintendent Sydney Johnson of the Hong Kong police. As a result of intensive enquiries since the arson aboard the *Pride of America*, it said, Hong Kong detectives had arrested two Chinese who had been employed aboard the vessel for its modification refit. Investigation had shown them to be mainland Chinese who had illegally crossed the border into Hong Kong only six months previously. Their families still resided in Shanghai.

On this occasion, Lu did not summon a conference. Instead he issued a brief statement. Without wishing to prejudice any court hearing, it said, the police announcement was regarded as proof of every claim made by Mr L. W. Lu, who looked forward with interest to a full judicial examination of the arrested men.

Both men were hesitant, each unsure of the other.

'I wasn't sure if you'd come,' said Rupert Willoughby.

Charlie Muffin walked farther into the underwriter's office, taking the outstretched hand.

'Never thought I'd get past the secretary,' said Charlie, indicating the outer office.

'She's a little over-protective at times,' apologised Willoughby. It was easy to understand his secretary's reluctance. Charlie wore the sort of concertinaed suit he remembered from their every encounter, like a helper behind the secondhand clothes stall at a Salvation Army hostel. The thatch of strawish hair was still disordered about his face and the Hush Puppies were as scuffed and down-at-heel as ever.

'Your call surprised me,' said Charlie. Willoughby was the only person who possessed his telephone number. Or the knowledge of what he had once been. And done.

'I had decided you'd never call,' he added.

'I almost didn't,' admitted Willoughby.

'So you're in trouble.'

'Big trouble,' agreed Willoughby. 'I don't see any way of getting out.'

'Which makes me the last resort?'

'Yes,' said the underwriter, 'I suppose it does.'

4.

Rupert Willoughby was a tall, ungainly man, constantly self-conscious about his height. He took great care with his tailoring, trying to minimise his stature, but then defeated any effort of his tailor in an attempt to reduce it even further by hunching awkwardly. He crouched now, untidy, his blond hair flopping over his forehead as he bent over his desk, occasionally referring to a file as he outlined the details of the *Pride of America* cover, every so often jerking up to the other man, as if in expectation of some reaction.

Beyond the desk Charlie sat with his legs splayed before him, head sunk upon his chest. By twisting his left foot very slightly, Charlie could see that the repair hadn't worked and that the sole of his left shoe was parting from the uppers. Which was a bloody nuisance. It meant a new pair and those he was wearing were at last properly moulded to his feet. It always seemed to happen like that, just when they got comfortable. Looked like rain, too.

'And so,' concluded Willoughby, 'my proportion of the syndicate makes me liable for £6,000,000.'

'Yes,' said Charlie. 'It appears you are.'

How much the man resembled his father, thought Charlie nostalgically. Practically an identical style of setting out a problem, an orderly collection of facts from which any opinion or assessment was kept rigidly apart, so that no preconceptions could be formed. Sir Archibald Willoughby, who had headed the department during almost all of Charlie's operational career and whom Charlie realised without embarrassment he had come to regard as a father-figure, had obviously groomed his real son very carefully.

'It's a lot of money to lose,' said the underwriter. The figure was too large to consider seriously, decided Charlie. He looked sideways. How much space in the room would £6,000,000 occupy? he idly wondered. The whole bookcase and the sidetable, certainly. Probably overflow on to the couch as well.

'And you want to avoid paying out?' Willoughby stared across the desk. His hand was twitching, Charlie saw.

'It might be difficult,' said the underwriter hurriedly. The admission embarrassed him and he actually blushed.

'You haven't got your share?' demanded Charlie.

'No.'

'Christ.'

'It's only temporary,' said Willoughby defensively. 'We've had a very bad two years.... whole series of setbacks.'

'But why take the risk in the first place?'

'I *had* to,' insisted Willoughby. 'A firm can be wiped out in a creditors' rush by no more than a City rumour that it's in financial difficulties. Besides which, there seemed no risk.'

'You're a bloody fool,' said Charlie.

'That knowledge doesn't help either,' said Willoughby.

'Your father left a fortune,' remembered Charlie.

'Already gone.'

'Loans then.'

'There's hardly a bank where I don't have an overdraft. And where I haven't gone over the limit.'

'So?'

'So unless there's a near-miracle, there's nothing that can stop me being drummed out of the Exchange.'

'Nobody knows?'

'Nobody. Yet. But it won't take long. This sort of news never does.'

'What's the legal opinion of Lu's claim?'

'We are completely liable,' said Willoughby.

'No room for manoeuvre?'

Willoughby shook his head. 'We might have had a chance had we included a political sabotage clause, the sort of thing that's been introduced into aircraft cover since hijacking started.'

'Why didn't you?'

'Because it's not normal, in case of ship cover... and I was in too much of a hurry to sign the policy.'

'Why?'

'Nelson managed to negotiate a 12 per cent premium. For Lloyd's, that's very high. I needed the liquidity.'

'Who's Nelson?'

'Our Hong Kong agent.'
'Good?'
'He got more of the cover than anyone else when it was put on the Hong Kong market.'
'Why?'
'Why what?'
'Why more than anybody else, and at such a good premium?'
'Because he's better, I suppose. Or because he tried harder.'
'What's he like?'
'Unusual chap,' remembered the underwriter. 'I've only met him three times. Colonial through and through. Born in India, father a governor of a minor state there before independence. Only time spent in England was at school, Eton and then Cambridge. He's so out of place here that two years ago he cut short the paid home leave that we allow our overseas men. Made some excuse about the climate.'
'Reliable?'
'Absolutely.'
'What does he say?'
Willoughby paused at the staccato questioning.
'It's so straightforward that he doesn't even see the need for an investigation,' he said.
'But you do?'
Willoughby leaned towards him.
'I've got to try,' he said. 'I've got to try anything.'
The soul-baring would be difficult for the man, Charlie knew. He'd hate admitting to being anything less than his father had been.
'How long before you've got to pay?' asked Charlie.
Willoughby made a movement of uncertainty.
'Lu's lawyers have already filed an intention to claim. We could probably delay until the two men who have been arrested are found guilty, but even to attempt that might create a dispute. I gather they've made a full admission.'
'So you haven't much time.'
'I haven't much of anything,' said Willoughby. 'Time least of all.'
'The last resort,' repeated Charlie. There was no point in buggering about. And Willoughby appeared to appreciate honesty anyway.
'Yes,' agreed the underwriter.
'Would you have avoided contacting me, if you could?'
Willoughby paused. Then he admitted, 'Yes. If I had had a choice, I wouldn't have made the call.'
Most people would have lied, recognised Charlie, unoffended. The man was trying to retain his integrity, anxious though he was.
'Well?' said Willoughby. He couldn't keep the plea out of his voice.
So much of his life had been spent getting hold of the shitty end of the stick that nobody else wanted to touch, reflected Charlie. How he

wished the approach had come through friendship, reminiscent of the man's father, rather than desperation.

'Why should I?' he said.

'*Why make people crawl, Charlie... why bully?*'

The part of him that had always embarrassed Edith most, he remembered. The part his wife didn't like and had always tried to correct.

Willoughby winced, imagining a refusal.

'No reason,' he accepted. 'The sort of things you once did...'

He paused, recalling what Charlie had done.

'It was silly of me,' he said. 'I should have realised you couldn't do it, that it would be too dangerous for you because of what happened.'

'You expect me to... because of my relationship with your father?'

'I *hoped* you'd try to help.'

'As the last resort.'

'Please,' said Willoughby.

Charlie stopped, suddenly angry with himself. He shouldn't do it, certainly not to a man whose father had befriended him to the degree that Sir Archibald had.

'Inverted snobbery...'

Another of Edith's accusations. Almost correct, too. Sir Archibald had recognised it properly. Warned him about it, even.

'*Inferiority complex, Charlie... not the confidence everyone imagines. Why, Charlie?*'

And Charlie couldn't answer because he hadn't known himself. Not then. Not until it was too late.

'I'm sorry,' he said.

'You've a right to be offended,' Willoughby accepted. 'It was madness of me to think of you, after all you've been through.'

'Not really,' said Charlie. 'You didn't put up barriers when I asked you for help once.'

That had been after Charlie was stupid enough to make a pilgrimage to Sir Archibald's grave. British intelligence had picked him up there and started the pursuit. What logic said it had been all right for them to set him up to be killed in East Berlin, then label him a renegade, to be hunted and assassinated because he had fought back and exposed them for their stupidity? Only Willoughby had understood, because the same men had caused his father's suicide. So only Willoughby had helped. Not true, he corrected himself. Edith had helped, as she had always done. And now Edith was dead.

Believing he had been rejected, Willoughby said, 'I'd appreciate your not mentioning this to anyone.'

'I haven't said I won't help,' said Charlie.

Willoughby blinked, his eagerness almost childishly obvious in his face.

'You could get to Hong Kong?' he asked hurriedly. 'I mean, there wouldn't be any difficulty with... about your identity?'

Charlie smiled at the other man's renewed embarrassment.

'The passport is genuine enough,' he said. 'It was the documents that obtained it that were phoney.'

Work again, thought Charlie. Different from what he'd been used to, but still work. It would be good to get back. And to end those aimless Sunday drives.

'I'd need the full authority of your company,' said Charlie. 'I'd never get official help without it.'

'Of course,' Willoughby assured him. 'And I'll let Nelson know you're coming... ask him to give you every assistance.'

Charlie stood.

'And thank you,' said Willoughby.

'There's no guarantee that I'll find anything to help you,' warned Charlie. 'It seems as straightforward as Nelson has said.'

'But you might,' said the underwriter.

The man was more desperate than he had imagined, thought Charlie, as he emerged into the secretary's office.

The summer rain suddenly burst against the window and he remembered the split sole.

'Where's the nearest shoe shop?' he said.

The girl looked up at Charlie in hostile bewilderment.

'A what?'

'Shoe shop,' repeated Charlie. Supporting himself against her desk, he raised his feet, so she could see the gap.

'Need a new pair,' he said unnecessarily.

The girl pressed back against her chair, face frozen in contempt.

'I'm sure I really have no idea,' she said.

Charlie lowered his foot but remained leaning on her desk.

'Never make a Girl Guide,' he said.

'And you'll never make a comedian.'

It would have to stop. Now he was trying to score off secretaries, just because they had posh accents. And losing.

At first Robert Nelson had tolerated Jenny's insistence, regarding it more as something like a secret intimacy between them. But as the months had passed and she had maintained the demand, he had come to regard it as a humiliation to them both.

She sat waiting on the opposite side of the table. Beside her lay the wallet, various pouches unzipped and ready.

'Housekeeping,' he said, counting out the money.

He watched her put it carefully into the top section of her wallet, sipping from his drink. He'd managed at last to persuade her there was no need for written details of the household accounts, so perhaps the other thing wouldn't be difficult.

'Dress allowance,' he said.

She nodded, smiling.

He took another drink, both hands clasped around his glass.

She sat, waiting.

'Please, Robert,' she said, frowning.

'Why, for God's sake '

His annoyance broke through, so that he spoke louder than he had intended.

'Please,' she said again.

He put the glass aside, determined against another outburst, spacing his words in an effort to convince her.

'Apart from a stupid piece of paper, you are my wife,' he said gently. 'I love you and want you to stay with me. Always.'

'I know,' she said.

'Then *why*?'

'Because it's always been... since I was young...'

'It's... it's obscene,' he protested, realising he had failed again.

'Please,' she persisted.

Angrily he pushed into his pocket, bringing out more notes and thrusting them on to the table.

'I-love-you money.'

'Thank you,' she said, putting the money into a waiting pouch.

How long would it take, wondered Nelson, for her to forget what she had once been?

5.

It was the tie that registered with Charlie, long before Robert Nelson got near enough for a formal greeting. So long ago, thought Charlie. Yet so easily recalled. Blue stripes upon blue, at an angle.

The two men who had set him up to be killed on the East Berlin border had been to Eton. And like Robert Nelson had always worn their ties, no matter the colour of their suits. An identification symbol; like road signs, something to be recognised by everyone.

They'd mocked his grammar school accent. And the way he'd

dressed. So they'd underestimated him, dismissing him as an anachronism; a perfect sacrifice. And been so disastrously wrong. Only one of them had survived. And that one had been disgraced. Twice. But he would still be wearing the tie, wherever he was, Charlie knew.

'I've kept you waiting,' apologised Nelson, reaching him at last through the airport crowd.

'I've only just cleared customs,' Charlie assured him, immediately conscious of the swirl of harassed agitation in which the insurance broker moved.

A strangely pale, almost flaky-skinned man, Robert Nelson was sweating, despite the thin suit and the partial air-conditioning, so that the wisped, receding hair was smeared over his forehead, accentuating the pallor.

Even before their handshake had ended, he was gesturing impatiently to porters whom Charlie had already engaged, sighing with frustration at people who had innocently intruded themselves between the luggage and twice muttering, 'Sorry, so very sorry,' to Charlie, in regret for some imagined hindrance.

The air-conditioning was better within the confined space of the waiting car and Nelson mopped his face and hands with an already damp handkerchief, smiling across the vehicle. It was an apprehensive expression, decided Charlie. Why? he wondered.

'I knew there would be an investigation,' announced Nelson, as if confirming an earlier discussion. 'Just knew it.'

'Routine, surely?' said Charlie. He looked at his watch. Whisky-breathed at ten in the morning?

'But you're not one of the normal investigators. Director level, Willoughby said.'

'No,' said Charlie. 'Not a normal investigator.'

Despite his assurances to Willoughby, there was still a risk that someone would discover just how different, he knew. His hand still had the slight shake that had started when he had approached the passport and immigration desks at the airport.

Nelson appeared to be expecting more but when Charlie didn't continue, he pointed through the window.

'You can just see the *Pride of America*,' he said.

Charlie gazed out into the bay, getting a brief view of the hull before the car dipped into the tunnel that would take them beneath the harbour to Hong Kong island.

'Looks a very dead ship,' said Charlie.

'It is.'

'Any scrap value?'

'Less than a million, I would estimate. I believe the Japanese are already interested.'

'Quite a difference from $20,000,000.'

'Yes,' agreed Nelson, as if appreciating some hidden point. 'Quite a difference.'

The vehicle emerged from the tunnel and turned along the Connaught Road towards the Mandarin Hotel. To the right, towards Kowloon, the seemingly disordered slick of sampans and junks locked one to another and stretched far out into the bay from the harbour edge. So tight was the jam that it was impossible to identify occupant with craft and the impression was of constant, heaving movement, like a water-borne anthill.

'They're called the floating people,' said Nelson. 'It's said that some are born, live and die without ever coming ashore.'

Charlie turned to his left, looking inland. A mile away, first the Middle Level, then the Heights jutted upwards to the Peak, the apartment blocks and villas glued against the rock edges.

'Easy to judge the wealth here,' said Nelson, nodding in the direction in which Charlie was looking. 'The higher you live, the richer you are.'

'What about Lu?'

'One of the richest taipans in the entire colony,' said Nelson. He's got a villa on the other side of the Peak, at Shousan Hill. Like a fortress.'

'Why a fortress?'

'Ensure his privacy.'

'I thought Lu enjoyed exposure and publicity.'

'Exactly,' said Nelson. 'It makes him an obvious target for every crank and crook in Asia.'

Nelson flustered around the arrival at the hotel, urging bellboys over the bags and actually cupping Charlie's elbow to guide him into the hotel.

The broker hovered beside him while he registered, instantly chiding the porters when they turned from the reception desk. Charlie sighed. Nelson's attitude could very easily become a pain in the ass, he thought.

It was the briefest of impressions as they waited for the elevator, but Charlie had been trained to react to such feelings and he twisted abruptly, examining the foyer.

'What is it?' demanded Nelson, conscious of the sudden movement.

'Nothing,' said Charlie.

He'd always had an instinct about surveillance. But this time he *had* to be wrong. How could he be so quickly under observation? And from whom? There was no reason. He was jet-lagged and irritated by Nelson's constant attention, that was it.

The lift arrived and Charlie started to enter, then hesitated. He'd survived by responding to impressions as fleeting as this. And while he'd changed vocations, the need for survival remained. More so. Now that he'd come out of hiding.

'Sure there's nothing wrong?' said Nelson.

Charlie stared back into the bustling foyer.

'Quite sure,' he said, still uncertain.

Nelson had reserved him a suite and Charlie examined it appreciatively.

'Never got this on Civil Service Grade IV allowance,' he muttered. Self-conversation was a habit he never bothered to curb. It usually became more pronounced when he was worried.

'What?' asked Nelson.

'Thinking aloud,' said Charlie. Obviously Robert Nelson had no idea of his company's financial difficulties.

'I had a bar installed,' pointed out Nelson hopefully.

'Help yourself,' Charlie invited him.

'You?'

'Too tired after the flight,' said Charlie, watching the other man reach for the whisky.

Islay malt, he saw. Sir Archibald had been drinking that, when he'd gone to his retirement home in Sussex the day before setting off to entrap the bastards who had taken over the department and reduced it to an apology of what it had once been.

There'd been bottles of it, in a sitting-room cupboard. The poor old sod had fallen into a drunken sleep and not been aware when he had left. According to the inquest report Sir Archibald had even swilled the barbiturates down with it.

'I specified a room with a view of the harbour. And Kowloon,' said Nelson, by the window.

'Thank you,' said Charlie. 'The ship, too.'

'Yes,' agreed Nelson. 'Everywhere I look I'm reminded of that damned ship.'

Charlie turned, curious at the bitterness.

'And beyond the New Territories is China,' continued Nelson, with his back to the room.

'I know.'

'You've been to Hong Kong before?'

'No,' said Charlie quickly, alert to questions about his past.

'Incidentally,' said Nelson, apparently unaware of Charlie's apprehensive reaction, 'Australia are 96 for 2.'

The broker had turned back into the suite and Charlie stared at him in astonishment.

'What?' he said.

'The Test,' said the broker, disconcerted by Charlie's lack of response. 'We get the reports on the BBC World Service.'

'Oh,' said Charlie. And no doubt discussed the finer points in clubs and at cocktail parties and couldn't have located Lord's or the Oval without a street map.

'You're not interested in cricket?'

'Not really,' admitted Charlie. What was it that the man was finding so much difficulty in saying?

Nelson looked at his glass, appearing surprised that it was empty.

'Go ahead,' gestured Charlie.

Nelson remained at the portable bar, looking across the room.

'I'm to be dismissed, aren't I?' he demanded suddenly.

Charlie frowned at him.

'What?'

'That's why you've come... someone who's not a normal investigator... a director. You've come to fire me because there was no qualifying clause in the policy.'

The fear tumbled from the man, the words blurred together in his anxiety.

'Of course I haven't,' said Charlie.

He reached down, easing off his shoes.

'You must excuse me,' he said. 'They're new. Pinch like hell.'

Nelson gazed at the other man, controlling the look that had begun to settle on his face. Old Etonians didn't take their shoes off in public, decided Charlie. Careful. That was an antagonism of an earlier time.

'Yours was not the final decision on the policy,' he reminded him, straightening. 'You drew it up, certainly. And admittedly it's an expensive oversight that there was no political sabotage clause. But London gave the final approval. You're not being held responsible.'

'I find that difficult to believe... I negotiated it, after all.'

'Very successfully, according to Willoughby.'

Nelson moved away from the bar, his suspicion of the remark obvious.

'What do you mean?'

'Wasn't 12 per cent high?'

'Comparatively so.'

'That's exactly what I want to do, compare. What were the other premiums?'

'I don't know,' said Nelson uncomfortably. 'It was sealed bids. Lu kept me waiting until the very last moment... wanted more time... all done in a terrible rush, really.'

So convinced was he of dismissal that despite Charlie's attempted reassurance, Nelson was still offering a defence.

'And you haven't enquired about the other premiums?'

Nelson shook his head, embarrassed at the oversight.

'Another cause for complaint,' he said, resigned.

'I've told you, no one's blaming you,' repeated Charlie. He would telephone Willoughby to get a confirmatory letter.

'It'll be a disaster for the firm, won't it?' demanded Nelson.

More than you know, thought Charlie.

'If they have to pay,' he said.

The qualification penetrated the other man's nervousness and he came closer to where Charlie was sitting.

'If?'

'I've flown seven thousand miles to decide if we should,' Charlie reminded him.

'But we've no grounds for resisting settlement,' said Nelson.

'Not yet,' agreed Charlie.

'Do you think I haven't examined every single thing that's happened since the damned explosion?' Nelson reacted as if his ability were being questioned afresh. 'There's nothing wrong with Lu's claim... not a bloody thing.'

'But you still don't know what the other premiums were.'

'I'm *sorry*,' said Nelson, exasperation breaking through.

'Can you find out?'

'The other companies might not want to disclose them.'

'Isn't there an old boy network?' demanded Charlie. Surely there were more blue-patterned ties in Hong Kong?

Nelson hesitated before replying.

'I'll try,' he promised. 'But I don't see what it would prove.'

'Might not prove anything,' admitted Charlie. 'Then again, it might be interesting. I think we should look a little deeper, that's all. Get under the surface.'

Nelson went back to the window, looking now not out over the harbour but down into the streets far below.

'This might be an English colony,' he reflected, 'but it's China down there, in almost everything but name...'

He turned back to Charlie.

'Westerners aren't allowed beneath any surface here. We're tolerated, that's all.'

'Nowhere can be as closed as that,' protested Charlie.

'Hong Kong is,' insisted Nelson. 'Believe me. If there were anything wrong with the fire, we wouldn't learn about it from the Chinese community.'

'But there isn't anything wrong, as far as you're concerned?'

Nelson shook his head.

'I wish there were,' he said. 'God knows I've tried hard enough to find something. But the evidence is overwhelming.'

'The police are being cooperative?'

'They've no reason not to be, with a case like they've got.' He indicated a briefcase.

'I've brought the file for you.'

Charlie smiled his thanks.

'So you think we'll have to pay out?'

Nelson's belief that the fire was uncontestable would have been another reason for imagining that a directorial visit was to announce his dismissal, realised Charlie.

'I *know* we'll have to pay,' confirmed the broker. 'Lucky Lu never suffers a misfortune that costs him money.'

'Lucky?'

'His wealth started with some deals that turned out spectacularly successful on the Hong Kong stock exchange. It's been Lucky Lu for as long as I can remember.'

'Sounds like a poof's favourite lavatory,' reflected Charlie, massaging his feet. It would take weeks to break in those damned shoes. It was fortunate he had postponed having the supports put in.

'You're very different from what I expected,' said Nelson suddenly. 'I think other people are going to be surprised, too.'

'Other people?'

'I assumed you'd want to see the police chief. Name's Johnson. I mentioned your coming. And I told Lu's people as well. Willoughby asked me to give you all the help I could.'

'Thanks,' said Charlie. He'd have preferred announcing his own presence.

'You're annoyed,' said Nelson, detecting the reservation in Charlie's voice, and growing immediately apprehensive.

'No,' lied Charlie. Poor bugger seemed worried at his own shadow; but then, so were they all, for differing reasons.

'Is there anything else I can do?'

Charlie shook his head.

'I suppose I'd better study the file. And get some sleep.'

The broker stayed for another drink, then left, promising to collect Charlie the following morning so they could attend the remand hearing of the two Chinese accused of arson.

Alone, Charlie closed all the curtains against the view and the sunlight, put a 'Do Not Disturb' notice outside the room and decided the file could wait.

He slept for about five hours and then woke, knowing it was still not midnight Hong Kong time and that he had long hours of sleeplessness ahead of him.

Edith would have enjoyed the luxury of the apartment, he thought, feeling his eyes cloud in the darkness. And tried hard to conceal her concern at the cost. Poor Edith.

Always so aware of the money. And of his resentment of her inheritance, sufficient to support them both.

And it had been resentment, he recognised. The perpetual feeling.

Idiotic, childlike resentment. He could even recall the words he'd shouted at her, careless of the hurt, when she had suggested he simply retire from the service that had decided he was expendable and live on her wealth.

'*And don't patronise me with your money... like you've always patronised me with your breeding...*'

That was why he had inveigled America into the border deal and then disappeared with the $500,000 defection fund. To ensure there would never be any dependence upon her. Why in God's name hadn't he realised how truly dependent he had been, instead of turning them both into exiles, terrified of every footstep?

'I'm sorry, darling,' he said. 'So very sorry.'

He didn't want to spend more than a month in Hong Kong. The grave would become too overgrown if he stayed away any longer.

Sighing, he snapped on the light and pulled the file towards him. He'd be bloody tired in the morning, he knew.

There had been two supplementary reports to the original account from the CIA's Asian station in Hong Kong and then a separate analysis prepared by specialists at the Langley headquarters in Virginia.

'Well?' demanded the Director.

'Certainly looks like Peking,' judged the deputy.

'Odd though.'

'Facts are there.'

'We've got to be sure.'

'Of course.'

'Why don't we send in someone with no preconceptions, to work independent of the station?'

'They won't like it.'

'I'm more interested in being able to advise the President and the Secretary of State that China is growing careless of detente than I am in the feelings of some station personnel,' said the Director sharply.

'Who?' asked the deputy.

'Someone who's keen, anxious to prove himself...'

Harvey Jones heard the telephone ringing as he pedalled up Q-Street at the end of his daily five-mile ride. He sprinted the last few yards, ran up the steps and fumbled the key into the lock to snatch the phone off the rest as the ringing was about to stop.

'There you are,' said the deputy director, annoyed at being kept waiting. 'Thought for a moment that you were going to miss the chance of a lifetime.'

6.

The authorities had not anticipated the interest in the remand hearing and had only assigned one of the smaller courts, with limited seating, so that entry had to be controlled by permit.

'I managed to get two,' reported Nelson in the car taking them to the administrative building. 'It wasn't easy, though. The press are screaming for all the seats.'

'We were lucky then,' said Charlie. Like the tie, the broker retained the harassed anxiety of the previous day. And a dampness was already softening his shirt and suit into creases. The man was still unconvinced his job was safe.

It was the discovery of the other premiums, Charlie knew.

'You're quite sure that the rest were only 10 per cent?'

Nelson saw the reiteration as criticism. He was annoyed, too, that such an obvious enquiry hadn't occurred to him in advance of the man's arrival from London.

'Yes,' he said tightly. 'Those I could find out about anyway.'

'Still convinced that there's nothing strange about the fire?' said Charlie.

'It's odd,' conceded Nelson.

'Odd enough to look further?'

'I've told you how difficult that will be.'

'There's the police,' said Charlie. And the personal danger in approaching them. Over-cautious, he told himself.

How could there be any danger, here in Hong Kong? It was, he recognised, an apprehension of authority. Any authority. It would always be with him. Like so many other fears.

The car began to slow at the approach to the administrative buildings.

'It shouldn't last long,' said Nelson.

'Remand hearings usually don't.'

'You've been to a lot?'

Charlie tensed, then relaxed. There was no danger in the admission.

'Quite a few,' he said.

But not the sort Nelson imagined. In the past it had always involved sneaking through side doors and adjoining buildings, to avoid the surveillance and cameras of those uncaptured at the Official Secrets trials of those who had been caught and who nearly always reminded Charlie of the grey, anonymous people at rush-hour bus queues. Which was why, he supposed, they had made such good spies. Until he had exposed them.

'Have you anything planned for tonight?' asked Nelson abruptly.

Charlie turned to him in the car.

'There's a very good Peking-style restaurant in the Gloucester Road and Jenny and I wondered if you'd like to be our guest.'

Chinatown with English country street names, reflected Charlie. Why, he wondered, had Nelson blurted the invitation with even more urgency than was customary?

'Jenny?' he queried.

'My... she's... someone I live with,' said Nelson awkwardly. As if the qualification were necessary, he added, 'Jenny Lin Lee.'

'I'd like very much to eat with you,' said Charlie. Again the need for hurried words. There was embarrassment mixed with Nelson's permanent agitation.

Because of the crush around the building, they left the car some distance away and as soon as they began walking Charlie felt the prickle of unseen attention. He stared around quickly, as he had in the hotel foyer, but again could detect nothing.

Apprehension of the cameras, he decided, as they got to the steps. Expertly Charlie manoeuvred himself behind Nelson, watching for a casually pointed lens which might record him in the background of a picture and lead to an accidental identification from someone with a long memory.

It was cooler inside the building, although Nelson did not appear to benefit.

'There's the police chief,' he said, pointing across the entrance hall to a tall, heavily built man.

'Superintendent Johnson,' called the broker.

The man turned, a very mannered, slow movement. Like Willoughby, the policeman had an affectation involving his height. But unlike the underwriter, Johnson accentuated his size, leaning slightly back and gazing down with his chin against his chest, calculated always to make the person he was addressing feel inferior.

'The senior colleague from London about whom I told you,' announced Nelson.

Johnson examined Charlie.

'*Senior* colleague?' he queried pointedly. He was immaculate, uniform uncreased, buttons gleaming and the collar so heavily starched it was already scoring a red line around his neck.

'Yes,' confirmed Nelson, appearing unaware of the condescension.

Hesitantly, Johnson offered his hand.

Charlie smiled, remembering Nelson's remark of the previous evening about the surprise of people he would encounter. Underestimated again, he thought contentedly.

'Investigating the fire,' added Nelson without thinking.

Johnson's reaction was immediate.

'It has already been investigated,' he said stiffly. 'And satisfactorily concluded.'

'Of course,' said Charlie smoothly. 'These things are routine.'

Johnson continued staring at him. Unconsciously the man was wiping his hand against the side of his trousers.

'Ever been in the Force?' invited Johnson.

Another recognition symbol, decided Charlie. Like a tie.

'No,' he admitted. It meant a closed door, he knew.

'Scotland Yard,' announced Johnson, as if producing a reference. 'Fifteen years. Never an unsolved case.'

'Just like this one?'

Johnson put his head to one side, trying to detect the sarcasm.

'Yes,' he said. 'Just like this one.'

'I rather wondered if it might be possible for you and me to meet... at your convenience, obviously,' said Charlie.

'I've already made all the relevant material available to Mr Nelson,' said the superintendent.

'I know,' said Charlie. 'I've read your reports. You've really been most helpful. There are just one or two things that seem unusual...'

'I've a busy diary...'

'Of course,' flattered Charlie. Pompous prick.

'Lot of commitments...'

'It wouldn't take more than fifteen minutes,' persisted Charlie. 'There's a huge sum of money involved, after all.'

'Talk to my secretary,' Johnson capitulated. 'We will see what we can do tomorrow.'

'You're very kind,' said Charlie. Between what would he be fitted? he wondered. Golf and the yacht club lunch?

An usher announced that the court was about to convene, interrupting them. There was a slow shuffle through the entrance, bottle-necked by two of Johnson's officers scrutinising the entry tickets. Nelson and Charlie were allocated to the well of the tiny court, just to the left and below the dock.

Charlie twisted as the men were arraigned, looking up at them. Why was it that criminals never had the stature expected of their crimes? The two accused Chinese entered the dock cowed and frightened, heads twitching like animals suspecting a trap about to close behind them. One wore just trousers and vest and the second had a jacket, grimed and shapeless from constant use, over a collarless shirt. The man's trousers were supported by cord. Charlie recognised the opium habit from the yellowed, jaundiced look of their eyes. Their bodies vibrated with the denial imposed since their arrest.

Charlie turned away, stopping at the sight of Johnson rigidly upright and towering above the other policemen at the far side of the dock. The sort of man, judged Charlie, who would stand up before he farted in the bath. Probably at attention. Johnson looked directly at him, his face blank.

At the demand from the usher, the court stood for the entry of the magistrate. Immediately he was seated, the clerk announced that the accusation would be read first in English, then translated into Cantonese for the benefit of the accused.

'The charge against you,' began the official, looking first to the dock and then back to the charge sheet, '...is that on June 10 you did jointly commit an offence of arson, namely that you did secrete aboard a liner known as the *Pride of America* incendiary devices and that further you did, separately and together, ignite at various situations aboard the said liner quantities of inflammable material. Further, it is alleged that you interfered with the fire precaution systems upon the said liner in such a way that additional quantities of inflammable material were introduced into the flames...'

He stopped, handing the sheet to the Chinese interpreter.

The man began the accusation, but was almost immediately stopped by a noise which Charlie later realised must have been the sound of the first man falling. He turned at the scuffling movement, in time to see the warders move forward to try to prevent the second Chinese, in the crumpled jacket, from collapsing beneath the dock rail.

There was a moment of complete, shocked silence broken only by the unseen sound from the dock of strained, almost screaming attempts to breathe, and then it was overwhelmed by the babble that erupted as reporters tried to get nearer the dock, to look in.

Then there was another commotion, as Superintendent Johnson began bellowing at his policemen to restore order.

A warder emerged from below the rail, and there was a second momentary lull in the noise.

'Dead,' he announced. 'They're both dead.'

He spoke apologetically, as if he might in some way be blamed for it.

Superintendent Johnson succeeded in interposing constables between the dock and people trying to stare in, then more officers arrived to clear the court.

It was not until they were back in the vestibule that Nelson and

Charlie were able to extract themselves from the hurrying funnel of people.

'What the hell does that mean?' demanded Nelson.

Charlie considered the question.

'It means,' he said, 'that there won't be a trial.'

'I don't understand,' protested the broker.

'No,' admitted Charlie. 'Neither do I. Not yet.'

Suddenly it seemed that there was going to be very little difference between what he was attempting to do now and what he had done in the past. Would he still be as good? he wondered.

The photograph of Charlie Muffin was passed slowly around the inner council, then finally returned to the chairman.

'Such a nondescript man,' said the chairman.

'Yes,' agreed Chiu.

'Incredible.'

'Yes,' said Chiu again.

'So the insurers aren't as satisfied as the police.'

'Apparently not.'

'Such a nondescript man,' repeated the chairman, going back to the photograph.

7.

Their Formica-topped table had been separated from others in the restaurant by wheel-mounted plastic screens trundled squeakily across the bare-boarded floors and they had sat upon canvas-backed chairs. But the food had been magnificent. It was, decided Charlie, a Chinese restaurant for discerning Chinese.

'It was good?' enquired Jenny Lin Lee anxiously.

'Superb,' said Charlie honestly, smiling at her.

She hesitated, then smiled back. A man trained to see through the veil that people erect at first encounters, he was intrigued by the girl. Her frailty was practically waif-like, yet he felt none of the protectiveness that would have been a natural response. Instead, he was suspicious of it, imagining a barrier created with more guile than most people were capable of. A professionalism, in fact. But at what could she be professional? Her hair, obviously very long, was coiled thickly but demurely in a bun at the back of her head. She wore hardly any make-up, just a touch of colour to her lips, and looked more like Nelson's daughter than his mistress. Certainly the broker behaved protectively towards her. But there was another attitude, too. A discomfort, decided Charlie. Definitely a discomfort.

Charlie was aware that he had held back because of his uncertainty, contributing to the awkwardness of the meal.

'Would have tasted better with this,' insisted Nelson thickly, raising his minute drinking thimble. Charlie had refused the Mao Tai, preferring beer. Jenny had chosen tea, so the insurance broker had consumed nearly all the bottle.

'Nothing like whisky, though,' said Nelson, as if the qualification were necessary. 'That's what they call it, you know. Chinese whisky.'

'Yes,' said Charlie.

'There's no better restaurant in the colony for Peking Duck,' said Jenny quickly.

She'd realised Nelson's increasing drunkenness and moved hurriedly to take attention from the man. They seemed equally protective towards one another, thought Charlie. It appeared an odd relationship. But then, who was he to judge? He'd never managed a proper relationship in his life. And now he would never have the chance.

'It really was very good,' he said.

'It's cooked over charcoal... and basted in honey,' she said.

'Australia are 160 for 5, by the way,' said Nelson, adding to his thimble. He looked over the table, grinning apologetically.

'Sorry,' he said. 'Forgot you're not a cricket fan.'

'What are you interested in?' asked Jenny.

Another rescue attempt, thought Charlie.

'Hardly anything,' he shrugged.

'There must be *something*,' persisted the girl.

Should have been, thought Charlie. Edith's complaint too. The one he thought he could solve with the appropriated money.

'*Enjoy ourselves now, Edith... my money, not...... nothing we can't do.*'

Except stay alive. And he'd killed her. By being bloody stupid. He'd killed her as surely as if he'd pressed the trigger. And he wouldn't forget it, he knew. Not for a single minute of a single day.

'No,' said Charlie. 'Nothing.'

New discomfort grew up between them at the collapse of the conversation, covered within minutes by the arrival of a waiter, clearing dishes and the rotating table centre upon which they had been arranged.

Jenny waited until fresh tea and more cups had been set out and then excused herself, pushing through the screen.

Very little to stay for, thought Charlie.

'Jenny's a very lovely girl,' he said dutifully.

'Of course she is,' said Nelson.

Charlie frowned, both at the choice of words and the truculence. Nelson was quite drunk.

'Now we've learned about the 12 per cent I know I'll be dismissed for this damned policy,' declared the broker obstinately. He was gazing down into his cup, talking more to himself than to Charlie.

'I've told you…' Charlie started, but Nelson talked on, unheeding.

'And then they'll laugh. My God, how they'll laugh.'

'Who?' demanded Charlie.

'People,' said Nelson, looking at him for the first time. 'All the people. That's who'll laugh.'

'At what, for Christ's sake!'

'Jenny and me… but to my face, then. Not like now… behind my back.'

'But why?'

'Because they consider Robert has strayed outside a well-ordered system.'

Charlie turned at the girl's voice. She was standing just inside the screen. She must have realised they had been discussing her, yet she was quite composed.

'Sorry,' mumbled Nelson. 'Very sorry. Just talking…'

'I think it's time we left,' she said, to Nelson. The tenderness in her expression was the first unguarded feeling she had permitted herself all evening.

'Yes,' agreed Nelson, realising he had created an embarrassment. 'Time to go home.'

He tried to get his wallet from his pocket, but Jenny took it easily from him, settling the bill. She seemed practised in looking after him.

Nelson walked unsteadily between them out into Gloucester Road. There was a taxi at the kerbside and the broker slumped into it, sitting with his head thrown back, eyes closed.

'He doesn't usually drink this much,' apologised the girl.

'It doesn't matter,' said Charlie.

'Oh, it does,' she said urgently. 'You mustn't think he's like this all the time. He's not, normally. It's because he's worried about dismissal.'

'I know. I've tried to make him understand, but he won't listen.'

'It would mean the end of everything for him, to be fired.' She didn't appear to believe him either, thought Charlie. What the hell did he have to do to convince them?

'He tried to explain to me, back in the restaurant. But it was difficult for him.'

She seemed to consider the remark. Then she said, speaking more to herself than to Charlie, 'Yes, sometimes it's difficult for him.'

'Thank you for the meal,' said Charlie, as she started to enter the car. 'It was a splendid evening.'

She turned at the door, frowning.

'No it wasn't,' she said. 'It was awful.'

On the Kowloon side of the harbour Harvey Jones stared around his room at the Peninsula Hotel, his body tight with excitement. Specially chosen, the deputy director had said. To prove himself. And by Christ, he was going to do just that.

Sure of the security of his locked room, the American took from his briefcase the documents identifying him as an official of the United States Maritime Authority, transferring them to his wallet. A perfect cover for the circumstances, he decided.

It was going to be difficult to sleep, despite the jet-lag. But he had to rest, if he were to perform properly. Carefully he tapped out a Seconal capsule, swilling it down with water from the bedside jug.

He hoped the fire wasn't as straightforward as it appeared. He wanted there to be a startling explanation. Something that would surprise everyone. Impress them, too, when he revealed it.

8.

Clarissa Willoughby stared over the dinner table at her husband, throat working with the approach of the predictable anger.

'What do you mean, broke?'

'Just that.'

The woman laughed, a disbelieving sound.

'But we can't be.'

'For the last two years we've been continuously unlucky,' said the underwriter. 'It's been nobody's fault.'

'It must be somebody's fault,' she insisted.

He shook his head, not wanting to argue with her but knowing it was practically unavoidable. It had been ridiculous to expect her understanding, because Clarissa had never understood anything, except perhaps the importance of the Dublin Horse Show compared to Cowes Week or what dress was right for the Royal Enclosure at Ascot but unsuitable for Henley.

'It's a combination of circumstances,' he said inadequately. 'Unless we can find something wrong with this ship fire, I can't avoid going down.'

'Going down?'

'Bankrupt. And struck off the Exchange…'

'Oh Christ!'

'I'm sorry.'

'Sorry!' she mocked.

'What else do you expect me to say?'

'There must be something…?'

'I've used all my own money.'

'The banks, then…'

'Won't advance another penny.'

She thrust up from the table and began to move jerkily about the room. She was very beautiful, he thought. Spoiled and selfish and arrogant, but still very beautiful. And she wasn't a hypocrite, either. She'd never once told him she loved him.

'My friends will laugh at me,' she protested.

'Yes,' he agreed. '*Your* friends probably will.'

He hadn't meant to emphasise the word. She swung back to him.

'What does that mean?'

'It doesn't mean anything,' he said wearily.

'Will your friends behave any better?' she demanded. 'Do you know anyone you can rely upon?'

Not a friend, accepted Willoughby. Just one man whom the underwriter felt he would never completely understand.

He looked up at his wife. How would she react to Charlie Muffin? It would be a cruel experiment; for Clarissa, not Charlie.

'What are you going to do?'

'Delay settlement as long as possible.'

'Why?'

'In the hope of there being some reason why we don't have to pay out.'

'Is that a possibility?'

He examined the question, slowly shaking his head.

'No,' he admitted. 'It doesn't seem that it is, from what we know so far.'

'So you're just trying to put off the inevitable?'

'Yes,' he said. 'I suppose I am.'

'Christ,' she said again. 'I can hardly believe it.'

She lit a cigarette, puffed nervously at it and then stabbed it out into an ashtray.

'I'm still finding it difficult,' he conceded.

'I want to know, at least a week before,' she declared.

'Know what?'

'When the announcement is going to be made about your bankruptcy... before all the fuss begins.'

'Why?' he asked sadly.

'I would have thought that was obvious.'

'Why, Clarissa?' he insisted.

'You surely don't expect me to stay here, in London, among all the elbow-nudging and sniggering...?'

'I'd hoped you might.'

'You should know better than that.'

'Yes,' he agreed. 'Of course I should.'

'What a mess,' she said. 'What a rotten, shitty mess.'

'Yes,' he said. 'It is.'

She stopped at the table, staring down at him. 'Is that all?'

'All?' he asked.

'All you're going to do? Sit around like a dog that's been beaten once too often and just wait for the final kick?'

'There's nothing more I can do.'

'What a man!' she sneered.

'I've said I'm sorry.'

'How soon will you hear about the fire?'

'I don't know,' he said.

'I won't forgive you for this,' she said.

The remark reached through his depression and he laughed at her.

'I don't see anything funny,' she said.

'No, darling,' said Willoughby. 'You wouldn't.'

Robert Nelson had become an unconscious weight by the time Jenny manoeuvred him into their apartment. She stumbled with him into the bedroom and heaved him on to the bed. He lay there, mouth open, snoring up at her.

She smiled down.

'Poor darling,' she said.

With the expertise of a woman used to handling drunks, she undressed him, rocking him back and forth to free trapped clothing and finally rolling him beneath the covers.

She undressed, hesitated by the bedside and instead put on a kimono, returning to the lounge. The curtains were drawn away from the windows. She slid aside the glass door and went out to the verandah edge, standing with her hands against the rail. Below her the lights of Hong Kong glittered and sparked, like fireflies. She looked beyond to where a blackened strip marked the harbour. It was impossible to see the partially submerged liner, but she knew exactly where it would be. She stared towards its unseen shape for a long time, her body still and unmoving.

'Oh Christ,' she said at last. It was a sad, despairing sound. She turned back into the room, her head sunk against her chest, so she was actually inside before she realised it wasn't empty any more. Fright whimpered from her and she snatched her hand up to her mouth. Jenny stood with her back against the cold window, eyes darting to the faces of the three men, seeking identification.

'No,' said the eldest of the three. 'We're not people you're likely to know.'

He spoke Cantonese.

'Oh,' she said, in understanding.

'Surprised we are here?'

'Yes.'

'Frightened?'

'Yes.'

'It's right you should be.'

'What do you want?'

'For this stupidity to stop.'

'Stupidity?'

'The ship. Don't pretend ignorance.'

'What can I do?'

The man smiled.

'That's a naive question.'

'There's nothing I can do,' she said desperately.

'What about the man who's come from London?'

'He's supposed to be investigating,' she conceded, doubt in her voice.

'And what is he likely to discover?'

'Nothing,' she admitted.

'Precisely,' said the man.

'So he must be shown.'

'By me?'

'Who else?'

'How?'

'You're a whore. Used to men. You shouldn't have to ask that question.'

There was distaste in the man's voice. Momentarily she squeezed her eyes closed, to control the emotion.

'You can't make me,' she said. It was a pitiful defiance, made more childlike because her voice jumped unevenly.

'Oh don't be ridiculous,' said the man, irritated. He gestured towards the bedroom door beyond which Robert Nelson slept.

'Do you feel for him?'

'I love him,' said Jenny. This time she didn't have to force the defiance.

'If you don't do as you are told,' said the man quietly, 'we will kill him.'

Jenny stared across at the leader of the group.

'You do believe me, don't you?' he said.

'Yes,' she said. 'I believe you.'

'So you'll do it?'

'Do I have a choice?'

'Of course not.'

Cantonese was the language of another meeting that night, because most of the people assembled in one of the three houses that John Lu owned in Kowloon were street Chinese and uncomfortable with English. It had been right that he should make the announcement, according to tradition, so his father had remained on Hong Kong island. Freed of the old man's intimidating presence, the boy had adopted the same cold authority, enjoying its effect upon the people with him.

'Is that understood?' he demanded.

There were nods and mutterings of agreement.

'Even the New Territories, as well as Kowloon and Hong Kong,' he emphasised.

'We understand,' said the man in the front.

'Everyone must know,' insisted the millionaire's son. That was as important as the tradition of making the announcement.

'They will,' promised the man who had spoken earlier.

9.

Charlie had expected his appointment to be cancelled after the court deaths of the two Chinese, but when he telephoned for confirmation Superintendent Johnson's secretary assured him he was still expected.

Unable to lose the feeling that he was being watched, Charlie walked to police headquarters by a circuitous route, frequently leaving the wider highways to thread through the shop-cluttered alleyways, their incense sticks smouldering against the evil spirits, all the while checking behind and around him, irritated when he located nothing and growing convinced, yet again, that his instinct had become blunted.

There was another feeling, even stronger than annoyance. He'd always thought of his ability to survive as instinctive, too. It was an attribute he couldn't afford to lose.

'Perhaps I should burn incense,' he muttered, recognising the indication of fear.

The police headquarters were as ordered and regimented as the man who commanded them, the regulation-spaced desks of the head-bent clerks tidy and unlittered, the offices padded with an almost church-like hush.

Johnson's office was the model for those outside. Never, decided Charlie as he entered, would it achieve the effect of being occupied and worked in; it was more like an exhibition case.

Even seated behind the predictably imposing desk, Johnson had perfected the stretched-upright gaze of intimidation. The police chief indicated a chair to the left of the desk and Charlie sat, waiting in anticipation.

Almost immediately Johnson looked at his watch, for Charlie to know the pressure upon his time.

'Appointment in thirty minutes,' he warned.

'It was good of you to see me so promptly,' Charlie thanked him. 'Especially after what happened in court.'

Such men always responded to deference, Charlie knew.

'Murder,' confirmed Johnson.

'Murder?'

Johnson would need very little encouragement, guessed Charlie.

'Post-mortem examinations proved they both died from a venom-based poison... created involuntary lung-muscle spasms. Cause of death was asphyxiation.'

Charlie said nothing, remembering the strangled breathing.

'The Chinese farm snakes, you know. For food.'

'I know,' said Charlie.

'So venom is freely available in the colony. Chinese doctors even use it in some cases as a health remedy. It'll take more tests but we think it was either from a Banded Krait or a Coral Snake.'

'You said murder,' Charlie reminded him.

Johnson leaned back in the chair, refusing to be hurried despite his own restriction upon time.

'Know what solves crime?' he demanded.

'What?' asked Charlie. Had Johnson always been as overbearing as this? Or had he developed the attitude since he arrived in the colony?

'Routine. Just simple routine. Finding those responsible for the fire was merely a matter of gradually working through those Chinese employed on the refit, matching the fingerprints to those we found all over the sprinkler systems and the incendiary devices and then confronting them with the evidence. Simple, logical routine.'

'And now you've made an arrest for their murder?' said Charlie.

Johnson shifted, off-balanced by the question.

'Employing the same principle, we've satisfied ourselves we know the man responsible. We've eliminated every person who had contact with the dead men except one.'

'Who?'

'A prison cook. Ideally placed to introduce the poison. His name is Fan Yung-ching.'

'But you haven't made an arrest?'

'Not yet.'

'Because he's returned to mainland China?' suggested Charlie.

Johnson frowned at the anticipation.

'That's what we strongly suspect,' admitted the police chief. 'We've established that he disappeared from his lodgings and that his family have always lived in Hunan, on the mainland. Apparently he crossed about six months ago.'

'I'm surprised how easy it appears to be to go back and forth over the border,' said Charlie.

The superintendent leaned forward on his desk, always alert for criticism. Basically unsure of himself, judged Charlie.

'It's virtually impossible for us to control or even estimate the number that cross each year,' conceded the police chief. 'At least five thousand come in without Chinese permission, swimming across the bay. Double that number must enter with official approval.'

'Ten thousand!' said Charlie.

'Would it frighten you to know that the majority of Chinese crews on British warships and naval support vessels come from communist China, with merely accommodation addresses here to satisfy the regulations about their being Hong Kong Chinese?'

'Yes,' admitted Charlie. 'It probably would.'

'It's a fact,' insisted Johnson. 'And it frightens the Americans, too. Particularly during joint NATO exercises.'

'So you're convinced that the men who destroyed the *Pride of America* were infiltrated into the colony. Then killed by another Chinese agent?'

Johnson nodded, tapping another file neatly contained in red binding at the corner of his desk. The word 'closed' was stencilled on it, Charlie saw.

'To save the embarrassment that might have been caused by the trial,' the policeman confirmed.

Johnson had a pigeon-hole mind, decided Charlie.

'Once we confronted the two with the evidence of the fingerprints and the incendiary devices, they made full statements,' continued Johnson. 'Admitted they were told to cross, then wait until they were contacted… what espionage people call being…'

He hesitated, losing the expression.

Sleepers, you bloody fool, thought Charlie. He said nothing. His feet were beginning to hurt and he wriggled his toes, trying to become more comfortable.

'I forget the term,' dismissed Johnson. 'Anyway, they were eventually contacted, given the materials to cause the fire and did what they were told.'

'Just as you think the prison cook did?'

Again Johnson looked curiously at the doubt in Charlie's voice.

'From other people at the man's lodging house, we know that the night before the remand hearing another Chinese came to see him, that he handed the cook a package and that afterwards the man seemed agitated and frightened. We've got fingerprints from his room which match those on the rice bowls from which the men ate before they came to court...'

'And that, together with his mainland background, fits neatly into the pattern?'

'I've considered all the evidence,' Johnson defended himself.

'I've seen most of it,' Charlie reminded him.

'And mine is the proper conclusion on the facts available.'

'But doesn't it seem just a little clumsy?' asked Charlie.

'Clumsy?'

'The two who fired the liner were opium smokers, weren't they?' asked Charlie, recalling the indications at the court hearing.

'There was medical evidence to that effect,' admitted Johnson. 'Many Chinese are.'

'And almost illiterate?' pressed Charlie.

'There was no education, no,' conceded Johnson.

'What about the cook?'

'Apparently he smoked, too. We haven't been able to establish his literacy, obviously.'

'Then to use your guidelines, it's not logical, is it?' said Charlie. 'Or even sensible?'

'What?' demanded Johnson, resenting the argument.

'In a fanfare of publicity,' said Charlie, 'one of the world's most famous passenger liners is brought here and a man renowned for years of anti-communist preaching announces that it's to become a prestige university at which he's going permanently to lecture against the Peking regime...'

'I'm aware of the facts,' interrupted Johnson.

'Then don't you think it's odd,' broke in Charlie, 'that a country which decides to stifle that criticism – a country which according to you can without the risk of interception move ten thousand people into this colony and therefore, presumably, include in that figure the most expert sabotage agents in any of its armed forces – should select for the task three near-illiterate, drug-taking Chinese whose capture or discovery was practically a foregone conclusion? And by so doing guarantee worse publicity than if they'd let the damned ship remain?'

Johnson laughed, a dismissive sound.

'A logical argument...' he began.

'Routine logic,' interposed Charlie.

'Which regrettably doesn't fit the facts,' concluded Johnson. 'You must defer to my having a great deal more knowledge of these matters than you.'

'But they just *wouldn't* do it, would they?' insisted Charlie, cautious of any mention of his earlier life.

'Give me an alternative suggestion,' said Johnson.

'At the moment I don't have one,' said Charlie. 'But I'm going to keep my mind a great deal more open than yours until I've better proof.'

'And you think you're going to get that in Hong Kong?' sneered Johnson, carelessly patronising.

'I'm going to try.'

The large man rose from his desk, staring towards the window.

'You're a Westerner,' he said, turning back into the room after a few moments. 'A round-eye... even if there were anything more to discover, which I don't believe there is, you wouldn't stand a cat in hell's chance of penetrating this society.'

The second time he'd had that warning in forty-eight hours, thought Charlie. It was becoming boring.

'And if I can?'

Johnson shook his head at the strange conceit in the unkempt man sitting before him.

'Come back to me with just one piece of producible evidence that would give me legal cause to reopen the case and I'll do it,' he promised. 'Just one piece.'

He hesitated.

'But I tell you again,' he added, 'you're wasting your time.'

The 12 per cent premium on its own wasn't evidence. Not without the reason to support it. It could wait until another meeting. And Charlie was sure that there would be one.

'Have you asked the Chinese authorities for any assistance in locating the cook?' asked Charlie.

'There's been a formal application,' said Johnson. 'But we don't expect any assistance. There never is.'

'So what will happen?'

'We'll issue an arrest warrant. And perhaps a statement.'

'And there the matter will lie... still a communist-inspired fire?'

Johnson smiled, condescending again.

'Until we receive your surprise revelation, there the matter will lie,' he agreed. 'Irrefutably supported by the facts. There's no way you can avoid a settlement with Mr Lu.'

On the evidence available, decided Charlie, the policeman was right. Poor Willoughby.

He saw Johnson look again at his watch and anticipated the dismissal, rising from his chair.

'Thank you again,' he said.

'Any further help,' said Johnson, over-generous in his confidence. 'Don't hesitate to call.'

'I won't,' promised Charlie.

Superintendent Johnson's next appointment was approaching along the corridor as Charlie left. Politely, Charlie nodded.

Harvey Jones returned the greeting.

Neither man spoke.

The telex message awaiting Charlie at the hotel said contact was urgent, so although he knew it would he five o'clock in the morning he booked the telephone call to Rupert Willoughby's home. The underwriter answered immediately, with no sleep in his voice.

'Well?' he said. The anxiety was very obvious.

'It doesn't feel right,' said Charlie.

'So we can fight?'

The hope flared in the man's voice.

'Impressions,' qualified Charlie. 'Not facts.'

'I can't contest a court hearing on impressions,' said Willoughby, immediately deflated. 'And according to our lawyers that's what we could be facing if we prolong settlement.'

'I know that,' said Charlie. 'There is one thing.'

'What?'

'Lu agreed to pay you a 12 per cent premium…'

'I told you that.'

'I know. What's your feeling at learning everyone else only got 10 per cent?'

There was no immediate response from the underwriter.

'That doesn't make sense,' he said at last. 'We were the biggest insurers, after all.'

'Exactly.'

'So there is something more than impressions?' said Willoughby eagerly. Again the hope was evident.

'It's not grounds for refusing to pay,' insisted Charlie.

'But what about the court deaths?'

'The police chief is convinced he's solved that… and that it doesn't alter anything.'

'What about the 12 per cent, linked with the deaths?'

'I didn't tell him about the premiums,' admitted Charlie.

'Why the hell not?'

'Because there is no link. So I want to understand it, first.'

'We haven't the time,' protested Willoughby. 'How long?'

'A week at the very outside,' said the underwriter.

'That's not enough.'

'It'll have to be.'

'Yes,' accepted Charlie. 'It'll have to be.'

'Have you seen Lu?'

'Not yet.'

'Surely he's the one to challenge about the 12 per cent?'

'Of course he is.'

'Well?'

'By itself, it's not enough,' Charlie insisted.

'So what are you going to do?'

'I don't know,' admitted Charlie.

'That's not very reassuring.'

'I'm not trying to be reassuring. I'm being honest.'

'I'd appreciate forty-eight-hour contact,' said Willoughby. And spend the intervening time working out figures on the backs of envelopes and praying, guessed Charlie.

'I'll keep in touch,' he promised.

'I'm relying on you,' said Willoughby.

Charlie replaced the receiver, turning back upon it almost immediately.

'Damn,' he said. He'd forgotten to ask Willoughby to send a letter to Robert Nelson, assuring him of his job. Not that the promise would matter if he didn't make better progress than he had so far. He'd still do it, though. The next call would be soon enough.

He was at the mobile bar, using it for the first time, when the bell sounded. Carrying his drink, he went to the door, concealing his reaction when he opened it.

'I thought you'd be surprised,' said Jenny Lin Lee, pouting feigned disappointment. Then she smiled, openly provocative, the hair which the previous night she had worn so discreetly at the nape of her neck loose now. She shook her head, a practised movement, so that it swirled about her like a curtain.

'I am,' said Charlie.

'Then you're good at hiding things,' she said, moving past him into the suite without invitation.

'Perhaps we both are,' said Charlie.

Clarissa stood looking down at her husband expectantly when Willoughby put the phone down.

'Nothing,' he said, shaking his head. 'Some inconsistencies, but nothing that positively helps.'

'But the court murders?'

'It doesn't change anything, apparently.'

'How good is this man you've got there, for Christ's sake?'

The underwriter paused at the question. He knew little more than what he had heard from his father, he realised. Certainly the escape in which Charlie had involved him had been brilliantly organised. But then Charlie had been fighting for his own existence, not somebody else's.

'Very good, I understand,' he said.

'Little proof of it so far,' complained the woman.

That was the trouble, thought Willoughby. Proof.

'Give him time,' he said unthinkingly.

'I thought that was what we didn't have.'

'No,' admitted the underwriter, 'we don't.'

'You won't forget, Rupert, will you?'

'No,' he promised. 'I won't forget.'

'A week's warning, at least.'

'A week's warning,' he agreed. Why was it, he wondered, that he didn't feel distaste for this woman?

10.

Jenny Lin Lee had pulled her hair forward and because she sat with her legs folded beneath her it practically concealed her body. He was still able to see that beneath the white silk cheongsam she was naked. She took the glass from him, making sure that their hands touched.

'I got the impression last night that you didn't drink,' he said.

'Robert needs a sober guardian.'

'Where is he now?'

'At the weekly dinner of the businessmen's club,' said Jenny disdainfully. 'One of the few places that will still let him in.'

Purposely she moved her hair aside, so that more of her body was visible. She looked very young, he thought.

'There are some that don't?' he asked.

'Apparently.' She shrugged, an uncaring gesture.

'Why?'

'You mean he didn't tell you?' she demanded, revolving the glass so that the ice clattered against the sides.

'Tell me what?'

'The great embarrassment of Robert Nelson's life,' she intoned, deepening her voice to a mock announcement. 'He's in love with a Chinese whore.'

It was an interesting performance, thought Charlie. So it had been a professionalism he'd recognised the previous night. Why, he wondered, had it been so difficult for him to identify? He of all people. Not that he would have used the word to describe her. Because she wasn't. Not like the girl in front of him.

'Say hello to your uncle, Charlie, there's a good boy... what's your name again, love?'

But not a whore. Never have called her that. Not now. She hadn't even taken money, not unless it was offered her. And only then if the rent were due or the corner store were refusing any more credit or some new school uniform were needed. And she would always describe it as a loan. Actually put scribbled IOUs in the coronation mug on the dresser. He'd found fifty there, when his mother had died. All carefully dated. And dozens more in the biscuit tin, the one in which she put the rent money and the hire purchase instalments. One of the names, he supposed, had been that of his father. She wouldn't have known, of course. Not for certain. She would have been able to remember them all, though. Because to her they hadn't been casual encounters. None of them.

He didn't believe she'd wanted physical love. Not too much anyway. It was just that in her simple, haphazard way, she couldn't think how else it would enter, except through the bedroom door.

She'd tried to explain, pleading with him. She'd been crying and he'd thought the mascara streaks had looked like Indian warpaint.

He'd been the National Service prodigy then. Transferred because of his brilliance as an aerial photographer from RAF Intelligence to the department that Sir Archibald was creating.

And so very impressed with the accents and the attitudes of the university entrants. Impressed with everything, in fact. And so anxious to belong. He hadn't challenged them, of course. Not then. That had been the time when he was still trying to ape their talk and their habits, unaware of their amusement.

And been frightened that the sniffling, sobbing woman who didn't even have the comfort now of any more uncles would endanger his selection because of the security screening he knew was taking place.

'Can't you understand what it's like to be lonely, Charlie... to want somebody you can depend on, who won't notice when you're getting old...'

He'd grimaced at the mascara. And called her ugly. The one person who could have given her the friendship she'd wanted, he thought. And he hadn't understood. Any more than he'd understood what Edith had wanted from him, until it was too late. Why had he never been able to dream Edith's dreams?

How long, he wondered, would it take Robert Nelson?

'Strayed outside the well-ordered system,' he quoted.

She nodded.

'The Eleventh Commandment,' said Jenny. 'Thou shalt fuck the natives but not be seen doing it.'

'And you don't love him?'

'What's love got to do with being a whore?'

'Very little.'

'He's convenient,' she said. 'And the bed's clean.'

'Do you really despise him?'

'I despise being paraded around, to garden parties where people won't talk to me and to clubs where I'm ignored, so he can show me off like someone who's recovered from a terminal illness.'

'Why don't you tell him that?'

'I have. He says I'm imagining it and he wants me to be accepted.'

'Why not leave?'

'Like I said,' she sniggered, 'the bed's clean. And the money is regular.'

'But not enough?'

'There's never enough money... that's one of Lucky Lu's favourite expressions.'

Charlie slowly lowered himself into a chair facing the girl, feeling the first tingle of familiar excitement.

'I hadn't heard that,' he encouraged.

'You'd be amazed, with all the publicity, at the things people haven't heard about Lucky Lu.'

The entry into the society that everyone said would be denied him? Charlie frowned. He'd always suspected things that came too easily.

'Like what?' he prompted.

'You got money?' asked the girl.

'As much as you want,' offered Charlie, misunderstanding the demand.

She stood, smiling.

'You spend a lot and you get a lot,' she promised, walking towards the bedroom.

Charlie remained crouched forward in the chair, momentarily confused. Before Edith's death, there had been many affairs, the sex sometimes as loveless as that being offered by the woman who had disappeared into the bedroom. But for almost two years there had been a celibacy of grief. He'd always known it would end. But not like this. Mechanically almost. But she had hinted a knowledge about Lu of which even Nelson seemed unaware; a knowledge he'd never learn if he rejected her.

'I don't believe you can reach from there,' she called.

He grimaced at the awkward coarseness, then stood hesitantly, walking towards the bedroom. There was nothing, he realised. No lust. No feeling. Certainly not desire. Just apprehension.

She'd discarded the cheongsam and was sitting back on her heels, near the top of the bed. She'd swept her hair forward again, covering herself except for her breasts, which pouted through like pink-nosed puppies.

'You only keep your clothes on for short-time. You don't want a short-time, do you?'

Rehearsed words, he thought. Like prompt cards in a child's classroom. Would his mother have ever been like this? No, he decided. She wouldn't have even known the expressions. He was sure she wouldn't.

Reluctantly he took off his jacket and tie, edging on to the bed.

'What do you know about Lu?' he asked. He wouldn't be able to make love to her, he knew.

She put her hands on his thigh, feeling upwards, then gazing at him, pulling her mouth into an artificially mournful expression.

'That's not very flattering for a girl,' she complained. Immediately there was the prostitute's smile.

'We'll soon improve that,' she promised.

She moved her hand up, reaching through his shirt, then stopped.

'What's that?' Charlie looked down.

'String vest,' he said.

'A what!'

'String vest. Supposed to keep you cool in hot weather.'

'Good God!'

She began to laugh, genuinely now, and he smiled with her.

'Doesn't seem to work, either.'

'Let me see,' she insisted.

Feeling foolish, he took off his shirt and she began to laugh even more, pointing at him with an outstretched finger and rocking backwards and forwards on her heels.

'You look ridiculous,' she protested. 'Like a fish, a fish wrapped up inside a net…'

He did, thought Charlie. A flat fish. Very apt.

He reached for her outstretched hand, intending to repeat the question about Lu, then realised that the amusement had changed, becoming more strident, edging towards hysteria.

'What…?' he began and then saw she was crying, her eyes flooded with emotion.

'Oh fuck,' she said desperately. 'Fuck, fuck, fuck.'

She pumped her hand in his, in her frustration, and then came forward, pressing her face into his shoulder. Charlie put his arms around her, holding her against him. Her skin was very smooth and he could feel her tipped, soft breasts against him. There was still no reaction within him.

'It was a good try,' he said quietly. Normally there was anger at realising he had been wrong. This time it was relief.

She sobbed on.

'Why?' he said.

'Robert's so worried,' she said, her voice uneven and muffled against his shoulder. 'He's convinced he'll be dismissed, because of the premium.'

'But why this?'

She pulled away from him.

'I'm sorry,' she said.

'It wouldn't have worked.'

'I could have pretended... whores do all the time.'

'I couldn't.'

It was a sad smile, but controlled now.

'No,' she said. 'You couldn't, could you?'

'I still want to know why.'

'Wanted to compromise you... then plead for Robert. Ask you not to recommend that he be fired. Blackmail you even. Another whore's trick.'

'He's not going to be sacked,' insisted Charlie. 'I've told him that, more times than I can count. In a few days, I'll get Willoughby to reassure him by letter.'

She was back on her heels now, gazing at him. Crying had puffed her eyes, he saw.

'It's my fault, you know,' she blurted suddenly.

'What is?'

'The fire... everything, all because of me.'

Charlie leaned forward, taking her hand again.

'Jenny,' he said urgently, 'what are you saying?'

'Lu's people are talking openly to the Chinese about it. They have to, you see. For Lu's family to recover face, it's important that everyone knows...'

'Jenny,' he stopped her. 'Tell me from the beginning. Tell me so that I can understand...'

She sniffed and he groped into his pocket for a handkerchief. She kept it in her hand, tracing her fingers over his wrist, a little-girl gesture.

'Lu doesn't just get his money from shipbuilding and property development and oil,' she began slowly. 'That's crap, part of the great benefactor publicity machine...'

'What else?'

'He owns a good third of the bars and brothels in Wan Chai,' announced the girl. 'Maybe more. They're quieter, now that the war in Vietnam is over and the Americans aren't coming here... and the Sixth Fleet has gone. But there's still enough business. Not that they matter, by themselves. He's got at least two factories here in Hong Kong manufacturing heroin from the poppy resin that comes in from Thailand and Burma... it's called Brown Sugar. Or Number Three...'

She paused, then went on, 'He's the biggest supplier in the colony and ships to America and Europe as well...'

Another pause.

'You know what a Triad is?'

'Something like a Chinese Mafia?'

She nodded.

'Lu's a paymaster for at least three Triads, with branches not just here but in Europe as well.'

'How do you know all this?'

She ignored the question.

'And then there's the name. Lucky Lu. It doesn't come from the luck he had on the Hong Kong stock market, like all the publicity says. He runs the casinos and mahjong games throughout Hong Kong and Kowloon...'

The sad smile again.

'The Chinese are the biggest gamblers in the world,' she said. 'Only Lucky Lu is always the winner.'

'How do you know all this?' repeated Charlie. Almost enough to return to Johnson, he decided, though he still wanted a link with the 12 per cent premium.

Her head was pressed forward now, so that she didn't have to look at him, and when she spoke her voice was muffled once more.

'Before meeting Robert,' she said, 'I was with Johnny Lu... the son that controls Lucky's vice businesses. I was his number one woman...'

'I've seen his pictures,' said Charlie. 'He seems to be almost his father's shadow.'

She hesitated.

'Johnny told me not to go,' she remembered distantly. 'Told me I wouldn't be accepted. He was right...'

'Why was the ship fire your fault?' demanded Charlie.

'Robert didn't get the major share of the insurance because he was better than anybody else,' said Jenny. 'He got it because Lu planned it that way... planned it so that the man who took his son's woman and caused the family loss of face would be the greatest sufferer when the ship burned... that's why the premium was higher.'

At last, thought Charlie. It was all so remarkably simple.

'Lu did it himself?'

She shook her head at the naivety of the question. 'Of course,' she said. 'If you knew more about the Asian mind you'd know that loss of face is the worst insult a Chinese can suffer. Something that's got to be avenged…'

'And having ensured that it wouldn't cost him a penny, he even managed to stage it so that his famous anti-communist campaign would benefit?' he said, in growing awareness.

'Because he is *such* an avowed anti-communist, it made the story even more believable, didn't it?' she said.

'What about the shipyard workers, and the prison cook?'

'Chosen because they were mainland refugees,' she said. 'Frightened people who'd got deeply into debt at Lu's gambling places and were given the way to settle…'

'And as a safeguard against the shipyard men recanting on the rehearsed story, which they would almost certainly have done in court, he had them killed?'

'Yes.'

'Why didn't you tell Robert all this?' asked Charlie suddenly. 'Why wait so long?'

'And let him know that the Chinese as well as the European community in Hong Kong were laughing at him for falling in love with a whore? He's suffering enough as it is.'

'But it means we can contest the claim. Robert would have realised that.'

'Oh, you poor man,' she said. 'This is street gossip, bar talk. The only proof is the cook, who's probably in Hunan by now. Or dead, like the other two. This isn't anything you can fight Lu with…he's won. Like he always wins'

She was right, realised Charlie. About the proof anyway. He still had nothing.

'I'm buggered if he'll win,' said Charlie.

'I told you to show how Robert had been tricked,' said the girl. 'To show why he shouldn't be fired. Not to fight any court hearing.'

'There'll be a way,' promised Charlie.

'I'd like to believe that. God, how I'd like to believe that.'

Charlie heard the noise first. He spun off the bed, crouched towards the linking door und then remained there, staring up foolishly at the figure of Robert Nelson framed in the doorway.

'Oh no,' said the girl quietly. 'Dear God, no.'

'If you set out to do this sort of thing, you should ensure your corridor doors are secured,' said Nelson.

He was striving for enormous dignity, realised Charlie. A nerve twitching high on his left cheek was the only hint of the difficulty he was having in controlling himself.

Charlie motioned towards the now cowering girl. At last she'd tried to protect herself with the bed cover. She was crying again, he saw, softly this time.

'We didn't... there was nothing...' he started, but the broker talked over him.

'That's not really important, is it?'

'Of course it's important,' shouted Charlie. 'She came here because she loves you.'

'It looks like it.'

'Don't be a bloody fool.'

'Like the Chinese think I am, as well as everybody else?'

'You heard...' started Charlie but again Nelson refused him.

'Enough. And I'm as determined as you are that Lu won't succeed in his claim.'

He looked to the girl.

'I don't want you back at the apartment,' he said evenly.

'Please...'

'Just pack your stuff and get out. Tonight.'

'For Christ's sake,' protested Charlie. 'This is ridiculous. What's wrong with you?'

'Nothing,' said Nelson. 'Not any more. And when I establish that Lu's claim is false, there won't be any more laughter either.'

So Nelson didn't understand. Any more than he'd been able to, all those years ago.

The broker turned away from the bedroom, but Charlie called out, halting him.

'Where are you going?'

'To find one of the Chinese spreading the story she recounted and get him to swear an affidavit incriminating Lu,' said Nelson, starting towards the outer door again.

'Stop him!' begged Jenny.

'Robert,' yelled Charlie, hurrying into the adjoining room. 'That won't work. Wait. We'll go to the police first. They're the people...'

Nelson slammed the door, without looking round, leaving Charlie standing near the tiny bar.

'Assholes,' he said.

She was at the bedroom door when he turned. Because she had only worn the cheongsam it had taken her seconds to dress. She had stopped crying, but her eyes were still swollen.

'Your handkerchief,' she said, holding it out.

'You can keep it if you want.'

She shook her head. 'Whores don't cry for long.'

She shrugged, a gesture of defeat.

'He expected to catch us,' she announced.

'What?'

'Robert. He expected to find us. He never really trusted me... He thought I couldn't forget the old ways. That's why he came in without knocking. Always unsure…'

Just as Edith had always been unsure, thought Charlie, never quite able to believe their marriage was for him anything different from everything else he did, another way of proving himself equal.

'But why me?'

'You'd have been the obvious choice.'

'He'll have recovered in the morning,' said Charlie hopefully.

Jenny shook her head.

'No.'

'Where will you go?'

'I'm known in all the bars,' she said bitterly.

'Wait. Until tomorrow at least.'

'Maybe.'

'I'll contact you tomorrow,' he said. 'After I've seen the police.'

She gave him a pitying look.

'You don't stand a chance,' she insisted.

'People have been telling me that for as long as I can remember,' he said. It was good to feel confident again. It had been a long time. More than two years, in fact. Not since he'd started to run.

Charlie's second telephone call stopped Willoughby as he was leaving his Knightsbridge flat for the City. The underwriter listened without interruption as Charlie repeated what the girl had told him, without naming her as the immediate source.

'Dear God,' said Willoughby softly.

'There's still no proof,' warned Charlie, immediately detecting the feeling in the other man's voice.

'It would mean we wouldn't have to pay a penny…'

'I said there's no proof.'

'But you can get it, surely?'

'I can get the police to investigate. To be produced in court, it will have to be something official.'

'Do that then. And, Charlie…'

'What?'

'Thank you.'

There was no way to prick the man's optimism.

'Something else,' Charlie said.

'What?'

'I want you to write a letter to Nelson, assuring him that his job is safe.'

'Why?'

'It's important.'

The inner council were impressed, realised Chiu Ching-mao, looking around the faces before him.

They had remained unspeaking during the playback of Charlie's bedroom discussion with Jenny Lin Lee and for those who did not speak sufficient English, Chiu Ching-mao had provided Cantonese transcripts.

'The encounter was excellently monitored,' said the chairman, when the tape ended. 'Congratulate your people upon installing the devices so well.'

'Thank you,' said Chiu. 'I will.'

'So now the Englishman knows the truth?'

'Yes.'

'I wonder what action he'll persuade the police to take?' Chiu knew he wasn't expected to give an opinion and said nothing.

'Why did the girl try to seduce the Englishman?' asked the chairman suddenly. 'Why didn't she just tell him about the fire?'

'I assumed what she said on the recording was the truth... that she wanted to compromise him into protecting the employment of the man she's living with,' suggested Chiu.

The chairman shook his head.

'Stupid woman,' he said. 'Will Nelson cause any problems?'

'I've tried to use it to our advantage,' said Chiu.

'How?'

'John Lu hasn't the cunning of his father,' said Chiu. 'I've calculated upon him panicking.'

'By doing what?'

'Letting Lu's people know what Nelson is trying to do in the waterfront bars.'

'Yes,' agreed the chairman. 'It can't do any harm.'

11.

Charlie was still in his dressing-gown when Superintendent Johnson telephoned.

'I was about to call you,' he said, recognising the police chief's voice.

'I'd like to see you,' said Johnson.

'When?'

'As soon as possible.'

Charlie hesitated. 'What for?'

'It had better wait until you get here.'

'It sounds formal.'

'It is.'

'Thirty minutes,' promised Charlie.

It took him twenty. The building was still wrapped in its ordered calm as Charlie followed the clerk through the hushed corridor to Johnson's office. This time the man stood as Charlie entered, his manner different from their previous meetings. Johnson pointed to the same chair and Charlie sat down, curious at the changed attitude.

'Unpleasant news,' announced Johnson bluntly.

'What?'

'Robert Nelson was found by a harbour patrol-boat just before dawn this morning. Drowned.'

'What!' repeated Charlie, incredulous.

'He's dead, I'm afraid.'

'She told me to stop him...'

'I didn't hear what you said,' complained Johnson.

'He was murdered,' said Charlie.

Johnson spread his hands, shaking his head as he did so. 'Of course it's a shock,' he said. 'He drowned. An accident...'

'I don't believe it was an accident,' insisted Charlie.

Johnson sighed, annoyance overriding the artificial sympathy. The superciliousness was returning, Charlie realised.

'Any more than you believe what happened to the ship?' demanded the policeman, intending sarcasm.

'I *know* what happened to the ship,' said Charlie. 'Lu planned its destruction.'

'Oh for God's sake!'

'Wait,' pleaded Charlie. 'Hear me out... and then see if you think Nelson still died accidentally.'

Johnson settled behind his desk. Predictably he looked at his watch.

Charlie watched the policeman's face as he recounted the story that Jenny Lin Lee had told him, omitting only the circumstances in which Nelson had found them in the hotel suite, but when Johnson did react it was in a way quite unexpected by Charlie.

The police chief laughed, head thrown back to emphasise his mockery.

'Preposterous,' said Johnson. 'Utterly and completely preposterous.'

'But the facts...' started Charlie.

'There are *no* facts,' Johnson crushed him. 'Just one small inconsistency, the apparent willingness to pay a premium higher than that agreed with the other insurers. But that doesn't prove anything.'

'It proves *everything*!'

'Lu is unquestionably a multi-millionaire,' said Johnson. 'The insurance money will only just cover the purchase of the *Pride of America*. The money honouring the contracts with the professors and staff he engaged for his university he has had to pay himself, so he's actually out of pocket. He'll recover £10,000,000. But will have spent more. Insurance frauds are for profit, not exercise. The 12 per cent would be proof if it showed he had made a profit. And it doesn't.'

'But the point is loss of face.'

'That's Chinese business.' Johnson was unimpressed. 'You'll get nowhere in this colony trying to prove a crime by invoking folklore and tradition.'

'How the hell do you prove a crime in this colony?' demanded Charlie.

Johnson stiffened at the intended rudeness.

'When I took over the running of the police force,' he said, speaking slowly, 'it was riven by corruption and scandal. I cleaned it up into one of the most honest in the world... by strict observance of Home Office regulations. And common sense.'

'And common sense dictates that you don't probe too deeply into the affairs of one of the richest and most influential men in Asia?'

'Not when there isn't a good enough reason for so doing,' said Johnson. 'To operate here, there has to be a balance, knowing when to act and when to hold back. Since I became chief of police, the crime rate has never been so low. I respect the Chinese. And they respect me. It's a working relationship.'

'And you'll not instruct your vice squad to probe Lu?'

Johnson shook his head.

'I had a crime of arson,' he said. 'I arrested the culprits, who admitted it in legally recorded statements. The escape of their murderer is an embarrassment, but understandable in the circumstances of Hong Kong. I see no need to launch a meaningless, wasteful investigation.'

'What about Robert Nelson's death?'

'There has already been a post-mortem examination,' said Johnson. 'There was nothing besides the water in his lungs that could have caused his death.'

'He was murdered,' insisted Charlie.

'Your company's representative in this colony was a dissolute...' said Johnson.

He hesitated, uncertain whether to continue. Then he said, 'There are certain rules by which colonials are expected to live. Unfortunately Mr Nelson chose to ignore those rules. By openly cohabiting with a Chinese girl – and not just an ordinary Chinese girl at that – he cut himself off from both societies.'

'I've already had the rules explained to me,' broke in Charlie. 'You can screw them as long as no one knows and you keep your eyes closed.'

'Don't mock or misquote a system about which you know nothing,' said the policeman. 'It maintains the status quo of this colony.'

'So Nelson was an embarrassment whom no one will really miss?'

'It's no secret that he drank heavily. The medical examination showed an appreciable level of alcohol in his body.'

'Oh come on!' jeered Charlie. 'Blind drunk, he stumbled into the harbour.'

Johnson was making a visible effort to control his annoyance.

'I've no doubt whatsoever that the inquest verdict will be accidental death.'

'I'll prove you wrong,' Charlie promised.

'By Chinese folklore and the comic-book ramblings of a Chinese prostitute?' said Johnson. 'Isn't it time you simply accepted your liability, settled whatever claim is being made for the loss of the ship and stopped running around making a fool of yourself?'

Johnson's refusal meant there was no chance of obtaining any official rebuttal of Lu's claim, realised Charlie. And seven thousand miles away a poor bastard was having the first easy day since the fire and imagining he was safe.

'Please,' he tried again; accepting the error of antagonising the other man. 'Surely there's sufficient doubt for some sort of investigation?'

'Not in my opinion.' Johnson was adamant.

'Let's not risk the *status quo*,' challenged Charlie, facing the hopelessness of persuading the man.

'No,' agreed Johnson, still holding his temper. 'Let's not.'

'Aren't you frightened of pressure from London?' demanded Charlie.

Johnson's face tightened at the threat.

'This colony is self-governing.'

'It's a Crown colony, still answerable to Whitehall,' said Charlie.

It was a stupid attempt, he recognised. How could he risk going to the London authorities? Even if Willoughby tried, there would be a demand for the underwriter's source. He might be safe in Hong Kong, but he could never sustain a London enquiry.

'If there is any interest from London, I'm sure I can satisfy it,' said Johnson.

He'd destroyed any hope of getting assistance from the policeman, Charlie knew. And he could think of no one else.

'Is there anything you want officially done about Nelson?' he asked, anxious now to end the meeting.

'Formal identification.'

Unspeaking, Charlie followed the police chief through the cathedral-quiet corridors and into the basement. He'd been too often in mortuaries but was never able to inure himself to the surroundings. The habitual casualness of the attendants offended him, as did the identification tags, always tied like price tickets to the toes.

The drawer was withdrawn and the sheet pulled aside. At last Robert Nelson had lost the expression of permanent anxiety, thought Charlie.

'Yes,' said Charlie.

'What about his clothes?' asked an attendant, as Charlie turned to leave.

Charlie looked back. The man was indicating a jumble of sodden clothing visible inside a transparent plastic bag.

'I'll send for it,' said Charlie. The bundle had been tied together with the Eton tie.

Jenny opened the door of Nelson's apartment hurriedly, the hope discernible in her face.

'Oh,' she said. There was disappointment in her voice, too.

'I'm glad you stayed,' said Charlie.

'I promised,' she said. 'But he isn't here.'

'I knew he wouldn't be.'

She stood aside for him to enter.

'What's happened?' she anticipated him, remaining by the door.

'He's dead, Jenny.'

She nodded.

'Of course,' she said.

She shrugged. 'I tried so hard to protect him. That's all I wanted to do, to stop him getting hurt.'

'In the harbour,' said Charlie inadequately. 'Drowned.'

She was standing very still, refusing any emotion.

'It'll be thought an accident,' she said.

'Yes,' he said. 'That's how they're treating it.'

'But he was murdered, of course.'

'I know.'

'I wonder which of them did it?' she said. She spoke quietly, to herself.

'Which of them?' demanded Charlie.

She looked directly at him, as if considering her words. 'Nothing,' she said finally.

'What is it, Jenny?'

'Nothing,' she said again.

'Help me,' pleaded Charlie.

'I tried,' she said sadly. 'For nothing. So no more mistakes.'

She paused.

'Poor Robert,' she said. 'Poor darling.'

'I'll make the arrangements,' said Charlie.

'Yes.'

'I'm sorry, Jenny. Really sorry.'

She made a listless movement. The resignation was almost visible.

'Did you tell the police about the fire?' she asked.

'They didn't believe me,' said Charlie.

'So nothing is going to be done about that, either.'

'Not by the police, no.'

'I told you,' she reminded him. 'I told you Lu would win. He always does.'

'I'll upset it,' said Charlie. 'Some way I'll upset it.'

'No you won't,' she said. 'You'll just get hurt. Like Robert. And like me.'

'Do you want me to stay?'

She looked at him curiously. 'Stay?'

'Here, for a while.'

She shook her head.

'I told you before,' she said. 'Whores don't cry for long.'

'Why keep calling yourself that?' said Charlie angrily.

'Because that's how I've always been treated,' she said. 'And how I always will.'

When Charlie got back to the hotel, he found there had been three attempts to contact him from London by telephone.

'And there's been a telex message,' added the receptionist. Remaining at the desk, Charlie tore open the envelope.

'Lu today issued High Court writs,' it said. It was signed by Willoughby.

Charlie had started towards the lift, head still bent over the message, when he felt the hand upon his arm.

'I've been waiting for you,' said the man. 'Gather you're as interested in the ship fire as I am.'

'Who are you?' asked Charlie, recognising the accent and feeling the immediate stir of anxiety deep in his stomach.

'Harvey Jones,' said the man, offering his hand. 'United States Maritime Authority.'

My ass, thought Charlie, instinctively. And this time, he knew, there was nothing wrong with his instinct.

'It was never part of the original proposal,' protested Lu. As always, he spoke quietly, despite his anger.

'It was an over-reaction,' admitted his son. His habitual nervousness was even more pronounced.

'Which you could have prevented.'

'I'm sorry.'

'You're stupid,' said Lu. 'Is there a risk of the police treating it as murder?'

'There's been no announcement. It was done carefully.'

'The absence of an announcement doesn't mean anything.'

'I know.'

'So you've permitted an uncertainty.'

'Yes.'

'Do you know what would have happened to anyone who wasn't my son?'

'Yes.'

'And even that wouldn't be an obstacle if it became a choice between us.'

'I know.'

'There mustn't be any more mistakes.'

'There won't be.'

'I'm determined there won't be,' said Lu. 'Quite determined.'

12.

Charlie was forcing the calmness, sitting deep into the chair with his hands outstretched along the armrests, watching Harvey Jones pace the room.

Trapped, Charlie decided. Not quite as positively as he had been beside Sir Archibald's grave. Or during the chase that had followed. But it was close. Too close. And all his own fault. He hadn't considered it properly, realising the obvious American reaction to the possibility of communist China deliberately destroying something so recently US property.

He'd managed to conceal the nervousness churning through him, Charlie knew. But only just. The American was already worryingly curious. Otherwise he wouldn't have stage-managed the lobby meeting. So it would only take one mistake. And Jones would isolate it. Charlie was sure of that, because he recognised the American was good. Bloody good. Which meant he had to be better. A damned sight better.

So far, he had been. With the caution of a poacher tickling a trout into the net, Charlie had put out the lures. And Jones had taken them. But even then it had needed all Charlie's experience to spot the tradecraft in the other man. For him Charlie felt the respect of one professional for another. He hesitated at the thought; a professional wouldn't have allowed the miscalculation which had brought about this meeting.

'I'd have expected someone with Johnson's experience to see the bit that doesn't fit,' suggested Jones.

'What was that?' asked Charlie. He would have to be cautious of apparently innocent questions. Cautious of everything.

'That Peking would hardly have used ignorant hop-heads for a job like this.'

'Johnson told you?'

Jones completed a half-circuit of the room. The movement was as much of a test as the questions, Charlie recognised; an attempt to irritate him by its very theatricality.

'Made a joke of it,' said the American, inviting some annoyed response.

'Johnson seems to think almost everything I say is amusing,' said Charlie.

'Oh?'

Shit, thought Charlie. He had to continue.

'I asked him today to investigate what I really think happened to the *Pride of America*,' he said, covering the awkwardness. Perhaps volunteering Jenny's story wouldn't be so much of a mistake. Jones would become suspicious of obvious evasion.

'And what do you think really happened?'

'That Lu planned the fire. And the destruction of the ship.'

'What!'

Jones eased into a facing chair, halted by the announcement.

Again leaving out the girl's attempted seduction, Charlie recounted the story. He was getting very adept at it, he thought. To tell Jones could be another lure, rather than a mistake. The man's reaction would be a further confirmation. Not that he really needed it.

'Jesus!' said Jones.

'Clever, isn't it?' said Charlie.

'But how the hell can you prove it?'

The man had failed, thought Charlie. If Jones really had represented the US Maritime Authority, he'd have been as interested in proving it as Charlie. And accepted it as a joint operation. Jones would realise the mistake and recover quickly, he guessed.

'I can't prove it,' admitted Charlie.

'Johnson isn't interested?'

'Called it preposterous.'

'Which it is.'

Clever, assessed Charlie. Now he was forced to talk further, always with the risk of a slip.

'But it fits better with opium-smoking illiterates,' he pointed out.

'That really was damned smart of you,' repeated Jones.

The American was still manipulating the conversation.

'It seems obvious,' Charlie said uneasily.

'Not to Johnson, who's supposed to be the expert.'

'He's got a policeman's mind... trained only to accept fact.'

'What are you trained in?' demanded Jones openly.

'Trying to avoid £6,000,000 settlements,' said Charlie.

Jones smiled.

Amusement? wondered Charlie. Or admiration at escaping again? There was as much danger in showing himself an expert in this type of interrogation as there was in a misplaced word.

The American rose, to pace the room again.

He went towards the bar and Charlie said, 'Would you like a drink?'

'Never touch it.'

Because it might blur his faculties, no matter how slightly, guessed Charlie. And he judged Jones to be the sort of man who didn't like to lose control of anything, most of all himself. About him there was an overwhelming impression of care. It was most obvious in the pressed and matched clothes, but extended to the manicured hands and close-cropped hair and even to the choice of cologne that retained his just out-of-the-bathroom freshness.

'Can I help you to one?' offered the American.

'No,' said Charlie. Jones didn't want to impair his thinking, he reflected. And he couldn't afford to.

'Thought about asking for an independent autopsy?' asked Jones. 'If you could discover any injury to Nelson inconsistent with his being drowned it would be something upon which Johnson would have to act.'

An invitation to reveal his expertise, saw Charlie, the apprehension tightening within him.

'No,' he said. 'I hadn't thought of that.'

'Might be an idea,' said Jones.

'Yes,' agreed Charlie. 'It might.'

'How much time do you think you have, now that Lu's issued writs?' asked Jones, nodding to Willoughby's telex message that lay between them on the table.

He'd endangered the underwriter by letting the American read the cable as they had travelled up in the lift, Charlie realised belatedly. It had been a panicked reaction, to gain time. Now, unless he allayed the uncertainties, it would be automatic for Jones to have their London bureau check Willoughby. And in his present state, the underwriter wouldn't be able to satisfy any enquiry.

'Not much,' said Charlie. 'Our lawyers will want to begin preparing an answer to Lu's claim almost immediately. And they won't be able to do that on what I've got available.'

'So you're in trouble?'

But just how much? wondered Charlie.

'Looks like it,' he said.

'I'll be intrigued to see what you do,' said Jones.

'What would you do?' demanded Charlie, turning the question.

Jones made an uncertain movement.

'I'm in a more fortunate position than you,' he said. 'There's no money riding on what I do.'

'What, then?' insisted Charlie.

Jones was at the window. He turned at the open question. 'Just a group of government officials who want to know if Peking put a match to a liner hardly out of American ownership.'

Now Jones was making mistakes, thought Charlie, as the different confirmation came of his earlier assessment. Or was he? Perhaps it was an invitation to Charlie to become more careless.

'Why should that interest them?' he pressed. 'The sale had gone through, after all.'

'But only just,' said Jones. 'Hardly be a friendly act towards America, would it?'

'And that worries a shipping authority sufficiently to send you all the way here?'

'You'd better believe it,' said Jones glibly.

But I don't, thought Charlie. It would be wrong to let the disbelief be too obvious.

'So what are *you* going to do?' he repeated. It was time to attempt some insurance of his own. Or at least as much protection as possible.

Jones returned to his chair, apparently realising the failure of his wanderings to irritate Charlie.

'Like you, I'm stuck with the official version,' said the American.

'But I don't accept it. What about you?'

'I like your story better than Johnson's,' conceded Jones.

'Why not ask Johnson's help?' suggested Charlie. 'He might change his mind if he got a second request so quickly.'

Jones made a dismissive gesture with his well-kept hands. 'He'd know it originated from you. And he didn't strike me as a man prepared to change his mind very often.'

'Perhaps you're right,' said Charlie. About now, he decided.

'We could work together,' said Jones, promptly on cue.

Charlie maintained his relaxed pose, smiling across at the other man. Jones had realised his earlier mistake.

'You're welcome to anything I learn,' promised Charlie. 'And if you come up with anything, I'd like to know about it.'

'I was actually thinking of something closer,' said Jones. I know you were, thought Charlie. Aloud, he said, 'I was never much for teamwork.'

'We could both benefit,' Jones argued.

He already had, Charlie decided. Having led Jones into making the suggestion, then rejecting it, he would know from the closeness of the man's attention just how strong Jones's uncertainty of him remained. Which was the maximum insurance for which he could hope.

'Or get in each other's way,' said Charlie. 'I think it's better we work independently. But perhaps exchange what we come up with.'

'So you're a loner?'

'Every time.'

'How many times have there been?'

'What?' said Charlie, momentarily confused by the question.

'How long have you worked for insurance companies?'

'Must be twenty years,' assured Charlie, wanting to change position in the chair but knowing the other man would recognise the nervousness it would betray.

'Long as that?'

'Hardly entrust a £6,000,000 investigation to a newcomer, would they?'

'Not unless he had particular qualities... like being able to see something that the police don't regard as unusual.'

'Seemed obvious, like I told you.'

'Sure,' agreed Jones. 'You told me.'

Charlie waited, but the American didn't continue. The man was letting the silence build up, trying to disturb him as he had attempted with the pointless meandering around the suite.

Remembering the way the encounter had been forced upon him, to *become* annoyed would be entirely natural, realised Charlie, just in time.

'Right,' he said positively, standing up. 'If there's nothing more with which I can help you at the moment...'

'If you're quite sure there isn't?' interrupted Jones, making his most direct approach since they had begun talking.

'And I have a funeral to arrange,' continued Charlie, refusing to respond to the innuendo.

Once more Jones stood, accepting his dismissal.

'Kind of you to let me barge in like this.'

'No trouble at all,' said Charlie.

'We'll keep in touch.'

'Of course.'

'I'm at the Peninsula.'

'I'll remember that.'

'Damned clever of you, seeing the flaw in Johnson's case,' reiterated Jones, shaking his head in feigned admiration and wanting to prolong the meeting as much as possible.

Now it was Charlie's turn to use silence.

'I'll get along then,' said Jones finally.

'Yes,' Charlie encouraged him.

Charlie stood unmoving for several moments after the door had closed behind the American. Then he went to the bar. The bottle vibrated against the glass edge as he splashed the whisky out, drank it in one gulp, then poured a second.

Good, he judged. But good enough? There was no way he could be sure. Certainly Jones had been pressing until the very end. But it would be wrong to read too much into that. It was basic procedure, the sort of persistence he would have shown himself in the same circumstances.

He paused at the thought. As frightened as he had been, there had been something enervating about the confrontation. Perhaps the feeling of a matador facing an insufficiently weakened bull and knowing it could kill him. Charlie snorted, disgusted with himself. That was melodramatic bullshit, he thought; the sort of posturing of which he knew he had been guilty in the past.

He was not fighting bulls. He was fighting for his life. Again.

He wanted to run. The awareness came suddenly, surprising him. He was no more prepared to die now than he had been on the East Berlin border or during the pursuit by the Americans or the British or during any of the missions upon which he'd been sent by the underwriter's father.

A man who relied so much upon instinct, Charlie recognised his determination to survive as the strongest force within him.

So how *could* he survive? Certainly not by running. That would provide whatever confirmation Jones needed and start the chase all over again. Resolve everything quickly then. Far quicker than Willoughby was demanding. But how, against Johnson's official refusal to reopen the case?

'You're fucked, Charlie,' he told himself. 'Without even being kissed.'

He booked the call to London, stared at his glass considering another drink and then rejected the idea. It never helped.

Willoughby's response was immediate. The man must spend all his time waiting by the telephone.

'Nelson's dead,' announced Charlie, quietening a flurry of questions from the underwriter.

'Oh God,' said Willoughby.

'Yes.'

'What happened?'

It took Charlie only a few moments to tell the underwriter. Hardly long enough, he thought. A man's life, dismissed in a minute or two.

'And Johnson still won't help?' demanded Willoughby, when Charlie had finished.

'Not upon anything. And to be fair to the man, I don't suppose there's any logical, police reason why he should.'

'But you said...'

'That I didn't have any proof,' Charlie reminded him. If Harvey Jones instituted any investigation in London, Willoughby would collapse, thought Charlie again.

'I haven't much more time,' said the underwriter, defeat etched into his voice. 'I'll have to make an announcement soon.'

Perhaps neither of us has got much more time, thought Charlie.

'I realise that,' he said.

'What about Nelson trying to prove the girl's story,' said Willoughby desperately. 'That's a motive. Cause enough for some sort of police investigation. That and the premium?'

'But there's no evidence of what Nelson was trying to do... apart from my word. Death was by drowning. And he'd been drinking.'

'So there's still nothing with which we can dispute the writs?'

'Not yet.'

'I was very hopeful.'

'I warned you not to be.'

'It just seemed so good...'

The broker's death registered fully for the first time.

'Poor Robert,' said Willoughby. 'Christ, what a disaster.'

'There's something else,' said Charlie.

He had to warn Willoughby of the danger of Harvey Jones, he knew.

Charlie had expected alarm but it was more hopeless resignation in the underwriter's voice when he had finished telling of the American's visit.

'You could be wrong,' said Willoughby. 'He really could be employed by the maritime agency.'

'No chance,' said Charlie, refusing Willoughby any false reassurance, despite his awareness of the man's need. 'I've spent all my life seeing people like Harvey Jones for what they really are.'

'And he suspects you?'

'Of course not. At the moment he's just curious.'

'But why?'

'He's trained to spot inconsistencies. And he saw it straightaway in the official account, just like I did. It's only natural he should wonder about someone who thinks like he does.'

'What the hell are we going to do, Charlie?'

'I don't know.'

'Get out,' insisted Willoughby suddenly. 'The only thing you can do is run.'

'I've already thought of that,' admitted Charlie. 'It would be the worst thing I could do.'

'What then?'

The idea was only half formed in Charlie's mind, but at least it indicated some intention.

'I think it's time that I saw Lucky Lu.'

'I'm not sure that's strictly legal, now that he's issued writs.'

It probably wasn't, thought Charlie. But being strictly legal had never been a consideration in the past.

'We don't have time to worry about legal niceties,' said Charlie.

'Be careful then. Be bloody careful.' Charlie hesitated at the words.

'I will,' he promised. Or dead, he thought.

It would have helped, decided Harvey Jones, had he had someone with whom he could have discussed the meeting. But the instructions had been explicit. So he had to reach a judgment by himself. The man was unusual, certainly. But was he any more than that? The apparent awareness of interrogation techniques was intriguing. But there were many sorts of people who might have experience of that. Lawyers, for instance. And insurance investigators would have had a lot of contact with the law. A smart lawyer would have spotted the inconsistency about the Chinese dockyard workers, too. Or again, someone who spent a lot of time involved with them.

Specially chosen; to prove himself. That's what the deputy director had said.

And he didn't want to prove himself an idiot by suggesting British Intelligence were in some way interested, with a cover as good as his own.

He'd wait, he decided. Until he was sure. And only when he was convinced would he cable Langley and get them to run a check in London, so that there could be some official instruction for them to work together. Ridiculous to operate separately, after all.

Jones smoothed the robe around him, looking across to where his suit hung crisp and fresh after its return from the hotel valet.

That was another thing he'd found difficult to accept about the man. For someone important enough to be investigating a £6,000,000 insurance claim, he was a scruffy son of a bitch.

Meant one thing, though. With a description like that, it wouldn't take the computer long to come up with the man's proper name. So they could even approach London with an identity, in case the bastards tried to deny their interest.

13.

The reception area was enormous and everywhere there were pictures of L.W. Lu.
Charlie examined them with the professionalism of his teenage training, appreciating the care that had gone into their taking and selection. The biggest, a gigantic enlargement occupying nearly the whole wall behind the desk of identically uniformed girls, showed the millionaire with two American Presidents and another, only slightly smaller, with Henry Kissinger. Along another wall were a series showing Lu individually and then in groups with all the British Commonwealth leaders during the Singapore conference. And the area to the left was given over to a pictorial history of Lu's charity work, showing him at the two orphanages he had established for Vietnamese refugees after the fall of Saigon and touring wards of the hospitals which were maintained entirely by the charitable trust he had created.

'Christ,' said Charlie mockingly, moving forward and looking for the lift he had been told would bypass the other eighteen floors of the skyscraper block from which Lu Industries were controlled and take him direct to the penthouse office.

He located it by the guards. Both were armed, he saw. A separate receptionist, male this time, sat behind them at a small desk.

'You have an appointment for eleven o'clock with Mr Lu?' he said, before Charlie could speak.

'Yes.'

'We were told to expect you.'

The lift door opened by some control which the man obviously operated but which Charlie could not see. As he entered, he saw the man reach for a telephone to announce his arrival above. Predictably, there were more photographs lining the lift panels, this time showing Lu at the launchings of his various tankers and passenger ships. The facing wall had pictures of the *Pride of America* leaving New York, another of its Hong Kong arrival and a third showing Lu in a small boat alongside the destroyed hull. John Lu really did resemble his father, thought Charlie, studying the photographs. Except for the smile. The younger man was a miserable-looking sod. Charlie paused, considering the judgment. Not really miserable, more apprehensive.

Despite the obvious entry he could have expected from the Willoughby company name and the warning from the increasingly distracted underwriter in a hurried telephone call earlier that morning that Lu's London office had made contact to establish he had directorial authority, Charlie had still been intrigued at the speed with which the millionaire had agreed to see him. He'd anticipated a delay of several days instead of the instantaneous agreement.

Another man, uniformed like his colleague on the ground floor, awaited Charlie when the lift doors opened.

'Please,' he said, inviting Charlie to follow.

This time the photographs around the walls were of world leaders. Charlie identified the nearest as President Giscard d'Estaing and Pierre Trudeau. And on easels this time because the wall area was entirely glass, giving a 180-degree view of Hong Kong, Kowloon and the mainland beyond.

There were uniformed and armed guards in the corridor and even in three outer offices through which they had to pass to reach the door to Lu's personal suite. It would be virtually impossible to make an unauthorised entry, Charlie realised.

Lu's office was very large, created from the corner of the building with the views of Kowloon and the New Territories. Rotating smoked-glass slats running from floor to ceiling gave the room an unexpectedly subdued lighting compared to the brightness of the other rooms through which he had passed. And there was a further surprise. Here there were no photographs. A bookcase occupied one of the two unglassed walls, broken only by a doorway, and along the other were showcases containing models of boats.

Lu rose as Charlie entered, hurrying around his desk, hand outstretched, teeth glinting.

'Welcome,' he said, the hiss in his voice only just evident. 'Welcome indeed.'

For how long? wondered Charlie.

The millionaire personally led him to a couch away from the desk, then sat down in a matching easy chair. He was a puppy-dog fat, polished sort of person, thought Charlie. But it was only surface plumpness. Beneath it he recognised a very hard man.

'Some refreshment?'

'No thank you,' said Charlie.

'Nothing at all?'

'Nothing.'

Charlie looked around the office again.

'What is it?' asked Lu.

'I was expecting your son to be present.'

'John?'

'You appear to spend a lot of time together.'

'No father could ask for a more dutiful son,' he said.

'Isn't son-to-father loyalty a Chinese tradition?'

Lu paused.

'Filial attachments are important in Asia,' he agreed. 'But unfortunately the ties appear to be becoming less important to the young of today.'

'I've learned quite a lot of Chinese tradition since I've been here,' said Charlie.

'You've been here some days?'

'Yes.'

'Then I'm surprised.'

'Surprised?'

'That you haven't called upon me sooner.'

'I don't understand,' said Charlie.

Lu made an expansive gesture.

'Surely this meeting means that there is to be no unpleasantness between your company and myself.'

'Unpleasantness?'

'Over this business of the writs.'

'I don't think I can promise that,' said Charlie, guardedly. The mechanical efficiency to which he'd so far been exposed probably meant that somewhere a tape recording was being made of the encounter. It was the sort of precaution he would have taken.

Momentarily Lu's smile dimmed.

'That's disappointing,' he said. 'But inevitable, I'm afraid.'

'You haven't come to agree settlement?'

'No.'

Lu was forcing the discussion, realised Charlie. To get the response he wanted from the man, he needed time to seed some uncertainty.

'What then?' demanded the millionaire.

Shock him, decided Charlie.

'To warn you that under no circumstances will my company consider paying out one cent of the claims you have filed against us,' he declared.

Lu settled back in the chair, shaking his head in apparent sadness. Not the reaction he had tried for, thought Charlie.

'Do you know,' said Lu, reflectively, 'I really can't remember when anyone had the temerity to *warn* me about anything.'

'I gather you lead a fairly protected life,' said Charlie, gesturing to the outer doors.

Lu sighed, too obviously, at the intended sarcasm.

'So very unfortunate,' he said, still maintaining the smile.

The sibilance was more noticeable, realised Charlie. So there was at least some slight annoyance. It wouldn't be enough.

'As unfortunate as the death of Robert Nelson?'

Lu nodded.

'I heard of the death of your man here,' he said. 'Such an able person... obtained more of my business than anyone else.'

'Why, Mr Lu?' said Charlie.

The smile was finally extinguished.

'Because I respected him and chose to give him the business.'

'At 12 per cent, when the rest of the sealed bids quoted 10?'

For a moment the millionaire faltered.

'I can afford to give my business to whom I choose,' he said.

'That's not business, Mr Lu. That's charity. Or stupidity. Or an indication that you didn't expect the money to be out of your hands for very long. Just long enough for it to be the bait for which it was intended?'

'I'm really not accustomed to rudeness,' said Lu threateningly.

'I'm not being rude,' said Charlie. 'I'm asking a very pertinent question.'

'After the sealed bid tenders had been taken up,' said Lu, 'we discovered that we were still uncovered to the extent of £6,000,000. Mr Nelson's offer had not at that stage been accepted. Rather than reopen the other policies, which might have left us with even less cover dangerously near the sailing date from New York, I decided to give it to him. It was an oversight, really. It was all done at the very last moment.'

'He told me about the rush,' said Charlie. 'And I think you are talking bullshit.'

Lu winced at the crudeness. That hadn't worked either, thought Charlie.

'I'm not really concerned with what you will accept or not,' said Lu. 'I'm rich enough to do as I wish with my money.'

'No one's that rich.'

'I am. And I'll remind you that I'm used to being treated with proper respect, because of it.'

'And I'll remind you that I'm not being disrespectful,' said Charlie. He was, he knew. Intentionally so. There had to be some way to penetrate the man's control.

'That's for me to decide,' said Lu.

'There will be several things for you to decide today,' agreed Charlie.

'Don't strain my patience,' said Lu.

'Now you're issuing warnings,' said Charlie.

'With far more ability to enforce them,' said Lu.

'As you did with Robert Nelson?'

Lu sat impassively, hands cupped in his lap. It wasn't working, realised Charlie. Lu had sensed the manoeuvre and was refusing to react.

'I know that Nelson was murdered,' announced Charlie. 'And I know why.'

Do *something*, for Christ's sake, he thought.

'All of which,' said Lu, 'would I'm sure be of great interest to the police. My only concern is in the settlement of my claim for the destruction of my ship, sorry as I am about Mr Nelson's death.'

'You destroyed your own ship,' declared Charlie. 'And had Robert Nelson killed when he tried to establish the reasons being spread by your people among the Chinese community.'

The patronising smile came back.'

'I've made a mistake,' Lu said. 'I've admitted a madman to my office. And I'm usually so careful.'

'As careful as you were in having the shipyard workers killed, knowing they could never withstand any cross-examination in court.'

'More than one murder!' mocked Lu.

There had always been a desperation about the bluff, accepted Charlie. But he'd expected to unsettle the man far more than he had done. He should have resisted Lu's pace and prolonged the verbal fencing, he realised. It was his own fault that he'd hurried the confrontation. More than hurried. Panicked, in fact. Because of his nervousness of Harvey Jones. There had been a time when he wouldn't have made such a mistake, no matter what the pressure.

'You and perhaps more importantly your son have lost face once,' persisted Charlie. 'Try to press this claim in court and I'll ensure you'll be ridiculed not just in Asia but throughout the world. Are you prepared to risk that?'

'I haven't the remotest conception what you're talking about,' said Lu, shaking his head.

'I will guarantee that in the English High Court my company will oppose your claim,' said Charlie. 'I'll see to it that every suspicion comes out. We'll label Robert Nelson's death for what it was. We'll demand to know in open court why you were prepared to pay 12 per cent on a £6,000,000 cover and get a better answer than the one you've given me. We'll show the real reason... that your anti-communist campaign was always to be paid for by British insurance companies...'

'Such nonsense,' intruded Lu. 'You're talking absolute nonsense.'

'But we won't just stop there,' carried on Charlie. 'We'll ask questions about the gambling. And the brothel-keeping. And the heroin factories that supply America and Europe.'

'Is there no crime for which I'm not to be held responsible?' sneered Lu. He infused boredom into his voice.

'I don't know of a man who uses publicity more effectively than you,' said Charlie, ignoring Lu's jibe. 'Are you prepared to risk the loss of face that such a court hearing would cause?'

Lu stood and for a moment Charlie thought he intended summoning the guards from the outer offices. Instead the man went to the desk, selected a cigar and returned to the chair, fumbling for the gold cutter on his watch chain.

'I congratulate you,' announced Lu unexpectedly.

Charlie waited.

'It really was a most effective attempt,' continued the millionaire. 'Almost deserved to succeed.'

'*Will* succeed,' Charlie corrected him, imagining a change of attitude at last.

'Oh no,' said Lu. 'I'm no longer treating you as a fool and neither must you regard me as one.'

The attitude *had* changed, realised Charlie. But not as he had hoped.

'I've already told you,' said Lu, 'that I'm a very careful man. I begin nothing without the guarantee of success.'

He stopped, waving a flame before his face. Charlie glanced towards the desk. He hadn't seen Lu turn off any recording device. But that's what the man had done, he was sure, under the guise of getting a cigar.

'I'm not arguing you wouldn't win judgment,' said Charlie. 'I'm saying it would be a court action that would destroy you and your reputation...'

'And I asked you not to treat me like a fool,' repeated Lu, sadly. 'We both of us know there will never be a court hearing.'

'You'll withdraw the claim?'

Lu laughed at him, in genuine amusement.

'No,' he said.

'I won't withdraw the claim. I'll press it, as hard as I am able. Because I know damned well that no lawyer, no matter how much filth or innuendo he hoped to smear, would risk fighting in court the case I am able to bring.'

'I... I...' tried Charlie, but Lu raised his hand imperiously, halting him.

'You need evidence,' said Lu. 'Better evidence than some doubt about a rich man's foible in paying more than he should for a policy he needed in a hurry. You'd need witnesses prepared to give evidence about a planned crime. And if you had that, it wouldn't be you sitting here. It would be the police.'

Gently he tapped the ash from his cigar.

'Your lawyers might listen to your romanticising,' said the millionaire. 'They might even be curious. But they'd never introduce it into a court hearing. Your company will settle. For the full amount. Because they have no option. My policy is legally incontestable. There's never been any risk of my being humiliated. Nor will there be. Ever.'

He'd lost, accepted Charlie. Completely. Another thought came, suddenly. Robert Nelson had died simply for attempting to establish the accusation at street level; he had actually challenged the man.

'You checked up on me with my London office before agreeing to meet me?' he said.

Lu nodded. 'I told you I leave nothing to chance.'

'And they knew I was coming here today, to confront you with what I believed to be the truth.'

Lu's smile broadened.

'You're giving me another warning,' he said.

'Were anything to happen to me, so soon after Robert Nelson's death and my visit here, the police might be forced into finding the proof that our lawyers might need to take the case to court.'

It meant *admitting* defeat. But that had been established anyway. Now Charlie needed protection.

'Yes,' agreed Lu. 'They just might. I'll remember that.'

At least, decided Charlie, rising and moving towards the door, for the moment he was safe. Safe, from Lu anyway. But there was still Harvey Jones.

'You'll recommend your company to drop their resistance and settle?' said Lu expectantly.

Charlie stopped, turning.

'No,' he said shortly.

'You can't win, you know.'

'So people keep telling me.'

'Perhaps you should listen to their advice.'

'Perhaps.'

'Don't become an irritant, will you?' Lu cautioned him. Maybe he hadn't created as much protection as he had hoped, thought Charlie.

'Unfortunately,' he said from the door, 'it seems to be a facility I have.'

'Yes,' said Lu, determined to master every exchange. 'It could be unfortunate.'

After Charlie had left the room the millionaire remained seated in the chair in which he had confronted him, and that was how John Lu found him when he entered from the adjoining office.

'Well?' asked the father.

'Kill him,' said the son immediately.

'Fool,' snapped Lu. 'You spend so much time with scum that you even think like them now.'

'But he's got it. He's got it all.'

The millionaire shook his head.

'He's got nothing. Not a shred of proof. And there's nowhere he can get it.'

'What about the woman?'

'You chose badly there, didn't you?' demanded Lu, avoiding a direct answer.

The younger man, who had remained standing, shuffled awkwardly.

'She'd talk,' he admitted.

'About what?' said the millionaire dismissively.

'But she knows!'

'And everything we've got is concealed by companies layered upon companies and by nominees operating through other nominees,' reminded Lu. 'There is nothing directly linking us to anything. Who's going to start investigating us, on the word of a whore?'

'She could be a nuisance,' said John, in rare defiance.

'Oh, I think she should be punished,' agreed Lu, as if correcting a misapprehension.

The son smiled.

'But properly this time,' warned Lu.

'Of course.'

Jenny Lin Lee would want to know of the arrangements for the funeral, Charlie decided. There was no reply throughout the afternoon to his repeated telephone calls, so after the inquest at which he gave evidence of identification and which returned the verdict which Superintendent Johnson had anticipated, he went to Robert Nelson's apartment.

The doorbell echoed back hollowly to him.

The caretaker was happy to open the door for fifty dollars and Charlie's assurance that he represented the dead man's company.

Already the rooms had a stale, unlived-in smell. Expertly he went from room to room; nowhere was there a trace of the girl. Known in all the bars, she'd said. Which ones? he wondered.

As he turned to leave the apartment, his foot touched something, scuffing it along the carpet. Bending, he picked up a letter with a London postmark and the Willoughby company address embossed on the back, for return in case of non-delivery.

Aware of its contents, he opened it anyway, reading it in seconds. Sighing, he put into his pocket the underwriter's letter assuring Robert Nelson that his position would not be in any way affected by the *Pride of America* fire.

'Not much,' muttered Charlie savagely, closing the door.

14.

Since the encounter with the American, Charlie had become over-conscious of the feeling of being watched, making sudden and too obvious checks, so that had he been under surveillance any observer could have easily avoided detection. Desperation. Like trying to bluff Lu. And this new idea. Further desperation, he recognised, forced upon him by the difference of the past from the present.

Before, the only consideration had been Charlie's rules. Now it was Judge's Rules; the need not just to learn the truth and then act to his own satisfaction, but to that of barristers and law lords. It imposed a restriction to which he was unaccustomed; like trying to run with a shoelace undone. There seemed a very real possibility of falling flat on his face.

People spilled from the pavement into Des Voeux Road, slowing the cars to a noisy, protesting crawl. Charlie used the movement of avoiding people to check around him, then abandoning the futile attempt, knowing that in such a throng any identification would be impossible.

He had expected the legation of the People's Republic of China to be an imposing building, perhaps even with a police guard. But so ordinary was it, slotted in among the shops and the cinema, that he was almost past before he realised be had found it.

He pushed slowly forward through the milling Chinese, smiling at his first impression; it was just like a betting shop. Even to the counters round the sides, at which people were filling in not their horse selections but their applications to return to mainland China.

He ignored the side benches, going straight to the reception desk. It was staffed by three men, dressed in identical black-grey tunics.

'I wish to see Mr Kuo,' said Charlie. When the clerk did not react, Charlie added, 'Mr Kuo Yuan-ching.'

'He knows you?'

'I telephoned. He said I was to call.'

The man hesitated, then turned through a small door at the rear. Charlie moved to one side, to make room for the continual thrust of people. A hell of a lot of the five thousand seemed to regard it as a wasted swim.

He was kept waiting for nearly fifteen minutes before the clerk returned and nodded his head towards the rear office. With difficulty Charlie squeezed past the counter and went into the room.

It was as spartan and functional as that through which he had just come. A desk, three filing cabinets, one upright chair for any visitors, the walls bare and unbroken by any official photographs, even of Mao Tse-Tung.

'May I?' asked Charlie, hand on the chair back.

The head of the Chinese Legation stared at him without any expression of greeting, then nodded. Like confronting a headmaster for the first time, thought Charlie. Christ, his feet hurt.

'You will take tea?' said the official.

It was a statement rather than a hospitable question.

'Thank you,' said Charlie, accepting the ritual. Kuo rang a handbell and from a side door almost immediately appeared another tunicked man carrying a tray dominated by a large Thermos. Around it were grouped teapot and cups.

'Proper Chinese tea,' announced Kuo, pouring.

Charlie took the cup, sipping it.

'Excellent,' he said politely. He had rushed almost everything else and made a balls of it, he thought. And this was his last chance, hopeless though the attempt might be, under the newly recognised rules. So the meeting could proceed at whatever pace the other man dictated.

Kuo topped up the pot from the Thermos, then sat back, regarding Charlie again with a headmasterly look.

Charlie gazed back, vaguely disconcerted. Kuo was a square-bodied, heavily built man, dressed in the regulation tunic but with no obvious signs of his rank. Under its cap of thick black hair, the man's face was smooth and unlined.

Kuo nodded towards the telephone.

'You spoke of wanting help?'

'Yes,' said Charlie.

'What kind of help?'

'I represent one of the syndicate members who insured the *Pride of America*...'

'Who now stand to lose a large sum of money.'

'Who now stand to lose a large sum of money,' agreed Charlie.

'And you don't want to pay?'

Can't pay, thought Charlie, sighing. There was something almost artificial in the communist criticism of capitalism, he decided. As ritualistic as the tea drinking.

'We're trying to avoid paying out wrongly,' he explained. 'And at the moment, we might be forced to.'

'How is that?' demanded Kuo.

'The liner was not set alight by agents of the People's Republic of China,' declared Charlie.

For the first time there was reaction from the man; no facial expression, but a hesitation before he spoke again.

'If it is an assurance of that which you want, then of course you have it,' said Kuo. 'The accusation has been ridiculous from the start.'

For someone of Kuo's control, it had been a clumsy response, thought Charlie.

'I want more than assurance,' he said.

'What?'

'Proof.'

Kuo leaned forward over the desk, pouring more tea.

'How long have you been in Hong Kong?' he asked, settling back into his chair.

'Little over a week,' said Charlie.

'Then you must have seen the police?'

'Yes.'

'And Mr Lu?'

'Yes.'

'So we must be almost at the bottom of the list,' decided Kuo.

Charlie considered his reply. Was Kuo seeking an apology, imagining some insult in the order of priority? There seemed no point in evading the accusation.

'Yes,' he admitted. 'At the bottom.'

Briefly, unexpectedly, Kuo smiled.

'You're very honest,' he said.

'If I thought I'd achieve more by lying, then I would,' said Charlie.

Again the smile flickered into place.

'Very honest indeed.'

Charlie sipped his tea. Again he'd made the proper response, he realised, relieved.

'Even if you are prepared to help me,' Charlie went on in explanation, 'it might not be possible for you to do so.'

'Why?'

'I believe Lu destroyed his own ship,' said Charlie. 'I believe that he used gambling debts to force the shipyard workers into doing it and then had them murdered by someone else who had also got into debt…' Charlie hesitated, Kuo remained impassive on the other side of the desk.

'Believe,' repeated Charlie. 'But cannot prove to the satisfaction of the English court in which Lu is suing for payment. But there might be a way to obtain that proof…'

'By seeing if a prison cook named Fan Yung-ching has returned to his family in Hunan?'

Charlie nodded, letting the curiosity reach his face.

'We are not entirely ignorant of the affair,' said Kuo.

'Then help me prove the truth of it,' Charlie urged him. 'The real truth.'

'You expect my country to help a capitalist institution save a fortune!'

'I expect China to have a proper awareness of the harm that could be caused to its relations with Washington if this remains unchallenged,' said Charlie.

'An insurance official with a politician's argument,' mused Kuo.

'A logical, sensible argument,' Charlie corrected him. He sounded as pompous as Johnson, he thought.

'Come now,' said Kuo. 'Lu has the irritation of a droning insect on a summer's day. Are you seriously suggesting an impediment between my country and America from someone as insignificant?'

'The *Pride of America* was built with an enormous grant from the American government. And then sustained by an equally enormous grant, until it became blatantly uneconomical. Millions of dollars of American taxpayers' money supported that ship. And there was a *pride* in it. The destruction, within weeks of leaving America, is far from insignificant. And I'm sure there are people within your Foreign Ministry who feel the same way…'

Charlie paused, tellingly.

'And if you didn't think so, too,' he said, 'you wouldn't be as familiar with the details as you obviously are.'

Again there was the brief, firefly smile.

'Not only honest,' said the Chinese, 'but remarkably perceptive as well.'

'Am I wrong?'

Kuo fingered his teacup, finally looking up. 'No,' he admitted, matching Charlie's earlier honesty. 'You're not wrong.'

'Then help me,' said Charlie again.

'How?'

'If the cook has returned to…' began Charlie.

'He has,' Kuo cut him off.

Charlie felt the sweep of familiar excitement at the awareness that he could win. Lu's boastful words, he remembered. But that's all it was, a boast. In himself, Charlie knew, the need was far deeper. Sir Archibald had recognised it; one of the few who had. And used it, quite calculatingly. But openly, of course. 'Go out and win, Charlie.' Always the same encouragement. And so he'd gone out and won. Because he'd had to. Just as he'd had to win, and win demonstrably, when he'd realised Sir Archibald's successors were trying to beat him. And then again, when they'd begun the chase. 'Go out and win, Charlie.' No matter who gets hurt. Or dies. Poor Edith.

Charlie began concentrating, considering another thought; he'd expected the Chinese to be properly concerned, but to have established already the return to China of the Hunan cook showed a determined investigation.'

'Superintendent Johnson told me he had sought assistance from you,' said Charlie.

'He wants the man returned to the colony.'

'And that's not possible?' probed Charlie gently.

'It might not be thought wise.'

'I wouldn't need his return to fight Lu in the English High Court,' Charlie assured him.

'How, then?'

'Give me an entry visa to China,' said Charlie. 'Let me interview the man, in the presence of your officials and someone from the British embassy in Peking who can notarise the statement as being properly made and therefore legally admissible in an English court.'

He'd been involved in British espionage for two decades, reflected Charlie. And in that time used a dozen overseas embassies. There could easily be an earlier-encountered diplomat now assigned to Peking who might recognise him. He would, thought Charlie, spend the rest of his life fleeing through a hall of distorted mirrors and shying away from half-seen images of fear.

Kuo indicated the teapot, but Charlie shook his head. The man added to his own cup, apparently considering the request.

'You must tell me one thing,' he said.

'What?'

'If we make this facility available to you... if he makes a full confession about what happened, can you absolutely guarantee that Lu's claim will be publicly discussed in an open court, so that the man will be exposed for the fraud he is?'

Now Charlie remained unspeaking, balancing the demand. It was impossible to anticipate what the cook would say. Or his statement's admissibility in court, despite the attempted legality of having a British embassy official present. It would be sufficient to beat Lu. But more probably in private negotiations with lawyers, rather than in an open court challenge.

'It would mean Lu's claim against my company would fail,' predicted Charlie.

'But not that the man would be taken to court, for everyone to witness?'

'I cannot guarantee that.'

'I respect you again for your frankness,' said the legation head.

'You knew that, without my telling you,' said Charlie.

'Yes,' said Kuo. 'I knew it.'

Charlie controlled the almost imperceptible sigh; another test passed.

'I would try to ensure that my company made a public announcement of any withdrawal by Lu,' promised Charlie. 'And that would by implication show the claim to be false.'

'But isn't it sometimes a condition of out-of-court settlements that there should be no publicity?'

'There appears little you haven't considered,' said Charlie.

'No,' agreed Kuo. 'Very little.'

'Does that mean you can give me an immediate decision about a visa?'

Kuo shook his head at the eagerness.

'Oh no,' he said. 'I have to refer to Peking.'

'So there could be a delay.'

'There normally is.'

'But this isn't a normal case,' said Charlie.

'No.'

'So when would you expect to get a decision?'

'What would you say if I asked you to return this time tomorrow?'

'I would say that you seem to have been expecting me.'

Kuo laughed, his face fully relaxed for the first time.

'We were,' he said. 'In fact, I'm surprised it's taken you so long.'

The wind began to freshen in sudden, breathy gusts as it always does before the summer downpours in Hong Kong and the priest started to hurry, frowning above his prayer book at the clouds bubbling over the Peak. Why shouldn't he? thought Charlie. Despite a congregation of only one, the man had persisted with a full service, even the fifteen-minute promise of the glory awaiting Robert Nelson compared to the unhappiness of the life he had known. So why should he get wet? From the left the gravediggers hovered, shovels in hand, as anxious as the priest that the grave should not become waterlogged.

Charlie shook his head, refusing the invitation to cast the first sod down upon the coffin.

The priest smiled slightly, happy at the saved minute. 'And so,' he intoned, 'I commit the body of Robert Nelson to the earth and his soul to Heaven...'

He turned expectantly to Charlie, who was unsure what to do. Finally he backed away, realising it was over. The priest fell into step beside him.

'Surprised at the turn-out,' he said genially.

'Yes,' agreed Charlie. He'd worked methodically through the bars of the Wan Chai and then Kowloon, trying to locate Jenny Lin Lee. And got shrugs and blank faces and assurances that she was unknown.

'Particularly for someone so respected in the community.' Charlie looked sideways. The priest smiled back ingenuously. The man didn't know, decided Charlie. But then, how could he?

'Perhaps they were busy,' said Charlie.

The priest frowned.

'That's not usually an obstruction among the European community here,' he replied automatically.

'At least he'll never know how little they cared,' said Charlie, jerking his head back in the direction of the grave.

The priest stopped on the narrow pathway, face creased in distaste.

'That's hardly respectful of the dead,' he complained.

'Neither is a business community ignoring the funeral of a man who's worked here all his life,' snapped Charlie. Wasn't there ever a circumstance in which he did not have to weigh and consider his words? he thought wearily.

'Quite,' said the priest, immediately retreating. 'Very sad.'

The path split, one way going back to the church, the other to the lychgate exit. The first rain splattered the stones as they paused, to part.

'Goodbye,' said the priest, grateful to have escaped getting wet.

'Thank you,' said Charlie.

He was almost at the covered gateway before he saw Harvey Jones. He stopped, careless of the downpour.

'I startled you,' apologised the American.

'Yes,' said Charlie.

'I'm sorry.'

Charlie said nothing. He should have seen the man, he thought. Been aware of his presence at least. Perhaps his instinct *was* failing.

'Hadn't you better get under cover?' said Jones. 'You're getting soaked.'

Charlie pressed under the tiny roof, turning back to look over the churchyard to avoid the American's direct attention. The gravediggers were scrabbling the earth into the grave, careless of how they filled it. The poor bugger even got buried messily.

'Arrived too late to join the service,' said Jones, still apologising.

'You'd have been lost in the crowd,' said Charlie sarcastically. 'Why did you come?'

'Wanted to see you.'

'Why?'

Because the man's curiosity was increasing rather than diminishing, thought Charlie, answering his own question.

'See how you're getting on,' said Jones.

Liar, thought Charlie.

'You'd have kept drier waiting at the hotel.'

'Nothing else to do,' said the American easily. 'Perhaps it was the rain that kept everyone away.'

'He wasn't very popular,' said Charlie.

'Certainly not with someone.'

Charlie ignored the invitation.

'How's the investigation going?' asked Jones, forced into the direct demand.

'Nowhere.'

'Pity.'

'Yes.'

'Didn't suggest a separate autopsy?'

'What?' said Charlie, forgetting.

'Separate autopsy,' repeated Jones. 'Try to find something upon which Johnson could have worked?'

'Decided it would be a waste of time.'

'So what *have* you done?'

Spent all my time trying to avoid you, thought Charlie.

'Poked about,' he said.

'And found what?'

'Nothing. What about you?'

'Nothing.'

It was as if his anxiety were forcing the breath from him, making it impossible for him to create proper sentences. It would not be difficult for Jones to notice the attitude. And for his curiosity to increase. The rain began lessening. Soon he would be able to escape.

'Still might be better if we worked together,' suggested the American.

'I prefer to stay on my own,' said Charlie.

'Wonder what the Chinese think about it?' said Jones suddenly.

Charlie made an unknowing gesture.

'Why not ask them?'

'Might well do that. Do they have representation here?'

'I believe so,' said Charlie, playing the game. So Jones had been out there somewhere in the crowd and seen him enter the legation. And wanted him to know. Why? An offer to identify himself, like wearing a school tie?

'Yes indeed, I might well do that,' repeated the American.

'Let me know how you get on,' said Charlie.

'Of course,' promised Jones. '*I'll* keep my side of the bargain.'

Another invitation, Charlie recognised.

'It's stopped raining,' he said, nodding beyond the lychgate.

'Can I give you a lift?'

'I've got a taxi waiting,' said Charlie.

'I'll let you know what Kuo Yuan-ching says,' promised Jones, as he walked from the churchyard.

'Who?' said Charlie, avoiding the trap.

'Kuo Yuan-ching,' said the American again. 'I gather he's the man to see.'

Alone at last, Charlie stretched back against the seat as his car started its switchback descent towards the Central district. The tension made him physically ache. He blinked his eyes open, reflecting upon his encounter with Harvey Jones. Because he was tired, he was making mistakes. There was no reason why he shouldn't have told the American of his visit to the Chinese official. All he had done was risk being found out in a lie and possibly arousing the man's suspicions further. And he guessed Jones had plenty of doubts already.

'You're not thinking fast enough, Charlie,' he told himself.

'So he's behaved exactly as you predicted?' said the inner council chairman.

'Yes,' said Chiu. Modestly, he kept the satisfaction from his voice.

'You will deal with him personally?'

'I think it's best.'

'And ensure every preparation is made?'

'Yes.'

'I wonder how clever this Englishman is?'

'It doesn't really matter now, does it?' said Chiu, the conceit audible.

'I suppose not,' agreed the chairman.

15.

Charlie got off the train at Sheung Shui and looked towards the Shum Chun river that formed the border. Almost as far as the Lo Wu bridge there was a confused crush of people. He began to walk towards the crossing but immediately had to step aside for a herd of pigs which was being driven into the New Territories.

Impossible to control, remembered Charlie. That's what Johnson had said about the border traffic. Difficult even to decide which way most of them were going.

There was no logical reason for any challenge, but Charlie still felt the involuntary stomach-tightening when he offered his passport at the British end of the control. The official glanced at him briefly, compared the picture, checked the visa and waved him on. Would he ever lose the apprehension? he wondered, walking on to the bridge towards China. Better if he didn't. Frightened, he reacted quicker.

At the Chinese check, he offered not just his passport but the letter which Kuo Yuan-ching had given him earlier that day. Immediately there was a smile of expectation and at a gesture from the official another Chinese walked forward from a small room behind the passport booth.

'My name is Chiu Ching-mao,' the second man introduced himself. 'I am to be your escort to Peking.'

He retrieved Charlie's passport, waving to indicate that he should bypass the queue that stretched before him. Obediently the people parted and Chiu stretched out to take Charlie's overnight shoulder grip and briefcase.

Feeling vaguely embarrassed at the special treatment, Charlie surrendered the bags and fell into step with the other man.

'We expected you earlier,' said Chiu. Like the men in the Hong Kong legation, he wore the regulation grey-black tunic. He was a thin, bespectacled man, with an intense way of examining people when he spoke, as if suspecting the responses they made.

'I didn't expect so many people,' admitted Charlie. He nodded towards another herd of pigs. 'Or livestock.'

'Trade is extensive in this part of China,' said Chiu watchfully.

The treaty guaranteeing British sovereignty was not accepted by Peking, remembered Charlie.

'Of course,' he said, wanting to avoid a political polemic.

The official seemed disappointed.

Once free of the immediate border, it was easier to move, despite the bicycles. They appeared to be everywhere, cluttering the kerb edges and thronging the oddly traffic-free roads.

Seeing Charlie's look, Chiu said, 'To cycle is to remain fit.'

'Yes,' said Charlie. If he let the man get it out of his system, perhaps he'd stop.

'We have a long way to go,' said Chiu, looking at his watch..

'I know.'

'But we can still make our connections,' added the Chinese. 'We will go by train to Canton and from there fly to Peking.'

'I appreciate very much the trouble you have taken,' said Charlie.

'My ministry regards your visit as important,' said Chiu.

'Ministry?'

'I am attached to the political section of the Foreign Ministry,' elaborated the man.

Different from normal, recognised Charlie. They really were going to enormous trouble.

At the station they appeared to be expected, bypassing the normal barriers with an attentive escort of railway officials.

The train seemed almost as crowded as the border bridge, but Chiu went confidently ahead of the railwaymen until he found the empty carriage he was apparently seeking and stood back for Charlie to enter.

'Reserved,' he announced.

So much for equality for all, thought Charlie. He sat back as Chiu dismissed the officials in a tumble of Chinese, staring through the window at the last-minute rush before departure. For the first time in almost a fortnight, he thought, he did not have the impression of being watched. It was a tangible relief.

He turned to the man opposite.

'I am still surprised that my visa approval was so prompt,' he said, sweeping his hand out to encompass the carriage. 'And at all this assistance.'

'I have already said your visit is regarded as important,' Chiu reminded him.

'Less than a day is still fast,' insisted Charlie.

'Not for China,' said Chiu, seeing the opportunity.

The train lurched, shuddering forward clear of the station. Like most rail systems upon which he had travelled throughout the world, it appeared to go through every back garden. But there was a difference; here, each garden was immaculate and cared for, like entries in a horticultural exhibition. Which was the purpose, decided Charlie. But a public relations exhibition, not a horticultural one.

Once in the open country, they travelled along the spine of high embankments. On either side, in the regimented paddy fields, peasants crouched knee-deep in the irrigation water beneath the cover of their lampshade hats.

'You will be staying in the Hsin Chiao hotel, in what was once the Legation district of Peking,' announced Chiu.

The only hotel in the city with a bar, remembered Charlie. He wondered if he'd have anything to celebrate.

Anticipating another diatribe as Chiu moved to speak, Charlie said quickly, 'It is surprising that you've allowed me access to this man in preference to the Hong Kong police.'

'The police would demand his return,' said Chiu, as if that were explanation enough.

'But that would surely achieve the same effect as letting me obtain a statement... better, even. It would guarantee a court hearing.'

Chiu looked across at him tolerantly.

'It would also establish a precedent,' he said.

They were interrupted by the opening of the carriage door. Charlie turned to see a file of white-coated men.

'I've arranged for lunch to be served here in the compartment,' explained Chiu.

Neither spoke while the table was erected between them and the dishes laid out.

'There are knives and forks, if you wish,' said Chiu solicitously.

'Chopsticks will be fine,' said Charlie. There appeared no courtesy the Chinese authorities had overlooked.

As they started to eat, Charlie said, 'So the man will go unpunished?'

Chiu paused, chopsticks before his face.

'Oh no,' he insisted quietly. 'People who bring disgrace to China never go unpunished.'

The special treatment continued when they reached Canton. A car was at the station to take them directly to the airport. There they again skirted all the formalities, driving past the departure building to the waiting aircraft. Predictably, their seats were reserved.

'The man is being brought from Hunan, to enable your meeting to take place in the capital,' announced Chiu, as they belted themselves in for take-off.

'That's very helpful,' said Charlie.

'We thought it better.'

'The British embassy...' started Charlie.

'Ambassador Collins has promised an official to notarise the accounts of any meeting,' finished Chiu, enjoying the constant indications of their efficiency. 'My Ministry has already approached them.'

'Collins?'

A movement went through Charlie, as if he were physically cold. Not the same man, he thought wildly. It couldn't be. Just a coincidence, that's all. He smothered the hope; now he was thinking like Willoughby. Unrealistically. And he'd already done too much of that.

Could still be a coincidence, he decided. Not a particularly unusual name, after all. Then again, it might not be. About due for ambassadorial promotion when they'd met. The First Secretary at the Prague embassy, remembered Charlie. Prissy man, resenting the London instruction to provide whatever help Charlie might demand. The department were giving him that sort of authority then, still believing the defection to be the biggest intelligence coup of the decade. The visit to Czechoslovakia had been to arrange the final details of the crossing.

'You know him?' asked the Chinese.

'No,' said Charlie. I hope not, he thought. There'd even been an argument between them.

Chiu stared at him curiously.

Just when everything had at last seemed to be going so easily, thought Charlie. Why hadn't he checked at the High Commission in Hong Kong? Taken one telephone call, that's all. He'd even anticipated the danger, in Kuo's office. Careless again. Unthinking.

The aircraft doors thumped closed and the No Smoking and seat-belts signs flicked on. There was nothing he could do. Not a bloody thing.

'My Ministry have taken a very unusual decision in admitting you,' said Chiu. 'We hope it will work out satisfactorily.'

'So do I,' said Charlie sincerely. In so many ways, he thought. He'd certainly need the hotel bar. But not for a celebration.

Harvey Jones leaned against the rail of the ferry taking him from Hong Kong to Kowloon, gazing down into the churned waters of the harbour. Far away the *Pride of America* looked like one of those beached whales that sometimes came ashore along the Miami coastline, driven to suicide by sea parasites infecting their skins. His parents had sent him pictures in their last letter from Fort Lauderdale, the one in which they'd assured him of how happily they were settling down into retirement.

Pity he couldn't send them a postcard. Be had security, he knew. Perhaps he'd visit them, when he got back. He might even have something about which to boast. Then again, he might not.

Jones drove his fist in tiny, impatient movements against the rail. Why, he wondered, were the damned Chinese being so helpful to the bloody man? And they *were* being helpful. Openly so. He hadn't even had to make it obvious that he'd followed the man to the legation offices. Kuo had freely admitted it. Almost volunteered it.

'...*special chance... to prove yourself...*'

He was being beaten, decided Jones. By a tied-in-the-middle-with-string hayseed of an agent who should have been put out to pasture long ago. And he *was* an agent, no matter how closely he tried to hide behind the insurance investigator crap. Jones was sure of it.

The American stared up, irritated by another realisation. To ask Washington to pressure London for cooperation now would be an open admission of failure. Best to wait. At least until the man came back. It would be easy to gauge whether the visit had been worth while. That was it. Just wait and trick the bastard into some sort of confession. Then put the arm on him.

The ferry nudged against the dock and Jones got into line to disembark.

Still failure, though. Whether he did it now or later.

It wasn't going as he had hoped, he admitted to himself reluctantly. In fact, it was turning out to be a complete fuck-up.

Jones had cleared the quayside by the time Jenny Lin Lee finally left the same ferry. For a moment she stared across towards Hong Kong island, then started towards Kowloon.

Already they would know she had arrived. Been warned to expect her, in fact. Just as the hotels and then the bars in the Wan Chai had been warned to refuse her, forcing her lower and lower.

She turned right, along the Salisbury Road and in front of the Peninsula Hotel which Jones had just entered and on towards the harbour slums.

That's where the Mao Tai shacks and the short-time houses were. All she could expect now. Or would be allowed. No Europeans, of course. Or even clean Chinese. Just the blank-eyed, diseased men of the fishing junks and the shipyards.

She could avoid the pain, she knew, feeling for the assurance of the hypodermic in her shoulder bag. There would be no difficulty in obtaining it, not until she'd really established a dependence. Then it might be difficult. Impossible, eventually. But that hadn't happened yet. Weeks away. And she had to take away the feeling.

16.

Fan Yung-ching, the former prison cook, was a wizened, dried-out old man, tissue-paper skin stretched over the bones of his face and hands, making him almost doll-like. A very ugly doll, thought Charlie.

The man crouched rather than sat on the other side of the interview bench, skeletal hands across his stomach as if he were in physical pain. Which he probably was. Fear leaked from him, souring the room with his smell. Soon, decided Charlie, the man would wet himself. Charlie had been in many rooms, confronting many men as frightened as this. Always, at some stage, their bladders went. He hoped that was the only collapse. Often it wasn't.

It was a small, box-shaped chamber, crowded because of the number of people who had to be present.

The interpreter who would translate Charlie's questions was immediately to his left, arms upon the table, waiting with a notepad before him. Behind, at a narrow bench, sat Chiu Ching-mao. With him was the official from the legal section of the British embassy.

Geoffrey Hodgson, the man had introduced himself. Typical diplomat-lawyer posted because of an ability with languages.

Charlie looked at the lawyer and Hodgson smiled hopefully, just as he'd smiled when he confirmed in unwitting conversation the ambassador's former posting to Prague.

'Expects you at the embassy after the interview,' Hodgson had said.

No escape then.

It would have been four years, Charlie calculated. And not more than three hours together. The man would have encountered thousands of people in that time. And would not know the outcome of Charlie's visit to Czechoslovakia anyway, because of the embarrassment to the department.

Scarce reason to remember him. Wrong to panic then. Pointless anyway. At least he knew in advance. It gave him a slight advantage; too slight.

Charlie continued his examination of the room. At a third table sat two bilingual notetakers, tape-recording machines between them.

As efficiently organised as everything else, decided Charlie.

'Shall we start?' he said.

'There should be an oath, if the man has a religion,' warned Hodgson.

Fan shook his head to the interpreter's question.

'An affirmation, at least,' insisted Hodgson. It was an unusual situation and he didn't want any mistakes.

'He understands,' said the interpreter.

The man paused as one of the notetakers made an adjustment to the recorder, then quoted the undertaking to the old man. Haltingly, eyes locked on to the table in front of him, Fan repeated his promise that the statement would be the truth. He was wiping one hand over the other in tiny washing movements. He was too frightened to lie, Charlie knew.

The affirmation over, Fan hurriedly talked on, bobbing his hand in fawning, pleading motions.

'He begs forgiveness,' said the interpreter. 'He says he was forced to do what he did... that he did not know it was a poison he was introducing into the men's food. He was told that it was a substance merely to make them ill, to cause a delay to the trial...'

It was going to be more disjointed than he had expected, realised Charlie. He turned to Hodgson.

'Would there be any difficulty about admissibility if the transcript is shown to be a series of questions and answers?'

The British lawyer pursed his lips doubtfully.

'Shouldn't be,' he said, 'providing that it couldn't be argued that the questions were too leading. You must not suggest the answers you want.'

Charlie turned back to the cook.

'Does he know the man who gave him the substance?'

'The same man who threatened me,' replied Fan, through the interpreter.

'What is his name?'

'Johnny Lu.'

Charlie reached into his briefcase, bringing out one of the many photographs of the millionaire's son it had been automatic for him to bring. It had been taken at the press conference just after the liner sailed from New York and showed the man next to his father.

'This man?' he asked.

Fan squinted at the picture.

'Yes,' he said finally.

Charlie looked towards the recorders.

'Can the transcript show he has identified a picture of John Lu taken aboard the *Pride of America*,' he requested formally.

The proof, Charlie thought. The proof that Johnson had demanded. And which would save Willoughby. What, he wondered, would save him?

'Why did he threaten you?' he said, coming back to the old man.

'I owed money... money I had lost at mahjong. I did not have it...'

'What was the threat?'

'That he would have me hurt... badly hurt.'

'Tell me what he said.'

'That if I will put what he gave me into their food, he would not let me be hurt... that it would cancel my debt.'

'Were you at any time told what to do by anyone representing the government of China?'

Fan looked hurriedly to the interpreter and then across at Chiu, to whom the other Chinese in the room had been constantly deferent.

He shook his head.

'You must reply,' insisted Charlie.

'No,' said Fan.

'What about the men who died... those accused of causing the fire?'

It was a remote chance, but worth trying.

'I do not know,' said Fan.

'Did they gamble?' pressed Charlie.

Fan nodded. 'Sometimes with me.'

'Be careful,' interrupted Hodgson, from the side. 'If just one section is challenged,' it could have the effect of casting doubt on the whole statement.'

'Did they win or lose?' Charlie asked the Chinese, nodding his acceptance of the lawyer's warning.

'Sometimes win. Sometimes lose,' said Fan, unhelpfully.

'Did John Lu cancel your debt?'

'He told me to go to him to get a paper. But I did not.'

'Why?'

'I was frightened I would get killed. I ran away.'

Fan gave an involuntary shudder and a different smell permeated the room. He'd been right, realised Charlie. It always happened.

'What did John Lu say would happen to the men who had caused the fire?'

'Just that they would become ill... nothing more.'

'Why did he want that?'

'He said it would get into the newspapers... that it was important.'

'Why?'

'I do not know.'

Charlie wanted nothing more from the man. It had seemed ridiculously easy. But the rest of the day wasn't going to be.

He sat back, looking to Chiu. 'Thank you,' he said.

'That's all?'

The Foreign Ministry official appeared surprised.

'It is enough,' Charlie assured him.

'Much trouble has been taken,' said Chiu. 'A mistake would be unfortunate.'

'To go on might create just such a mistake,' said Charlie, looking to Hodgson for support.

The lawyer nodded agreement.

'You came pretty close on one or two occasions as it was,' he said.

'How long will it take to notarise this statement?' asked Charlie.

'Fifteen minutes,' said Hodgson. 'Won't take much longer to prepare it, either, I wouldn't think.'

Charlie came back to Chiu.

'So I could return to Hong Kong first thing tomorrow?' he said. He had to limit his stay in Peking to the minimum, he had decided. Even if he identified him, Collins would have no reason to attempt his detention. The risk was in querying his presence with London. And by the time that was answered, he could be clear of Hong Kong. Running again.

Chiu was still unhappy with the brevity of the account, Charlie knew.

'If you wish,' said the Chinese, stiffly.

He did wish, thought Charlie. It wasn't just the new danger of the ambassador. He shouldn't forget the curiosity of Harvey Jones. At least he could escape that now. One problem replaced by another.

Charlie turned to the trembling figure sitting opposite.

Fan still gazed steadfastly down at the table, not realising the questioning was over.

People who bring disgrace to China never go unpunished, Chiu had said. Hardly surprising the poor bastard had pissed himself.

'Will you tell him I am grateful?' Charlie asked the interpreter. 'He has been of great assistance.'

Fan stared up at the translation. Even he was bewildered that it was over so quickly.

Charlie rose, ending the interview.

'Right,' said Hodgson briskly. 'Let's get along to the embassy, shall we?'

First, thought Charlie, he'd need a toilet.

'Quite the most unusual city to which I've ever been,' volunteered the lawyer, in the car taking them to the embassy.

'Yes,' said Charlie. It didn't appear to have a centre. Rather, it was sprawl upon sprawl of squares.

'Do you know that underneath all the buildings and offices there are nuclear shelters?' said Hodgson.

'No.'

'It's a fact,' insisted the lawyer. 'The Chinese are paranoid about an attack from Russia. They reckon they can clear the entire city in fifteen minutes.'

That's what he needed, mused Charlie. A bomb-proof hole in the ground to which he could run at the first sign of danger.

'We've arrived,' announced Hodgson.

To what? wondered Charlie. Despite his preparedness, he still faltered at the entrance to the ambassador's study, knowing as he did so that the reaction would look strange but momentarily unable to control the urge to turn and run.

'Come in, come in,' encouraged the ambassador. 'Not often we get visitors from home. And under such strange circumstances.'

Collins had altered very little, Charlie decided. Not physically, anyway. He continued into the room, taking the out-stretched hand. The man's face remained blank. Please God let it stay that way, prayed Charlie.

'Sherry?' fussed Collins, indicating the decanter.

'Thank you,' accepted Charlie. Not more than three hours, he thought again. How good was the man's memory?

'Astonishing business, this fire,' said Collins, offering Charlie the glass.

'Very.'

The man's manner had changed since their last meeting, even if his appearance hadn't. He was more polished than he had been in Prague; showed more confidence. But it would only be surface change, guessed Charlie. Still be a prissy sod.

'The Chinese chap made a full confession, did he?'

'Full enough,' said Charlie. 'It will be enough for us to challenge Lu's claim in the High Court.'

'Have to make a report to London about it,' said the ambassador, as if the idea had just occurred to him.

'Of course,' said Charlie uneasily. 'I understand the Hong Kong police have asked officially for assistance.'

Collins nodded.

'No reply yet to my Note,' he said.

He suddenly put his head to one side. 'Have we met before?'

Charlie brought the sherry glass to his lips, knowing an immediate reply would have been impossible for him.

'Met before?' he echoed dismissively. 'I don't think so. Not often I take sherry with a British ambassador.'

At least the strain didn't sound in his voice. Sweat was flooding his back, smearing his shirt to him.

Collins laughed politely.

'Odd feeling there's been another occasion,' he insisted.

'There must be so many people,' said Charlie.

'Quite,' agreed Collins.

'Do you anticipate the authorities will send the cook back?' said Charlie, trying to move the man on.

'They helped you,' pointed out the diplomat.

'But only to obtain a statement. I gather they feel to turn the man over to the Hong Kong police would be establishing a precedent for any future cases. And they are unwilling to make such a sweeping commitment.'

'Quite,' said Collins again.

The ambassador was still examining him curiously.

'And as far as they are concerned, a High Court challenge will be as good as any criminal court proceedings,' said Charlie.

'Ever been to Lagos?' blurted Collins snapping his fingers in imagined recollection.

'Never,' said Charlie. The perspiration would be visible on his face, he knew. And the room was really quite cold.

Collins moved his head doubtfully at the rejection.

'Usually got a good eye for faces,' he apologised.

'I'd have remembered,' said Charlie.

'Quite,' said Collins.

Since their last meeting, the man had affected an irritating air of studied vagueness, thought Charlie.

'How long you staying in Peking?'

'I've got what I came for,' said Charlie. 'I'm leaving as early as possible tomorrow morning.'

'Oh,' said Collins, in apparent disappointment. 'Going to invite you to dinner tomorrow evening. As I said, not often we get visitors from home.'

'Very kind,' Charlie thanked him, 'but we've got to file an answer in the London courts as soon as possible.'

'Quite.'

Just a stupid mannerism? wondered Charlie. Or the thoughtless use of a favourite word, to feign interest while he tried to recall their other meeting?

'Stockholm?' tried Collins, gesturing with his finger.

Charlie shook his head.

'Never been there,' he said. The man would persist, Charlie knew. He looked the sort of person who played postal chess and did crossword puzzles, enjoying little challenges.

Charlie looked obviously at his watch.

'I've a four o'clock appointment at the Foreign Ministry with Mr Chiu,' he improvised. He hadn't and there was a danger of the ambassador's discovering the lie. But it was the best escape he could manage And there was an even greater danger in continuing this conversation.

'I'll check with Hodgson,' said Collins, taking the hint.

He spoke briefly into the internal telephone, smiling over at Charlie as he replaced the receiver.

'All done,' he said.

Almost immediately there was a movement from behind and the lawyer entered at the ambassador's call, carrying a file of documents.

'The Chinese original,' he said, holding out the papers, 'and a British translation. Both notarised by me and witnessed by the First Secretary. I've also annotated the identified photograph and sworn a statement that it was the one seen by the man.'

'You've been very kind,' said Charlie, including the ambassador in the thanks.

'That's what we're here for,' replied Collins, rising with Charlie.

The ambassador walked with him to the study door. Charlie was aware of his attention.

'Amazing,' said the ambassador, when they reached the hallway. 'Just can't lose the feeling that I know you from somewhere.'

'Thank you again,' said Charlie.

'Sure about tomorrow night?'

'Quite sure. I'm sorry.'

Charlie hesitated immediately outside the embassy buildings. He was trembling. Almost noticeably so. He straightened his arms against his sides, trying to control the emotion. After his discovery at Sir Archibald's vault, when he had realised they were chasing him, there had been times when he had felt helplessly trapped in a contracting room, with the walls and ceiling slowly closing in upon him. It had been frightening, claustrophobic. For a long time he had not encountered it. But it was very strong now.

'Well?' demanded Clarissa Willoughby.

'I'll have to make the statement soon,' admitted the underwriter.

'Even before you finally hear from Hong Kong?'

'It's a criminal offence knowingly to go on trading without funds to meet your obligations,' said Willoughby.

'Criminal!'

'Yes.'

'Christ, I couldn't stand you appearing in court as well.'

'I didn't think you intended to stand anything.'

'I don't,' said the woman.

'Where are you going?'

'I haven't made up my mind. Does it matter?'

'I suppose not.'

'I feel very sorry for you, Rupert. I really do.'

She spoke in the manner of a person discovering that a friend's pet was having to be put down, thought the underwriter.

'Thank you. When do you intend to leave?'

'End of the week, I suppose,' said the woman. She smiled.

'You really are being remarkably civilised,' she said.

'Isn't that what we've always been?' he said, the bitterness showing for the first time. 'Remarkably civilised.'

'If it confirms Lu's involvement with the fire, then surely it's enough? For our purpose, anyway,' said the chairman.

'I suppose so,' said Chiu.

'What *else* is there?'

Chiu shrugged.

'You're right,' he agreed.

'And on behalf of the council, I would like to thank you,' said the chairman formally.

Chiu smiled, gratefully.

'The statement still has to be put to its proper use,' he reminded them.

'I don't think we should worry about that, do you?'

'I hope not.'

17.

The wind was stronger than the previous day, so the dust from the Gobi drifted in pockets through the capital, gritting the buildings and plants with a light, greyish-yellow dust. Charlie saw that a few people wore face masks or pulled scarves up around their mouths. He sat in the Hsin Chiao foyer, his briefcase and shoulder grip already packed beside him, knowing he was early but impatient for Chiu's arrival. Because the hotel was organised on the Russian style, with each floor having its own reception staff, the main foyer was remarkably empty. The furniture was frayed and shabby and the walls were patched with quick repair work; it reminded Charlie of a retirement hotel way back from the seafront at Eastbourne.

The Chinese official stopped just inside the entrance when he saw Charlie already waiting.

'I am not late,' stated Chiu.

'I couldn't sleep,' said Charlie truthfully. 'So I got up early.'

'The car is waiting.'

As the vehicle nudged out into the shoals of bicycles, Chiu said, 'Fan Yung-ching is still available.'

'I have what I came for,' said Charlie. 'It will be sufficient, believe me.'

'It would be difficult to arrange another meeting, if anything had been overlooked,' warned Chiu.

What were they going to do with the poor old bugger? wondered Charlie.

The car moved out of the Legation district, with its pink-bricked buildings and into the huge T'ien An Men Square.

'There is much to see in Peking,' offered Chiu, gesturing towards the red-walled Forbidden City.

'I don't think I've time,' said Charlie.

'There is the monument to the Heroes of the Revolution,' said Chiu, pointing through the car window. 'The cornerstone was laid by our beloved leader, Mao Tse-tung.'

Charlie nodded politely. It reminded him of the Russian statue to their war dead in East Berlin. The department's attempt to kill him, remembered Charlie. He'd actually stood by the Russian monument and watched the innocent East German he'd cultivated for just such a purpose drive the marked Volkswagen towards the checkpoint. Poor sod had believed he was driving towards an escape to the West.

'*How can a man as sensitive as you sometimes be so cruel?*'

Several times Edith had asked him that, unable to understand his peculiar morality of survival. As Sir Archibald's secretary in the early days, before their marriage, she'd heard it talked about in the department. Admired even, as essential for the job. But she hadn't admired it. She'd been frightened of it. He didn't think she had ever been completely sure that it hadn't affected their marriage, suspecting Charlie of a calculated willingness to use her as he seemed willing to use everyone else.

Not even at the very end had she truly believed that it was inherent in him, something of which he was more ashamed than proud.

'You would not care to stop to see the monument?' said Chiu. 'Or perhaps the Museum of the Revolution?'

'No, thank you,' said Charlie. 'I'd rather get straight to the airport.'

Again the formalities were waived and they were the first on the Canton-bound aircraft. Neither spoke while the other passengers boarded, but as they trundled towards take-off, Chiu said, 'You had a good meeting with your embassy?'

Charlie looked at the man beside him. That was the problem, he accepted. He'd never know. Not until it was perhaps too late.

'Very,' he said. 'The ambassador is making a report to London about your helpfulness.'

'It will probably mean a fresh application for the man to be returned to Hong Kong.'

'Probably,' agreed Charlie.

He closed his eyes, hoping the other man would stop forcing the conversation. He was very tired, realised Charlie. But not from the restless, almost unsleeping night. It was an aching mental and physical fatigue, his mind and body stretched against relaxation not just by the need to anticipate the obvious dangers, but to interpret the nuances and half-suspicions. He'd swung the pendulum too far, he thought. The rotting inactivity about which he had whined to Willoughby seemed very attractive now. But wouldn't, he supposed, if he were pushed back into it. Which didn't, at the moment, seem very likely.

He managed to feign sleep until the arrival of the meal.

'We will be in Canton soon,' promised Chiu.

And after that, Hong Kong. To what? wondered Charlie. 'I can't thank you enough for the help you've given me,' he said sincerely.

'Let us hope it has not been wasted,' said Chiu, the criticism obvious.

'Yes,' agreed Charlie, unannoyed. 'Let's hope.'

Because there was special clearance in Canton, they were aboard the express within an hour of touchdown. The same peasants seemed bent beneath the same hats in the same fields, thought Charlie.

'I will keep Mr Kuo and your Hong Kong legation informed of what happens,' promised Charlie.

'What do you intend doing?'

'I'll lay the information before the Hong Kong police, obviously,' said Charlie. 'It will be more than sufficient for them to begin enquiries. Then tell our lawyers in London that we have proof upon which they can immediately enter a defence to Lu's claim.'

And then flee, he thought.

Chiu nodded. 'With no guarantee that there will be either a criminal or a civil hearing at which Lu can be denounced.'

'It's almost a certainty, in one court or another,' said Charlie carelessly.

'*Almost* a certainty,' echoed Chiu, throwing the qualification back.

At the border, Chiu escorted him to the bridge.

'Again, my thanks,' said Charlie, facing the man near the jostling booth. There seemed to be more people than when he had entered China.

'It was in both our interests,' said Chiu.

Charlie turned, offering his passport, but was again waved through without inspection. He walked across the bridge, glad of the distant sight of a train already in Sheung Shui station. He felt a flush of relief. Then, immediately, annoyance because of it. He had become so nervous that he saw omens of good fortune in something as ridiculous as a waiting train, like a housewife planning her day around a newspaper horoscope. He hadn't realised the strain had become that bad.

He was about a hundred yards into the New Territories when instinct made him react, seconds before the attack became obvious. He swivelled, automatically pulling the overnight bag and briefcase in front of his body as some sort of protection. There were three of them, he saw, marked out against the rest of the Chinese by their Westernised silk suits. The sort that Lucky Lu favoured, thought Charlie fleetingly.

They were spaced expertly, so that it would be impossible to confront one without exposing himself to the other two. And approaching unhurriedly, very sure of themselves. The man to the right was even smirking.

Charlie turned to run, but collided at once with an apparently surprised man carrying a jumble of possessions in a knotted rug. It burst open as it hit the ground, cascading pots and pans and clothing and the man started screeching in bewildered outrage. Charlie tried to dodge around him, brushing off the man's grasping protests, but hit another group who drew together, blocking his escape and gesturing towards the shouting peasant.

He'd never get through, he realised, turning back. The three were still walking calmly and unhurriedly towards him, blocking any dash back to the border. The smiling man had pulled a knife. Narrow-bladed, so there would hardly be any puncture wound. Little risk of identifying blood splashes, after the attack. Very professional, judged Charlie.

The peasant was babbling to his left and Charlie swept out, thrusting him aside. The advancing men stopped, warily.

They believed he was seeking space in which to fight, Charlie knew. It wouldn't be a mistake they'd make for longer than a few seconds.

All his life Charlie had existed in an ambience of violence. But always avoided actual involvement, relying upon mental agility rather than physical ability. A survivor unable to fight his own battles. It was not cowardice, although he was as apprehensive as anyone of physical pain. It was an acceptance of reality. He just wasn't any good at it. Not close up, hand-to-hand brutality. Never had been. No matter how persuasive the lecture or good the instruction, he had never been able to bring himself to complete the motion in training that would, in a proper fight, have maimed or killed. The practice, grown men grunting around a padded floor in canvas suits, had even seemed silly. He'd actually annoyed the instructors by giggling openly.

'One day,' Sir Archibald had warned in rare criticism, 'there might be the need.'

But he'd still been careless, because the department had had a special section for such activity, men who regarded death or the infliction of pain as a soldier does, uninvolved and detached, a function of their job. He'd only achieved the attitude rarely. To survive, in East Berlin. And to avenge Edith's murder. And even then it had been remote. He had wanted Edith's killer to die. But not to see the fear of realisation upon his face; the sort of fear that the three men could see in him now.

Now there was the need.

They'd started forward again. More confidently. The one with the knife said something and the other two began to grin as well.

They definitely knew, realised Charlie.

'Help!'

He screamed the plea, desperately, instantly aware that other people around had joined in the shouts of the man with whom he had collided, smothering the sound of his voice.

'Help! For God's sake, help!'

The crowd pulled away from him and for the briefest moment

Charlie thought it was because of his yell. Then he saw it was an almost rehearsed enclave, with the three men facing him just six feet away. And that there were more assailants than he had at first identified.

The handle of his overnight bag was looped with a strap, so that it could be supported on his shoulders. He gripped the top of the strap, whirling the bag around his head in clumsy arcs, forcing people away from him.

They drew back, easily, isolating him in a circle. Twenty at least, decided Charlie. Probably more. No way of knowing.

'The briefcase,' demanded the Chinese with the knife.

He reached out, beckoning.

Charlie stared back, panting. His eyes locked on the knife in the man's hand. He thought of the pain it would cause, thrusting into his body, and his stomach loosened.

'Give me the briefcase,' insisted the man. Again he motioned impatiently.

The other two had spaced further out, so that he was faced with a wider attack.

The knife man moved to come forward and again Charlie swept the bag around in a wild, warding-off sweep. Aware that the artificial protests from the peasants had stopped, he screamed again, 'Help. Please help me!'

He could even see the border, in the direction in which he was facing. Less than a hundred yards. The police and officials appeared unaware of what was happening.

It was a cry of shock, not pain, and as he fell Charlie saw that it was one of the long poles from which he'd seen many of the peasants supporting belongings and goods that had been swept across the back of his knees, crumpling his legs beneath him.

The overnight bag hampered him now, the strap becoming entangled with his wrist, and before he could free himself one of the three men he had first seen had got to him, clamping his arm to his side.

Charlie butted him in the face with his forehead, hearing the grunt of pain. He'd hurt himself, too, he realised, blinking. He tried to scramble up, but felt himself being grabbed behind by unseen hands. Because his eyes were watering, he could only half-focus on the man with the knife. Bending over him. Only feet away.

'I said I wanted the briefcase.'

It was a scream of fear this time, with no articulate words. Charlie thrust back into the people holding him from behind, trying to escape the knife, stomach knotted for the moment of pain. He kicked out, but half bent as he was he missed the man's groin, hitting him harmlessly on the thigh. And then the attacker he'd butted grabbed his leg, twisting him completely over.

Charlie lay face down, sobbing his helplessness. He was almost unaware of the briefcase being snatched from him because of the pain that exploded in his head as something began smashing into his skull, urgent, hammering blows.

But not the pain that he had imagined from the knife, he thought, as he drifted into unconsciousness. Hardly any hurt at all, now that they'd stopped hitting his head.

So death wasn't as painful as he'd always thought it would be.

'Got it!'

Hodgson, who had brought their copy of the Chinese statement into the ambassador's study so that the man could refer to it when preparing his report to London, stared down at Collins.

'I'm sorry, sir?'

'That man. I knew I'd met him before.'

'Oh.'

'Prague,' declared the ambassador. 'Four years ago in Prague.'

Hodgson waited, not knowing what was expected of him. Collins had his eyes closed with the effort of recollection. 'Attached to our Intelligence service,' he added. 'Actually had some sort of altercation with him.'

The ambassador opened his eyes, frowning at the memory. 'What's he doing as a director of a Lloyd's underwriting firm?' he demanded, as if the young lawyer would have the answer instantly available.

'I don't know,' said Hodgson. He hesitated, then risked the impertinence.

'Surely it can't be the same man?' he said.

Collins maintained his distant look.

'Certainly looked like him,' he said, his conviction wavering.

'It would take years to attain the seniority that he appeared to have,' pointed out Hodgson.

'Quite,' conceded Collins, turning back to his desk. 'Quite.'

18.

He hadn't died.

The awareness came to him with the first burst of searing pain, as if his head were being crushed between two great weights. He tried to twist, to get the pressure to stop, but that only made it worse and then he heard a sound and realised he was whimpering.

'It'll ache,' said a voice. Muzzy. As if the words were coming through cotton wool.

Charlie could feel the strong light against his face and squinted his eyes open carefully, frightened it would cause fresh pain. It did.

There appeared to be a lot of people standing over him, but his vision was blurred, so he could not distinguish who they were.

'How do you feel?' asked the voice.

'Hurts,' managed Charlie. 'Hurts like buggery.'

His voice echoed inside his own head, making him wince. 'We've given him an injection, now we know there's no fracture. It'll get better soon.'

Charlie tried focusing again, feeling out with his hands as he did so. A bed. Hospital, then.

'Do you feel well enough to talk?'

Another voice. Superintendent Johnson.

Cautiously this time, Charlie turned in the direction of the sound. Still difficult to distinguish the man, but the height was obvious.

'Yes.'

'There's a shorthand writer present. He'll record what you say.'

'All right.'

'Who did it?'

'Chinese.'

'Could you recognise them again?'

Charlie considered the question. In his fear, all he'd looked at was the knife. And their clothes. There was the one with the smile; he'd seen his face closely enough.

'Probably,' he said.

'Mainland Chinese?'

'They wore Westernised clothing,' said Charlie. 'Silk suits.'

'Did they speak?'

'One did. English.'

Whatever drug they'd given him was taking effect. The pain was lessening. And Johnson was becoming easier to see.

'Hong Kong then?'

'It would seem so.'

'Why?'

'I'd got the proof.'

Charlie blinked at the announcement, wanting very much to see the policeman's face. Johnson was gazing down at him, keeping his face clear.

'Proof?'

'The cook was made available to me in Peking. It was just as the woman said. Everything.'

'You brought the statement back?'

'In the briefcase. That was what the man kept saying. He wanted the briefcase.'

'When the border guards got to you, you only had a shoulder grip.'

'So they got it.'

'And the proof.'

Was there almost a sound of relief in Johnson's voice? No, decided Charlie. That was unfair.

'I won't admit I was wrong. Not yet,' said Johnson, identifying his attitude.

'I didn't ask you to,' said Charlie.

'I'll need more than a statement made by a man to whom I'm refused access. I need facts. So far we haven't even the affidavit you claim was sworn.'

Charlie almost shook his head in denial, stopping at the first twinge of warning.

'It was notarised to make it legally admissible by a lawyer from the British embassy,' he said. 'They have a copy. You could get it from the Foreign Office, in London.'

'What did the cook say?'

'That the poison was given to him by John Lu... that he'd been told it would only make them ill. And that it would cancel his gambling debt.'

'Just as the woman said,' repeated Johnson reflectively.

'It will be sufficient to make the enquiries,' insisted Charlie. He could see everything clearly now. Apart from Johnson and the short-hand writer, there was another policeman by the door. Standing near the third officer were a nurse and a white-coated man whom Charlie assumed to be a doctor. They were both Chinese.

'Yes,' agreed Johnson. 'It will be sufficient to start enquiries. Do you think the Chinese will send the cook back?'

'Definitely not,' said Charlie.

'It'll be difficult, trying to proceed on a case like this, with the legal muscle that Lu can employ, with only a sworn statement.'

'Can you guarantee a court hearing?'

The constant demand, from every Chinese official he'd met. Johnson was right, accepted Charlie. And the Foreign Office statement would only be a copy. Would the company lawyers be prepared to go into court on anything less than the original?

'Yes,' said Charlie. 'It'll be difficult.'

'I'd like a fuller statement, later on,' said the police chief.

'Of course.'

'Maybe tomorrow?'

Johnson put the question more to the doctor than to Charlie.

'Certainly the X-rays show there's no fracture,' said the white-coated man cautiously. 'But there's undoubtedly concussion. I'd like to keep him under observation for a few days.'

'Tomorrow,' insisted Charlie. There was an uncertainty in his mind, a doubt he could not even formulate. Little more than instinctive caution. But it was there, nagging more intrusively than the pain. And there was something else. The danger of the ambassador's memory. And Jones's curiosity.

'That might not be wise,' protested the doctor. 'You're lucky not to be more seriously hurt.'

'How lucky?'

Charlie put the question to Johnson. The policeman stared back at him curiously.

'What do you mean?' he asked.

'How long was it before the border guards got to me?'

Johnson made an uncertain movement.

'We don't know. They didn't see the beginning of the attack, obviously. By the time they got there, you were unconscious and there wasn't a sign of anyone who'd attacked you.'

'Or the briefcase?'

'Or the briefcase,' confirmed Johnson.

'One of the men had a knife,' said Charlie. 'The one who did the talking.'

Johnson looked at the doctor.

'Nothing but head injuries,' insisted the man. 'And minor grazing consistent with being knocked to the ground.'

'There was a knife,' insisted Charlie. 'I saw it.'

They didn't understand, he thought.

'So they obviously got the briefcase without having to use it,' said Johnson easily. 'We can get it all down in the statement.'

'I wish you'd give yourself more time,' said the doctor. They thought the knife was a hallucination, decided Charlie.

'I can sign myself out, as I could in England?' he asked.

'Yes,' said the doctor.

'I'll agree to stay overnight,' promised Charlie. 'But tomorrow I'll leave.'

It would be ridiculous even to try tonight, he knew. He'd collapse and lengthen the period in hospital.

'You've had at least four severe blows to the head,' said the doctor.

'But there's no fracture.'

'Concussion can be as bad.'

'A night's rest will be sufficient.'

'Why don't I call tomorrow?' suggested Johnson, moving to intercede. 'To see how you are.'

'At the hotel,' said Charlie finally.

The doctor's hostility spread to the nurse who remained after everyone else had left. She moved jerkily around the room, showing her irritation in the briskness with which she moved, tidying up after the policemen.

'Would you like a sleeping draught?' she asked.

'Please,' said Charlie. Without help, he knew, he'd never rest.

She returned within minutes with some brown liquid in a tiny medicine glass, waiting by the bedside until he swigged it down.

He relaxed back upon the pillow she plumped for him.

'Good-night,' she said.

'Good-night.'

'Something is not right, Charlie,' he said to himself, after she had gone. But what the hell was it?

He began to feel the approach of drowsiness. He turned on the pillow, looking towards the door through which the girl had just left.

Jesus, he thought, as sleep overtook him, I hope that girl is not a gambler.

The ache was still there, but far less than the previous night. Little more than a hangover discomfort. And he'd endured enough of those. The growing belief that he knew what was happening helped. Always the same excitement, the awareness that he had realised something that no one else had. He needed more, though. A damned sight more. But at least he had found the direction in which to look for it. At last. And Charlie's Rules, too. Not Judges'.

'I wish you'd stay,' said the doctor.

'There are things I must do.'

'What?'

'Reports to be made to London, apart from the statement to the police,' he said glibly.

'Nothing that couldn't wait.'

'I'll be careful,' said Charlie. And would have to continue to be, no matter what happened.

The doctor moved his shoulders, abandoning the attempt.

'These might help,' he said, handing Charlie a phial of pills. 'And if you start vomiting, get back here immediately.'

'I will,' promised Charlie.

The nurse of the previous day entered, frowning when she saw that Charlie was already dressed.

'Damned glad you don't play mahjong or follow the horses,' Charlie greeted her.

The girl stared at him.

'What?' she said.

'Forget it,' said Charlie.

'Sure you're all right?' demanded the doctor.

'Positive,' insisted Charlie. It had been a bloody silly thing to say. Irrationally, it had been his first thought upon awakening and from it had come the conclusion that was exciting him.

'You won't change your mind?'

'No.'

Charlie walked slowly to the hospital elevator, conscious of the movement against the corridor floor jarring up into his head. There was a slight nausea deep in his stomach, but he knew it was not from the head wounds. He was actually aware of the customary discomfort from his feet; that had to indicate some improvement.

He reached the hospital reception area and had just realised the need for a car when he heard the shout and turned expectantly.

'Hi there,' called Harvey Jones.

'Hello,' said Charlie.

He'd anticipated the approach, but thought it would be back at the hotel. He'd underestimated the man's keenness.

'Heard you got mugged,' said the American. 'How is it?'

'Still painful,' admitted Charlie. 'Who told you about the attack?'

'Superintendent Johnson. I've been keeping in touch with him.'

'Oh?'

'Thought you might get into contact when you returned from Peking.'

'You knew I was there, then?'

'Sure,' admitted Jones easily. He motioned towards the forecourt. 'I've got a car. Can I give you a lift?'

'Thank you,' said Charlie.

He relaxed gratefully into the passenger seat, feeling the ache in his body now, as well as his head, and aware how much it had taken from him to travel even this short distance. The doctor had been right. He should have stayed.

'How did you know I'd gone to Peking?' pressed Charlie.

'Kuo Yuan-ching told me.'

The American had been easing the car out into the jammed streets but he risked a sideways glance to assess Charlie's reaction.

'Quite open about it, was he?'

'Why shouldn't he have been?'

'No reason,' agreed Charlie. 'Did you try for a visa?'

Again there was a glance from the American, to gauge any sarcasm.

'Yes,' he said shortly.

'But he wouldn't give you one?'

'Said it might take months to process. That's why I wanted to know the moment you got back.'

'Why?'

'We promised to pool everything we found, remember?'

'I remember,' said Charlie. 'What have you come up with?'

The car was bogged in traffic and the American turned completely towards Charlie.

'You smart-assing me?'

Charlie returned the look, his face open with innocence.

'No,' he said. 'Why should I?'

The traffic moved and Jones had to look away.

'We're going to work together soon. And you'd better believe it,' said the American.

Now it was a blatant threat, recognised Charlie.

'I took a statement from the cook,' he said, trying to turn the other man's annoyance.

'And?'

'It confirmed everything we knew but couldn't prove.'

'So it wasn't Peking?'

'Definitely not.'

'And you've got the statement?'

'That's why I was attacked. The briefcase containing the Chinese original and the transcript signed by an English embassy official were stolen. There was a photograph, too, identifying John Lu.'

This time it was Charlie who was studying the American, watching his expression. Jones continued staring straight ahead, moving his fingers lightly against the steering wheel in his impatience with the vehicles around him.

'Lu's men?' demanded Jones finally.

'He'd be the only man to gain by stealing it.'

'That's what Superintendent Johnson thinks.'

'You must have had quite a discussion with Johnson?' If Jones had known about the statement and its theft, why had he wanted him to repeat it? Some sort of test, supposed Charlie.

'Johnson's being very helpful,' admitted the American.

'Why?'

'I think he believes it's going to be tough to prove anything against

Lu, even now... and that he's going to need all the assistance he can get.'

'And you can provide that assistance?'

Admit it, you bastard, thought Charlie, seizing the opening. You've hinted the Agency might help, in return for favours.

'It's possible,' said Jones.

Charlie sat back, letting the discussion go. His headache was worsening. Even though it was difficult without water, he gulped down two of the tablets he had been given at the hospital, coughing when they stuck drily in his throat.

'Anything wrong?' asked Jones anxiously.

'No,' lied Charlie.

They gained the tunnel running beneath the harbour and the car increased its speed. How much had happened in the two weeks since he'd made the same journey with Robert Nelson, reflected Charlie. So many tunnels. So much misunderstanding.

As they emerged, Charlie looked across to the Lu office block.

Guessing where Charlie's attention lay, Jones said. 'He'll be worried sick.'

'Will he?' said Charlie.

The American laughed at the caution.

'The whole damned thing is about to come down around his ears,' he insisted.

'I wish I were as sure,' admitted Charlie. 'A signed statement was tenuous enough. Now even that's gone.'

You're a shit, Charlie, he thought. But he'd never made the pretence of being anything else. Except a survivor. And that's what he was doing now. Surviving. He hoped. Please God that he'd got it right.

Jones eased the car into the edge of Connaught Road and Charlie got out unsteadily in front of the Mandarin Hotel.

'We'll keep in touch,' said Jones, leaning across the passenger seat.

'Yes.'

'And take care.'

'I shall,' Charlie assured him.

19.

Because of the time difference between Hong Kong and London, Superintendent Johnson had left his office late. He had been held up awaiting confirmation that a copy of the Peking statement would be despatched to him as soon as it arrived from China in the diplomatic bag. Just as he reached his apartment on the Middle Level, the first contact came from the station inspector.

When he learned it had been an anonymous telephone call to police headquarters, Johnson refused to over-respond. But he listed his instructions carefully, ordering that the forensic and photographic sections should be alerted, in case it were genuine. And that his official car should be sent back.

Then he sat, still in uniform. Waiting.

The second call came within thirty minutes. There was positive confirmation, the duty officer reported. Nothing was being done until his arrival, as he had insisted.

Johnson had been trained at Hendon. And sometimes even here he referred to the long-ago lectures and notes. Remembering them now, he sat in the back of the car as it made its way towards Stubbs Road and the Peak, eyes closed, consciously trying to clear his mind of any preconception and suspicion about the fire and the courtroom murders and the claims of a down-at-heel insurance investigator.

He'd need an open mind, he knew. It was going to be a difficult one; the most difficult ever. Particularly now the Foreign Office in London was involved. The sort of thing he tried so hard to avoid. He gripped and ungripped his hands, a frustrated gesture. It was all so damned vague, like imagined shapes in the fog. And the lectures had told him to ignore things that weren't clear. He needed facts. Just plain, straightforward facts.

He stirred, moved by another thought; whatever he was driving towards, it certainly seemed that he had been wrong about the fire and the men who had admitted responsibility. Which was going to be bloody embarrassing. Yet the facts had been there, as obvious as the fingers on his hand. Too obvious. And he'd made a mistake. Superintendent Johnson, who was well aware that had he remained in England he would never have risen above the rank of ordinary inspector, didn't like making mistakes. He worried that other people would realise his limitations and laugh at him.

He nodded with satisfaction at the road block established half a mile from Lu's mansion on Shousan Hill, acknowledging the wave as his recognised car swept through. But it would be the only one allowed past, he was confident. He'd repeated the instruction during the second call. It was the sort of routine at which he was very good.

An inspector was waiting at the already opened gate to Lu's home.

'Well?' demanded Johnson, getting from his car.

'Everything as you asked, sir,' said the man. 'Nothing's been touched. Servants and guards assembled in one spot, so they couldn't interfere with anything.'

'How many?'

'Fifteen. John Lu is one of them.'

'Yet they heard nothing.'

'Lu apparently relied upon an extensive electrical system.'

'So what happened to it?'

'Here,' the inspector invited him.

Johnson followed the man to a corner of the surrounding wall. It was topped all the way by thick wire mesh.

'Normally enough electricity going through that to kill an elephant,' said the inspector.

'What stopped it working?'

With a nightstick, the inspector indicated an obscured corner, near brickwork which swept out to begin the imposing entrance through which one had to drive to reach the house.

'There's a conduit box there,' he said. He waved an impatient hand and an officer in one of the waiting cars gave him a light operated from the vehicle's battery. 'It's been bypassed, so that there was no current passing through this section here…'

In the light of the torch, Johnson could see avoidance leads clamped by their bulldog clips to the live wires, and beyond them the hole that had been carefully cut through the mesh.

'On the other side,' said the inspector, 'there's the main junction box for this side of the house. Every alarm system has been circuited in the same way.'

'An expert?' said Johnson.

'Professional,' agreed the officer.

'What about the clips?'

'Haven't let the forensic people get to them until your arrival,' said the man. He hesitated.

'But I think you'll find they're of American origin,' he said, wanting to prove himself.

'American?' demanded Johnson sharply.

The inspector partially retreated at his superior's reaction.

'That's my guess,' he said.

'What about the house?'

'It happened in what appears to be the main lounge. I've men guarding it. And an ambulance on the way.'

'Ambulance?'

'One of them is still alive.'

Johnson waved the inspector towards his car, entering from the other side and telling the driver to go on. Normally, he realised, the grounds would have been floodlit, but the interference with the power supply had created an odd, patchwork effect.

The scientific experts were grouped just inside the main entrance to the house. When they saw Johnson's car arrive, they straightened expectantly.

'Give me a moment,' he said, moving past them.

He stopped just inside the door of the room the inspector indicated, to get an overall impression.

'Holy Jesus,' he said softly.

It had been a protracted, desperate fight. A glass-topped table in the middle of the room was splintered and crushed, presumably by the weight of a stumbling body. There were bloodstains, too, which continued to an overturned couch and then led to a wall near the fireplace.

Here all the ornaments and decorations had been swept aside in the struggle and more blood smeared the walls. A delicate Chinese brushworked painting that had concealed the wall safe hung lopsided, the hook almost torn from the wall. The safe gaped open and inside Johnson had the briefest impression of bundles of money banded together in tight blocks.

But he wasn't interested so much in the safe.

At its foot, his body wedged in a strange awkwardness against the skirting board, lay Harvey Jones. The man's leg was twisted beneath him; he'd broken it when he fell, thought Johnson, his mind registering the details with a clinical, later-to-be-produced-in-court accuracy.

Near the man's outstretched left hand was a tall pedestal ornament, its heavy base messily bloodstained. There was a matching ornament on the other side of the fireplace; Johnson saw, cracked where it had fallen to the ground.

He knelt, to get closer to the body. Jones's eyes were still open, in a shocked expression of death, and the police chief could just see the bullet entries. One, high in the left shoulder, was little more than a flesh wound, but there was another, lower in the chest. And from the amount of blood it was clear there was a third that he couldn't immediately see.

Johnson had begun to straighten before he noticed the document.

He crouched again, trying to read it without displacing it before the photographs were taken. There was a slight splash of blood on one corner. And the man's arm obscured the beginning. But it was quite easy for Johnson to read at least a third and identify the signature of Geoffrey Hodgson alongside the seal of the British embassy in Peking.

He stood, slowly. So he wouldn't have to await the arrival of the diplomatic bag.

'Here,' called the inspector.

The Chinese millionaire lay so that his crumpled body was almost completely concealed by the desk. From it came the snorted breathing of someone deeply unconscious and by moving around behind him Johnson could see the deep triangular gash at the side of Lu's head.

The police chief looked across at the ornament by Jones's outstretched hand. The base could have created just such a wound.

Facts, he recognised contentedly. Presentable, unarguable facts. Soon it would be time to bring the photographers and scientists in, to commence the simple, logical routine.

'Quite a fight,' suggested the inspector.

Drawers had been jerked from their runners and in two places Johnson could see where the locks had been forced, crudely jemmied open by some strong leverage. The contents were strewn haphazardly over the desk, as if someone had been looking for something particular and discarded what he didn't want without caring where it landed.

Again Johnson crouched, grunting with the difficulty of getting his large body beneath the narrow leg-space of the desk. About six inches from Lu's right hand lay a pistol.

Johnson lowered himself to it, sniffing, immediately twitching his nose at the smell of cordite.

'Czech,' commented the inspector. 'M-27.'

'Rough-looking weapon,' said Johnson, rising.

'But could be fitted with a silencer,' said the inspector, indicating the attachment.

There was movement at the door and Johnson turned.

'The ambulance is here,' reported the guarding policeman.

'Let them come in,' said Johnson. 'And forensic and photographic, too.'

The experts entered in a bunch.

'Photographs first,' stipulated Johnson, sure of his case and therefore sure of himself.

The white-coated ambulance men entered with their stretcher.

'The man's here,' said Johnson. 'But before he's moved I want a paraffin test on his hands, to establish that he's recently fired a gun.'

Immediately one of the plain-clothes men opened a bag and began walking towards the desk.

'Superintendent Johnson.'

The police chief turned at the inspector's summons.

'This would seem to be the point of entry,' said the officer. A neat semi-circle had been cut from the glass near the interior catch of the ceiling-to-floor window.

'That's it,' agreed Johnson.

'Not difficult to see what happened.'

'Quite obvious,' agreed Johnson. 'Intruder surprised by the householder in the middle of a robbery, is shot but manages to bludgeon the man to the ground, then dies of his injuries as he tries to retrieve from the safe what he's looking for.'

'Looking for?'

'Something I thought was going to create the most difficult case I'd ever been called upon to handle,' admitted the police chief. 'But now it looks like one of the easiest.'

The inspector pointed towards the dead man at the far side of the room.

'Quite an expert, wasn't he?'

'Oh, he was an expert right enough,' said Johnson.

The inspector turned at the confidence in his superior's voice.

'Did you know him?'

Johnson smiled.

'He worked for the American government,' he disclosed. 'The Central Intelligence Agency.'

'Oh,' said the inspector doubtfully. 'That could cause some problems, couldn't it?'

'I don't see why,' said Johnson.

The facts were there after all. No one could argue with them. Plain as the fingers on his hand.

Charlie Muffin was finally sick. He stood sweating over the lavatory bowl, agonised by the head pain that came with each stomach-stretching retch. When he could finally leave the bathroom it was difficult to see and for a moment he thought he was suffering from the double vision with which he'd awakened in hospital.

He sat quietly on the edge of the bed, blinking the wetness from his eyes. He was limp with perspiration. And smelt. Like the confused old man in the Peking interview room.

Charlie reached out for the pills the doctor had given him, concerned at how few remained in the bottle. It would be sensible to go back to hospital. Sensible. But impossible.

He undressed carelessly, leaving his clothes puddled on the floor. He didn't bother to get beneath the bed covering because he knew he wouldn't sleep.

It was going to be a long time until the morning, he thought.

20.

Johnson took the document from Charlie, nodding with satisfaction at another established fact.

'No doubt at all?'

'No,' said Charlie. 'That's definitely the statement I took from the cook in Peking.'

'And the one that was stolen from you at the border?'

'Yes.'

'And this is the photograph, identifying John Lu?'

'Yes.'

The police chief sat back expansively. 'That's it then. Everything explained.'

'It would seem so,' agreed Charlie. There was no pain now, but if he moved his head quickly he still felt a slight dizziness. It had all been brilliantly conceived, he thought. Which meant he was still in great danger.

'You'll always have to run, Charlie, always…'

'Be a defence to the killing, of course,' said Johnson. 'Reduced to manslaughter or even, with a good counsel, justifiable homicide in the protection of his property.'

'Yes.'

'In fact Jones's killing is unimportant compared to the door it opened.'

The fitting epitaph, thought Charlie sadly. 'Here lies Harvey Jones, whose death served a purpose.'

'It would seem I owe you an apology,' conceded Johnson unexpectedly. 'You were right.'

'It would have been difficult to prove,' he admitted, indicating the statement. 'Even with that.'

'But not now,' said the police chief.

'No,' said Charlie. 'Not now. What about John Lu?'

'The widest open door of them all.'

'What do you mean?'

'He was among those detained at the house last night. So he couldn't run. And so he panicked. Started making admissions before we even asked questions.'

'You were lucky.'

'Luckier than we thought. His lawyers are trying to do a deal now, to salvage something from the mess into which he talked himself.'

'What sort of deal?'

'His evidence against his father, together with all the details of the crime empire, in exchange for a guarantee against prosecution.'

'Not very Chinese, son turning against father, is it?' Johnson laughed. The policeman was very happy with himself, thought Charlie.

'I told you not to take any notice of that folklore rubbish,' he said.

'Yes,' said Charlie. 'You told me. Will you accept his offer?'

'Make an unbreakable case.'

The policeman sat forward as the thought came to him; 'And it would be the end of any claim against you, if he'd agree to be a witness.'

'Yes,' said Charlie. 'It would.'

'He hated his father apparently,' said Johnson.

'Hated him?'

'Always. Have you told your people in London?'

Charlie nodded.'

'I telephoned before coming here,' he said. Willoughby had almost sobbed with relief.

'It'll be a hell of a case when it finally comes to court.'

'Yes,' said Charlie.

Johnson saw a lot of personal credit coming from it.

'And not just because of Lu and who he is,' continued Johnson. 'You didn't have any idea that Jones was an American Intelligence agent, did you?'

'No,' said Charlie. 'No idea at all.'

'He was,' confided Johnson. 'There's an enormous diplomatic flap.'

'I suppose there would be,' said Charlie. He looked at his watch.

'Coming to the remand hearing?' Johnson invited him.

'Yes,' said Charlie, rising.

It was difficult to keep in step with the large man and Charlie's head began to hurt again.

'I wondered if you would do me a favour,' he said.

Johnson slowed, looking sideways. 'Of course.'

Now the man was almost over-compensating in his friendliness, thought Charlie.

'I want to find the woman,' said Charlie.

'Woman?'

'Jenny Lin Lee, the woman who was with Nelson.' Johnson stopped completely, turning across the corridor towards Charlie.

'She's not at Nelson's flat any longer,' explained Charlie.

'You think she's gone back whoring?'

Charlie knew he would never be able to think of that word as anything but offensive and ugly.

'Yes,' he said.

'Shouldn't be too difficult,' promised Johnson, setting off towards the court again. 'Call me tomorrow.'

'I will,' said Charlie. 'Early.'

He'd already booked his return flight to London. He was taking a risk even now. But there were other things to do.

It was the same court as that in which the two Chinese shipyard workers had appeared and again there was a crush for admission. because he was with Johnson, Charlie entered ahead of everyone else, with a choice of seats.

'I gather Lu is flying lawyers in from London when the case opens,' said Johnson.

'When will that be?'

'I shall apply for remands until we reach a decision with the son. But it shouldn't take too long. I've got an unarguable case.'

Just as he'd had with the fire and the poor sods who'd got killed, thought Charlie. How was it that people like Johnson got into positions of power? There was a great similarity between the police chief and the people who'd taken over the department after Sir Archibald's death.

'Unarguable,' agreed Charlie.

Johnson identified the sarcasm.

'Surely you don't think this is wrong?' he demanded.

Charlie hesitated, avoiding an immediate reply.

'You've got a good case,' he said finally.

The ushers began to admit the public and Charlie moved away, towards the seat he had occupied when he and Nelson had been in court.

He turned as Lu was brought in. The millionaire's head was turbaned with bandages and a medical attendant was in the back of the dock, as well as the warders. Lu stared defiantly towards the magistrates' bench, hands gripping the top of the dock.

The court rose for the magistrates' entry and immediately the clerk read out the charge of murder against Lu.

Johnson rose as the man finished.

'I would make a formal application for a week's remand,' he said officiously. 'At which time I anticipate the police being in a position to indicate when they could proceed.'

The local solicitor representing Lu until the arrival of the London counsel hurried to his feet. He was wearing an Eton tie, Charlie saw.

'I would like it entered into the court records at this first hearing that my client utterly denies the preposterous charge against him,' said the man. 'Were it based on fact, there would be a producible defence against it. But it is not. I would therefore make application for bail, asking the court to consider my client's position in this community. He would, of course, be prepared to surrender his passport.'

'Having regard to the seriousness of the charge, together with other matters still under investigation, the police oppose bail most strongly,' objected Johnson instantly.

'Bail refused,' declared the magistrate chairman. As the solicitor moved to speak, the man went on, 'You have the right, of course, to apply to a judge in chambers.'

'An application will be made,' said the solicitor.

'He won't get it,' Johnson said to Charlie, as the court cleared.

'No,' said Charlie, uninterested. It was almost time for his appointment.

'Know what the defence is going to be?'

Charlie paused at the court exit, turning back to the police chief.

'What?'

'That he knows nothing whatever about what happened to Harvey Jones...'

Johnson laughed, inviting Charlie's reaction.

When Charlie said nothing, Johnson added, 'Ridiculous, isn't it?'

'Yes,' agreed Charlie. 'Ridiculous.'

'No risk at all?'

Willoughby nodded at his wife's question.

'No risk at all. Not any longer.'

She came towards him, arms outstretched.

'Why, darling, that's wonderful.'

He refused to bend towards her and because of his height, she wasn't able to pull herself up to kiss him.

'Oh,' she said. 'Punishment?'

'What did you expect?'

'There's no need to be... to be...' she stumbled.

'Uncivilised?' he offered.

'Or sarcastic.'

He closed his eyes, helplessly. Why couldn't he just tell her to get out? She'd been going, after all.

'Do you still want me to leave?'

'You know the answer to that.'

'Do you still want me to leave?' she persisted.

'No,' he conceded, his voice a whisper.

'Then you mustn't be cruel to me.'

'You're a cow,' he said.

'Which is a very rude and offensive word. But I've never pretended to be otherwise.'

The usual defence, he thought.
'What about this man who's done it all?'
'Charlie?'
'Charlie! What a delightfully coarse name! Is he coarse, darling?'
'Strange, in many ways,' allowed Willoughby.
'I simply must meet him.'
'Yes,' agreed the underwriter. 'You must.'
'Very soon.'
'All right. Very soon.'
'Rupert.'
'What?'
'Say you love me.'
'I love you.'

21.

Kuo Yuan-ching looked cautiously across the desk, head to one side in what Charlie had come to realise was an habitual pose. 'I'm intrigued at your visit,' said the Chinese.

'You shouldn't be,' said Charlie. It would be wrong to let this man imagine any superiority.

Kuo let an expression reach his face, but refused to respond directly to the remark. Instead he said, 'Everything would seem to have been resolved far better than you had hoped.'

'And you'll get your court denunciation.'

'It would seem likely,' admitted Kuo.

'It's inevitable,' predicted Charlie. 'Especially now that John Lu wants to save himself by turning Queen's evidence.'

'Then we're both satisfied.'

'No,' said Charlie. 'I'm not satisfied at all.'

'Not with having saved £6,000,000!'

'That's not what I meant.'

'What, then?'

'I know what happened,' announced Charlie.

Kuo remained expressionless, hands resting lightly on the table top.

'Doesn't everybody?' he said.

'No, Mr Kuo. Hardly anybody.'

The man shook his head, raising his hands in a gesture of bewilderment.

'You baffle me,' he protested condescendingly.

'For a long time, you baffled me,' said Charlie. 'And then I thought of the incredible help and all the concern about Lu being publicly denounced. And then I remembered what Mr Chiu told me, as we were going to Peking.'

'What was that?'

'"People who bring disgrace to China never go unpunished,"' quoted Charlie.

Kuo nodded, seriously.

'That's true,' he agreed. 'We're sometimes a vindictive nation.'

'I've often been accused of the same fault. Perhaps that's how I finally realised the truth.'

'Is vindictiveness necessarily a fault?'

'It's taken me a long time to recognise it,' admitted Charlie. Too long, he thought.

'I'm still waiting to be surprised,' prompted Kuo. 'Apart from the fact that I should have been wounded by the knife, the border attack was very convincing, even to the suits your people wore. Just like Lu's men. But not to use the knife was a mistake…'

'Our people!' echoed Kuo.

'Your people,' insisted Charlie. 'No one except the Chinese authorities knew when I would be returning across the border, with the statement implicating Lu. So it couldn't have been anyone else, could it?'

There was a disparaging expression upon Kuo's face. 'But why should we steal from you an affidavit we went to such enormous trouble to ensure you obtained?' he said.

'To guarantee, even if it meant murder, the public disgrace of Lu,' said Charlie. 'A disgrace that I *couldn't* guarantee, not even with the statement.'

'A very wild flight of fancy,' said Kuo mildly.

'No,' argued Charlie. 'Not wild at all. Just a sensible interpretation of Peking's determination to maintain its rapport with America… a rapport important enough to risk the death of an American agent… an agent whom you took particular care to let know the facilities I'd been given and who you knew would make an effort to retrieve incriminating evidence if enough people pointed him to it. And enough people did…'

Charlie paused.

'Which was why I wasn't knifed,' he accepted. 'I had to set the bait, didn't I?'

Kuo pushed his chair slightly away from the table, making a small grating sound.

'It actually removed the risk of having to snatch him off the streets, with all the problems of failure that that might have created, didn't it? All you had to do was follow him, until he got to Lu's house?'

'People who know more about it than I do said you were extremely clever, Mr Muffin,' said Kuo conversationally. 'But I don't think any of us believed you'd work it out as far as you have. You really are a surprising man.'

Charlie sat motionless, numbed by the identification.

'Why bewilderment, Mr Muffin? You'd expect Peking to have extensive files on all American and British operatives, wouldn't you?' said Kuo, still casual. 'Just as they have files about our people.'

Charlie still couldn't respond.

'It was little more than a routine cross-reference with your picture, almost as soon as you arrived in the colony to question the fire, that gave us your identity,' said the Chinese.

He had assumed control, decided Charlie.

'And you were right,' continued Kuo. 'We had far more reason than any British insurance company to expose Lu. So nothing could be left to chance.'

The almost constant impression of surveillance, remembered Charlie. So his instinct wasn't failing. He felt the relief of a man fearing blindness who is assured that all he needs are reading glasses.

'Your coming really fascinated us,' admitted Kuo. 'Particularly as your file had you marked as dead.'

He leaned forward across the desk.

'And such an interesting file,' he said. 'We could easily appreciate why London and Washington would want you killed.'

Russia would have leaked the humiliation of the British and the Americans, Charlie knew; they'd seen it from the beginning as a propaganda coup. He was not surprised that Peking knew the details.

'You made very full use of me, didn't you?' he said, at last.

'As much as we possibly could,' conceded Kuo. 'The arrival of the man Jones made it perfect for us.'

'Otherwise mine would have been the body found in Lu's lounge?'

Kuo's face opened with the obviousness of the answer.

'It would have had to be, wouldn't it?' he said. 'And you would have had as much reason to try to retrieve the document as the American. More maybe.'

'But I'm not being allowed to escape, am I?' guessed Charlie.

'Escape?'

'Within twenty-four hours this colony will be inundated with men from Washington, investigating the death of one of their operatives,' predicted Charlie. 'To point them towards me would round the whole thing off very neatly, wouldn't it?'

'You're a very suspicious person, Mr Muffin.'

'I have to be.'

Kuo nodded.

'Yes,' he agreed. 'Of course.'

'Do you intend exposing me?' demanded Charlie. Kuo sighed, a man facing an unpleasant duty.

'It's very unlikely that they'd see the flaw you recognised. No one was as completely involved as you, after all. But there's always the outside possibility. And as I've said, we can't leave anything to chance.'

'So to be handed me might deflect their curiosity?'

'You must admit,' said Kuo, 'Washington would be very interested.'

Moving slowly, so the man would not misunderstand, Charlie put his hand into the inside pocket of his jacket and took out an envelope.

'As interested, perhaps, as they would be in these?' he said.

Kuo's control was very good, thought Charlie. There was not the slightest indication of emotion as the man went carefully through the photographs.

The first showed quite clearly Harvey Jones bypassing the alarms at Lu's house. There were more, of Chinese this time, at the same spot on the wall. The picture of the American's apparently unconscious body being bundled into the lounge was slightly blurred because of the distance from which it had been taken, but Jones was still recognisable. There were several pictures of a car, with the number plate clearly identifiable.

'The registration would prove it to be the vehicle assigned to this legation, wouldn't it?' asked Charlie.

'Oh yes,' agreed Kuo. He looked up. 'Infra-red photography?'

'I was professionally trained,' said Charlie. 'I actually entered the department because of it.'

'They're very good,' said Kuo, as if he were admiring holiday snapshots.

'The only difficulty is the need to keep the film refrigerated until just before use and then getting it developed as soon as possible afterwards,' said Charlie. 'Fortunately in a place like Hong Kong I had no difficulty buying an 0.95 lens.'

'The negatives and more prints are obviously in a safe place?' said Kuo, bored with the phoney civility.

'Obviously,' agreed Charlie, unworried by the threat. He looked at his watch.

'One set will almost be in London by now,' he said. He was back in an environment he'd believed he'd left for ever. He felt very much at home.

'With a complete account?' queried Kuo.

'Very full,' confirmed Charlie.

'You could have saved Jones,' the Chinese accused him suddenly.

'I tried,' said Charlie. But only after he had guaranteed his own survival.

'The telephone call to the police?'

Charlie nodded.

'But I was too late,' he said. As always.

'I wondered about the call,' said Kuo. 'It was much sooner than that which we had planned to make. We were almost caught.'

'I know,' said Charlie, taking more pictures from his pocket.

Kuo was shown twice by the identifiable car.

'Really very clever,' he congratulated Charlie.

'As I said, I have to be.'

'Just as I had to be there,' said the Chinese, in explanation. 'We realised the risk, of course. But I had to see the affidavit was put in the right place. And guarantee the little, important things... like ensuring the firing traces would be found on Lu's right and not left hand.'

'Nothing could be left to chance,' remembered Charlie.

'Exactly.'

'Keep the photographs,' offered Charlie. 'I expect you'll want other people to see them. Mr Chiu, for instance.'

Kuo nodded, putting them into a drawer in the desk.

'I congratulate you,' said Kuo.

Charlie didn't feel any pride. Just relief. And regret. The regret of which Edith had never thought him capable.

'It would seem,' said Kuo, 'that we will part in friendship.'

'Not exactly friendship,' qualified Charlie. 'More in complete understanding.'

Kuo smiled. 'It's been an interesting experience, Mr Muffin.'

'For both of us,' agreed Charlie.

Johnson had wanted to send someone with him, but Charlie had refused the protection.

The shack was actually against the Kowloon waterfront, part of the tin-drum and cardboard shanty town to the east of the city.

Charlie felt the attention as soon as he entered, stopping just inside the door to adjust to the darkness. And not just attention, he realised. Hostility, too.

The mutter of conversation began again, but everyone was still watching him, he knew. Everyone except Jenny. She was at the bar, head bent in apparent interest in something before her.

He picked his way through the trestles at which the Chinese sat, careful not to come into contact. It would need little excuse for an argument to erupt.

As he got near to the girl, he saw that the hair of which she had once been so proud was greased with dirt and matted in disorder.

'Jenny,' he said quietly.

Her glass was almost empty. She was staring down into it, but her eyes were fogged and unseeing.

'Jenny,' he tried again.

The barman positioned himself in front of him.

'Beer,' said Charlie.

The man looked at the girl and Charlie nodded. There was still no reaction when her glass was refilled.

He reached out, touching her arm. She was very cold, despite the oven-like heat of the place. She responded at last to his touch, squinting sideways. There was no immediate recognition.

'Twenty dollars,' she said distantly. 'Very good for twenty dollars.'

'Jenny,' he said again, trying to reach her.

'Hong Kong, not American,' she recited. 'Fuck all night. Just twenty dollars.'

There were no puncture marks on her arms. He looked down and saw the needle bruises around her ankles, near the big vein.

'Know you,' she said thickly.

The cheongsam was the one she had worn the night she had come to his room. It was very stained and the thigh split had been torn, so that it gaped almost to her groin.

'Came to fire Robert.'

She smiled with the pride of a child remembering a difficult multiplication table.

'Lu lost,' said Charlie. 'Too many other people did, as well. But Lu lost.'

There was no comprehension.

'Robert came here,' she said, mouthing the words slowly. 'That night. He came here.'

He reached out again, trying physically to squeeze some reaction from her.

'Lu has been arrested,' he said.

'Very brave, coming here by himself. Round-eyes aren't allowed... now they've made me come here... work here... punishment...'

Charlie lodged against the barstool, looking at her sadly. The heroin had almost completely blanketed her mind. She would take months to cure. Months of patient, constant care. He looked at his watch. The flights bringing in the American investigation teams to supplement those already in the colony would be arriving within three hours.

It would have to be someone else.

She blinked her eyes, as if remembering something.

'All night,' she said. 'Only twenty dollars. Anything you want.' She snatched out, suddenly desperate when she saw him move. 'Fifteen then. Anything you want for fifteen.'

He shrugged her hand away, threading between the unsteady tables again. It didn't matter if he collided with anybody, he realised. They had wanted him to find her and see what had happened.

'Bastard,' she screamed, behind him. 'Fired Robert.'

Yes, thought Charlie, stepping unsteadily out into the street. He was a bastard. Literally. And in every other way. Usually he wasn't as ashamed of it as he was now. She wouldn't have understood had he tried to explain he wasn't abandoning her.

22.

Willoughby needed movement to let off his excitement, striding without direction about the room. For the first time he was holding himself upright, Charlie saw. He was remarkably tall.

'Unbelievable,' said the underwriter, groping for words sufficient to express himself. 'A miracle, nothing short of a miracle...'

The grandfather clock in the corner of Willoughby's office chimed the half-hour and Charlie looked across to it. Still another hour before the appointment. The chiropodist would probably insist upon the supports being put into his shoes. Mean another new pair, he supposed. Wonder how difficult it would be, adjusting to an artificial lump beneath each foot?

'People got hurt,' Charlie reminded him, puncturing the other man's euphoria. 'Too many people.'

Willoughby stopped the pacing, looking seriously at Charlie.

'And not just in Hong Kong,' said the underwriter, obscurely.

'I don't understand,' said Charlie. Despite the chiropodist, he could still get to Guildford before the rush-hour. He hoped Edith's grave hadn't become too neglected.

Willoughby shook himself, like a dog throwing off water. 'It's not important. Incidentally, there was quite a lot of money due to Robert Nelson. I sent it to our new broker...'

'There was a woman,' said Charlie hopefully. 'It's important to arrange something for her...'

'Jenny Lin Lee?' interrupted Willoughby.

Charlie nodded.

'She's dead.'

'Oh.'

'Massive drug overdose, apparently,' said the underwriter. 'The police have decided it was self-administered, so there's no question of any crime.'

Already stencilled 'closed' and filed in one of Johnson's neat little cabinets by one of his neat little clerks, thought Charlie. Again he'd been too late.

'She knew Lu would win some sort of victory,' said Charlie softly.

'What?'

'Nothing,' said Charlie.

'I'll always be indebted to you,' declared the underwriter, sitting at last at his desk.

'It took me a long time to realise how long I'd been away,' said Charlie. 'Almost too long.'

He would never know about the Peking ambassador, he thought. Not until it was too late, anyway.

'I wouldn't like it to end,' said Willoughby. 'In fact, Clarissa wants to meet you.'

'Clarissa?'

'My wife. Let's meet socially, very soon.'

'Thank you.'

'I'm sorry for the way all this began, Charlie. It was wrong to treat you as I did.'

'Forget it.'

'I'd like the association to continue.'

Charlie shifted uncertainly. How soon would it be before the fear diminished and the boredom began eating away at him again?

'I don't know,' he said. 'I made a lot of mistakes.'

'But won in the end.'

'Only just.'

Which was all he could ever hope for, decided Charlie. To win. By a small margin.

The Do-Not Press
Fiercely Independent Publishing

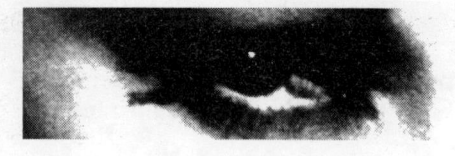

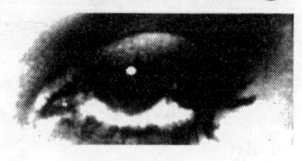

Keep in touch with what's happening at the cutting edge of independent British publishing.

Join The Do-Not Press Information Service and receive advance information of all our new titles, as well as news of events and launches in your area, and the occasional free gift and special offer.

Simply send your name and address to:
The Do-Not Press (Dept. CC)
PO Box 4215
London
SE23 2QD

or email us: thedonotpress@zoo.co.uk

There is no obligation to purchase and no salesman will call.

....

Visit our regularly-updated Internet site:

http://www.thedonotpress.co.uk